Praise for *Ch*

T0179907

"*Christmas at Spruce Hill Farm* is a delightful story overflowing with holiday spirit. Kathryn Springer writes with warmth and charm."
—RaeAnne Thayne, *New York Times* bestselling author

"*Christmas at Spruce Hill Farm* is a warmhearted delight! A snowy inn, a Christmas tree farm, and a wonderful happy ending. Holiday stories don't get any sweeter than this!"
—Lee Tobin McClain, *New York Times* bestselling author

"Flawed characters with real problems, a touch of romance, lots of heart, and even more snow. The perfect Christmas read."
—Linda Goodnight, *New York Times* bestselling author of *The Rain Sparrow*

"Kathryn Springer does it again. *Christmas at Spruce Hill Farm* is like curling up with a soft blanket, a full supply of hot cocoa and a batch of warm-from-the-oven sugar cookies. It has all the wonderful feels of Christmas!"
—Lenora Worth, author of *The Christmas Quilt*

"Springer delivers all the feels! A cozy holiday setting, the drama of family dynamics, not one but two great heroes, and a pair of bold, smart women who discover love in the last place they expected to find it. A holiday treat for every reader who loves happily-ever-afters!"
—Allie Pleiter, *Publishers Weekly* bestselling author

Also by Kathryn Springer

The Gathering Table

For additional books by Kathryn Springer,
visit her website, www.kathrynspringer.com.

Christmas AT SPRUCE HILL FARM

KATHRYN SPRINGER

LOVE INSPIRED

Stories to uplift and inspire

LOVE INSPIRED®

Stories to uplift and inspire

ISBN-13: 978-1-335-01675-1

Christmas at Spruce Hill Farm

Recycling programs
for this product may
not exist in your area.

For questions and comments about the quality of this book, please contact us at CustomerService@Harlequin.com.

® is a trademark of Harlequin Enterprises ULC.

Love Inspired
22 Adelaide St. West, 41st Floor
Toronto, Ontario M5H 4E3, Canada
www.LoveInspired.com

Printed in U.S.A.

This book is for Pete, the best husband, dad and grandpa,
who prays for me and with me, makes meals when I'm on deadline,
and always encourages me to keep going when I'm tempted to give up.
I'm so blessed to be on this journey with you!

Chapter One

Lucy Gable woke up to five inches of snow, a text message from the airline letting her know that her afternoon flight was delayed and a best-selling author who was MIA.

And since Lucy didn't have a shovel or a private plane at her disposal, the missing author was the only thing she had control over at the moment.

Right. Just keep telling yourself that, Luce.

Because over the past six months, Brynn Dixon seemed to have lost interest in everything. Interviews. Sales numbers. Social media.

Starting her next book.

Lucy's heart broke from its choreographed rhythm and performed a little tap dance inside her chest. A mysterious condition that had started shortly after her employer began spending more time on the patio than she did at her desk.

Hopefully, Brynn had gone downstairs to take advantage of the continental breakfast the manager of the boutique hotel had promised at check-in.

Lucy shivered, slipped on the lightweight cardigan that she found herself wishing *wasn't* so light and was almost to the door when her cell phone began to ring.

The flutter, which had started to subside, stirred to life again, keeping time with the name displayed on the screen.

Lucy had always looked forward to her chats with Ainsley Adams, but lately the freelance publicist had been growing frustrated with Lucy's attempts to free up some space on Brynn's jam-packed calendar.

"Brynn Dixon is a queen, Lucy," Ainsley had declared the last time they'd spoken. "As Brynn's personal assistant, your job is to keep the court running smoothly. Mine is to expand her territory."

Lucy was tempted to ignore the call but knew it would only prolong the inevitable.

"Hi, Ainsley."

"We have a problem."

It was 7:00 a.m. Ainsley had no idea she was talking to someone who'd already surpassed her quota of problems for the day.

Lucy glanced at the winter wonderland outside the window again.

Whose brilliant idea had it been to schedule a book tour in December? In a state known for unpredictable weather?

Oh, that's right.

Hers.

"What's wrong?" Switching her phone to Speaker, Lucy stepped into the common living room that separated the two suites for the second time that morning. Still no sign of Brynn, but further investigation yielded a red leather coat hanging in the wardrobe, proof that her employer hadn't ventured beyond the walls of the hotel.

This time.

"I've been monitoring the message boards after the signing last night, and what I'm seeing is the beginning of a mutiny."

"A mutiny?"

"A lot of unhappy readers," Ainsley clarified.

The publicist had a flair for the dramatic. And based on past experience, Ainsley's definition of *a lot* could easily translate into *two or three*, so Lucy refused to panic.

In spite of the single-digit temperature, there'd been standing room only in the coffee shop that hosted last night's event. Granted, it was a *small* coffee shop, but that was entirely by design.

This year, in an effort to appease Ainsley and Brynn's publisher, Lucy had come up with a different kind of book tour. Four "Mistletoe Stops" in towns that could have been the setting for Brynn's newest release. Towns a little off the beaten path. A little less populated.

In true Ainsley fashion, though, the woman had taken Lucy's idea and run with it. Asked readers to nominate their hometowns for the Mistletoe Stops and then unleashed the avalanche of emails onto Lucy's already-full plate.

Not that Lucy had minded. She'd sifted through the entries and deliberately chosen towns with main streets and independent bookstores. Corner cafés instead of conference centers.

Because while the last tour had been deemed a success thanks to large venues packed with enthusiastic, energized fans, Lucy realized it had had the opposite effect on the author herself. Although Brynn hid it well, Lucy had been working as her assistant long enough to tell she was completely drained. After every event, Brynn would retreat to her room or slip out of the hotel when no one was looking. Behavior totally out of character for the vivacious woman who'd always enjoyed spending time with her fans.

Maybe it was burnout. Maybe it was writer's block. But in Lucy's mind, the remedy was the same. Rest.

Another message from the airline suddenly popped up on-screen and she saw the word *Canceled* before the notification banner disappeared.

Okay. Maybe they should have stayed in Tennessee. Tennessee had small towns. What it rarely had was snow… But Brynn had seemed intrigued by the thought of a white Christmas, and Lucy would take *intrigued* over *indifferent* any day.

She walked over to the desk, flipped open her laptop and did a quick, one-handed hunt-and-peck search for another airline.

"Lucy? Did you hear what I said?" Ainsley's voice held a bit of an edge now, a blade honed from years of getting her way.

"Mutiny," Lucy murmured. She mentally scrolled through images from last night's event. "The owner of the coffee shop served homemade Christmas cookies and cinnamon lattes. The readers took selfies with Brynn and got an autographed copy of *Meet Me under the Mistletoe* to take home. There were twinkly lights and Christmas carols playing in the background, too."

"All of that sounds great," Ainsley said. "But apparently there was one missing ingredient."

"What's that?" Lucy clicked a few more links and mentally tucked away another fun fact about Wisconsin: the state had a lot more small towns than airports.

She opened a new tab and started to search for rental cars.

"Trace Hunter."

"*Trace?*" Lucy almost choked on the word. "What do you mean they want Trace? Trace isn't… He's not even the hero in Brynn's book!"

"Well, everyone is demanding that he be the hero in her next one," Ainsley said. "There's already a buzz, Lucy. Preorder sales are going to be off the charts."

Lucy pressed one hand against her heart. Not a tap dance. Freestyle kickboxing. "Brynn hasn't said anything about her next book."

Including if she planned to *write* one.

"I know you were sure a meet and greet with the hero

wouldn't work this time…" Ainsley let her disapproval dangle in the air. A reminder that Lucy was the one who'd made the decision to temporarily nix what had become the highlight of Brynn's previous book tours. "But this is a great promo opportunity. It shouldn't be too hard to find someone to play Trace for the rest of the Mistletoe Stops on the tour."

Now Lucy was panicking.

"Trace is a *secondary* character," she felt compelled to point out again. "Not to mention he…he's a *thief*!"

"Reformed thief," Ainsley corrected. "Now he's a PI who retrieves things from the bad guys in his spare time. Kind of like a modern-day Robin Hood."

Lucy's back teeth snapped together. "He's cynical and brooding—"

"And handsome."

"Sure," Lucy muttered. "Just ask him."

"He's daring. Charming—"

"A rule breaker *and* a heartbreaker."

"Until he meets his one true love."

Lucy stifled a groan.

Ainsley had obviously fallen for Trace Hunter, too.

"I'll contact the talent agency we've worked with in the past," Ainsley continued. "I'm sure they can find some candidates that fit Trace's description, and Brynn can choose the one she likes best."

"Even if she agrees, there isn't enough time. The tour ends the day before Christmas Eve. That's less than two weeks away."

"One appearance, then, if it comes to that. Trace will be the grand finale. The best and last gift under the tree."

Ainsley was a great publicist. She was also as tenacious as a pit bull when she locked onto an idea.

"I can't make any promises…and I can't speak for Brynn, either."

"Seriously, Luce, you and I both know that she really stepped outside the box this time. Trace isn't her typical hero, but I think that's why he's so appealing. Why would Brynn introduce a new character near the end of the book if he wasn't going to get his own happily-ever-after?"

"Brynn—" Lucy closed her lips to seal off the rest of the sentence.

Because she couldn't tell Ainsley the truth.

Brynn hadn't introduced her next hero in those final chapters because she hadn't written them. Lucy had. Finishing Brynn's novel had fallen outside of her usual responsibilities, but Lucy had agreed because Brynn needed her help.

And the character that had captured everyone's attention had come straight from Lucy's imagination.

She should have known Trace Hunter would be trouble the moment he'd sauntered onto the page in chapter twenty.

Chapter Two

"**W**ould you like some coffee, Ms. Dixon?"

Brynn really had to get better at this. The plaid wingback chair facing the window in the library had looked like the perfect hiding place when she'd slipped downstairs to have a quiet chat with God before the day officially started.

"It's Brynn, remember?" She smiled up at the manager of the hotel. *Sweet Susanne.* It was the way Brynn had taught herself to remember people's names over the years. She attached an adjective to their first name. "And yes. Coffee sounds wonderful."

"Looks like we're getting the snow the meteorologist predicted." Susanne shook her head. "'Tis the season, though. It's supposed to taper off by noon, but there's another storm coming fast on the heels of this one."

"We usually don't get more than a dusting in Nashville."

"Around here, our *dusting*," Susanne said and put air quotes around the word, "is two or three inches."

"Someone said she was staying here" came a loud whisper

from the hallway. "I brought along my copy of *His Promise to Keep* just in case."

"The dining room is starting to fill up so you might be more comfortable in here." Susanne glided toward the door, effectively blocking Brynn from view. "I'll be right back with a carafe and some pastries."

"Thank you." The manager, bless her heart, must have realized Brynn's fans expected her to make an entrance wearing one of the sequined dresses and the white leather cowboy boots that had become her signature style, not mismatched sweats and every-which-way hair.

She wiggled deeper into the chair and turned toward the window again, enchanted at the way the wind tossed snowflakes through the air like sparkling bits of confetti. It was beautiful. Serene, even.

Although, Lucy had probably called the airline several times by now, checking on the status of their flight.

Brynn didn't know what she'd do without her.

For years, Brynn had resisted hiring a personal assistant. But keeping up with technology that seemed to change as often as the latte flavors at her favorite coffee shop had forced her to give in. A decision she'd never regretted. Lucy was capable and efficient and kept Brynn's life running smoothly so she could concentrate on upending the lives of the characters who populated her books.

More than that, though, in spite of the twenty-year gap in their ages, Lucy had become a friend.

Which was the reason why Brynn instantly recognized the footfall coming down the hall. Lucy moved from place to place like a hummingbird—so quickly it didn't appear as though she were moving at all.

The footsteps paused outside the door of the library. Susanne had closed it when she'd left, and Lucy wasn't the kind of person who forced things open. Another one of the many reasons why Brynn liked her.

"I'm in here," Brynn called out, adding a silent apology to God for having to put their chat on hold for a bit.

The door opened and Lucy appeared, ready for the day in slim, ankle-length slacks, a boat-neck sweater and ballet flats, all in the basic black that made up ninety-nine per cent of her wardrobe.

With her dark hair in a pixie cut and a porcelain complexion that magnified black velvet eyes, Lucy had a vintage Audrey Hepburn–vibe going on. Knowing Lucy, though, it wasn't an attempt to draw attention to herself. In fact, Brynn suspected it was just the opposite, the dark clothing an attempt to fade into the background, like a member of a crew changing sets between the first and second acts of a play.

"Good morning." Brynn felt a yawn coming on and shaped it into a smile. "I woke up early and decided to explore a little."

Lucy returned the smile, but Brynn felt a pinch of guilt when she saw the flash of relief in her assistant's eyes.

Probably because she'd been playing hide-and-seek with Lucy over the past few months, too.

"Our flight's been canceled." Lucy frowned at the falling snow and then at the cell phone in her hand. "I'm waiting for the rental car company to call me back."

"No Uber?"

"Susanne laughed when I asked, so I took that as a no." Lucy fingered the pendant around her neck. She never outwardly fretted or worried, but Brynn had noticed that Lucy reached for the necklace whenever an unexpected wrinkle developed in the fabric of her day. As if tracing the edges of a small, heart-shaped piece of silver could somehow smooth it away. "I'm sorry about this."

"Never be sorry you have to stay a few hours longer in a place that smells like a chocolate croissant." Brynn motioned to the wingback chair's twin.

Lucy lit on the edge, caught Brynn's pointed look at her phone and set it down on the mahogany table. "Ainsley called a few minutes ago."

Ambitious Ainsley.

There was no denying her publicist was creative and brilliant when it came to her job. But unlike Lucy, Ainsley's main goal was to keep Brynn's name at the top of the lists and social-media platforms so she could enjoy all the benefits of the view. And because Ainsley loved nothing more than to see Brynn hopscotching her way through every big city in the country, it hadn't been hard to figure out that this particular book tour had been Lucy's idea. Small Midwestern towns with a few extra days between signings so Brynn had more downtime.

"She wanted an update on the signing last night?" Brynn guessed.

Lucy reached for the pendant again. "Actually—"

"Miss Gable?" The door opened, and Susanne poked her head into the library. "Do you…um…have a minute?"

Lucy glanced at Brynn, no doubt wondering if she would take advantage of the sixty seconds and attempt another escape.

"I'm not going anywhere." Brynn drew an invisible *X* over her heart.

An easy promise to keep when the fatigue she'd been battling on a daily basis had slipped through her defenses again.

Lucy nodded, a little reluctantly, and slid one more concerned look in Brynn's direction before she followed Susanne out of the room.

Brynn knew that Lucy knew something was wrong. She lived in a spacious, self-contained apartment above the carriage house on Brynn's property, and they got together every morning to make sure their calendars were in sync. Lucy had noticed when Brynn had started napping more than writing. Worked

Brynn's schedule around the doctor's appointments and tests that had resulted in more questions than answers.

Stress, Brynn's primary-care physician had finally determined. She was working too hard and needed to slow down a little. But Brynn had been tired before, and this felt…different.

Right or wrong, though, she still hadn't told Lucy that her symptoms had gotten worse. Not only had the fatigue slowly stolen her energy, it had also worked its way to her brain, clouding her thoughts—and her creativity—and burned like hot coals in her joints.

While Brynn was wiggling her fingers and toes to prove she still had some level of control over her body, Lucy's cell phone started to ring. An unknown number appeared on the screen. Knowing Lucy would be upset if she missed a call about the rental car, Brynn swiped her finger against the screen.

"Hello?"

"It's David McCrae, and I need to talk to you about this… book tour."

If the crisp masculine voice on the other end of the line hadn't already piqued her curiosity, the short but significant pause where an adjective should have been proved irresistible for the writer inside of Brynn.

"All right." Brynn could pretend to be Lucy for a few minutes. "What would you like to know?"

"How do I get out of it?"

Brynn blinked. Lucy handled all the details whenever they traveled, and Brynn showed up at the designated space on time, autograph pen in hand. A division of labor that played well to both their strengths.

"I'm sorry?" Brynn had to make sure the fog wasn't affecting her hearing. "Did you say you want to get out of it?"

"Yes. I can't imagine someone like…" Another pause, as if he were searching for a name this time.

Southern manners dictated she help the man out.

"Brynn Dixon?"

"Sure. I guess so. Anyway, Spruce Hill Farm—"

"Farm?" Brynn interrupted, even more intrigued. Images of chickens and cows danced in her head.

"Christmas-tree farm." He sounded a little suspicious now. "The inn is on the property, but I'm not sure the author would be comfortable here. It's not really set up for guests that require a lot of pampering."

Pampering?

For a person who'd never met her, David McCrae had made an awful lot of assumptions.

"But it *is* an inn?" Brynn pressed. "With running water? Electricity?"

"Of course." He sounded a little disgruntled by the line of questioning. "But there's no day spa or room service. And as far as entertainment goes, the best I can offer is a jigsaw puzzle in the gathering room."

The gathering room.

In her mind's eye, Brynn saw furniture with comfy pillows, a table with plenty of space for books and a steaming mug of hot chocolate. Flames dancing in a fireplace, casting shadows on the wall.

"The farm is kind of isolated, too," David McCrae continued. "Frost is two miles away—"

Brynn couldn't help it. She interrupted again, charmed by the name. "Frost?"

A long silence. And then, "You don't know the name of the town you're scheduled to visit?"

"They all kind of blur together."

Especially now.

Brynn rubbed her temples to disperse the fog collecting inside her head.

"Based on what I was told, the author writes romance novels

and her…Ladies of the Evening…show up in droves for book signings. The only space I'd have for a group that size is the barn, and it's pretty drafty this time of year."

Brynn choked back a horrified laugh.

"Ladies in *Waiting*," she corrected. "Because they're waiting for her next book?"

"I'll have to take your word on that."

It was one thing to suggest that Brynn required room service and mani-pedis, but to suggest she wasn't a good writer almost took the sweet right out of her tea.

"Maybe you shouldn't have tossed your name into the hat if you didn't want to be included in the Mistletoe Stops," she pointed out.

Or here was another thought.

Maybe a man who tried to discourage guests from checking into his inn shouldn't be *running* one.

"*I* didn't enter the contest. My daughter did. She thought it would boost business."

Even if the fog wasn't messing with the wiring in Brynn's head, the unexpected rumble of affection in *my daughter* prevented her from making a sassy comeback about why his business might *need* boosting.

But David McCrae wasn't off the hook yet.

"So in other words," Brynn said slowly, "you want us to voluntarily withdraw from the tour and disappoint your daughter so you don't have to."

"I like to think that I'm doing both of us a favor." He didn't sound the least bit repentant. "Like I said, the accommodations are a little on the rustic side."

"Not to mention isolated."

"Uh-huh. Not much going on at all. Even the chickens and the horses get bored."

Not only chickens but horses, too.

"Isolated and rustic and quiet," Brynn mused.

"*Really* quiet."

Brynn smiled.

"It sounds absolutely perfect, Mr. McCrae."

Chapter Three

"I'm sorry for interrupting, but the man insists on speaking to Ms. Dixon, and I wasn't sure what else to do. I didn't notice him at the meet and greet last night, and he's not a registered guest..." Susanne said as she shepherded Lucy through the lobby and down a carpeted hallway.

"You did the right thing," Lucy reassured her. "I've dealt with these situations before."

While the majority of Brynn's readers were well-behaved and polite, on rare occasions a fan showed up at an event, unedited manuscript in hand, or followed Brynn on social media and wanted to play the role of her best friend for the day. That's when Lucy stepped in. She wasn't a bouncer by any stretch of the imagination, but growing up as the oldest of six had fine-tuned her skills in the area of conflict resolution.

"He refused to give me his name when I asked, too." Susanne paused outside a door at the end of the hall, and her voice dropped to a whisper. "He said he wanted to surprise her."

Lucy ignored the trickle of unease that skittered down her

spine and forced a smile. "You take care of your breakfast guests. I've got this."

"All right, but please let me know if you need anything." Susanne cast one more dubious glance at the closed door before she retreated.

Lucy pulled in a breath and turned the knob. Swallowed a squeak when the man standing in front of the window pivoted toward her.

Maybe she shouldn't have sent Susanne away.

Lucy wasn't the kind of person who judged the proverbial book by its cover, but a thirtysomething guy in faded jeans and a gray hoodie, with a mane of tawny hair that matched the tangle of beard covering the lower half of his face, didn't look like one of Brynn's usual fans.

He crossed the room in two strides and stopped at the edge of her personal space. Lucy wasn't petite like Brynn, but she would have had to slip on a pair of stilettos in order to look him in the eye.

"The manager said you were asking to speak with Ms. Dixon." Lucy lifted her chin to make up for the difference and pressed out a polite smile. "I'm afraid she'll be checking out soon and won't have time to meet with visitors."

"I'm not—"

A strangled cry came from behind Lucy, and she whirled around. Brynn stood in the doorway. One hand covered her lips, the other was already reaching for the man who'd managed to sneak past Lucy.

He closed the distance between them first. Wrapped his arms around Brynn and lifted her right off her feet.

Instead of protesting, Brynn laughed. A light, airy sound Lucy realized she hadn't heard for quite some time.

The moment Brynn's feet touched the floor again, she poked a finger at his chest. "How... When did you get here?"

There was a glimmer of wry amusement in the aquamarine eyes that met Lucy's over Brynn's head. "A little while ago."

Lucy might not have recognized the face, but now she recognized the voice. Smooth and mellow with a hint of smoke.

But why would Caleb Beauchamp show up now?

Unfortunately, Lucy knew the answer to that question the moment it popped into her mind.

Most likely because he'd run short on cash.

Lucy had never met the man in person, but for the last three years she'd been wiring checks—extremely generous checks—to him. Mexico. Belize. Greece. France. Jamaica. The destination changed with every calendar month as he jetted around the globe on Brynn's dime.

Brynn had donated to scholarship funds for creative-writing majors in the past, but if that were the case, as far as Lucy knew, Caleb Beauchamp was the only long-term recipient of her employer's generosity.

Caleb would follow up with the obligatory thank-you call after the money was delivered, but Lucy couldn't help but notice that the last few times Brynn had been on the phone with him, she'd kept their conversations short.

Leaving Lucy to surmise that Caleb Beauchamp had started to deplete her employer's already-limited energy in much the same way he was depleting her savings account. A little at a time.

Brynn's gaze suddenly swung toward Lucy. "Were you two in on this together?"

"*No.*" The word came out a little more forcefully than Lucy intended. "I had no idea he was coming here."

And would have tried to prevent it if she'd had any inkling Caleb would show up in the middle of the book tour.

This was the second time he'd caught her off guard.

Caleb must have noticed something had changed with Brynn, too, because he'd managed to find out Lucy's personal cell-phone number and contacted her instead. Wanted to know

Brynn's schedule and expressed concern as to why she'd been slow to return his calls.

Even if Lucy hadn't signed a confidentiality agreement when Brynn hired her, she wouldn't have shared that information. Their relationship, whatever it was, wasn't any of Lucy's business, but it was her job to keep her employer's life as stress-free as possible. So she'd told Caleb the truth—Brynn was getting ready to go on a book tour—while keeping the details of said tour purposely vague.

But apparently not vague enough.

"I came up with this plan all on my own," Caleb confirmed. The glimmer of amusement turned into laughter and spilled into the tiny creases that fanned out from his eyes almost as if he'd read Lucy's mind. "And we hadn't quite gotten to the formal introductions yet."

"Then, allow me to do the honors." Smiling, Brynn stepped between them. "Caleb, this is Lucy, a close friend and the one who keeps my personal and my professional life running smoothly. And, Lucy, somewhere under all of this—" she reached up and sketched a quick outline of the beard and windswept surfer hair "—is Caleb Beauchamp...my son."

Chapter Four

Her *son?*

Lucy had practically memorized Brynn's bio, and there was no mention of a son.

Or a husband, current or ex-, for that matter.

While Lucy tried to find an internal file in which to place this new information, she realized she wasn't the only one who looked a little shocked by Brynn's announcement.

The questioning glance Caleb Beauchamp volleyed at Brynn was returned with a nod and a bright smile. And a nudge toward Lucy.

Caleb dutifully stretched out his hand, and when his fingers wrapped around Lucy's, she couldn't help but notice the expensive watch secured by a leather band around his wrist.

"It's nice to meet you, Lucy."

If only she could say the same.

The timing of Caleb's arrival was…suspicious.

Lucy searched his face, looking for a semblance of her employer, but the only similarity Lucy could see was a smattering of copper embers, several shades lighter than Brynn's fiery curls, glowing in the tangle of his beard.

Maybe he wasn't Brynn's biological son. Maybe he was the child of a close friend or family member who'd somehow wormed his way into Brynn's affection. A tenuous connection based on shared history and not DNA...

"We're both left-handed," Caleb murmured. "We don't like butter on our popcorn, either, but I suppose that doesn't count."

At the moment, the only thing Lucy was counting was the number of minutes or—*please-God-no*—hours it would take to secure a rental car and continue on their journey to Jackson Lake, their next Mistletoe Stop. Leaving Caleb Beauchamp, the newest ingredient in the stew of problems Lucy had to solve, to return to some exotic locale so he could continue to work on his tan.

"I can't believe you're here," Brynn said, unwittingly voicing Lucy's thoughts out loud. "How did you find me? You didn't drive in this awful weather, did you? Have you had breakfast yet?"

Lucy had heard Brynn encourage teenagers to pursue their dreams, challenge aspiring writers to never give up and win over the toughest critics with her sweet Southern charm. This was the first time she'd ever heard Brynn sound like...a *mom*.

Caleb grinned, and there it was, hiding in plain sight. A dimple just below his right cheekbone, the perfect match to Brynn's. "Your readers have been talking about it, and I followed the Instagram photo trail. Yes, but I've been in worse. And I talked the flight attendant into an extra bag of pretzels."

I'm sure you did, Lucy thought. *You and your Southern drawl and your...your dimple.*

And here she'd thought that circumventing Ainsley's scheme to bring the fictional Trace Hunter to life would be her greatest challenge for the day.

★ ★ ★

Caleb could almost *see* the wheels turning in Lucy Gable's head.

Not so easy to get rid of me when I'm standing in the same room with you, is it? he wanted to say.

He shouldn't have been surprised that Brynn's personal assistant would be traveling with her. Or that the hotel manager had sent her instead of Brynn to intercept him.

There'd been no one behind the desk when he'd entered the hotel lobby. Caleb had followed the sound of laughter to the breakfast room, expecting to find his mom making friends over coffee and pastries. Instead, he'd caught the eye of the manager, who'd quickly escorted him down the hallway to a room as far away from the guests as possible while still technically being inside the building.

Okay. So maybe he *did* look a little rough.

Crossing several time zones could have that effect on a guy. So did a few sleepless nights and a last-minute change in plans.

Caleb blamed Lucy Gable for all three.

Maybe he shouldn't have bypassed Brynn and called her assistant, but something was going on, and Caleb had hoped Lucy would provide some insight as to what that something was.

Instead, she'd informed him that "Ms. Dixon" was about to leave on her holiday book tour and that everything was "fine."

Caleb didn't particularly like the word. A generic term that could either be the truth or a cover-up.

He didn't like getting the runaround, either, and Brynn's assistant was pretty good at it.

Caleb had pushed back a little, but Lucy the Gatekeeper had denied him access to any more information. While he'd been formulating a different strategy, she'd said a polite goodbye and hung up on him.

He'd tossed his backpack into the cargo hold of the plane and almost taken out Mel in the process. He hadn't been able to dodge the mechanic's question—*What's got your cables in a twist?*—though.

In hindsight, he should have known Mel wouldn't believe a half-hearted *Nothing* any more than he'd believed Lucy's *Fine*.

But he was almost thirty-two years old. It seemed a little juvenile to admit that Brynn hadn't been asking as many questions about what was going on in his life. Or that she didn't return his calls or texts right away. They'd gone for years—twenty-five of them to be exact—without contact before he'd found her seven years ago. It wasn't like Brynn was shutting him out completely. And she had a lot on her plate, as Lucy Gable had been quick to point out.

In many ways, their relationship was still new, and Caleb was trying to figure things out. When he'd first met Brynn, spending time with her had almost felt like he was betraying the memory of the loving woman who'd adopted him. And even though Caleb was careful to call Brynn by her name in public, it was becoming more and more natural to think of her as "Mom."

To think of himself as her...son.

Which was why he'd called Lucy to begin with.

"I'm not sure," Caleb had finally admitted to Mel. "How's that for an answer? But something seems off with Brynn."

"If you're concerned, adjust your schedule and go home," Mel had said with her usual bluntness. "Christmas is kind of the perfect time for that. I think someone even wrote a song about it."

Once the seed of the idea was planted, Caleb was surprised at how quickly it had taken root and grown into a full-fledged plan. Less than forty-eight hours later, he'd been on a flight back to the States.

It had taken a little detective work on Caleb's part to find out Brynn's exact location, but fortunately, given the staggering number of fans who tuned into their favorite author's comings and goings, a few clicks told Caleb everything he needed to know. He hadn't been forced to rely on Lucy at all.

Caleb's gaze shifted to Brynn's assistant again.

Lucy had moved a respectful distance away to give them some space, but there was a guarded look in her dark-as-midnight eyes.

How long had she worked for Brynn?

Two years? Three? Long enough to earn her trust. To make herself indispensable. Long enough that Brynn had let her guard down and referred to Lucy as a friend.

Long enough to entrust her with a secret that had the potential to change both of their lives if it came out.

A tentative knock on the door preceded Susanne's entry.

"Ms. Dixon?" Her brow was furrowed, as if she wasn't sure what she was going to find on the other side. Her gaze bounced between Lucy and Caleb before settling on Brynn again. "I put together a breakfast tray and left it in the library so you can have some privacy."

Privacy?

Brynn loved being around people. Loved hearing their stories and asking questions about their lives, not hiding away and being waited on like some high-maintenance celebrity.

Now Caleb was even more glad he'd listened to Mel and come back to the States.

"Thank you so much, Susanne." Brynn smiled. "I hope there's enough for three."

"Of course." The manager returned the smile and her gaze lit on Caleb again as she backpedaled toward the door. "I'll brew another pot of coffee."

After she'd left the room, Caleb could feel Lucy studying him, no doubt looking for further evidence that he really was related to Brynn.

Maybe now that she knew the truth, though, she wouldn't be so quick to get rid of him.

"Brynn, I can finish packing before we check out," Lucy offered.

Or maybe not.

Caleb's gaze shifted to Brynn. "You're leaving today?"

"That's the plan."

Lucy was the one who answered his question, but the telltale glance she cast out the window told Caleb she wasn't as confident as her tone.

"Please, don't rush off, Lucy," Brynn said. "You haven't eaten breakfast yet, either, and if I know you, you already started packing when we got back from the coffee shop last night."

Lucy didn't deny it, but she looked torn between making her employer happy and expediting their departure.

"Caleb won't mind if you join us," Brynn added.

Caleb did, actually, but he could play nice, too.

"That would be great."

Lucy's expression remained neutral, but Caleb had a feeling she wasn't thrilled with Brynn's suggestion, either.

He trailed behind the women as Lucy bypassed the main dining room and led them down another hallway into a comfortable room. A wall of glass overlooked a pond behind the hotel. Blue twinkle lights spilled from a stone fountain in the center and flowed across the ice, mimicking the movement of water. A bronze heron with a bright red bow around its neck was poised to greet guests at the end of the snow-covered path.

For Caleb, who'd just spent the last month in a place where the sculptures were created by wind and sand and the temperatures topped a hundred degrees, there was something enchanting about the scene.

Brynn sank into one of the chairs, and Lucy immediately reached for the carafe of coffee.

"Thank you—" A cell phone began to ring, startling all of them. "Oh, that's right. This one is yours." Brynn laughed and shook her head as she retrieved a phone from the pocket of her sweater. "That's why I'd gone looking for you." She handed it to Lucy, who moved toward the window while she took the call.

"Hello?"

Caleb couldn't hear the other end of the conversation, but out of the corner of his eye he saw Lucy's shoulders stiffen. She murmured a polite thank-you before she hung up.

"The rental company?" Brynn guessed. "Do they have a car for us?"

"No, someone took the last one about an hour ago, but I'll talk to Susanne about a late checkout and keep looking."

Oops.

"Sorry...that's my bad," Caleb said.

Lucy's gaze swung to him. "*You* rented it?"

"It's a good thing, though, right? Because now we can all travel together."

"You're coming with us?"

Caleb found it a little disconcerting that both the women in the room asked the question at the same time. He could understand Lucy Gable's dismay—especially if there was a reason why she'd been so evasive when they'd spoken on the phone. But the shadow that skimmed through Brynn's eyes at his announcement tripped another internal alarm.

For several years, Brynn had been trying to pin him down for a visit. And now, when he was here—for Christmas, no less—she was suddenly hesitant to have him around?

"I thought I'd tag along with you for a while." He smiled at Brynn. "If that's okay."

"We're on a book tour," Lucy blurted out.

"I promise I won't get in the way..." Caleb fished the keys from the pocket of his jeans and jingled them as a reminder. "And right now, it looks like I'm the only one with a car."

Chapter Five

Lucy wanted to toss her cell phone into the nearest snowbank.

She'd never put much stock in Murphy's Law, especially when it came to Monday mornings, but now she was beginning to think there was some truth to the old saying. Because every time her phone rang, there'd been a crisis waiting for her on the other end.

Ainsley. The airport. Movin' On Car Rentals.

The number showing on the screen wasn't in her contact list, and Lucy found herself hoping the caller was a robot who wanted her to book a Caribbean cruise instead of an actual person this time.

"Hello?"

"Hello… Am I speaking to Lucy Gable?"

"Yes, you are."

"Oh, good." A sigh, proof the person on the other end of the line was an actual person, filtered into her ear. "I was hoping I'd catch you before you left the hotel. This is Helen Anderson. The mayor of Jackson Lake?"

"Ms. Anderson. Of course."

Jackson Lake was the next stop on the Mistletoe tour. Helen Anderson had been a fan of Brynn's books since college and, after seeing Ainsley's post, had exceeded the one-hundred-words-or-less guideline and practically written a thesis singing the praises of her hometown.

"I was going to call you after we checked out this morning." Lucy pinched the phone between her shoulder and ear and tucked her pajamas into her suitcase. Made a mental note to purchase some in flannel. "Our flight this afternoon was actually canceled, so we'll be driving to Jackson Lake instead. We might not make it in time for dinner, but I'm hoping I can meet with you tomorrow morning to nail down the details for Ms. Dixon's book signing."

"Well…that's actually the reason I'm calling."

Something in Helen's tone had Lucy's fingers tightening around the phone.

"One of the trees in the town square fell and took out a power line during the night. It sounds like it's going to take a while before they're able to restore power," Helen said. "Thanks to the storm, the crews were already dealing with some outages in the northern part of the county, so we're not at the top of the list."

The knot that had formed in Lucy's stomach loosened a little. Compared to what she'd had to deal with so far, a temporary power outage didn't seem too bad.

"I assume the town hall has a backup generator?"

The mayor's superfan status notwithstanding, one of the reasons Lucy had chosen Jackson Lake from the dozens of entries that had poured in was that Helen mentioned the town hall had been a church the year Jackson Lake was founded. And the bride of the very first couple who'd exchanged vows there?

Helen's great-great-grandmother.

Another dash of romance for the Mistletoe Stop tour.

"Well…we talked about putting one in the budget, but they're expensive. If we lose power or a pipe breaks, we move our meeting to the café down the street."

Lucy could work with that.

It had been standing room only at the coffee shop the night before, but no one had seemed to mind. In fact, Lucy noticed the smaller space felt cozier. Made the evening seem like a gathering of good friends instead of an event.

And if Jackson Lake lived up to the reputation of most small towns, it had a flourishing grapevine. Spreading the word about a last-minute change in the location shouldn't be difficult to accomplish.

"How many people do you think the café can hold?"

Helen cleared her throat. "I'm sorry… I guess I wasn't clear, Ms. Gable. The town hall isn't the only building without power. The outage affected all the businesses on Main Street and most of the private residences, too. And the café is closed during the month of December so Vivienne Larson can spend Christmas with her daughter in Orlando."

Snow. Downed trees.

Lucy was beginning to think they were weather-related plagues meant to stop the Mistletoe Stop tour in its tracks.

She walked over to the window and saw Caleb scraping ice off the windshield of a compact car that looked like a toy sandwiched between the pickup trucks parked on either side of it.

No wonder it had been the only vehicle left at the rental company.

"Please tell Ms. Dixon that I'm sorry about all of this. Everyone in Jackson Lake had been looking forward to meeting her in person, especially our Lattes and Lit book club."

Had been looking forward to meeting her?

"I don't understand. Are you *canceling* the entire event?"

"Well…"

Lucy winced. She'd already figured out that when Helen

started the sentence with that word it meant another adjustment to the already-adjusted plan.

"We really don't have any choice. And with this next storm moving in, I'm not sure what kind of turnout we'd have, to be honest. When I went shopping yesterday, the aisles were filled with people stocking up on supplies. I had to buy a loaf of pumpernickel bread because everything else was gone, and my husband doesn't care for pumpernickel at all."

Neither did Lucy, but at the moment there were more pressing details to consider than the empty shelves in the bakery section of the grocery store.

"I made a reservation at the Lilac and Lace B and B in Jackson Lake. Do *they* have a generator?"

There'd only been one place to stay in the area, and like Susanne's boutique hotel, the bed-and-breakfast had a smaller number of rooms and a cozy, more intimate atmosphere.

Lucy had purposely added an extra week at the Lilac and Lace following the signing so Brynn could relax before her next appearance.

"I don't think so," Helen said. "The building is on the historic register, and Betsy likes to keep things authentic."

Helen was probably right. When Lucy had looked up the website, one of the things that made the bed-and-breakfast unique was that it had started out as a boarding house near the turn of the century.

"Under the circumstances, though, I'm sure Betsy will give you a refund. And if it helps," the mayor added brightly, "the Ladies in Waiting of Jackson Lake plan to show up at the next Mistletoe Stop. They want to support Brynn, and meet Trace Hunter, of course."

If Lucy heard that name one more time…

"I'm sorry, but Trace won't be at the meet and greet."

"Oh." Disappointment weighed down the word. "One of the members of the book club mentioned she'd seen it on a chat."

Ainsley.

Lucy would have to search the message boards and shut down the rumors before things got totally out of hand.

"I appreciate the update, Ms. Anderson," she said. "And I'm sorry about the outage. I hope everything gets back to normal soon."

Helen chuckled. "This *is* our normal, I'm afraid. We'll be fine, don't you worry. And once this next storm passes through, you and Ms. Dixon will be fine, too."

Fine.

Lucy didn't particularly care for the word.

"Thank you." She hung up the phone and resisted an inexplicable urge to look out the window again.

Brynn had a son. Lucy was still trying to wrap her head around that.

Brynn had appeared genuinely thrilled to see him, but when Caleb had announced that he would drive them to their next stop, some of her enthusiasm had faded.

Which was why, family or not, Lucy still didn't trust him.

But she *was* stuck with him, at least for now.

After closing her suitcase, Lucy finished straightening up the room and then rapped on Brynn's door.

"It's open."

Brynn was sitting in a chair by the window, her favorite fringed leather jacket draped over her lap. The slight slump of her shoulders made Lucy determined not to add to whatever burden she was already carrying.

And she wouldn't let Caleb Beauchamp add to it, either.

"Is there anything you need?" Lucy took a quick inventory of the room. Although Brynn's suitcase stood at the foot of the bed, ready to go, the dresses Lucy had hung up when they'd arrived were still in the wardrobe.

In recent weeks, Lucy had noticed that Brynn seemed more forgetful.

Shortly before they'd left Nashville, Lucy had set up a phone interview between Brynn and the editor of a popular women's magazine. Lucy had left the house to run some errands and, when she'd returned, found Brynn sitting outside on the patio. When she'd asked about the interview, the blank look on her employer's face only confirmed what the doctor had told Brynn: getting distracted, forgetting things, both were common side effects of stress. But Brynn had looked so stricken when she realized she'd missed the appointment, Lucy became that much more determined to make sure nothing like that happened again.

"It looks like the snow is starting to subside a little." Lucy unzipped the garment bag on the bed and reached for the dress Brynn had worn the night before, a sheath of emerald green sequins that stretched from neckline to knee and reflected light like an '80s disco ball.

"I hope the bed-and-breakfast in Jackson Lake is as nice as this," Brynn said. "Susanne is such a wonderful hostess I wouldn't mind staying a little longer."

Lucy wished they could, too, but Susanne had mentioned that a couple on their honeymoon had already booked the suite for the rest of the week.

"Helen Anderson—she's the one who entered the contest— called a few minutes ago." Lucy slipped another dress off its hanger. "It looks like we'll have to tweak our plans a little."

"*Tweak* sounds better than *cancel*," Brynn said. "What happened?"

Lucy summed up her conversation with the mayor, and when she got to the part about the lack of alternative venues, Brynn looked thoughtful rather than concerned.

"What do you suggest we do?"

"If the businesses on Main Street don't have power, then the B and B I booked doesn't, either." Lucy reached for another dress and noticed a shoe peeking out from under the bed. She discreetly scooped it up and reunited it with its mate. "It doesn't make sense to drive all the way to Jackson Lake, though. According to Helen, the outages can last awhile, and we have a week and a half before your next book signing."

"A week and a half," Brynn murmured.

"I know. It's a long time," Lucy admitted. Longer than the extra two days they'd planned to spend in Frost before the event. "We could find another place to stay in the area tonight, and I'll book a flight back to Nashville. Since we're heading south, not north, the weather won't be a factor, and we'll have plenty of time to make it back for the signing. By then, the weather will be better here, too."

It had to be, Lucy reasoned. Snowstorms were spaced out a bit, right? They didn't follow one right after the other like waves on the ocean. "I can rebook our flight to an airport that's closer to the town."

If there *was* an airport. But given their options, this plan made the most sense.

"Or…we can extend our stay at Spruce Hill Farm instead," Brynn said.

Driving straight to the last Mistletoe Stop hadn't even made Lucy's list.

Of the four towns she'd chosen for the tour, Frost was the smallest. Population 1,150, if Lucy remembered correctly.

But Grace McCrae had promised that her hometown's heart more than made up for its size, and that if Frost was one of the stops on Brynn's Mistletoe Stop tour, she wouldn't regret it.

"It's a two-and-a-half-hour drive," Lucy said slowly. "And it's possible our rooms won't be available this early, either."

"Or they might." Brynn's lips lifted in a smile. As if the thought of spending a little more time in Frost was a good thing.

And maybe it was, now that Lucy thought about it. Not only would Brynn get the additional downtime her doctor had claimed was crucial for her emotional well-being, this latest wrinkle might encourage the man who'd hijacked the rental car to resign as their chauffeur and turn the keys over to Lucy.

"Lucy…" Brynn's smile faded a little. "I realize that meeting Caleb must have been a bit of a shock."

Lucy sucked in a quiet breath. She hadn't been sure Brynn would bring it up.

"Yes," she admitted carefully. "But that's your personal life, and you get to decide what—" *or who* "—you want to share."

"Thank you," Brynn murmured. "But sometimes those choices aren't ours alone to make. I gave Caleb up for adoption after he was born, and we only met a few years ago. I should have told you sooner, but I—I'd made a promise."

Lucy knew all about promises. Keeping them wasn't always easy. Sometimes it required sacrifice. Taking a different path instead of pursuing your dreams.

But what had Brynn promised? And why?

Even if Lucy had dared to ask the questions, the opportunity disappeared when the door opened and Caleb walked into the room.

Caleb's gaze lit on Brynn. It was obvious something had changed in the ten minutes he'd slipped outside to brush the snow off the rental car. In the library, he couldn't help but notice she'd barely touched the food on her plate and the coffee Lucy had poured for her had gotten cold. Now the sparkle had returned to her eyes.

Caleb would like to think she was looking forward to going on a road trip together, but he had a feeling it was more than that.

"Did I miss something?" he asked Brynn.

"Our next Mistletoe Stop was canceled. There isn't enough time to replace Jackson Lake with another town, so Lucy and I were discussing our options."

"Nashville?"

"That was one of them, but we're thinking about going straight to the next town."

The idea obviously appealed to Brynn, but Lucy's expression wasn't as easy to read. In fact, the only time Caleb detected a ripple on the surface of Lucy Gable's calm exterior was when he tossed a pebble in the water.

Good.

Because Caleb had a plan, too. Stir things up a little and see what was underneath.

"Works for me." He watched Lucy perform a quick sweep of the room before she closed Brynn's suitcase and zipped it shut. "What's the window between now and the next storm? How far are we going?"

"Almost three hours, depending on the road conditions?" Brynn looked at Lucy for confirmation, and she nodded.

Caleb glanced at the Breitling on his wrist. The watch face looked as intimidating as the cockpit of a fighter jet, but it had proved invaluable when a guy was hopping between countries and time zones. It had also been a gift from Brynn when he'd completed flight school. A gift Caleb would have refused to accept if the possibility of hurting his mom's feelings hadn't outweighed the feeling that he didn't deserve it.

"If we leave now, we should be able to make it."

Lucy looked at Caleb's watch, too, and then her eyes met his. "I'll call the inn and find out if our rooms are available now. I didn't know you'd be joining us so I can't promise they'll have an extra one, though."

Reminding Caleb once again that he'd invited himself along on this trip.

"I was fortunate enough to get the last car. Maybe I'll get the last room, too."

Lucy was silent for a moment. Reloading, no doubt, because trying to make him feel guilty hadn't hit the mark.

"Frost will seem a little tame after Paris, so you might not find a lot in the way of entertainment."

Paris?

He hadn't been in… Oh, right. Caleb had forgotten Lucy was the one who handled Brynn's day-to-day finances, too. He'd spent two nights on the ground catching up on paperwork and networking with contacts before his next flight, but Lucy must have come up with her own theory about the way he'd spent his time there.

Oh, well. Caleb was used to people accusing him of being a slacker. Including members of his own family.

"Don't worry about me," Caleb said easily. "I've been burning the candle at both ends lately, so a little R & R sounds great."

Lucy nodded. "I'll ask about another room, then."

Would she?

Considering her track record, Caleb had his doubts.

But while he was wondering if he could trust Lucy, he couldn't shake the feeling she didn't quite trust him, either.

Chapter Six

The narrow country road that boasted more steep drops and hairpin curves than a bobsled course came to an abrupt stop at a heavy wooden gate. On the other side, fresh tire tracks cut a swath between the neat rows of evergreen trees fanning out from either side of the driveway.

Brynn's gaze followed the tracks, and her breath caught in her throat.

Perched on a hill was a sweet little wedding cake of a house, three tiers high, with a rusty, star-shaped weather vane as the topper. Icicles dripped between each layer of the white clapboard siding. If it hadn't been for the shutters and the front door, both painted a warm buttery yellow, the house would have blended in perfectly with the snow-covered landscape.

Brynn believed in love at first sight. Had written countless books about it. But this was the first time she'd experienced it for herself.

"This can't be right." Caleb frowned at the map on the dashboard as if it had deliberately taken them off course. "It doesn't look like a bed-and-breakfast. The gate has a lock on it. There's no sign…unless you count the one that says *No Trespassing* tacked on the tree over there."

"This is it," Brynn said.

The property matched David McCrae's description. Isolated. Quiet. Rustic. And remembering their conversation, a locked gate didn't surprise her at all.

No. What surprised Brynn were the tears scalding her eyes. And the feeling that this place was exactly where she was supposed to be. *Needed* to be.

And suddenly, the snowstorm predicted to wreak havoc on the northern part of the state seemed more like divine intervention.

"I don't know why the gate would be locked," Lucy said from the back seat. "I called this morning and left a voice mail, asking if our rooms would be available if we arrived today. Someone from the inn left a message while we were loading up the car and said we were all set."

"Maybe you should call again and let them know we're here," Caleb suggested.

Lucy was already on her phone. "This is Lucy Gable," Lucy said in the polite but matter-of-fact tone that people used when they were responding to a recorded message instead of a human being. "I called earlier about a change in Ms. Dixon's travel itinerary. We're actually here…at the gate…and I was wondering if you could text the code—"

"It's a padlock," Caleb murmured.

"Or send someone to open it for us," Lucy continued without missing a beat. "Thank you, and we look forward to checking in soon."

Out of the corner of her eye, Brynn saw Caleb's lips twitch.

She had no idea why her two favorite people in the world seemed to be at odds. Caleb and Lucy were close in age, and even though her assistant was quiet, she was also thoughtful and kind and passionate about her job. Traits she and Caleb had in common.

Brynn guessed the tension had something to do with the fact that Caleb had shown up unannounced and then invited himself along on the book tour. Lucy was flexible when the situation called for it, but she was extremely protective of Brynn, too.

But then, so was Caleb.

Which made the timing of his visit a little challenging for Brynn, too.

She'd planned to tell him. Eventually. When there was an actual diagnosis instead of a growing list of symptoms that her doctor had hinted might be more in Brynn's head than her body.

Caleb had been fifteen years old when his adoptive mother had lost her battle with cancer. Brynn didn't want to worry him, especially when she didn't know what she was dealing with. Didn't want to worry Lucy, either.

It would have been one thing if all those covert glances bouncing back and forth between Caleb and Lucy was their way of getting to know one another. But Brynn could tell they were watching her, too. With the intensity of two amateur detectives searching for clues.

If only she could find something that would bring them together and take their focus off her...

A loud buzz overrode the hum of the car's engine. A snowmobile burst between a row of trees and spun a half circle, churning up a cloud of snow in the driveway. Two headlights glared at them from the opposite side of the gate.

The driver, a modern-day cowboy in faded denim and Kevlar chaps, hopped off the machine. He strode toward them, one gloved hand extracting a ring of keys from the pocket of his fleece-lined coat. A helmet concealed the man's face, and Brynn decided that was probably a good thing because his muscular frame practically vibrated with impatience.

She waved a thank-you when he opened the gate, and in response, he pointed toward the house, straddled his sled and disappeared from sight again.

"Do you want me to look for other accommodations?" Lucy broke the silence. "We may end up a little farther from town, but there has to be something available."

"No." Brynn watched a gust of wind capture the weather vane and break into a lively reel on the roof. "I love it."

Caleb looked skeptical, too. "Are you sure?"

"I'm sure." So, so sure.

"All right." Caleb put the car in gear, and the tires spun in place, almost as if it were giving Brynn a few more seconds to change her mind.

"There's a sign." She spotted a piece of wood the size of a cutting board nailed to one of the trees.

"Axes Available Free of Charge." Caleb read the hand-lettered words out loud. "I might be wrong about this, but don't most bed-and-breakfasts offer, um, a complimentary *breakfast?*"

In the back seat, Brynn heard a noise that sounded suspiciously like a low growl. She couldn't be sure, though, because in the three years Lucy had worked for Brynn, she'd never heard her growl.

"Spruce Hill is a Christmas-tree farm *and* a bed-and-breakfast," Lucy said. "It also happens to be close to Frost, one of our winning entries."

"Frost," Caleb repeated. "I suppose the name alone scored the town a few extra points."

"Not really. Readers were asked to write a brief essay on why their hometown should be a Mistletoe Stop, and Grace McCrae's was...sweet."

David McCrae had said he hadn't entered the contest, his daughter did.

A family business, then?

Either way, it looked to Brynn like they could use some.

There were no other vehicles in sight. No lights or pine boughs woven through the railing on the wide front porch. Christmas wasn't that far away, but the only decoration Brynn could see was the bright red handle of a shovel impaled in one of the snowbanks that flanked the walkway.

"I'll unload the bags after we check in," Caleb said.

He was giving Brynn another opportunity to change her mind, too.

She shrugged into the crimson leather coat she'd chosen for the trip, assuming (hilariously) that its faux-fur collar would add another level of protection from the falling temperatures. She took the front steps one at a time, hoping Lucy and Caleb would think she was being mindful of slippery spots and not because every joint in her body was screaming at her for daring to move.

The yellow door that had welcomed Brynn from a distance was bare, too, except for a nail where a wreath should have been.

She reached out and tested the knob.

At least it wasn't locked.

She pushed the door open, and another gust of wind followed her inside, ruffling a stack of papers on the oak secretary desk in the corner of the lobby.

Brynn looked around, surprised—but not disappointed—by what she saw. It would have been tempting to go a little over-the-top and stick with the decor of a bygone era, but whoever had had their hand in the process of converting the farmhouse into an inn had skillfully updated the interior while staying true to its roots. Cream-colored walls formed the backdrop for a palette of soft blues and greens. The vintage bulbs in the chandelier overhead cast an amber glow on hardwood floor. There were a few homey touches, hand-hooked rugs and a barnwood frame behind the desk that displayed a quilt instead of the usual watercolor print. Comfortable and cozy without the kitsch.

While Brynn was soaking in her surroundings, Lucy made a beeline for the desk.

"Someone left us a note." Lucy picked up a piece of paper and skimmed the contents. "David McCrae had to deal with an emergency, but our rooms are ready and he left the keys. Gable Cedar. Dixon Balsam." She glanced at Caleb, who'd come in behind her, dragging suitcases in spite of what he'd said about waiting. "I requested a third room, but I don't see a key for Caleb."

Was the hopeful note in Lucy's tone a figment of Brynn's imagination?

No. Caleb's brow lifted, a hint that he'd heard it, too.

"After you're settled, I'll drive into Frost and find a gas station," he said. "And a hardware store with a camping section in case I need to buy a sleeping bag for the car."

"Lucy...you can ride along with Caleb, if you'd like," Brynn offered. "There might be something you need, too."

"My emails are piling up," Lucy said quickly. "And I have to call Ainsley back."

Brynn let her win this round. In spite of their rocky start—which Brynn knew she could take some of the blame for—there would be plenty of time for Caleb and Lucy to get to know each other better.

"I'll bring up the suitcases first," Caleb offered. "If your keys are there, I don't think anyone will mind if you find your rooms and unpack."

Before Lucy could protest, he started up the flight of stairs to the second floor.

Brynn followed, wishing there weren't so many of them.

The landing at the top branched out into two narrow hallways. A sign with an arrow pointing left guided them to the guest rooms.

There were tiny wooden trees on the doors in lieu of numbers so she waited while Lucy and Caleb had a lively debate over which one was the balsam and which one was the cedar.

Brynn could have settled the matter with a quick search on her phone but decided not to intervene. Arguing was a *form* of communication.

Caleb set the luggage down outside their rooms, but Lucy lingered in the hallway a moment.

"Would you like me to help you unpack?" she murmured to Brynn.

If Caleb hadn't been standing there, Brynn would have accepted Lucy's offer. It was one thing to have David McCrae think she was a diva, but Brynn didn't want her son to wonder why she couldn't hang up her own clothes in the closet.

"Thank you, but no." Brynn waved at the door. "You go ahead and catch up on things. I'm fine."

"All right." Lucy hesitated. "But if you need anything—"

"Let one of us know," Caleb finished the sentence, reminding Brynn that Lucy wasn't the only one looking out for Brynn's best interests.

I love them both, Lord, but right now, I don't even know what's best for me.

But Brynn trusted that He did, and that was enough to carry her through the day even if the future was as foggy as her brain.

Lucy's bedroom door snapped shut, and Brynn sank onto the edge of a poster bed that took up half the room. The pillows were as thick and puffy as cumulus clouds, the down duvet buttoned into a flannel cover for the season. There was an antique nightstand and a chair tucked in the corner with the slanted ceiling. Through a diamond-shaped window, Brynn could see a weathered outbuilding behind the house.

A sigh slipped out before she could prevent it.

Spruce Hill Farm was perfect, just like she'd known it would be.

Brynn contemplated closing her eyes for a few minutes before she unpacked. But even though the tower of pillows looked inviting, she'd been sitting for hours and decided to go downstairs to see if David McCrae considered a coffeepot a standard amenity or if it fell under the category of pampering.

After exchanging her boots for slippers, Brynn opened the door and eased into the hall. An attempt to be stealthy, knowing Lucy would appear in a heartbeat if she thought Brynn needed something.

There was no one downstairs to give her a tour of the inn so Brynn had no choice but to do some exploring on her own.

Like most older homes, the first level was a warren of narrow hallways and rooms. Brynn peeked into the one adjacent to the lobby. Comfortable chairs circled a low coffee table like spokes around a wheel, but there was no sign of the jigsaw puzzle their host had promised. A fireplace with a gas insert took up one corner of the room, and in the other was an antique sideboard with—Brynn checked—two empty carafes.

She backtracked and tiptoed through an enormous eat-in kitchen that smelled like burnt toast, her goal the set of Dutch doors she hoped led to the common dining room.

Instead, she stepped into a cozy slice of heaven on earth.

There weren't any tables at all unless you counted an old wooden pallet positioned between the chairs and the sofa. A fireplace made of jagged gray- and cream-colored stones that looked like they'd come straight from the field took up the center of one wall. An empty coffee mug sat on the hearth where a fire still simmered behind a mesh screen.

Brynn passed a gallery of black-and-white photographs on the wall, squeezed between two mismatched chairs with pillowy cushions and found her way blocked by a lopsided cardboard box on the floor next to the sofa. Tucked inside a nest of shredded paper was what appeared to be a cache of homemade Christmas ornaments.

Brynn was leaning down to inspect a cotton-ball snowman with tiny twigs for arms when the doors rattled and a furry missile hurtled toward her.

A split second before impact, the dog veered off course to investigate the empty coffee mug instead.

"Sorry," Brynn chuckled. "I've been looking for some, too."

The dog padded over to her, and she knelt down to give its ragged ear a scratch. It was a mixed breed of some sort, with a mottled gray-and-brown coat and a snow-white patch over one eye. In response to her greeting, the dog performed a tap dance, shedding a mixture of snow and pine needles and sawdust on the rug at Brynn's feet.

"Aren't you a sweetie pie?" She was one of those people who loved animals but had never had one of her own. She was either holed up in her office or at an airport, and neither one of those settings made for happy pets...

"You aren't supposed to be in here."

A man appeared in the doorway, and Brynn stood so quickly she almost lost her balance.

Their eyes met across the room, and she realized he hadn't been speaking to the dog.

Chapter Seven

Brynn had never seen their host's face but even without the snowmobile helmet there was no mistaking the crisp, no-nonsense voice.

The man himself, on the other hand... Nowhere near the old curmudgeon Brynn had imagined he would be.

David McCrae was...well, downright gorgeous, actually.

Early to midfifties, with close-cropped dark hair and rugged features. A lean but muscular physique that paired well with the fleece jacket and jeans.

His gaze swept over her, pausing a moment to linger on the comfy slippers made to look like cowboy boots. A birthday gift from Caleb that traveled with Brynn everywhere she went. They probably did look a little unusual with cream-colored leggings and a cashmere sweater, though.

The dog whined and lifted a paw for Brynn to shake, almost as if it were trying to apologize for David's gruffness.

"Not now, Patch."

The dog sighed and flopped down on the rug at Brynn's feet. Patch?

Personally, Brynn would have come up with something a little more…creative. A name chosen to reflect the dog's unique personality, not describe its markings.

"Sorry." David stepped into the room. "He likes to think of himself as the official greeter."

"Someone has to be," Brynn said sweetly.

Something flickered in David's eyes—*touché*, perhaps?—before they narrowed. "Lucy Gable? The woman I spoke with on the phone?"

The moment of reckoning.

"Lucy is my assistant, and she wasn't available so I answered her phone."

"And you are…"

"Brynn Dixon."

The diva, she was tempted to add.

She could see David replaying their conversation in his mind, and the color in his windburned cheeks turned a shade darker.

Because she believed in second chances more than first impressions, Brynn extended her hand.

David hesitated for a fraction of a second before he crossed the room and stopped in front of her.

His fingers folded around Brynn's, and she could feel the gentle scrape of calluses against her palm. Eye-level with a button in the middle of his jacket, Brynn breathed in the scent of the outdoors. Snow and fresh-cut pine and woodsmoke.

David released her hand, breaking the connection. He'd just come in from the cold, but for some reason, Brynn was the one suppressing a shiver.

"A tree fell down and blocked one of the side roads. I was in the middle of cutting it down when I saw your car pull up to the gate," David said. "And check-in isn't until three in the afternoon."

"I realize we're a little early—"

"A week and a half."

Brynn had been referring to the time of day but couldn't deny that he was right.

"Our third stop had to cancel at the last minute because of a power outage, and with another storm on the way, we didn't have a lot of options."

"Look, Ms. Dixon—"

"It's Brynn. Remember?"

"Brynn," he repeated. "As you can see, I'm not exactly prepared for guests."

This was a bed-and-breakfast. Shouldn't he always be prepared for guests?

Brynn didn't have a chance to ask because Lucy swept into the room.

"That staircase is like hiking up to Clingmans Dome, but I don't see an elevator anywhere. I'll find out if there's a room for you on the main floor. The Wi-Fi password is *keepontrying,* which I thought was a joke until..." She pulled up short when she realized Brynn wasn't alone in the room. "Hello."

"Lucy, this is David McCrae." Brynn made the introduction just in case Lucy hadn't made the connection. "Our host."

David inclined his head.

Pink tinted Lucy's cheeks. "Mr. McCrae. It's nice to meet you." Patch trotted over, seeking attention, and she obliged with a quick pat on his head. "Most of my communication has been with Grace, and I feel like I know her already. Is she here?"

"No, she isn't." David's voice sounded tight. "Grace is a freshman in college and won't be home until her Christmas break starts."

The flicker of surprise in Lucy's eyes told Brynn she hadn't been privy to that particular detail, but she recovered with her usual poise.

"I'm really sorry for the change in plans, and I hope our being here early isn't too much of an inconvenience."

David acknowledged her apology with a brief it-is-what-it-is nod.

"The third room we requested?" Brynn spoke up. "For Caleb Beauchamp?"

Brynn felt, rather than saw, David sigh.

"It will be ready soon. I have to fix the thermostat, but I guess that's easier than adding an elevator," he said. "By the way, there aren't any guest bedrooms on the first floor. The gathering room and the library are shared spaces, but everything else—" a pointed look at Brynn "—including the kitchen is off-limits."

Brynn glanced at the hearth. She'd thought *this* was the room David had mentioned on the phone.

Which made her guilty of trespassing.

By the end of their stay, Brynn had a feeling she'd be guilty of a lot of things.

She smiled at David McCrae.

Something told her that regret wouldn't be one of them.

Chapter Eight

He was terrible at this.

David walked over to the woodpile and tossed another log on the fire, sending a shower of sparks up the chimney.

Lynette would have greeted the author and her entourage at the door. With a smile. There would have been low lights and candles burning. Sterling-silver carafes filled with hot chocolate and coffee flavored with a dash of cinnamon. A fire in the gathering room to make them forget about the temperature outside.

The woman had had skills.

So did David, but his involved guiding boats through roller-coaster waves higher than a two-story house. Diving into water so cold it stripped the air from your lungs. Battling the elements to bring someone safely back to shore.

But when it came to successfully navigating the twists and turns, the subtle undercurrents, of social situations?

David would take the roller-coaster waves and frigid temperatures any day.

When he and Lynette moved to Frost and turned Spruce Hill

Farm into a bed-and-breakfast, it was with the understanding that she would be in charge of the guests and the kitchen and David would take care of the maintenance and financials.

Marriage was about compromise, after all. It was a division of labor that David could live with.

He preferred staying in the background, and Lynette had known how to make people feel at home. No matter how demanding a guest could be, she'd treated them all like family.

And she was the glue that had held theirs together.

When David had decided on a career in the coast guard, he'd given up on the idea of marriage and a family. Other guys in his unit made it work, but transferring from base to base and leaving for long periods of time seemed a lot to ask from the person you'd vowed to love and cherish.

Until he'd met Lynette.

He'd been stationed in Bayfield at the time. It was July, a busy time of year for tourists who were drawn to miles of rugged shoreline and pristine water. Unfortunately, Lake Superior didn't always play well with others, and David's team had responded to a call about a kayaker in distress near one of the Apostle Islands.

The kayak had capsized by the time the cutter located it, and they'd pulled two people from the water. A father whose only experience with the sport came from watching online videos, and his seven-year-old son. Only the little boy had survived.

David had stumbled into one of the local cafés at ten o'clock that night, his mind, body and spirit numb. Hadn't noticed the slender brunette until she set a cup of coffee down in front of him.

And then she'd proceeded to collect the candles from every booth in the diner—even the ones in use—and used them to create a smiley face in the center of David's table.

"It looks like you need one of these," she'd told him.

The craziest part was that Lynette wasn't a waitress. She'd

been in town that weekend to attend the wedding of a friend from college and had stopped by the café for a piece of pie after the rehearsal.

While David worked his way through the blue-plate special that had mysteriously appeared in front of him, Lynette had joined him at the table. She'd sneaked fries off his plate and somehow made David smile when it felt like he'd never be able to manage that simple action again. And then she'd asked if he would be her plus-one for the wedding.

The day had started out with a rescue...and then Lynette had rescued him. David hadn't known what he'd needed until he'd met her.

They'd married six months later, and she followed him to Alaska and then back to the Great Lakes. Grace came along when David was promoted to lieutenant commander. It tore him apart every time he left, but Lynette reminded him more than once that serving in the military was a choice *both* of them had made.

David promised that when he retired from the coast guard, Lynette would get to choose where they would live.

She'd chosen Frost.

Opening a bed-and-breakfast at the age of forty-five wasn't quite the way David had pictured spending his days, but he'd had no doubt his wife would make it a success.

Lynette listened, she laughed, and she loved well.

That's what Pastor Zach had said at her funeral.

Grief washed through David again. For the last three years, it had marked his days like the relentless ebb and flow of the tide.

If it weren't for Grace, David wondered if he would have splintered into a million little pieces a long time ago.

Grace.

Just thinking about his daughter triggered a rush of affection. He missed her. Missed her teasing and her laughter and her starry-eyed optimism.

The optimism that had brought Brynn Dixon to Frost.

Grace had been twelve years old when Lynette's grandparents had decided to sell the house and the Christmas-tree farm that had been in the family for almost a generation to them. Some kids her age would have balked at the amount of work involved, but Grace had pitched right in. Helped Lynette choose paint colors and furniture. Tagged along with David into the plantation and mastered the art of tending and trimming Christmas trees.

The inn had held its grand opening six months before the accident that had claimed Lynette's life. Their daughter, with her sweet spirit and sunny personality, had stepped into Lynette's shoes at the age of fifteen.

David had suggested closing the inn for a while, but Grace wouldn't hear of it. Reservations trickled in over the months that followed, and since most of the guests checked in for the weekend, Grace became the official greeter. Spent hours in the kitchen after school, practicing and perfecting Lynette's recipes, freeing David up to focus on maintenance issues that cropped up like weeds in an older home.

Between the two of them, they'd managed all right. But it hadn't taken more than a few weeks—*days*—after Grace left for college to confirm what David already knew.

Spruce Hill was Lynette's dream, not his.

And he knew she wouldn't want Grace to feel obligated to keep it alive, either.

Chapter Nine

Lucy should have insisted they stay at a hotel between Mistletoe Stops.

It was her fault for not doing her research, but the way Grace McCrae had described her hometown... Frost had sounded like the perfect place to wrap up the tour right before Christmas.

What she hadn't included in the essay was her age or that her father would be their host. A host who didn't seem to be the least bit excited about the additional income he'd earn because of their change in plans. Brynn's meet and greet was supposed to take place at the inn, but Lucy felt like an interloper, not a guest.

She was still a little surprised that Brynn had been so adamant about staying. Lucy wasn't sure if it was the energy required for another move or if Brynn really didn't care that the bed-and-breakfast tucked in the middle of a Christmas-tree farm didn't *have* one.

Every room in Susanne's boutique hotel had been decorated for the holiday. Twinkly lights and fresh greenery. Elegant pillar candles flickering on the mantel. Bistro tables dressed in plaid satin. It even *smelled* like Christmas. Warm gingerbread cookies in the afternoon and cinnamon rolls for breakfast.

Maybe she should have gone into Frost with Caleb and taken a quick look around the town. There might not be another place to stay, but it wasn't too late to scope out an alternate venue for the book-signing event.

But that would mean asking Caleb for a ride—or to borrow his car—and Lucy's personal goal was to avoid the man as much as possible.

He'd shown up in the middle of a book tour—unannounced—and invited himself along, which only proved there was a fine line between flexible and frustrating, as far as Lucy was concerned. But Brynn had seemed genuinely thrilled to see Caleb, leaving Lucy with no choice but to put up with him.

Her only consolation was that it wouldn't be for very long.

Caleb Beauchamp might pretend he didn't mind spending time in Frost, but based on the number of stamps in his passport, he'd go stir-crazy if he stayed in one place for very long. And a small-town B and B in northern Wisconsin didn't offer much in the way of entertainment.

Space, either.

Lucy paused midstep and took an inventory of her surroundings. Floor-to-ceiling bookcases lined the library's paneled walls. There was squishy leather furniture, the kind made for books and snowy days. It would have provided the perfect backdrop for a meet and greet with Brynn's readers, except for the fact that it wasn't a lot bigger than the guest rooms upstairs. Neither was the gathering room that David McCrae had described as a shared space.

Lucy took a lap around the perimeter of the room. She always did her best thinking while she was moving.

Growing up, she'd learned not to fight the current of nonstop activity in her home. The revolving door of nurses and therapists. The neighborhood kids, friends of her younger siblings, who swooped in to raid the fridge or use the bathroom at all hours of the day.

Homework. Shopping. Ballet, the grocery budget, band lessons, the bedtime brushing-and-flossing routine. Lucy had kept everything afloat so her mom could focus her attention on her little sister, Janie.

When Lucy needed time alone, she'd escaped into the pages of a mystery novel.

Which reminded her of Trace Hunter.

Which reminded her of the two voice mails Ainsley had left on her phone since they'd started out that morning. The publicist had also sent Lucy a link to the virtual coffee shop where Brynn's readers hung out. Ordinarily, the lively conversations centered around her latest novel, but if Lucy needed proof that Ainsley hadn't exaggerated about Trace's popularity, it was right there in black and white, along with hundreds of hearts and smiley-face emojis.

When are we going to meet Trace?

#TeamTrace

I want more than a trace of Trace.

Will Trace get his HEA?

But the worst comment?

Is our prolific queen of storybook romance going to dip her pen into the suspense genre?

That particular reader's incredible leap had opened a whole new thread, but Lucy had only skimmed through the first two or three before she'd started feeling nauseous.

Trace wasn't supposed to get a happily-ever-after. He was part of a larger plot. A very *small* part. She'd never intended that the bad boy turned private investigator would have his own story.

Lucy hadn't intended to write his story at all.

But Brynn had come down with the flu before her last deadline and never quite bounced back. Over the next few months, Lucy had taken her to doctor's appointments and then to a specialist, but none of the blood tests or scans or consultations could pinpoint the cause.

Brynn, who'd never missed a deadline, was granted an extension, but it was imperative she meet the second one. Lucy had reluctantly come to the rescue because Brynn believed she was qualified to write the last five chapters of what would be Brynn's next best-selling novel simply because she loved to read.

Mysteries.

She loved to read mysteries.

And maybe, once upon a time, Lucy had started writing one of her own. But she'd set that dream aside because she'd had responsibilities, and there hadn't been room in her life for both.

She'd had a responsibility to Brynn, too, and that meant finishing Paisley and Fletcher's story. The couple had spent three-quarters of the book falling in love, and Lucy had no idea how to fill those final chapters creating their dream wedding, so someone had stolen Paisley's heirloom necklace at her bridal shower.

Then, while Lucy was staring at the blinking cursor on the monitor, Trace introduced himself.

Lucy had paced the floor while Brynn read the end of the book and almost fainted when she announced it perfect.

Nothing felt perfect anymore, though, and it was all Trace's fault.

Lucy still hadn't told Brynn about the messages. There hadn't been time, really. Just like there wasn't time to find an actor to play the role of Trace Hunter before Brynn's final meet and greet.

Lucy wasn't just unhappy with her fictional hero—*secondary character*—at the moment, she also couldn't imagine anyone who could step into Trace's fictional shoes.

The cynical PI wasn't anything like the sweet, easygoing Fletcher who'd won Paisley's heart. Trace was a risk-taker, focused and determined and a little irreverent...

"If you rub that necklace a few more times, will a genie appear?"

Lucy's head snapped up, and her fingers froze on her pendant as Caleb sauntered into the room.

Chapter Ten

Don't ask him why, but Caleb knew she'd be here.

What he hadn't known, though, was that the unflappable, efficient Lucy Gable was a pacer.

He'd actually gotten a little dizzy by the time she'd finished her third lap around the room.

Lucy's hands dropped to her sides, and the necklace broke into a free fall before settling in place over her heart. "I spoke with Mr. McCrae, and there's a room ready for you down the hall from ours." Her hand disappeared into an invisible pocket in the side of her pants, and she pulled out a metal key. "I already set your duffel bag outside the door."

It was a *backpack*. And a traveling companion that had held up through fire, a water baptism in the Amazon and a game of tug-of-war with a pack of nosy capuchin monkeys, thank you very much…

"Just in case you want to, uh, clean up before dinner," Lucy added.

The scruff on Caleb's jaw began to itch, a reminder that he hadn't had time to pivot with the sudden change in plans, either.

"I haven't talked to Mr. McCrae about meals other than breakfast, but the website said something about light appetizers later in the afternoon, so I'll send you a text when I find out."

A text.

Wait… Caleb's eyes narrowed.

Did his mom's personal assistant think he needed a handler, too? Or was this a polite way of getting rid of him?

Sorry, Caleb thought. *You're stuck with me until I figure out what's going on with Brynn. And how—or if—you factor into it.*

Lucy's cell phone rang, and her brows dipped together when she glanced at the screen.

"Excuse me," she murmured. "I have to take this call."

"No problem." Caleb reached down and experimentally poked one of the sofa cushions. It sprang back like a lump of bread dough ready for its second rise. The perfect consistency for a nap. He sat down and propped his feet on the ottoman.

Lucy turned her back on him and walked over to the window.

"We're in Frost," he heard her say. "I know, but the other venue isn't available because a tree fell on some wires, and the power is out…I know, I tried. But these are small towns and there aren't a lot of options, so I had to come up with another plan."

Caleb leaned back and closed his eyes.

If a person had a cell phone in their possession and opted not to leave the room, was it eavesdropping if he overheard the conversation?

Caleb didn't think so.

"No, I haven't asked Ms. Dixon if she's read the messages yet."

Ms. Dixon?

So formal.

So…familiar.

Caleb had heard Lucy use that particular tone when she'd walked into the room where the manager had stashed him after he'd arrived at the hotel.

"The inn is very small, so I'm not sure if there would even be a room available for Trace." Lucy paused to adjust the shade on the floor lamp in the corner. "She's resting right now, but I'll tell her you called."

Like she'd passed on the message that *he'd* called?

When Caleb had brought it up, Brynn had looked confused, and he realized that her personal assistant—whose job involved relaying messages—had neglected to mention it.

Caleb's eyes settled on Lucy again.

She made it sound as if Brynn was the one in charge, but it seemed to him that she was the one making most of the decisions.

"Even if Trace can't make it, the readers who show up for the meet and greet won't be disappointed," Lucy promised. "I'll make sure of it. Thank you for checking in."

The same thing she'd said to Caleb before she'd hung up on him.

Did the caller on the other end of the line realize they were being handled, too?

She ended the call, the phone disappeared in a sleight of hand and she turned to face him again. "Was there something else you needed?"

"Who is Trace?"

For a moment, Caleb wasn't sure Lucy was going to answer the question.

"A character in Brynn's book," she finally said.

"Ah." Caleb's copy had caught up to him in Belize, but he hadn't had time to read it yet. "And he's supposed to be at the signing."

Lucy wasn't fast enough to hide her surprise, and Caleb felt a twinge of satisfaction. He knew the drill. He'd met up with Brynn at several of her book tours in the past, before she'd hired Lucy. Before she'd hired *him* and he'd started spending more time in the air than he did on the ground.

Caleb had learned a lot about the woman who'd given him up for adoption by watching the way she interacted with her fans. The author known for writing small-town romance had a larger-than-life personality, white leather cowboy boots and a big heart.

She saw the best in everyone, too, which Caleb knew had caused some heartache in the past.

He might not have been able to protect her then, but he'd do everything in his power to make sure it wouldn't happen in the future.

"Yes," Lucy murmured. "According to Ainsley."

Ainsley Adams. "Mom's publicist."

Again, surprise. But this time Caleb wasn't sure if it was because he knew Ainsley's title or because Lucy still wasn't sure he had the right to call Brynn "Mom."

"The weather here is unpredictable, and the closest regional airport is an hour away. I don't want someone to get stuck there."

"The readers must be pretty disappointed," Caleb ventured. "Meeting the hero is a big deal at these things."

"Trace isn't… No one was expecting it this time. The Mistletoe Stop tour is unique. We're visiting small towns like the one featured in Brynn's newest book."

"*Small* is a pretty good description." Caleb tried to wrestle down a smile and failed. The entire population of Frost would fit in the hotel ballrooms where her previous events had been held. "So is *unique*. There's already a marquee outside the information center welcoming Brynn to town, by the way. *Merry Christmas and Happy Ever After*," he quoted. "Kind of catchy, right? You may want to pass that one on to Marketing."

Lucy smiled, and Caleb felt the impact like a punch to his gut.

It had registered in his male brain that Lucy was attractive, of course, but the smile that backlit her eyes and curved her lips transformed her features. Radiated a warmth that revealed another unexpected—and intriguing—facet of her calm, uber-efficient personality.

"If you're worried about the storm, maybe there's a guy in Frost who would play the part. It might generate some more press, and he wouldn't need a room, either." Caleb waited for an instant replay of that smile.

It disappeared instead.

"Who won't need a room?"

Caleb's first thought when he turned and saw Brynn framed in the doorway was that she was working too hard. Her cheekbones looked more prominent, a sign she'd lost weight, and there were shadows underneath her eyes that he hadn't noticed during their monthly video calls.

Guilt struck hard.

Caleb wanted the work he was doing to be successful. To make Brynn proud. But to accomplish that goal took him away from Nashville. How many times had he celebrated the birth of Christ away from home? Alone?

He couldn't remember, which was an answer in itself.

"Trace Hunter," Caleb said while Lucy appeared to be searching for the answer. "Your hero."

"He's not…" Lucy started to say, but the rest of the sentence was drowned out by Brynn's startled laugh.

"Trace?" She lowered herself into a chair. "I think you better fill me in on the details."

Lucy shot a glance at Caleb which he interpreted as a cue for him to leave.

He leaned back and crossed his arms behind his head instead.

"There's a…small…contingent of readers who think Trace is going to be in the next book, and they want to meet him," Lucy said slowly. "We both know he won't be, though…" She looked at Brynn as if she were waiting for her employer to agree with her.

Won't be.

That was a strange way to phrase it.

Caleb didn't quite understand all the ins and outs of publishing, but he knew that by the time one of Brynn's books hit the shelves, she had the next one well underway.

"Even if there was time to find someone to play the part, there isn't an airport nearby." Lucy began to recite the reasons she'd given him. "And with another storm coming, I don't know that it's a good idea anyway."

"I suggested she find someone in Frost," Caleb interjected. "That would solve the problem."

Lucy was looking at Caleb as if *he* were the problem.

"Except I've already asked Mr. McCrae not to tell anyone we arrived early so Brynn can...work without distractions."

People were distractions now?

Caleb waited for Brynn to contradict Lucy, but she smiled at her instead.

"Trace might not be the hero, but he *is* a character in the book," Brynn mused. "You've been thinking outside the box on this tour from the beginning, Lucy, so it might not hurt to give the readers what they want."

Lucy's eyes went wide. "But—"

"And we don't even have to look farther than this room." Now Brynn was looking at him. "Caleb can do it."

"*Caleb?*" Lucy almost choked on his name. "No. That won't work. Not at all."

Caleb would have agreed, except her strong reaction made him curious. Curious and, to be honest, a little offended. Which led to "Why not?"

"Why..." Lucy practically sputtered the word. "In the first place, you don't look anything like Trace. He has blond hair and..." She stopped.

"Blue eyes," Brynn helped her out.

Two for two.

"Tall? Short?" Caleb asked.

Lucy's gaze skimmed over him, and when their eyes caught and held again, her cheeks turned pink.

He arched a brow, waiting, until she finally muttered, "Six feet."

"Six-one-and-three-quarters. Close enough."

"He's clean-shaven, too," she added quickly.

"Good thing I have a razor in my backpack." Caleb couldn't help but press down on the last word a little.

Lucy didn't seem to notice.

"It isn't only about looks," she told him. "Trace was only in the last five chapters, but he…he's a complex character."

"I can do *complex*. How does this Trace guy make his living?"

"He's a private investigator who retrieves valuable items from criminals in his spare time," Lucy said.

"He's a thief?"

"Reformed… Never mind." She reached for her necklace. Caught herself and released it again. "Trace reflects the classic warrior archetype. No matter what he does, he's intensely focused on his mission."

Well, Caleb had a mission, too. To find out if his suspicions about something being wrong with his mom were correct. He decided to leave Lucy out of the decision-making process and looked at Brynn. "If you think having this Trace guy here would make the readers happy, then I'm happy to help. Like Lucy pointed out this morning, we have a lot of extra time here. You can give me some pointers."

"*You* have a lot of extra time," Brynn corrected. "I'll be curled up in front of the fireplace with my notebook. Lucy should do it."

Hold on…

Caleb wanted to spend more time with his mom, not the woman who'd looked skeptical when he'd claimed he could do *complex*.

"But he's *your* character. You're the writer."

"And writers write." Brynn smiled. "Lucy would make a great coach. As you can see, she happens to know a lot about Trace."

"I don't think—"

"All right."

Caleb's gaze swung to Lucy. After everything she'd just said, he couldn't believe she'd given in so easily.

Or that she looked almost…relieved.

Had Lucy realized that if she pushed back, Caleb would push back harder?

Had it been her intention all along to keep him from spending time with Brynn? Asking questions Lucy didn't want her to answer?

Had he just been played again?

Chapter Eleven

Brynn peeked into the kitchen. All the cabinet doors stood wide open, and David McCrae was sifting through the contents of a drawer next to the refrigerator.

He must have sensed her presence because he froze mid-search and turned in her direction.

Now that she'd been caught spying, Brynn had no choice but to brazen it out. "Looking for the last can of Who Hash?"

The rugged angles and planes of David's face shifted a bit before settling back into place.

Had she almost witnessed a real, honest-to-goodness smile?

For one sweet but all too fleeting moment the fog lifted, and Brynn felt almost normal again.

David abandoned the search and folded his arms across his chest, shields in place once again. "Was there something you needed?"

At the moment, an invitation to enter the kitchen. But since one didn't seem to be forthcoming, Brynn stepped over the threshold and broke the no-trespassing rule for the second time that day.

"This is beautiful." She looked around, admiring how the

rustic hickory cabinets and the raw edges of the granite counter-tops blended with gleaming stainless-steel appliances. A creative merging of both the old and the new had been applied to this space as well. "Do you do all the cooking yourself, or do you have a chef?"

"Neither," David muttered.

Which could explain the burnt toast she'd smelled when they'd arrived.

Mmm. A host who claimed to feed his guests but, based on the cryptic comment and the open cabinets and drawers, didn't look like he was familiar with his own kitchen.

"But breakfast is included with your stay." It must have occurred to David that an explanation was in order so Brynn wouldn't be raiding his fridge for leftovers. "Seven o'clock in the gathering room. Eight on the weekends. The menu is seasonal, though, so the ingredients depend on what's available locally. If there are any dietary restrictions, you better tell me now. I'd hate to serve Roast Beast to a vegetarian."

Brynn grinned. Not only had David picked up on her reference to the Grinch, but instead of being offended—wonder of wonders—he'd actually teased her back.

She didn't think he had it in him. Maybe the man's heart wasn't two sizes too small.

"When I was four years old, my grandmother took me to meet Santa for the first time. When he asked what I wanted for Christmas, I told him brisket."

David's lips curled at the edges. "Duly noted."

"It doesn't look like we'll be getting out much over the next few days, so I'm sure Lucy will be contacting a restaurant in Frost about catering our meals while we're here."

"Catering?" His eyebrows dipped together. "Look, Ms.... Brynn—"

"Hellooo? David? Knock, knock!"

He stiffened at the sound of a cheerful female voice coming from the screened-in porch off the kitchen. "Do you mind waiting in there?" Without waiting for an answer, David all but herded Brynn toward the room he'd informed her was off-limits to guests when they'd arrived. "This won't take long."

Brynn found herself on the other side of the swinging doors just as another one opened.

"There you are!"

Through the crack between the doors, Brynn caught a glimpse of a woman close to David's age. A thick silver braid trailed between her shoulder blades. Denim overalls that didn't disguise a willowy frame were rolled up at the bottom, exposing an inner layer of buffalo check flannel that matched her jacket. A style she still somehow managed to make look chic.

Camouflage hiking boots barely made a sound as she glided over to David. "I noticed a car parked out front and thought I better sneak in through the back door in case you were busy."

"Hello, Esther...and I am kind of busy at the moment."

Brynn knew she shouldn't be listening in on what the woman assumed was a private conversation, but then, David hadn't given her much of a choice. She withdrew to the sofa and patted the cushion, inviting Patch to join her. The dog jumped up and snuggled close, one floppy ear tilted toward the door, a true partner in crime.

"I see that." His visitor must have noticed the open cupboard doors. "Taking an inventory before our guest of honor arrives?"

"*Our* guest?" David asked mildly.

"Frost won the contest, so we're all willing to do our part. Brynn Dixon was the topic at our Friends of Frost meeting last night, and since you weren't there, I offered to stop over and tell you some of the ideas we came up with."

Brynn liked this woman.

Enthusiastic Esther.

"What kind of ideas?"

David, on the other hand, didn't sound enthusiastic at all.

"Frost Community Church is in charge of Christmas caroling on Main Street, but Darlene is going to talk to Pastor Zach about changing things up this year. She thinks people would enjoy an old-fashioned sing-along around a bonfire instead."

"You're going to start a bonfire on Main Street?"

"Of course not. We need a place with more room. A little more ambience, should I say?"

Brynn saw right where this was going, but it took David a split second longer to connect the dots.

"The inn."

Esther laughed. "We were hoping you'd offer!"

Brynn pressed her fingers against her lips. Oh, she wished she could see David's expression.

"Esther—"

Either Esther didn't hear the warning note in David's tone or it didn't deter her. "Brynn Dixon is scheduled to arrive a few days before the book signing, isn't she? A bonfire and some special activities would be a wonderful welcome to Frost."

"What kind of special activities?"

"We loved bringing the kids here when Rose and Wes ran things. Spruce Hill wasn't a B and B back then, of course, but Rose always said they loved being a part of making memories. They'd have a fire going and would serve Christmas cookies and hot chocolate. It was a tradition for a lot of families, and not only the ones who lived in Frost, either. People came from all over the area. And the sleigh rides." Esther almost hummed the words. "Martin has been snowshoeing behind the house and noticed you groomed some of the trails. It would be the perfect time to open the tree farm again."

Silence.

"The horses haven't pulled a sleigh since..." David stopped. Cleared his throat. When he spoke again, his voice sounded strained, as if he was keeping a tight rein on his emotions. "They're gigantic lawn ornaments now. I'm counting on Grace being here for that book-signing thing, but until then, I'll have guests that need attention. Meals. And what's the point of all this, anyway? To impress a woman you'll never see again?"

Now Esther was silent.

"Because Christmas is a time to come together," she finally said. "To spend time with family and friends and celebrate all the gifts that God provides by celebrating the gift of His son."

"You don't need sleigh rides to do that."

"No, but you know as well as I do that Frost has been struggling the past few years. How many businesses have shut down? How many of our young people leave and don't look back? Your own daughter is one of the exceptions. Someone who sees all the things Frost has to offer, not what it lacks. Isn't that why she entered the contest?"

"I have no idea why Grace entered the contest," David muttered.

"Well, I do. When I saw Grace at church over her Thanksgiving break, all she could talk about was all the big plans she had for this place after graduation. That girl knows Frost is special. Why would we pass up the opportunity to show Brynn Dixon it's special, too? She might be a celebrity, but she chose to come here, which tells me she's a small-town girl at heart. I say let's show her what we've got!"

Okay. Brynn really liked her.

"I'll *think* about it," David finally said.

"And I'll let you know when we're meeting again." Brynn caught a fleeting glimpse of the heels of hiking boots lifting off the ground as she hugged David McCrae. "Hopefully we'll see you there."

Enthusiastic *and* brave.

"Oh, I almost forgot. Hannah told me that if you want some mistletoe decorations, you should let her know soon. She's getting a lot of orders this year."

"And I want mistletoe because…"

"You haven't read Brynn's new book?" Esther sounded shocked.

"I'd never even heard of her until a few weeks ago."

"It's called *Meet Me under the Mistletoe*, and it takes place in a small Midwestern town like Frost. I'll lend you my copy if you promise to give it back. I want it autographed by the Queen of Storybook Endings herself."

"Don't tell me you're one of those Ladies—"

Oh, please get it right this time, Brynn silently pleaded.

"—in Waiting?" he said.

Brynn swallowed a sigh of relief as Esther laughed. "I've heard that's what Brynn's fans call themselves. I don't have a membership card or anything, but her stories are wonderful... And don't you give me that look, David McCrae. You can't form an opinion based on assumptions."

"On experience," he corrected. "Things don't always get tied up with a neat little bow, you know. And not everyone is guaranteed a happy ending."

Brynn had heard comments like those over the course of her career, but the bitterness that leached into David's voice told her that he wasn't talking about books anymore.

Esther must have heard it, too, because the only thing Brynn could hear was the crackle of the fire.

"But there are still things to celebrate," Esther said softly. "Love. Hope. God's provision. Gifts in the everyday moments. The best stories remind us of that."

"I appreciate you stopping by. Grace is in charge of decorating the inn for Christmas, but I'll pass on the message about Hannah's mistletoe."

And Esther got David's message, too. End of conversation.

"Thank you. I'll be in touch, David."

The back door snapped shut, and Brynn waited for David to appear. And waited a little longer.

Brynn ruffled Patch's ear and rose to her feet, a dozen questions bouncing around inside her head. Unfortunately, the person who knew the answers had forgotten about her. Or sneaked out another way.

She pushed through the doors and almost bumped into David. The cupboard doors were still open, but this time his gaze was fixed on something outside the window.

The set of his jaw told Brynn to leave him alone, but she couldn't help but feel a little responsible for reviving Frost's dormant Christmas spirit and resurrecting old traditions.

And some difficult memories for David, it seemed.

Before Brynn could apologize, he spoke first.

"Beverages and snacks will be available in the gathering room at four."

He smiled then, but Brynn wasn't fooled.

Just like Esther, she'd been politely dismissed.

Chapter Twelve

He'd done it again.

David sure knew how to clear a room. But guests—and neighbors—should respect a man's boundaries.

Grace may have told Esther that she planned to come back after graduation, but a lot could change in four years. Grace had her whole future ahead of her, and Lynette would have wanted her to embrace it, not cling to the past.

David's cell phone suddenly came to life and began to play Bing Crosby's "White Christmas." A ringtone his mischievous daughter had programmed into his phone when he'd left it unattended during her last visit.

The fact that Grace was calling instead of texting meant she wanted to talk.

The trouble was, David didn't. At least not until he'd had time to process Esther's outrageous request and Brynn Dixon's blatant disregard for boundaries.

But he couldn't ignore his only child any more than he could ignore the snow piling up outside the window, no matter how strong the temptation to delay the inevitable.

"Hi, sweetheart." Patch—the traitor who'd been cozying up to the woman who couldn't seem to stay where she belonged—nudged David's shin, and he reached down to scratch the dog's bristly chin. "I didn't expect to hear from you today."

"Hey, Daddy." The greeting was punctuated with a yawn.

David glanced at the clock on the wall.

Two o'clock.

"Sounds like someone needs a nap. Were you up half the night studying again?"

"Kind of," she murmured. "What are you up to?"

David knew that a vague response followed by a question was Grace's way of avoiding his.

"You pulled an all-nighter?" Yup. He'd gone into full-blown dad mode. Grades were important but so was getting enough sleep.

"I'm fine." Another yawn. "I promise I'll catch a nap after I turn in my essay exam…if you keep your promise."

At the moment, he was coming up blank.

"Promise?"

"To send a picture of our Christmas tree."

Right.

Grace had wanted to put the tree up right after Thanksgiving, but the holiday break had filled up quickly with visits from former high-school classmates who, like Grace, had come home to eat turkey and use the washing machine.

While David had loaded Grace's suitcase and the rest of the flotsam and jetsam that had accumulated during the four-day weekend into the trunk of her car, she'd disappeared into the plantation.

David had been about to track her down when she'd returned to the house, breathless and rosy-cheeked, and announced that she'd found the perfect tree. Marked it so he would know which one to cut down.

The house was always too quiet whenever Grace left, so

David had grabbed an axe and zigzagged between the rows until he spotted Grace's wool scarf tied around a balsam. A balsam with a gaping hole between the branches on one side and a slight tilt in its trunk.

The next time she'd called, he couldn't help but tease her a little.

He'd been expecting Martha Stewart and she'd gone all Charlie Brown on him.

"It doesn't have to look like the one in the gathering room," Grace had told him cheerfully. "When you put the ornaments on, they'll cover the bare spots. And promise you'll send a picture."

The memory of their conversation cycled through David's mind, and he glanced at the cardboard box on the floor. He'd lugged it up from the basement a few days ago but hadn't unpacked the contents yet.

"Yeah." David raked his hand through his hair. "There's another storm on the way, and I'm still dealing with the snow from this one."

Who was hedging now?

Because not only had David *not* sent a picture of the tree, he hadn't decorated it yet.

Or cut it down.

"That's okay." Grace yawned again. "And I get that you're busy. I'll have a billion things to do before Brynn Dixon gets there."

Like Esther, it didn't sound like she was dreading the extra work, either.

An image of a Brynn Dixon with her wild mane of auburn curls and lively emerald green eyes flashed in David's mind.

He was used to seeing women of a certain age dressed like Esther. Clothes that were more…practical. Not cashmere sweaters and slippers that looked like cowboy boots.

David had never met a romance novelist and wondered if they were all a bit...unconventional.

Didn't think the rules applied to them.

Looking for the last can of Who Hash?

Who knew that a dulcet Southern accent could make an insult sound so innocent?

A smile surfaced before David realized it was happening, and he tamped it down.

"Right now, you have one job. To concentrate on your exams," he told his daughter. "I'll hold down the fort."

"I know." Grace sounded way more confident in David's abilities than he did. "But I only have one exam on Friday morning. I was thinking...maybe I could drive up after I finish it and get a head start on the decorating."

That explained why she'd been burning the midnight oil.

"But you have another one on Monday you should be studying for over the weekend." And David would prefer that studying take place after a good night's sleep. "There will be plenty of time to decorate."

Which was why he wasn't going to tell his sweet but slightly impetuous daughter that Brynn Dixon had already checked into her room early: the moment they hung up, she'd toss some books and clothes into her suitcase, hop into the car and forget all about her exams.

"I have to plan the menu and do some shopping." Grace's voice thinned a little, her nervousness showing for the first time since she'd dropped the bombshell on David and announced that Frost had been chosen as a Mistletoe Stop on Brynn Dixon's book tour.

Which wouldn't have happened if she'd spent more time reading textbooks than romance novels.

But David decided it would be counterproductive to point that out and said instead, "There will be time for that, too. I'm sure you already have some ideas."

"A few," Grace said. "Brynn is from Tennessee, so I thought it would be fun to serve chicken and Mom's blueberry waffles. Give the recipe a Midwestern twist. What do you think?"

What did he think?

That blueberry pancakes and chicken didn't belong together on the same plate.

That this Mistletoe thing was distracting Grace. Messing with her priorities.

"I think I better let you go so you can take that nap," he said out loud. "And don't come home this weekend. We'll get everything done."

He had no idea how, with guests underfoot, but Grace had worked hard her first semester, and he wanted her to finish well.

"Okay."

David experienced a nanosecond of relief before round two began.

"There's something else I'd like to do this year."

David almost hated to ask. A shopping list he could handle. He could even make a decent batch of scones when he remembered to set the timer on the oven. Anything else, though, was stretching his skill set.

"Tell me what it is, and I'll do my best."

He always would where Grace was concerned. But sometimes a parent had to act in their child's best interests. David didn't want his daughter to return to Frost and take over a business whose success, like the others in town, was based on variables as unpredictable as the weather.

A few seconds passed and then a few more.

Just when David was beginning to think the call had dropped, she finally said, "The tree farm. Everyone in Frost is really excited about Brynn's visit, so I was thinking…maybe you could open it this year?"

David's gut twisted.

A coincidence? Or a conspiracy?

"Did Esther contact you?" David tried to keep his voice even.

"Mrs. Lowell?" Grace sounded confused that he'd jumped to that conclusion. "No. I read it in the notes."

"Notes?"

"From the last Friends of Frost meeting."

David had noticed the email in his inbox but hadn't taken time to skim through the contents yet.

Esther had continued to send a copy of the detailed minutes from their monthly get-togethers after Lynette passed away, even though he'd never attended any of the meetings. Lynette was the one who'd joined the committee made up of local businesspeople. In their eyes, she'd always been part of the community.

David had no ties to Frost, but Lynette had spent summer vacations with her grandparents at Spruce Hill Farm and knew most of the members by name. While David found it rather disconcerting that the collecting of information and passing it on seemed to be a favorite local pastime, Lynette had claimed it was one of the things she loved the most about living in a small town.

"I didn't realize they were sending the minutes to you."

"I talked to Esther when I was home for Thanksgiving, and they made me an honorary member. She said that I can join for real after I graduate."

Not what David wanted to hear.

Tell her the truth. Tell her it's time to sell. And for her to pursue her own dreams.

He shut down the thought.

Thanks to a famous author who'd decided to stop in Frost and sign a few books before going on her merry way again, he couldn't. Not yet, anyway.

"Kasey is the publicity coordinator and keeps me in the loop," Grace continued. "The last time she called, she mentioned how much she misses coming out to our place and find-ing a Christmas tree."

Kasey Lowell was Esther's niece. If David remembered cor-rectly, she'd stayed in Frost after graduation and worked at the daycare center a block off Main Street. Grace and Kasey had been friends since seventh grade, so it didn't come as a surprise the girls had stayed in touch. But the timing of the minutes—and her comment—gave the conspiracy theory more weight.

"Christmas isn't that far away. I'm sure everyone who wants a tree has one by now," David pointed out. He didn't remind Grace there was more to opening the tree farm than handing out axes. If he took people out in the sleigh, he'd need some-one to handle the money. Run the baler. And the Realtor had told David not to make any significant changes to the property before it went on the market.

"I know...but I miss it, too." Grace almost whispered the words. "Remember Mom would make a batch of hot chocolate the night before we opened because she claimed she couldn't serve it unless she knew it tasted good? And then we'd hitch up the horses and take the sleigh on a practice run? It was so much fun."

David's gaze moved over the photographs on the wall and locked on the close-up of an adolescent girl sitting bareback astride a draft horse, both arms locked around its neck. Her freckles had faded, and braces had closed the gap between her teeth, but the wide, infectious grin hadn't changed.

Everything had been fun because, like Lynette's grandparents before her, his wife had made it that way.

David had agreed to honor the reservations made before Lynette passed away, but he'd closed the tree farm to visitors that first Christmas. He couldn't watch families laughing to-gether, searching for the perfect tree, while David felt as if he were gasping for every breath. Learning how to survive with-out Lynette. The heart of *their* family.

When she'd been alive, the house had been filled with color swatches and paint cans. Laughter and the aroma of things baking. Ingredients that had made David's life richer. Now, every time he turned a corner, he ran into a memory. And it hurt.

Grace hadn't said anything when the tree farm had remained closed a second—and then a third—year.

He'd been secretly relieved she hadn't made it an issue.

Taken it as a sign that Grace wasn't as attached to Spruce Hill Farm as he'd thought she was. But this was a conversation that needed to take place face-to-face, so he told Grace the same thing he'd told Esther.

"I'll think about the sleigh rides."

"Really?" A squeal pierced David's ear. "What if someone still needs a tree? Can they cut one down?"

"I'll think about that, too."

"You could open the warming house! Serve hot chocolate."

"Now you're pushing it."

Grace giggled. "I'm stubborn…like someone else in the family."

In terms of character traits, it figured that was the one David would pass down to his only child.

"And, Daddy?"

Eighteen years old and she still called him that.

"Yes…"

"One more thing?"

"Third and final." David injected just the right amount of tease even as he braced himself for her next request.

"When you decorate the little tree? Save the star for me."

Chapter Thirteen

"Do you have a minute to chat?"

Lucy smiled at the sound of her sister's voice. Finally, a phone call that didn't involve natural disasters or chat rooms or contingency plans.

"Always." Catching up with Rachel was something she looked forward to, plus it would keep Lucy's mind occupied so she wouldn't be wondering what was going on upstairs. If Brynn was resting or writing. If a certain blue-eyed someone was *preventing* Brynn from resting or writing. "Are you done with work already?"

"It was slow, so my manager let me leave early. I'm taking a shortcut through the park."

"Nice." Lucy didn't have to close her eyes to picture the scene. She'd toured the campus before Rachel received her formal acceptance letter.

"What about you? Ordering room service on the bazillionth floor of some ritzy hotel?"

Lucy tried not to laugh. So far, there'd been no sign of the afternoon refreshments touted on the website. No sign of their host, either, now that she thought about it.

"Not this time." Lucy walked over to the wall of multipaned glass that overlooked the tree plantation in the gathering room. "I see snow and trees." Lots of trees.

"Snow?" Rachel sounded envious. "Where are you this time?"

"Frost, Wisconsin. Population one thousand one hundred and fifty."

Rachel laughed. "Seriously?"

"Seriously. It's our last stop on Brynn's book tour." Lucy didn't mention the series of events leading up to their early arrival. Rachel's weekly phone calls never lasted very long. Seven minutes to be exact—the amount of time it took to walk from the coffee shop to her apartment—but Lucy wasn't complaining.

"Mom is still upset you won't be home until Christmas Eve, you know."

Lucy felt a pinch of guilt. Unlike Caleb Beauchamp, she'd always taken her vacation the week before Christmas in order to spend more time with her family. Between the book tour and Brynn's health, though, she'd been forced to adjust her plans this year.

"I'll be home by dinnertime," Lucy promised.

"Good. Because you're the only one in the family who bakes and reminds us to wear our ugly sweaters and coordinates the white-elephant exchange. No one else has time for that stuff."

No one else made the time. That was the difference between Lucy and her siblings.

While they were growing up, it had fallen on Lucy to make Christmas special, and she must have succeeded because everyone, including their mom, still looked to Lucy to oversee everything from the purchasing of matching holiday pajamas to judging the ugly-sweater contest.

Truth be told, Lucy didn't mind. The trust her family placed in her to coordinate their annual traditions was flattering. And now that her siblings were scattered all over the country, it felt good to be needed, too.

"We could always skip the gift exchange this year." Lucy wasn't sure why she tossed out the idea when she already knew what Rachel's reaction would be. "No one shops for a gift until the last minute, anyway."

"No way. Yours is always the best one, and I know you bought and wrapped it already. Or did you put it in a gift bag?"

Lucy smiled. "Nice try, but I'm not telling."

Rachel chuffed. "I thought I was your favorite."

"You are." Lucy didn't hesitate. "You're my favorite Rachel."

Her sister laughed, just like Lucy knew she would.

"I'll send everyone a link to the gift I ordered for Mom and Dad," Lucy told her. "Now, how are classes going?"

"Great...and that reminds me. I'm finishing up a paper for my midterms. Will you have time to proofread it?"

"Sure." Lucy added a mental note to the growing list. "What's the deadline?"

"Um...midnight tomorrow."

"Rachel!"

"I know, I know. But it's your fault for sending me a copy of Brynn's latest book. I haven't been able to put it down. When is the next one coming out?"

"There isn't an official date yet." The same thing Lucy had been telling everyone who asked.

"I loved the way it ended," Rachel said.

"Thanks—" Lucy caught herself. "I'll pass that on to Brynn. Paisley and Fletcher's wedding did turn out pretty well."

After Lucy had gone cross-eyed poring over dozens of bridal magazines and scrolling through photos of bouquets and satin dresses for inspiration.

"I was talking about the private investigator. Trace." His name slipped out with a dreamy sigh.

"Trace—" Lucy's breath stalled in her lungs.

Because at that very moment, he strolled into the room.

"Lucy? What's wrong?" Rachel demanded. "Do you see a bear?"

A *bear*?

Lucy didn't have time for a science lesson about which animals hibernated during the winter.

"Sorry, Rach, but I have to go."

"Lucy—"

"I'm fine. Love you." Lucy blew a kiss into the phone and ended the call.

Caleb glanced at the cell clutched in Lucy's hand. "I'm here for my first coaching session."

"N-now?"

Caleb shrugged. "No time like the present. Brynn is upstairs resting, so I'm ready if you are."

Lucy had thought she was ready, too. But the mental script she'd prepared had gone completely blank the moment Caleb wandered into the room.

Because the smoky voice might have belonged to Brynn's jet-setting son, but she was looking at Trace Hunter. Blond hair damp from a recent shower, ocean-blue eyes…

A jawline sharp enough to cut glass.

True to his word, the man *did* own a razor. One that apparently wielded as much power as the sword Trace Hunter used when he practiced kenjutsu.

Because without the beard, Caleb Beauchamp was…

Another project, that's what he was. One of many Lucy had been assigned while working for Brynn.

It didn't matter if the project happened to be a person and not a speaking engagement or book tour, either. The same rules still applied.

Unfortunately, Rule Number One required studying the project from all angles. And that's when Lucy realized he'd done more than shave in the last few hours.

"You changed clothes." The statement sounded a little accusing, even to Lucy's ears.

"Yeah. But I packed pretty light this time," Caleb said, "so you'll have to tell me what this Trace guy would wear. Most of my stuff is still in my apartment."

Which apartment? Lucy was tempted to ask. Based on the number of places that served as pickup points for his monthly allowance, Caleb had quite a few to choose from.

"Well?" He struck an exaggerated catalog pose and flashed a smile that sent her pulse into a little skip.

Project, Lucy. Remember?

When Brynn had said that Lucy should be the one to coach Caleb, she'd wanted to protest, too. But after Brynn had explained why, hope had taken wing inside of Lucy for the first time in weeks.

Brynn did her best plotting the old-fashioned way. Curling up in front of the fireplace with her notebook was a sign that she was feeling more like herself again. If Lucy had to spend a little time with Caleb while they were here, it was a small sacrifice to make.

She took a step backward and tried to be objective as she took a quick head-to-toe survey of Trace's alter ego.

Gone were the hoodie and faded jeans. Caleb wore a heather-blue Henley, the sleeves casually pushed back to expose tanned forearms, and charcoal gray hiking pants with multiple pockets.

He looked amazing...ly like Trace.

"We can talk about clothes later." Lucy tossed Rule Number One aside for the moment. "Why don't I give you a copy of Brynn's book to start with? I'll mark the part when Trace is introduced. Chapter twenty. Or better yet, read the whole book. It will give you a feel for the overall story and the rest of the characters before we concentrate on Trace."

Lucy couldn't believe it. She was actually stammering.

Caleb shrugged. "I'm not much of a reader. Why don't you just give me the abridged version, and we'll go from there?"

Not a reader?

Lucy tried not to hold that against him. "All right."

Caleb dropped into one of the chairs near the woodstove. When Lucy didn't move, he tilted his head, a question in his eyes.

Right.

"The setting is a small town like Frost. Time frame November to December. In chapters one through twenty, the heroine, Paisley, falls in love with Fletcher. A week before the wedding, the heirloom necklace Paisley's mother gave to her as the Something Old is stolen, and Fletcher hires Trace to find it."

She couldn't admit she'd been pacing the floor, trying to figure out a way to save poor Paisley from a wedding guaranteed to be ruined by Lucy's total (and rather humiliating) lack of knowledge in the romance and true-love department.

Lucy had had a boyfriend her freshman year of high school. She and Isaac Monroe had grown up in the same neighborhood. At some indeterminate point during one of their many bike rides around the cul-de-sac and weekend study sessions, their friendship had turned into a mutual crush.

For two short months, Lucy had been the envy of her classmates. But their budding romance had taken a back seat to reality when her life was turned upside down on a sunny Saturday morning.

Isaac had wanted a girlfriend who could cheer him on from the bleachers or go out for pizza or a movie. Lucy had wanted to spend time with him, too, but someone at home always seemed to need her more. Their breakup hadn't been dramatic enough to warrant more than a passing mention in her diary. Isaac had stopped calling, and Lucy hadn't realized he'd stopped calling until she saw him kissing Shannon Benson outside of study hall one day.

"And Trace succeeds?" Caleb prompted.

"Of course." Lucy realized she'd sounded a little defensive when Caleb's brows shot up.

Trace's arrival in chapter twenty had saved Lucy from having to guess what it felt like to be so in love that the rest of the world faded into the background. It was possible, maybe, she did have a bit of a soft spot for him after all.

"Right. Warrior archetype. Complete the mission. Doesn't sound that complex to me." Caleb stretched out his legs and propped them on the ottoman, striking the same pose he'd used while eavesdropping on her conversation with Ainsley. "Why is Trace so popular with readers? Doesn't he just return the necklace and disappear?"

That's what Lucy had thought would happen, but Trace had insisted on hanging around until the end of the book.

"It takes a little longer than that. The necklace had more than sentimental value. It was worth a small fortune. One of Paisley's relatives had found it in the wreckage of a pirate ship during the Revolutionary War and gave it to his firstborn daughter. It became a family heirloom, passed down from bride to bride. Everyone thinks it was a crime of opportunity, but Trace is the one who figures out the thief was familiar with its history."

"A pirate ship," Caleb repeated. "Wow."

Lucy's heart bumped against her rib cage. "What does that mean? Wow?"

"It doesn't sound like Brynn. She's the Queen of Storybook Endings, isn't she? She doesn't usually mix true love with a mystery."

Lucy's eyes narrowed. "You said you weren't a reader."

"Not *much* of a reader. But what kind of son doesn't read his mom's books?"

Hmm. The same kind of son who benefits from the profits of said books but never has time for a visit?

"I'm just saying, why bring a PI into the story at all? Wouldn't

Fletcher have scored extra points if he'd found the necklace in a pawnshop and delivered it to Paisley on their wedding day?"

He would have. If only Lucy had thought of that.

"Fletcher is an architect. He doesn't know anything about the shady side of life. In order to stay true to his character, it had to be someone who had connections to questionable people. It's Trace's job to know what's going on in the city, and when he heard about the necklace, he showed up at Fletcher's house and offered to help."

He'd shown up at Paisley and Fletcher's private wedding reception, too, in a tuxedo to boot. The handsome, charming party-crasher.

Kind of like someone else Lucy knew.

Chapter Fourteen

Caleb didn't seem to realize he shared another trait with his alter ago.

"Questionable people," he repeated. "Got it. Because Trace is a thief."

"*Was* a thief," Lucy felt compelled to remind him. "But only because he was too young to know any better. Trace's parents earned their living by breaking the law, and it eventually caught up to them. They were sent to prison, and Trace went into the foster-care system. There were a few rocky years before he got his head on straight and became a private investigator. He feels guilty because his parents ruined people's lives, so when he gets a chance to right a wrong... Why are you looking at me like that?"

"Because you're talking about Trace Hunter like he's a real person," Caleb said. "Mom does that, too."

Lucy didn't know what to say...which meant she'd said too much.

"Brynn has a gift for bringing her characters to life." It was the truth. "It's one of the reasons people love to read her books." Lucy paused. He had that look on his face again. "What?"

"Brynn said you knew a lot about the character. Do you brainstorm with her? She told me once that when it comes to writing, and this is a direct quote, she likes to be *the only cook in the kitchen*."

Lucy hadn't expected that someone whose main source of communication with his mother was monthly checks and an occasional phone call would be familiar with Brynn's artistic quirks, but something in Caleb's tone warned Lucy they were heading into dangerous territory.

"I, uh, proofread some of the books before Brynn sends them to her editor." That was the truth, too.

So why was Caleb studying her as if she'd done something wrong?

"You have a pretty diverse portfolio. English major?"

Lucy's heart jumped into kickboxing mode again. She hadn't majored in anything but real life. Any skills she'd picked up had been born out of necessity. Correcting her siblings' homework. Taking care of the bills and the family budget.

Ordinary skills that didn't translate well on a résumé.

Caleb would wonder why Brynn had hired her—a high-school graduate—over candidates with multiple degrees and way more experience than Lucy. She'd wondered the same thing when Brynn offered her the job and had spent the last three years making sure she didn't disappoint the woman who'd taken a chance on her.

"No…" While Lucy tried to come up with a way to shut down what was beginning to feel like an interrogation and take control of the conversation again, rescue came from an unexpected source.

"Excuse me." David McCrae stood in the doorway, holding a wooden tray.

Lucy found their host rather intimidating, but at this particular moment she was grateful for the interruption.

"Come in." *Please.* "Whatever that is looks delicious."

David gave the contents a dubious glance. "I haven't been able to get to the grocery store in a few days, but I put together a few odds and ends to hold you over until supper."

"It's perfect." Lucy's stomach rumbled in agreement. "Thank you, Mr. McCrae."

For the snacks and saving her from Caleb's questions.

Doubt washed over Lucy again.

Not over her lack of a college degree but for adding yet another category to what Caleb had already referred to as her *diverse portfolio*.

But she wasn't a writer. She was a finisher of someone else's writing. An assistant who'd stepped in and completed a task. That this particular task happened to be a book that had rocketed to the top of several prestigious lists was the reason Lucy had trouble sleeping at night.

It wasn't as if Lucy had plagiarized Brynn's work. Brynn had *asked* her to finish the book. But Lucy had never expected it would complicate things.

Or threaten to expose the secret that Brynn had been trying so hard to keep.

If word got out that Lucy had written those last five chapters, then Brynn's readers—and her publisher—would want to know why. Which meant Brynn would have to admit she was suffering from burnout. Or something even more serious.

Over the past few years, Lucy had discovered that while Brynn was generous with her time and her talent when it came to her fans, in other ways she was a very private person.

The man sitting across from her was proof of that.

Why hadn't Brynn told anyone she had a son?

Before Lucy had come downstairs, she'd looked beyond the bio that was standard-issue in Brynn's press releases and went online to dig a little deeper into her history.

It was common knowledge that Brynn had grown up in Nashville. As the only child of a father who'd been third generation in a prestigious law firm and a stay-at-home mom known for her charity work, Brynn's early years looked almost idyllic on paper.

She'd taken a year off before starting college and traveled around Europe. After she returned, she'd spent the summer penning a story that had turned into her debut novel. It hit the bestseller list almost immediately, and she'd skipped college and kept writing, cementing her career as a romance novelist.

There was no mention of a child.

Caleb was only a few years older than Lucy, so Brynn would have been in her late teens, eighteen or nineteen at the most, when she'd given birth to him. But other than her parents, who'd relocated to New York City long before Brynn had hired her, there was no mention of a family anywhere. No mention of a pregnancy or a baby boy.

Still curious, Lucy had searched a little longer and found one clue buried in an old newspaper article. A reporter had asked Brynn where her "one and only love" was hiding, and Brynn had responded that he was in her heart but not her life. When he'd pressed her a little more, Brynn, who usually handled awkward situations with a gracious smile, had gotten teary-eyed instead.

That there'd been some kind of heartbreak or tragedy in Brynn's past had made fans more protective of her. They rallied around her, closing the door to any future questions on the subject. And making it easier for Brynn to protect her secret.

Another one she'd entrusted to Lucy.

Knowing Caleb was Brynn's son, her flesh and blood, only made their relationship more confusing, though.

Why was he taking money from Brynn? To support a certain lifestyle? And why didn't she mind? Did Brynn feel like she owed him something? Was she supporting Caleb out of guilt?

"There's apple cider and decaf coffee in the carafes on the sideboard, so help yourself."

David's comment yanked Lucy's thoughts in line, and she

put some distance between herself and Caleb as he set the tray down on the table.

"I'm sure Brynn is probably ready for a snack, too." Lucy reached for a plate, but Caleb beat her to it.

"I can take it up to her." He waved the book in the air. "Someone assigned homework for me to do."

Lucy was about to protest when David stepped in.

"I was hoping we could have a few minutes to talk about meals while you're here."

One of the things that happened to be on Lucy's to-do list.

"All right." She glanced at Caleb. "No cider, though. Brynn breaks out in hives if she eats apples."

Caleb dipped his head in a nod. Smiled.

"So do I."

Caleb balanced the tray on one hand and knocked on Brynn's door with the other.

Lucy had looked so hesitant when he'd offered to bring it upstairs, he was surprised he hadn't had to wrestle it from her grip.

"It's open."

Brynn's guest room looked comfortable, but it was half the size of the one she'd stayed in the night before.

She was sitting in a chair facing the window, a leather book embossed with hand-tooled wildflowers on her lap.

Caleb recognized it instantly. The verses she'd shared with him after they'd met had chased away the shadows and illuminated a new path, a better path, than the one he'd been on.

"Oh…Caleb." Brynn straightened and caught the Bible before it slipped from her lap. "I thought you were Lucy."

"I have to finish unpacking so I—" *won* "—offered to bring up the tray. She thought you might be working and not want to come down."

"She's thoughtful like that…and so are you."

Caleb wasn't so sure. He should have come back the moment he suspected something wasn't right.

Brynn might not have raised him, but apparently mind reading was a superpower every mother possessed to some degree, because she said, "Readers aren't the only people who contact me. Once in a while, I hear from a pastor or a teacher." A smile kindled in her eyes. "The occasional mechanic."

Mel.

He should have known she'd keep Brynn in the loop.

"I just go where I'm told."

"Hmm. I don't think you were told to fly a medical missionary and his family out of a hot spot a few weeks ago," Brynn mused. "But we can talk about that later." She moved the Bible to her nightstand and reached for a cracker. "How are you and Lucy getting along?"

The hot spot was a safer topic.

"I don't think she's excited about us working together." Caleb pulled up an armless wooden chair he wasn't sure would hold his weight and took a plate. Filled it with fresh fruit and paper-thin slices of cheese.

"I owe both of you an apology." Brynn slanted a look in his direction. "Surprise seems to be the order of the day."

Caleb didn't try to pretend he didn't know what she was talking about. "I was surprised," he admitted. "But it's your call."

"*Our* call," Brynn said. "I should have handled it differently. When I saw you…it didn't cross my mind to keep it a secret from Lucy. Even if there wasn't a confidentiality clause in her contract, I would trust her."

"And when she leaves?"

Caleb wished he could take back the words when a shadow passed through Brynn's eyes.

The circumstances may have been different, but they'd both learned that the people who were supposed to have your back didn't always stick around.

"*If* she leaves, yes, even then," Brynn finally said. "I trust Lucy, but you and I agreed that respecting your privacy comes first."

After they were reunited when Caleb was twenty-five, he hadn't been as concerned about his privacy as he was about Brynn's reputation. She didn't have a real throne, but her readers definitely put her on a pedestal. The sweet Southern girl next door who wrote wholesome, uplifting fiction.

A teenage girl getting pregnant out of wedlock had carried more of a stigma the year Brynn's debut novel was published. Any hint of scandal could have destroyed her career before it had a chance to succeed. More than thirty years had passed, but if Brynn's long-lost son suddenly appeared at her side, there would still be those people who claimed she'd built her brand on a lie.

There'd been another, more compelling reason to keep their relationship a secret, though. One Caleb was still reluctant to share with her.

"Lucy hasn't worked for you very long."

"Three years, but I don't know what I'd do without her. Once you get to know Lucy better, you'll realize there's nothing to worry about."

"You rely on her a lot."

Brynn's expression turned thoughtful. "I suppose I do."

"For a personal assistant, she's taken on a lot of responsibility." Caleb pushed a little harder. "I mean, she travels with you. She handles the financial end of the business. Proofs your manuscripts." That last one had caught him off guard.

While Lucy had gotten him up to speed on Trace's background, he'd realized the only way she'd be privy to that information was if Brynn herself had shared it with her.

Unlike a lot of authors, he knew that Brynn didn't have critique partners or beta readers. Her editor was the first person who saw her book.

And the expression on Lucy's face... She'd looked uncomfortable, almost guilty, when he'd questioned it.

"Lucy has amazing attention for details," Brynn said, coming to her defense once again. "Plus, if anything goes wrong, she's a fixer."

But what was she fixing?

That's what Caleb wanted to know.

Brynn was a wealthy woman and a generous one. She didn't have a family, either—at least not one that Lucy had known about until Caleb showed up.

It wouldn't be the first time someone had insinuated themselves into their employer's life, hoping for perks that extended beyond their weekly paycheck.

Was Lucy Gable looking out for Brynn's future...or her own?

Chapter Fifteen

"That's my coffee mug. And my fire."

"Yours is right where you left it." *Yesterday.* Brynn pointed at the hearth. "Mine—" she raised her mug "—was in the kitchen. And this fire is the only one I could find when I came downstairs."

She smiled at Patch, who, unlike his owner, looked happy to see her. The dog loped up to Brynn, tail wagging, whiskers tipped with frost.

David peeled off a flannel shirt and tossed it over the back of the sofa, revealing a long-sleeved thermal T-shirt underneath. And some pretty impressive biceps, Brynn couldn't help but notice.

Because studying people was a form of research. It's what authors did...

"There's a switch on the wall for the fireplace in the gathering room."

Brynn knew that. Just like she knew she'd taken a risk invading David's private living quarters again. She'd spotted him from her window, blazing a trail through the snow toward the barn. A pair of Belgian horses with shaggy coats the color of cinnamon stood behind the fence, waiting patiently for their breakfast.

Brynn, who was more than ready for her first cup of coffee, decided to see if David had brewed a pot before he'd left.

The sideboard in the gathering room was empty, but the smell of something baking had lured Brynn into the kitchen. Banana bread—she'd peeked—and a French press on the counter only steps from the peaceful retreat she'd discovered the day before.

Brynn had planned to be long gone by the time David returned, but the storm that had hit during the midnight hours and the one going on inside of her had kept her awake most of the night. Comfy cushions, a strong cup of coffee and the warmth radiating from the fireplace proved too much of a temptation.

"I like the real kind," Brynn said. "Y'all must go through a lot of wood up here."

"Enough." David ducked his head, but not before Brynn saw his lips twitch.

For stating the obvious or the *y'all* that had slipped out?

Brynn decided it didn't matter. David hadn't politely kicked her out, and she'd almost witnessed an honest-to-goodness smile again. She considered that a win-win. She took another sip of coffee as he tossed another log on the fire and caught a whiff of something other than woodsmoke.

"I think the banana bread is done."

David muttered a complaint and disappeared into the kitchen.

She heard the oven door opening and a muffled *ouch* before it snapped shut again.

Brynn's gaze shifted to the gallery of photographs on the wall, one of several interesting discoveries she'd made in the fifteen minutes she'd been alone.

Upon closer inspection, what Brynn had thought was a collection by a professional photographer turned out to be a collage of candid shots instead.

A sleigh filled with school-age children bundled up against the cold. Christmas trees leaning against the side of a weathered shed. An elderly woman tending an enormous cast-iron pot on a grate over a campfire. A close-up of an adolescent girl with a freckled face and a wide grin, sitting proudly astride a horse that looked like the ones on the other side of the fence.

Every photograph a black-and-white snapshot that captured Spruce Hill Farm's history…and a memory.

The conversation she'd overheard between David and Esther cycled through Brynn's mind again.

The Christmas-tree farm obviously held a special place in the hearts of the people who lived in Frost, but for some reason, David didn't feel the same way.

Brynn was still trying to figure the man out. He looked totally at ease straddling a machine built for snow and trails hemmed in by trees. In the kitchen, though, David McCrae appeared to be as out of his element as a mountain lion in captivity.

How had he ended up running a bed-and-breakfast? Was it by choice or by accident?

A family business wasn't always a blessing. Sometimes it was an albatross.

Brynn had hired Caleb to run Words with Wings, her nonprofit, because she knew he'd be perfect for the job. But if God had something else in mind for him, Brynn never wanted Caleb to feel obligated to stay. She wanted him to be happy, too.

The doors parted, and David returned. At some point between rescuing the banana bread and bandaging his finger, he'd found time to put on a black shirt with the inn's logo embroidered on the pocket.

Brynn wasn't fooled. Not one bit. Three cute little pine trees didn't change an outdoorsman into an innkeeper any more than a collar turned a wolf into a house pet.

"I'll be setting up breakfast in the gathering room. Unless you'd like a tray sent upstairs?"

Brynn would like to stay right where she was but doubted that was an option. Neither was telling David that climbing the stairs to the second floor would feel like tackling Mount Everest at the moment.

Brynn had only been awake a few hours, but she could feel the fatigue already creeping in, stealing her energy. She'd made a promise to herself not to let whatever was wreaking havoc with her body steal her joy, too.

Or David's insinuation that she was accustomed to special treatment.

"No, thank you." Brynn flashed a smile. "The gathering room is fine."

David's phone pinged, and he frowned at the screen. Typed a quick message back.

Another ping. Another frown. Two decisive taps.

If Brynn had to guess, it was the word *no*.

"People must wake up early around here."

"I've already gotten four messages and two voice mails this morning. One was from your assistant, by the way. I went over the breakfast menu with her last night, but now she wants to discuss kitchen privileges."

That didn't surprise Brynn. No wonder David had stared at her in disbelief when she'd asked about restaurants that could cater their meals. The night before, Lucy found a bar and grill that served pizza but was informed that Spruce Hill Farm was outside their delivery zone. It did, however, happen to be on the manager's way home, so he'd dropped it off after work.

Brynn had written about small towns like Frost, but she'd never called one home.

"I'm afraid we're used to Nashville," Brynn said. "All Lucy has to do is pick up the phone and food gets delivered right to the door."

David's cell pinged again. He looked down at it and then at the fireplace.

"Turning the sound off would be the better option," Brynn suggested lightly.

"Wouldn't matter," David muttered. "Either way, I'd have people showing up at my door."

"Like Esther?"

David's eyes narrowed, and Brynn realized she probably shouldn't have brought that up. But there was something about Esther that made Brynn want to get to know her better.

There are still things to celebrate.

Brynn had needed the reminder, too.

"You're the one who pushed me into a room that isn't sound-proof."

"I didn't push… Never mind. Your assistant doesn't want anyone to know you're here, and if you overheard my conversation with Esther, you must have realized the Friends of Frost get a little carried away when it comes to Christmas and celebrities."

Brynn ignored the celebrity part. She had loyal readers, but it wasn't like she had to worry about the paparazzi hiding behind a snowbank.

"It sounded to me like they want to revive a tradition that means a lot to people…including your daughter. She must be proud of her roots here."

David flinched, a sign Brynn had touched a nerve. "Her roots aren't in Frost. This place belonged to her great-grandparents, and we didn't move here until she was twelve years old."

We.

Brynn's stomach pitched. Had David and Grace's mother split up? Or had something else happened?

"But Grace must love it here or she wouldn't want to come back after she graduates from college."

"She's eighteen years old. She romanticizes things." David

was looking at Brynn as if she were somehow to blame for that. "But she's right in the middle of her midterm exams, and she should be concentrating on those. Believe me, if I'd known she—" He stopped, but Brynn filled in the blanks.

"Entered the contest." She tried to remember what David had said the day before when he'd tried to convince her to withdraw from the book tour. "You really didn't know anything about it?"

David's lips twisted. "Grace saw the announcement on social media, wrote some kind of essay about why Frost should be included in your tour and then forgot to check that email account for a month.

"When she saw that Frost had been chosen, she convinced your assistant that everything would be ready for your visit. She drove here for the weekend and told me about it. Promised I wouldn't have to do a thing, because her last exam was two days before you were scheduled to arrive."

But Brynn was already here.

She didn't regret their last-minute change in plans. She did, however, feel a little guilty that she was the reason David had been forced to change his. "And then we showed up early, so you don't feel prepared."

"Don't feel prepared?" David echoed. "I'm *not* prepared at all. For any of this."

"But it's Christmas. You must have guests this time of year. Don't you put up a tree? Decorate the rooms?"

For a moment, Brynn didn't think he was going to answer.

"Yes," he finally admitted. "But not this year. This year, I planned to put the house and the property on the market. The Realtor assured me there are a lot of people interested in buying land and I'd have an offer within forty-eight hours. When that happened, I was going to tell Grace and then surprise her with two weeks at the beach. We'd celebrate Christmas together *and* the sale."

Brynn felt the floor tilt underneath her feet. She sucked in breath to steady herself. "Your daughter has no idea you're planning to sell?"

"Just like I had no idea she'd become an honorary member of the Friends of Frost." David shook his head. "Apparently we need to work on our communication skills."

He wasn't the only parent in the room who could use a little help in that department.

Brynn was still trying to figure out a way to tell her son about the struggles she'd been having with her health.

Her brain had been short-circuiting lately, but suddenly the empty guest rooms and lack of holiday cheer made sense.

"You weren't going to accept any reservations this month, were you?"

"Nope. But Grace didn't know that." David scrubbed one hand over the stubble that had cropped up on his chin during the night. "I'm supposed to offer a *gourmet breakfast.*" He put air quotes around the words. "And the only thing I could find in the freezer was the loaf of banana bread Grace baked the last time she was here. Now she's threatening to blow off studying and come home early to get a head start on the decorating and the baking before you—and your fans—arrive. So you see my dilemma here."

Brynn did. It explained why David had tried to get out of hosting her final event, but she also suspected it went a whole lot deeper than decorating the inn for Christmas.

An idea began to form in Brynn's mind. One that would solve David's immediate problem and maybe hers as well. She'd wanted to divert Lucy's and Caleb's attention. The coaching sessions would only last so long. If they were busy, they wouldn't notice that Brynn *wasn't.*

She heard the sound of footsteps in the kitchen.

Lucy. Her timing impeccable as always.

"We're in here," she called.

Lucy entered David's living room with a smile already in place, as if there was nothing awkward about finding Brynn ensconced in their host's private quarters again. "Good morning, Brynn. Mr. McCrae."

"Good morning." Brynn returned her smile. "There seems to have been some kind of misunderstanding with David's daughter, Grace. I was just about to explain that even though Spruce Hill Farm is hosting the meet and greet, we take care of all the details, including the decorations."

Lucy blinked once before nodding. "That's right." Another warm smile, this one aimed directly at David. "You don't have to do a thing."

David's brows dipped together. "Grace seems to think she's in charge of all that."

"Like I said, a misunderstanding. It's important the experience revolves around a particular theme," Brynn said. "The readers who attend these events have certain expectations, and I don't want to disappoint them."

She should have been lifting a teacup, pinky pointed out, when she delivered those lines, but the stuffy, condescending tone must have been exactly right because Lucy's mouth dropped open.

Brynn, who'd made a silent pact with her eighteen-year-old self never to sound like her mother, was a little disturbed at how easily the words had flowed from her mouth.

"While Lucy works on the inside, you'll have time to do whatever you have to do outside." She caught David's gaze and held it. "Cut wood for a bonfire. Get the horses in shape to pull the sleigh. That sort of thing." She paused, waiting for David to catch up. When his eyes narrowed, she continued. "When Grace does arrive, it will be a nice surprise."

A memory, too.

The girl's last Christmas at Spruce Hill Farm, if the Realtor was right and the property sold right away.

David turned away, and Brynn saw him glance at the wall of photographs. Zero in on the teenage girl with the bright smile and pigtails, her arms wrapped around the draft horse's neck.

Grace?

If it was, Brynn felt sorry for both of them.

She didn't know why the thought of David selling the tree farm and the house bothered her.

Was he planning to stay in Frost? Or was he going to close the inn for good and move on?

David dragged his gaze from the photograph and his lips tightened again, a sign he wasn't looking forward to that particular conversation with his daughter, either.

"Caleb will want to help, too." Brynn knew she was ignoring boundaries again, but Esther and the rest of the committee was counting on her. So was Grace. The girl's roots might not be as deep as Esther's, but in the few years Grace had called Frost home, they must have taken root.

"Your driver isn't on my payroll," David pointed out.

Her *driver*? Brynn had to silently count to five so she wouldn't correct him.

"Caleb likes to be busy, and he's kind of a jack-of-all-trades," Brynn said. "I'm sure if you told him what needed to be done, he'd pitch right in."

Like Lucy, her son's timing couldn't have been more perfect. He walked past the window with the red-handled shovel Brynn had seen sticking out of the snowbank. "See what I mean?"

"What about you?" David tipped his head. "Are you going to volunteer to stack firewood?"

Actually, Brynn could think of at least a dozen things she'd love to do. Brush the horses' woolly coats. Decorate every room in the house with greenery and lights. Unpack the box of homemade ornaments stashed in the corner and try to fit together some more of the pieces of David McCrae's life.

But considering she'd barely been able to muster the energy to get dressed, Brynn was going to look like the diva that David thought she was.

"Sorry," she said lightly. "I'll be on the sidelines, working on my next chapter."

David didn't need to know that Brynn was talking about her life, not her next book.

Chapter Sixteen

"What's the first item on your agenda today?"

"Christmas decorations for the bed-and-breakfast." Lucy didn't have to consult her notes.

Technically, decorations hadn't been *on* Lucy's list until an hour ago, but they seemed to be the most pressing issue at the moment.

Brynn shook her head. "No. It's Lucy Gets a Raise."

Lucy grinned.

This was one of the reasons she loved working for Brynn.

Behind the sequins, flaming-red curls and the sweet Southern charm lurked a wry, self-deprecating sense of humor.

"You gave me a raise two months ago," Lucy reminded her.

"That was for coming up with the Mistletoe Stop idea. This one is for going above and beyond the call of duty." Brynn sighed. "It was the only solution I could think of at the moment."

Lucy settled into the chair opposite her employer. She hadn't broached the topic of her expanded duties during breakfast in the gathering room. David had been talking to someone on the landline in the lobby, and Caleb wandered in after shoveling to finish off the last piece of banana bread.

If Brynn was in need of a solution, though, it meant another problem had cropped up.

"I'm the one who should be apologizing," Lucy said. "Grace McCrae entered Frost in the contest, and I thought she would be here to handle all the details. Grace's father…" How to put this tactfully? "…doesn't seem to be as enthusiastic about hosting the event."

Or hosting at all, in Lucy's opinion.

"It wasn't showing up early that caught David off guard," Brynn said. "He hadn't been planning to accept reservations this month."

"I don't understand." In spite of a welcome as chilly as the temperature outside, the inn itself was warm and comfortable. "Was he going to update some of the rooms?"

"David wanted to put Spruce Hill Farm on the market. The Realtor thinks it will sell quickly, and he was going to surprise Grace with the news when she came home on Christmas break. Then he planned to whisk her away to the beach to celebrate."

"He…he was going to sell Grace's home right out from under her?" Lucy's stomach turned a somersault. "And he thought Grace would be *happy* about it?"

"He thought that keeping it a secret was the right thing to do."

It almost sounded like Brynn was defending him.

"Being honest with people is, too." Lucy winced the moment the words came out.

Pot meet kettle, Luce.

Brynn looked away. "Sometimes, when you make a decision to do or *not* do something, it's about protecting the people you care about."

That's how Lucy had gotten into her current predicament with the fictional Trace Hunter, but she had a feeling Brynn wasn't referring to David McCrae now.

"Grace was so excited when you picked Frost as a Mistletoe Stop that David put the sale on hold until after Christmas," Brynn continued. "But I feel responsible he's in this situation. He knows hosting the meet and greet means a lot to Grace, and he doesn't want to disappoint her."

Lucy had no idea how he was going to avoid it. The reason she'd assumed Spruce Hill Farm was a family business was because Grace had *said* it was when Lucy had contacted her after the contest closed.

"Did you read Grace McCrae's entry?" she asked carefully.

A shadow passed through Brynn's eyes. "I meant to…but no, not yet."

Lucy opened a file on her tablet and handed it to Brynn.

For a few minutes, the only sound in the room was the wind rattling the window, seeking entry. When Brynn looked up, Lucy saw tears shimmering in her eyes.

Lucy had had the same reaction the first time she'd read it, too.

"David hasn't seen this?" Brynn's fingers trembled when she gave Lucy the tablet back.

"Not unless Grace showed it to him."

Brynn sighed. "I don't think she did."

Lucy felt as if she'd been given a window into Grace's heart when she'd read her essay. She couldn't imagine how devastated the girl would be when she found out about the sale.

That's why Lucy was going to decorate every nook and cranny of the inn before Grace McCrae came home. Not because Brynn's readers expected a picture-perfect setting, though.

Because making Grace's last Christmas at Spruce Hill Farm one to remember was a promise Lucy had just made to herself.

Chapter Seventeen

"It's dark down there." Lucy waved the flashlight left and right, illuminating the cobwebs that crisscrossed the stairwell.

Caleb peered over her shoulder.

It was also cold, the size of a closet and, yes, a little creepy, but Lucy didn't have to sound so excited about it.

She took a few steps into the abyss and turned around, momentarily blinding Caleb with a beam of light. "Are you coming?"

Caleb hadn't decided yet.

He had no problem being confined to a small space thirty thousand feet above the ground. Being confined to a small space underneath it...that was an entirely different thing.

"I thought David said the decorations were in a storage closet."

"He did." Lucy ducked her head to avoid a low beam. "And the closet is down here."

Caleb had missed that part of the conversation.

Actually, he'd missed the whole thing when he'd been digging a path to the rental car.

Brynn hadn't given him many details, only that Lucy had

taken charge of getting the inn ready for Brynn's meet and greet with her fans. In a twist Caleb hadn't seen coming, he'd been drafted into service, too.

The stair sagged under his weight, and Caleb reached for the wooden handrail. It creaked in protest at the disturbance. Ducking to avoid a low beam in the stairwell, he continued his descent into the basement.

By the time he reached the bottom, Lucy had taken her flashlight and disappeared. When Caleb finally caught up to her, she was standing on her tiptoes, swiping at a piece of string dangling next to a bare light bulb on the ceiling.

Caleb appreciated her can-do spirit, but he was half a foot taller. He reached up and tugged on the string. It broke in half, and the bulb flickered irritably before it went out again.

"Try that one over there." Lucy pointed to another bulb positioned over a utility sink.

Caleb tugged a little more gently this time, and his reward was a glow that barely lit up the corner they were standing in.

Lucy turned off the flashlight and looked around. "David didn't say which room. Let's start with that door over there."

Caleb hadn't realized there were doors—three of them to be exact—that opened into other dark rooms.

So why was Lucy smiling?

"Is it my imagination, or is this fun for you?"

"I read my way through the entire *Nancy Drew* mystery series one year. She always found a clue in places like this."

"You look for clues, and I'll look for cardboard boxes marked *Christmas Decorations* so we can get out of here faster."

Lucy's smile faded. "You don't have to help me, you know."

He kind of did.

Not only because Brynn had asked him to, but because *What Would Trace Hunter Do?* was becoming his new motto.

Caleb had stayed up until midnight reading Brynn's book. Fletcher might have been the hero of the story, but in five short chapters, even a die-hard suspense fan like Caleb could see why the private investigator had stolen the show. Trace's search for the necklace was more entertaining than the lead-up to Fletcher and Paisley's wedding.

If his mom hadn't spent several decades building her brand in happily-ever-afters, Caleb had no doubt she could have been equally successful at writing whodunits.

"I have a few minutes." Caleb borrowed one of Trace's favorite lines, delivered with a straight face and tongue firmly in cheek, of course. With all the daytime investigating and nighttime righting of wrongs, the real mystery was how the character found a few extra minutes to shave.

He saw her expression and shrugged. "Hey, you're the one who assigned homework."

Lucy's smile bloomed for a moment, and then she spun a slow circle, taking an inventory of the room. "Hmm. Where to start?"

A rhetorical question considering she wasn't looking at him, but definitely a valid one, Caleb thought. The upper floors were almost minimalistic when it came to furnishings and decor, but the basement had become the collection site for cast-off furniture and boxes filled with items their host hadn't taken the time to sort through or wasn't ready to part with yet. Either way, picking their way through the maze made the search a lot more challenging.

"Door Number One?" he suggested. "People usually keep their seasonal stuff in a separate area."

At least Caleb's adoptive mom did, after a set of her favorite Christmas dishes had accidentally gotten mixed in with a donation to a local thrift shop one year.

"One it is." Lucy brushed the cobwebs off the knob and pushed it open, but Caleb managed to catch her arm before she stepped inside. He pointed to the shards of broken glass that littered the dirt floor.

"Sorry. I didn't want you to step on that."

Lucy went still for a moment. "Thanks." Her voice sounded a little scratchy, like she'd inhaled some of the dust floating in the air. "It looks like an old root cellar." She turned on the flashlight and trained it on the empty shelves. "On to the next one. It…it might be faster if we split up."

Caleb nodded in agreement. Given the number of boxes they were going to have to sort through, they could be down here the rest of the week.

A thought that, when taking into consideration the dust motes, spiders and shadowy corners, should have bothered Caleb more than it did.

"Fine. I'll take Door Number Two. If I can find it."

"Keep your eyes open for a broom."

Caleb spotted a mousetrap underneath one of the shelves and made a mental note to be on the lookout for furry little critters, too.

He waited until Lucy squeezed between two old dressers and disappeared from view before picking his way through a Jenga-like booby trap made from pieces of plywood and folding chairs.

On the other side of the basement was a utility room that held the water heater, furnace and a high-tech washing machine and dryer that looked out of place in a home with a root cellar.

"Caleb?"

Lucy's muffled voice reached Caleb while he was checking the boxes underneath the ironing board. So far, his search had yielded a cache of used paintbrushes and rusty tools but no Christmas decorations.

He retraced his steps to the center of the room. "Where are you?"

She sneezed instead of answering. Caleb followed the sound but was forced to take a detour around the dressers Lucy had managed to wriggle between. He found her a few moments later framed in Door Number Three.

She motioned at him to come closer. "There's a bunch of boxes in here, but none of them are marked."

Caleb followed Lucy as she waded deeper into the room. While she stood in the center, contemplating where to begin, he scanned the hedge of boxes that lined the perimeter of the room. Most of them were cardboard, but along one wall were three sturdy plastic bins that Lucy would have called clues.

Caleb picked one and pried off the lid. Just as he suspected. Inside the bin was a honeycomb of green and red tissue paper, a glass ornament tucked in the center of each one.

"Over here."

Lucy landed at his side in an instant and knelt down on the concrete floor to see what he'd found. "These are beautiful!"

Caleb shrugged. "If you really want to protect something from moisture or getting broken, you store it in plastic not cardboard."

"And you said you weren't a detective."

"I'm not." He laughed and reached out to pluck a cobweb from her hair.

"Are there any more?" Lucy ran her fingers through the short strands and released the scent of something light and flowery into the air.

"No." The word came out thin and a little scratchy. Caleb cleared his throat.

The dust. Had to be.

Lucy opened the second bin and grinned as if she'd just won the lottery. "Christmas lights." She snapped the lid back in place again. "I saw an outlet at the bottom of the stairs. You keep looking, and I'll plug them in and make sure they work before we haul everything upstairs."

Brynn hadn't been exaggerating when she'd said Lucy was a details person. She was obviously used to managing things—and people—too.

Caleb grabbed another tote. A thick layer of yellowed newspaper formed a buffer between the lid and the contents inside. His nose twitched as he peeled it back. Packed inside the large box were at least fifty smaller ones, the contents of each one written in permanent marker.

Bakery. Library. Stable. Bridge. Pond. Family.

The dust in the air collected in Caleb's lungs again, making it difficult to breathe.

He didn't have to open one of the boxes to know what was inside it.

Caleb's head jerked up at the sound of Lucy's voice.

"Two strands didn't make the cut, but I… What's the matter? You look like you just saw a ghost."

He pushed the box aside.

The Ghost of Christmas Past, maybe.

Chapter Eighteen

"Sorry, Nancy Drew. No apparitions." Caleb forced a teasing smile. "I think all this dust is clogging up my head."

"Are there decorations in that one, too?"

"Nothing you'd be interested in using."

The moment Caleb said the words he knew he'd made a mistake. Made her curious.

Lucy knelt down on the concrete floor and picked up one of the boxes. "Ice-cream parlor?"

"It's one of those light-up villages that takes forever to set up."

He knew that because his adoptive mom had started buying pieces the year she and his dad got married, and she'd continued to add a new one every year until...

"Really?"

Caleb wasn't surprised when Lucy reached into the box again and chose the one labeled *Library*. Out came a miniature brick building with an arched doorway and a tabby cat sleeping next to a stack of books in the window.

"I love it." Lucy handed him a box. "You can open this one."

"Are you sure you want to waste your time? We don't have

a lot of it, so we should probably stick with something simple. Like lights."

"I've decided our theme will be an old-fashioned Christmas," Lucy said.

"*Livery stable.*" Caleb read the words on the box. "I guess you can't get more old-fashioned than that."

"He said sarcastically," Lucy murmured.

Caleb shrugged. "All this just seems like...I don't know... overkill, that's all."

He could tell he'd chosen the wrong word when Lucy's eyes went wide.

"*Overkill?*"

"I thought you were just decorating the gathering room. There's barely enough room in there for people, let alone all this." Caleb waved his hand over the box. "But I can tell I'm talking to someone who probably has an ugly Christmas sweater tucked away in a drawer and breaks out the tissues for *It's a Wonderful Life* every year."

"There's nothing wrong with traditions." Lucy sat back on her heels. "My ugly Christmas sweater happened to win first prize last year, and *I* can tell that I'm talking to a Scrooge."

A *Scrooge?*

In Caleb's neighborhood, his adoptive parents had a reputation for making things merry and bright. Glenn and Marianne Beauchamp's house could have been the setting for a Christmas movie. He and his dad would untangle miles of lights and thread them between the branches of every tree in the yard, string them from the roof. When Caleb was finished, he would run back inside, his cheeks chapped red from the cold. His mom would have the hot chocolate ready, and she'd already be on her knees in the living room, unpacking the ceramic village and carefully releasing each piece from its Bubble Wrap cocoon. It took hours, but Caleb would help, setting up tiny buildings and bridges, miniature skating ponds and tiny trees that covered every flat surface and windowsill.

During the days leading up to Christmas, there would be cookies shaped like stars and snowmen cooling on wire racks in the kitchen and hand-knit stockings hanging from the mantel. Presents hidden in places that Caleb could never seem to find during clandestine searches when his parents were busy would pile up under the tree.

On Christmas Eve, they would go to church together, Caleb dressed in the crisp button-down shirt and khaki pants his mom bought for him every year. A greeter stood at the doors of the sanctuary, handing out candles. During the last carol, "Silent Night," the lights would dim, and one by one, the congregation would light the candle of the person sitting next to them until the entire room was illuminated by hundreds of tiny flames.

His mom would keep a watchful eye on Caleb and that candle no matter how old he was. When Caleb was in high school, he'd tease her a little, pretend he was going to drop it, just to hear her laugh.

Marianne Beauchamp had laughed a lot.

That's what Caleb remembered, even though the passage of time had started to blur the image of her face.

Looking back, Caleb realized he'd taken Christmas for granted, assuming every family put up lights and frosted sugar cookies. Read the Gospel of Luke passage before they opened presents in the morning.

All those memories and only one Christmas stood out from the others now. The one his mom wasn't there. The oncologist had given her six months to live, but God had cut it down to four, one of the reasons why Caleb had refused to accompany his father to the Christmas Eve service that year.

The other reason was Shae, a woman who'd lived in their neighborhood. An acquaintance at best, not someone his parents would have considered a friend.

But she'd become a frequent visitor after the funeral, bearing gifts of food and straightening up the house. Weeding and watering the roses that his mom had planted in the backyard. Small gestures that had made a grief-stricken bachelor rely on her help. And once he did, Shae had taken advantage of his loneliness, too.

For his dad's sake, Caleb tried to stay out of Shae's way, but she resented every moment that he and his dad spent together. Resented *him*.

"Caleb isn't even your flesh and blood, Glenn," Shae would complain. "He's nothing like you. He's moody and disrespectful. He doesn't want me here. No matter how hard I try, he makes that clear every time he ignores me and walks away."

No, Caleb had walked away because he knew the truth. Shae had found her golden ticket in his dad, a man who'd always worked hard, paid his bills on time. And when they married less than a year after his mom died, Shae had started to rack up bills of her own. She liked traveling and expensive jewelry and had zero desire to fill the void in a teenage boy's life.

The Christmases that followed were a reminder of everything Caleb had lost. He knew his mom would be heartbroken about the rift between Caleb and his dad. She would have told him to be kind to Shae...and himself. But Caleb was furious with his dad for marrying Shae and furious with God for not healing his mom. For not even giving her those few extra months.

The anger had crowded out everything good, and Caleb found there wasn't room for anything else...

"You aren't denying it."

Lucy's comment yanked Caleb off the shadowy path his thoughts had taken him down.

Oh. Right.

She'd called him a Scrooge.

"I prefer to think of myself as a realist."

"Stop quoting Trace!"

"I wasn't." Not this time, anyway. Caleb waved his hand over the box. "Look at the bar people try to set here. Christmas isn't like this. *Life* isn't like this. Acknowledging that leaves less room for disappointment."

Lucy looked disappointed in *him*.

She picked up a box with the word *Bakery* written in crooked letters across the top. A smile drew up the corners of her lips.

"Every Christmas my grandma would invite me over to her house, and we'd make cookies together. She had a coffee can filled with metal cookie cutters, and while she rolled out the dough, I'd pick out my favorites. By the time we were done, there'd be frosting and flour everywhere.

"The cookies didn't look anything like the ones you see in a bakery or in magazines, but Gran didn't care. It would have been easier to do it herself, but it was the time together that mattered to her. Now that she's gone, I pull out her cookie cutters at Christmas, and I remember the way her kitchen smelled. I remember her using the corner of her apron to wipe the flour off my nose. But mostly I remember that she was patient, and she listened to me, and her hugs smelled like vanilla and cinnamon."

Caleb didn't *want* to remember.

Maybe that was part of the problem.

"Sometimes all the extras can get a little out of hand," Lucy allowed. "But shutting yourself off from possibilities...from hope...in order to avoid disappointment doesn't leave a lot of room for joy, either."

Chapter Nineteen

Caleb's expression darkened, and Lucy wondered if she'd overstepped.

Her cell phone began to ring in the depths of her pocket, and Lucy fished it out. Glanced at the screen and smiled.

She pushed to her feet, wiggled out a cramp that had settled into her toes and held up the phone.

"I have to take this."

"Go for it." Caleb closed the flaps on the box with a decisiveness that told Lucy he was more than ready to move on from their discussion, too. "I'll look through some more of these containers."

"Thanks." Lucy mouthed the word as she hopped over an old guitar case. Time was of the essence when it came to Ben. If she didn't answer on the third ring, he ended the call and moved on with his day.

She swiped her finger across the screen as she reached the doorway.

"Hey, Boo." Only a big sister could get away with calling her twenty-one-year-old brother by his childhood nickname.

Lucy heard a noise behind her that sounded suspiciously like a snort. Or maybe a cough.

The air *was* kind of thick down here.

"Hold on a sec. I have to find a place with good reception," she told her brother. There was no one in sight when Lucy entered the lobby, but there were noises coming from the kitchen so she ducked into the gathering room. "What's up?"

"Can't I call just to say hello?" Ben complained.

"Of course you can." Not his usual MO, but who was she to point out the obvious? "Hello."

"Hello. Now that we got that out of the way... I'm proposing to Chloe."

"*Ben.*" Tears scalded the backs of Lucy's eyes and burned her nose. "I had no idea you two were getting so serious."

"Yeah...well. I know we haven't been together very long, but what can I say? Chloe is the one. My feelings for her won't change whether it's three months from now or three years."

Who are you, and what have you done with my brother?

The voice definitely belonged to Ben. It was the *words* he was saying that Lucy couldn't quite reconcile with the mischievous little boy who'd filled her shampoo bottle with bubble bath and used her jewelry box to store his bug collection.

"We love her, too." Lucy had been with Ben the first time the couple met. Chloe, a nurse's aide in the ER, was on duty when Ben and his mountain bike parted company on a trail over the Fourth of July.

Their parents had been traveling at the time, so Lucy was the one who'd gotten the call and driven him to the ER, her heart hammering in her chest as the hospital came into view.

Having previously spent days in the waiting room and sitting quietly at her sister Janie's side, listening to the hum of the machines that surrounded her bed, it wasn't a place Lucy had ever wanted to visit again. She'd probably looked as pale as Ben when they'd shuffled into the waiting room.

Chloe had been calm and attentive, patiently answering Lucy's questions and monitoring Ben until a nurse had wheeled him down the hall for X-rays. His ankle was badly sprained, not broken, and other than a few cuts and bruises, the only thing he'd really damaged was his pride.

Lucy had thanked Chloe when Ben was discharged, but her brother had gone one step further. He'd dropped off a bouquet of flowers the next day and invited her out for dinner. A move that should have signaled to Lucy there were changes ahead.

"Did you pick out a ring yet?" Lucy silently measured the length of the windowsill. She might not be able to set up the entire village here, but the library and lobby could use a holiday makeover, too.

"I asked the jeweler to design one," Ben told her.

The pinch of envy caught Lucy off guard. After all, her brother wasn't the first of her siblings to fall in love. Kristin was waiting for her fiancé, Josh, to return from his deployment so they could start planning their wedding. Sean and his high-school sweetheart, Amber, had been accepted at colleges on opposite sides of the country, but Sean kept in touch through flowers, phone calls and the occasional surprise visit, so Lucy had a feeling their long-distance romance would eventually turn into a lifelong commitment, too.

Lucy had thought about joining one of those online dating sites—for about a minute. But that would involve setting up a profile and actually, well, *dating*. Something that didn't fit with her already-busy schedule.

Everyone is busy, Luce.

Kristin had pointed this out when Lucy declined a blind date with one of Josh's fellow Marines who'd chosen to spend his leave in Nashville the previous spring. It was important to extend hospitality, though, so Lucy had sent him a list of her favorite restaurants and popular local hot spots instead.

It wasn't like she had a confidence problem. Lucy was extremely confident—when it came to her job. When it came to social situations, she was perfectly content to blend in with the wallpaper. Unlike Brynn, Lucy wasn't comfortable in the spotlight. Planning and scheduling, pitching ideas, those things came to Lucy as naturally as taking a breath. But put her in the same room—or basement—with a handsome guy and she didn't know what to say. Or, even worse, she rambled.

No wonder Caleb had looked relieved when her cell phone rang. He'd been literally saved by the bell.

"I'd send you a picture of the ring, but I can't pick it up until next week," Ben said. "I hope Chloe likes it. All the rings in the case looked the same, and I wanted something special. Something that looks like *her*. Do you know what I mean?"

Lucy cleared her throat to cover a sniffle. "I'm sure she'll love any ring you put on her finger because she loves you."

"You aren't crying, are you?" Ben asked suspiciously.

"No. Of course not. Have you thought about how you're going to propose?"

Given that Ben was a die-hard football fan, it was possible hot dogs and a jumbotron would be involved.

"Sure." He sounded a little offended by Lucy's question. "On Christmas Eve. But I'm going to need your help to pull it off."

"*My* help?"

"I'm only going to get engaged once. And I am your favorite, right?"

Lucy rolled her eyes, even though he couldn't see her face. "What do you have in mind?"

"We always have appetizers before the evening service, but I was thinking this year, we could have a nice dinner. You know, with candles and stuff?"

"Have you talked to Mom about all this?"

"I want to surprise her, too. Besides that, she and Dad will be going to the airport to pick up Janie."

As always, her sister's name triggered a rush of affection. Lucy kept in touch with Janie, sent care packages once a month, but hadn't seen her in person since she'd started her freshman year at a college in Texas.

"My plane doesn't land until three."

"Church doesn't start until seven. If we eat at five it'll give you plenty of time."

You, not *us*.

Now he sounded like her baby brother again.

But Lucy knew Ben's culinary skills were limited to cruising the frozen-food aisle and preheating the oven to three hundred and fifty degrees.

"All right." She made a quick note to add an amendment to her shopping list. The grocery store near their parents' home offered delivery, and she could always pull in Rachel and Kristin as backup if traffic was heavy or her flight was delayed. "I'll see what I can do. Anything else?"

Lucy had been teasing, but Ben said, "I'll let you know. And thanks, Luce. I really appreciate this. When you meet the one, I promise I won't fill the front seat of his car with packing peanuts."

The one.

Lucy was twenty-eight years old. She was the personal assistant to a romance novelist and didn't have time for a romance of her own. An irony that didn't escape her.

"I'm sorry I did that, by the way," Ben added.

"Only because you got caught and Dad grounded you for a week."

"It was two weeks, and Monroe deserved it for dumping you. I didn't pull off that job alone, by the way. Sean helped, but I didn't rat him out."

Now wasn't the time to rehash her failed relationship with Isaac Monroe, but Lucy was surprised Sean hadn't gotten an automatic grounding from their dad, too. Sean and Ben were twins and got into so much mischief together their neighbors had nicknamed them Thing One and Thing Two.

"I'll take it to the grave," she promised.

"I know you will." Ben paused. Cleared his throat.

"Love you—and I promise I'll be there Christmas Eve."

A loud thump behind Lucy muffled Ben's goodbye, and she whirled around. Caleb had cobwebs clinging to his shirt and a disgruntled look on his face.

Lucy hoped the box at his feet wasn't filled with ceramic buildings or gluing all the tiny pieces back together would be added to her list, too.

"Did you find anything else?"

"Lights," Caleb announced. "Two more boxes of ornaments, a Nativity set and a bunch of fake boughs."

"That's a good start." Lucy glanced at her watch. "I'm going to check on Brynn before I bring the rest upstairs."

"I can bring them up."

Lucy tried not to look surprised by the offer. Based on their conversation in the basement, she'd thought Caleb would be happy she'd given him an out. "Thank you."

"No problem." Caleb's smile didn't quite reach his eyes. "I'm a helpful kind of guy."

Lucy really wished Caleb would stop quoting Trace.

It was already a little surreal, having your hero step from the pages of a book and appear right in front of your eyes.

No. Not *her* hero.

Because Lucy's hero would be more like Fletcher. Steady. Dependable. Someone a girl could count on to stick around, not set off for parts unknown whenever he became bored with the local scenery.

Instead of leaving, Caleb tucked his thumbs into the back pockets of his jeans, and his gaze traveled around the room. "Are you going to start decorating today?"

"I'm not sure." Thanks to Ben, Lucy now had a million and

one things to do before Brynn's book signing. A million and two if Caleb was wondering about another coaching session. "But I emailed a list of the questions that readers might ask you during the meet and greet. You can take your time and look them over."

Caleb's brow shot up. "You *emailed* them? Our rooms are ten feet apart. All you had to do was knock on my door."

"I don't have access to a printer here." And email kept their relationship professional. It was saf—*easier* to remember that Caleb was only one of her many responsibilities when he wasn't saving her from broken glass and calling her Nancy Drew.

Removing a spiderweb from her hair.

For a moment, Lucy had forgotten that Caleb's concern about his monthly allowance had spurred the surprise visit, not concern for his mom. Forgotten Brynn had spent the last few Christmases alone because Caleb must have had something better to do.

"Okay." A glint appeared in Caleb's eyes, and Lucy wondered if she'd crossed some invisible line again. "After I haul up the rest of the boxes, I'll be sure to check my email."

"Great. I...I'll see you later, then." Lucy decided that leaving was better than rambling, so she went upstairs to her room and checked her own messages again.

A chatty email from Ainsley (no surprise there) that ended with an offer to come to Frost a few days before the book signing to *help out* wherever she was needed.

Lucy recognized a recon mission or, knowing Ainsley, an attempted takeover when she saw one. Ainsley might think the Mistletoe Stop tour wasn't getting the proverbial bang for Brynn's buck when it came to personal appearances, but that wasn't the goal this time.

And in spite of Ainsley's misgivings, Lucy had everything under control.

She moved on to the next message, an inquiry from a book

club in Florida asking about open dates in Brynn's speaking schedule for the upcoming year.

Lucy didn't even have to click on the file. After the Mistletoe Stop tour, Brynn's calendar was wide open.

Okay. So maybe not *totally* under control.

A sigh slipped out before Lucy could stop it and, with it, a prayer for guidance.

What should I do, Lord? About Brynn. Caleb. Grace McCrae. Ainsley.

Everyone needed something, and right now, Lucy needed a few extra hours in her day.

She slipped out of her room and padded down the hallway to the top of the stairs. She didn't know if Brynn was resting or so deep into her story that she didn't hear Lucy's quiet tap on the door. Lucy prayed it was the latter, but either way, she didn't want to disturb her.

When she returned to the gathering room, a hedge of boxes surrounded the coffee table, but there was no sign of Caleb.

The stab of disappointment Lucy felt was something she didn't want to examine too closely.

She located the box with the Christmas village first. A mountain of green and red tissue paper began to form at her side as she unwrapped tiny buildings and set them on the coffee table.

There were groups of carolers wearing Victorian-style clothing. Churches with bell towers and intricate stained glass windows. A trio of snowmen looking dapper in plaid vests and top hats.

Every box revealed a new treasure, and Lucy felt a swirl of anticipation every time she released one from its tissue-paper cocoon.

It seemed a shame the village only came out of storage once a year. A tiny Christmas Brigadoon.

Lucy unwrapped a rustic building with clapboard siding. A crust of silver glitter coated the shingles on its slanted roof.

There was a wreath in the window, but it was the words painted on a tiny chalkboard sign hanging on the door that caught her eye.

Grace's Famous Hot Chocolate.

Someone had personalized this addition to the village, but she doubted it was David McCrae. He didn't exactly strike her as the sentimental type.

Lucy traced the tip of her finger over a pair of pink hiking boots dusted with glitter that sat outside the door.

She had a feeling that small detail was significant, too.

The sign...the boots... They were more than a decoration. And they weren't only for visitors who might wander in and admire the display. The Famous Hot Chocolate shop reminded Grace that she was connected to this place.

Traditions weren't just memories. They were about connection. Shared history.

Unexpectedly, disturbingly, Lucy's thoughts shifted from Grace to Caleb.

When they were in the basement, he'd teased her about ugly sweaters and Christmas movies, but it was difficult to establish traditions when you never stayed in one place for more than a few weeks.

Did he like to travel? Or was he the restless type? Always looking for what he didn't have?

Whether or not Lucy approved of him, Caleb Beauchamp was a bit of a mystery...

"I have questions about your questions."

Chapter Twenty

Lucy jumped at the sound of Caleb's voice and almost dropped the vintage truck she'd just released from its tissue-paper wrapping.

"All right…"

Lucy waited, but Caleb was staring down at the village that had sprung up around her.

Overkill. That's probably what he was thinking.

What he said was "This one is broken." He reached down and picked up a carousel that all but disappeared in the palm of his hand.

Lucy leaned in for a better look and saw that he was right. A white horse with sprigs of holly braided through its mane had broken free from the splotch of glue holding it in place and was listing slightly to the left.

He was about to toss it back into the box, but Lucy grabbed his hand. "No. Don't. I can fix it."

Caleb didn't relinquish the carousel right away. Lucy hadn't realized her impulsive gesture would bring them practically nose to nose. Close enough to see the flecks of gold in his eyes that reminded her of sunlight dancing on the water.

And now she sounded like Paisley Winwood the first time she'd met Fletcher.

Whenever Brynn's characters were in close proximity, not only did they notice tiny details like that, the noticing tended to coincide with stomach flutters or tingles of awareness or jolts of electricity.

Never in any of the books Lucy had read had anyone experienced all three of those symptoms at the same time.

Lucy quickly released Caleb's hand and rocked back on her heels to put some distance between them. "Y-you said you have questions?"

Caleb looked confused for a moment, almost as if he'd forgotten why he'd sought her out. "Not the questions themselves. The *number.* I didn't realize it would be fifty."

Thirty-seven to be exact, but Lucy didn't correct him.

"The Mistletoe Stop tour is a little more casual than other book signings, but Brynn's readers have certain expectations as to how things are going to go. We try our best not to disappoint them."

"I don't want to disappoint anyone, either, so maybe you better tell me what I've gotten myself into here."

"After Brynn reads an excerpt from her book and mingles with her readers awhile, you'll be doing a short Q and A before the refreshments. The list I emailed are some of the most popular questions our heroes have been asked in the past."

Caleb grinned.

"What?"

"You just admitted I'm a hero."

"No, I di— Questions the *character* has been asked," Lucy amended. "And you have to answer them the way Trace would."

"I think I can handle that." Caleb picked up one of the unopened boxes and scooped out the nest of tissue paper before Lucy could stop him. "Hot dog cart?"

"It goes over there." She pointed to the small oval mirror

that doubled as a pond. "Caroling and ice-skating make people hungry."

"Okaaay."

Lucy caught the reflection of his smile in the glass and almost lost her train of thought again. He'd offered to bring the rest of the boxes upstairs, but she hadn't expected him to help with the decorating, too.

"Trace only appeared in the last five chapters of the book, so his character isn't as developed as Fletcher's," she said. "Readers didn't get an opportunity to know him very well, but they may still ask a lot of the same questions."

"I'm undeveloped." Caleb set a family of whitetail deer on the windowsill next to a snow-covered bungalow. "That means I can wing it, and no one will know the difference."

Lucy reached over and moved the doe two inches to the left, sheltering them under the boughs of a ceramic tree. "Yes…and no. We went over Trace's backstory, but readers usually care more about…" Heat crept into Lucy's cheeks. She ducked her head and grabbed another box before Caleb noticed.

At past events, Lucy had gone through dry runs with men who'd graced the covers of magazines without a blush or a stammer. Why did Caleb Beauchamp make her feel twitchy?

"More about?" Caleb prompted.

"His emotions. Why he acts the way he does. What makes him tick. What he thinks about life and love." She stumbled a little over the last word.

"Ah. The touchy-feely stuff."

"Right." Why hadn't she described it like that?

"Where should this go?" Caleb held out his hand. Cradled in his palm was a couple holding hands on a bench. "Are they waiting for the ski lift? Those ducks to cross the road? The line to go down at the hot dog stand?"

Lucy rolled her eyes. "You decide."

Although the bench would fit perfectly in the little gazebo.

"How about that gazebo?" Caleb asked.

Without waiting for an answer, he picked up the metal structure that was no larger than a demitasse cup and placed the couple inside.

Caleb's arm brushed against hers, and Lucy felt that flutter, tingle, jolt again.

She reached for her tablet instead of another box and pulled up her notes. It made for a flimsy shield, but it reminded Lucy that multitasking was a good thing—especially if it kept her mind on a fictional character instead of the man who was turning out to be just as complex—and appealing—as her fictional PI.

"How many questions am I supposed to take?"

"Five or six, depending on how we're running for time. Like I said, these are questions that readers have asked in the past." Lucy scanned the list again. "The ones you get might vary in topic a little, but if you have an idea how you'd respond based on this list, you can tweak the answers to fit. If you look like you're struggling, I'll step in."

"Struggling?" Caleb gave her a look. "This guy can handle himself. He's used to landing on his feet."

Challenge accepted.

Game on.

"Okay, Trace. What's your idea of the perfect date?"

"I don't date," Caleb said without missing a beat. "During the day I'm a private investigator, and in my spare time I find stolen items and return them to their rightful owners. It doesn't give me much time for a social life."

The matter-of-fact tone didn't match the wistful look in Caleb's eyes. The one that would cause hearts to melt like whipped cream on hot chocolate.

"But if you *did*…" Lucy dragged her gaze back to her notes again. "Rock climbing? Zip line? Mountain bikes?"

"None of the above," Caleb said. "My perfect date would be

outdoors but somewhere quiet. No interruptions. A sunset or stars."

Disturbingly enough, that would be Lucy's idea of a perfect date, too.

But in order to go on a date, a person had to *have* one, and since her busy schedule didn't allow much time for socializing, either, it appeared she and Caleb...*Trace*...had something in common.

"That sounds...nice." Lucy cleared her throat and chose another question from the list. "What are some of the qualities you would look for in that special someone? Assuming you had time to meet her, of course."

"Honesty."

Honesty.

Lucy didn't know why but the word scraped against her conscience.

Keeping Brynn's recent struggles with her health a secret was a promise she would have kept even without a confidentiality clause in her contract.

Maybe Caleb already knew about the doctor's appointments and specialists. But if he didn't, it wasn't Lucy's place to tell him...

"She'd have to have a sense of humor to put up with me, too." Caleb flashed a roguish smile that brought his dimple out of hiding.

She'd also have to be a risk-taker to trust her heart to a man with a smile that could make her forget her own name.

"How am I doing so far?"

"Fine," Lucy murmured.

He was actually doing great, but they were only on question three. She jumped to question fifteen. One of the tougher ones, but it was important that Caleb be prepared.

"What are three things you'd save in a fire? And you can't say people or pets. Those are a given."

For the first time, Caleb looked a little uncomfortable.

"Women really want to know this stuff?"

"Yes. It reveals your...*Trace's*...heart."

Caleb carried one of the boxes over to the windowsill and began to construct a path from pieces of faux cobblestone.

Lucy could tell he was stalling but knew it was better to take time and mull the question over now than stare blankly at an audience anxious to hear the answer.

Seconds ticked by, and just when Lucy had decided to help him out, he turned to face her again.

"The baseball glove that Dad gave to me on my seventh birthday. A photo album of my family vacations because everyone keeps a record of the moments they don't want to forget, even if they weren't perfect."

"Trace's parents went to prison when he was in his teens," Lucy reminded him. "They didn't go to baseball games or take vacations."

"But maybe there was a time when things were normal. When they felt like a family. Those are the memories he'd want to save."

The look in Caleb's eyes was the same one Lucy had seen after he'd found the Christmas village. Only now, she could give it a name.

Pain.

"Next question?"

Are you still in character?

That's what Lucy wanted to know but couldn't quite summon the courage to ask.

"Three things," she heard herself say. "You only gave me two."

"My backpack."

"Your...*backpack?*"

"Hey, I have to have something to put my baseball glove and photo album in when I run for the door." The roguish smile appeared again. "I'm a practical guy."

Trace, not Caleb.

Lucy shouldn't be finding it so difficult to separate the two. One man was a product of her imagination, the other...

A project, an inner voice prompted.

It shouldn't have been difficult to remember that, either.

"Readers loved Fletcher and Paisley's romance, but I think one of the reasons readers are so taken with Trace is because he's a bachelor. He doesn't have a love interest so—"

"Sure he does."

"No." Lucy drew out the word. "He doesn't."

"That event planner." Caleb tilted his head. "What's her name?"

The *event* planner?

Lucy mentally skimmed through the last few chapters of the book and...*oh*.

"Are you referring to the woman Paisley's mom hired to handle the wedding details?"

"That's the one."

"She doesn't have a *name*. The only thing she did was catch Trace sneaking into Paisley and Fletcher's wedding reception and threaten to call hotel security."

"They had a moment."

"They did not have a..." Lucy stopped.

"Take your time." Caleb looked smug. "I'll wait. But if you need some help, it starts with the words *Caleb was...*"

Right.

He was right.

Lucy couldn't believe it.

Just like Trace had sauntered into chapter twenty without so much as a by-your-leave, the nameless event planner had emerged from the glittering backdrop of Paisley and Fletcher's reception after an unfortunate collision between a bridesmaid and a server restocking canapés on the buffet table. One of the centerpieces had taken the brunt of the impact and tipped over, creating a river of water and roses and glass beads that flowed over the side of the table and onto the floor. The poor woman had gone to the conservatory to search for replacement flowers and stumbled upon Trace in the process.

And Trace...Mr. Focused on the Mission...had *flirted* with her.

The man had no qualms about using whatever tools were at his disposal if it brought him closer to achieving his goal, but the nameless event planner hadn't fallen for his charm.

When Trace—it was all coming back to Lucy now—had offered her a rose, she'd smiled—right before she'd called security to have him removed from the building.

How had she missed it?

And more importantly, why hadn't Caleb?

"I'm guessing Brynn knows her name," Caleb said. "She probably appears in chapter one of the book she's working on now."

Caleb had neatly turned the tables, and now she was on the receiving end of the questions.

Lucy forced herself to meet his eyes.

Big mistake.

Caleb was no longer pretending to be Trace, but he shared some of the same traits.

He was intelligent. Intuitive.

Suspicious.

Because Caleb made traipsing around the globe a career, he had a stake in Brynn's success. Her books funded his very comfortable lifestyle so it stood to reason that he would be interested in the next one.

Something Lucy wouldn't have forgotten if she'd been focused on *her* mission.

"I'm afraid I can't answer that question," she said. "Brynn doesn't discuss her work in progress with anyone."

"But you brainstormed together on this one. That's why you know so much about Trace."

Since it sounded more like a statement than a question, Lucy didn't feel obliged to give an answer.

"I should check in with Brynn. I can finish this later, but if there are any specific questions you need help with, let me know." She glanced at her to-do list. "I'll be sending you an attachment with the waiver we've required our heroes to sign in the past."

Caleb didn't tease her about the word this time.

"You want me to sign a *waiver*?"

"It's standard protocol," Lucy said. "You're giving us permission to share your image or video clips from the meet and greet across Brynn's social-media platforms."

Caleb stared at Lucy as if it hadn't occurred to him that agreeing to become Trace Hunter would involve more than a few hours of his time.

And then, to Lucy's absolute astonishment, he shook his head.

"No."

Chapter Twenty-One

David needed some space.

And since his home had been overtaken by guests and his private living room invaded by a green-eyed woman who was taking up way too much space in his thoughts, David found a temporary refuge in the cab of his pickup truck.

He plucked the thermos from the console between the seats, unscrewed the top and chugged the last of the lukewarm coffee he'd poured from the carafe in the gathering room.

The storm had shifted course during the night, setting its sights on Lake Superior and the Upper Peninsula instead. But David still had roads to clear from the last snowfall. The perfect excuse to disappear for a while. Patch usually came along for the ride, but the dog had opted to hang out by the fireplace. Or should he say hang out with Brynn?

The fact that David had been tempted to do the same unsettled him more than he wanted to admit.

He set the plow down and cleared the service road that made a loop around the back of the property.

The horses emerged from the barn and lumbered toward the fence, unaware that at this very moment there were forces working behind the scenes in an attempt to pull them out of retirement.

David could relate.

Opening the tree farm again should be the new owner's decision, not his. But Grace didn't know that, and she was the reason David still wasn't quite ready to say yes to opening the tree farm to guests.

Esther had talked about community and the importance of gathering together, but David knew there was more at stake. The businesses in Frost were struggling. What they needed was a transfusion. New blood.

Was it wrong that he didn't want his eighteen-year-old daughter to spill hers trying to keep her mom's dream alive?

Grace didn't realize all the challenges that came with running an inn. How it would keep her tethered to one place. Take over her weekends and holidays. She wouldn't be free to travel. Experience new things. She would hear guests talk about their adventures, but there would be limited opportunities to embark on any of her own.

Grace had been two weeks into her first semester when David's dad had called, telling him they'd decided to sell the condo in Sarasota. His mom had been having mobility issues, and unbeknownst to David, his aunt and uncle had been encouraging them to relocate to Arizona. They'd found an apartment in an assisted-living facility in their neighborhood that provided transportation, meals and a full-time nursing staff for its residents and had already contacted a moving company.

Before David had a chance to process that information, his mom had chimed in, wanting to know if David would be interested in buying their condo before they listed it with a Realtor.

David had stopped asking God for anything after Lynette

died, but if he'd been questioning the future of the inn, the call from his parents might have qualified as answered prayer.

One of David's greatest hurdles when it came to selling Spruce Hill Farm was not quite knowing what to do next. Until they'd moved to Frost, home had been wherever David was stationed at the time.

But Grace loved warm weather and sunshine. Lynette had been the daughter that Stephen and Alison McCrae had never had, and their door was always open to family. David's wife and daughter had spent several weeks with them in Florida every year, soaking up the sunshine and searching for shells on the beach, while David had spent the majority of his time in a smaller body of water that averaged a bone-chilling fifty-five degrees.

David had asked for a day or two to think it over, but he already knew what his answer would be. He'd convinced himself that Grace would be thrilled, too. They'd be living farther apart for a few years until she finished college, but Grace could spend summers and holiday breaks with him.

David wasn't cut out to be an innkeeper, but it turned out he was pretty good at the whole handyman thing. With all the people flipping houses these days, it shouldn't be hard for him to pick up a few odd jobs here and there to keep himself busy.

Moving to Florida would be a fresh start for both of them.

Grace knew her grandparents were moving to Arizona, but David had deliberately left out certain key details, like who was going to buy their condo, for instance, because he'd thought it would be fun to surprise her. When Grace came home for Christmas break, he would present her with an early gift—a plane ticket to Sarasota—and whisk her away to sunshine and sandy beaches. Grace loved watching the sunset from the balcony, and David would casually tell her that after he signed the final paperwork, she would be enjoying this view from now on...

And the Clueless Dad of the Year award goes to David McCrae.

His mission hadn't changed, but the expression on Brynn's face when he'd admitted he was going to sell Spruce Hill Farm told David he might want to come up with another way to break the news to Grace.

Like an honest, face-to-face conversation about Grace's future after everyone packed up and left.

David glanced in the rearview mirror before he backed up again and a flash of color in the plantation caught his eye.

Grace's scarf.

David still wasn't convinced there had been a so-called misunderstanding about Grace's responsibilities, but if Lucy Gable was willing to take over the decorating, that was fine with him. The next time Grace called, David could honestly say there was no need for her to rush home...and that, yes, he'd cut down her Charlie Brown Christmas tree.

The road between the rows of trees had drifted shut, forcing David to take an alternate route to get to it. The tires dug into the snow, almost as if they were forcing David to slow down as he drove past the weathered outbuilding that Lynette's great-grandfather had built by hand.

Seemingly of its own accord, his foot pumped the brake.

It had been a long time since David had ventured into the warming house where people had huddled together to pay for their trees and sip hot chocolate, but it occurred to David that a serious buyer would want to explore every inch of the property. For all he knew, critters could have made themselves at home inside the walls.

David turned off the ignition and hopped down from the cab. Fished the keys out of his pocket, searching for the one that opened the padlock before remembering he'd tucked it underneath the mat. Out of sight, out of mind, and thanks to the last storm, currently out of reach. He grabbed a shovel from the bed of the truck and tucked the blade underneath the pile of snow, working his way forward until he reached the entrance. He peeled back the mat and chipped away the crust of ice until he located the key.

The hinges on the door squeaked in protest when he pushed it open and stepped inside.

Stepped back in time.

At Lynette's funeral, well-intentioned people had encouraged David to take comfort in the memories. What they'd neglected to mention was that not all of them were the warm, fuzzy kind. Some of them were cold and hard and landed like a punch to the gut.

And some…like the half circle of oak benches arranged around the ancient wood-burning stove…weren't stored in his memories at all.

David had no idea where the benches had come from or how they'd gotten here.

Boards creaked underneath his boots as he crossed the room.

He peeled off one glove, traced his index finger over the rings and whorls in the gleaming wood.

Was his memory really that faulty? Or had the grief begun to affect his mind?

David's hand dropped to his side, and he walked over to the old workbench that been recommissioned as a counter near the entrance. There was a cash register, a relic from another era that spit out receipts on a strip of yellowed paper, and a stubby pencil tethered to a dog-eared ledger. It was the way Lynette's grandparents had kept track of sales, and why change what was working?

He flipped open the cover and saw a piece of paper tucked into the margin. Lynette's graceful handwriting was as familiar as his reflection in the mirror. The letters blurred at the edges and then sharpened when David blinked again.

Underneath the words *Phase Three* was a rough sketch of the warming house David had never seen before but knew without a doubt had come straight from Lynette's imagination.

David had teasingly referred to each stage of the inn's renovation as Lynette's Grand Plan, but they hadn't reached the halfway mark of Phase Two when she'd died.

He studied the sketch more closely. David knew she'd wanted to split the interior of the building down the middle. One side would be a gift shop where people could pay for their trees and browse through items made by local artists. The rest of the space would feature a gourmet hot-chocolate bar with cushioned benches arranged in a half circle around a wood-burning stove, coaxing people to linger awhile, chat while thawing out fingers and toes.

It was no surprise Lynette had started with the benches.

She'd always seen Spruce Hill Farm as something to share, when all David had wanted to do was share his life with her.

He threaded the padlock through the rusted metal clasp on the door and vaulted into the cab of the truck. By the time he'd dragged Grace's tree out of the plantation, shadows filled the pockets between the trees, reminding David that he was past due bringing his guests their tray of cheese and crackers.

He parked near the side entrance and let himself into the house through the door off the back porch. Told himself it was to avoid tracking snow through the lobby while acknowledging the possibility he was trying to avoid detection, too.

David definitely wasn't cut out to be a host.

He stripped off his coat and boots on the porch before entering the kitchen. Whatever was simmering in the stockpot on the stove was seasoning the air with an aroma that made David's stomach sit up and beg.

Brynn's uberefficient assistant, Lucy, had asked for kitchen privileges, and it appeared that she'd actually found something in David's refrigerator to cobble together for dinner.

He lifted the lid and peeked inside.

Chili, studded with chunks of onion and black beans.

Patch appeared out of nowhere and bumped against David's leg.

"Sorry, bud." He replaced the lid again. "This isn't for us."

Patch whined as if he'd understood and deserted him again, ambling toward the doors that had guarded David's privacy once upon a time.

Once upon a time.

Which reminded David there was probably a woman on the other side of those doors who made a very comfortable living creating, packaging and peddling stories that didn't reflect real life.

There are still things to celebrate… Gifts in the everyday moments. The best stories remind us of that.

Unbidden, Esther's words cycled through David's mind, and he shook them away.

Once upon a time, when he woke up every morning next to the love of his life, his family and faith intact, David had believed it was true.

Now, counting his blessings meant counting the days until the inn sold and he could escape the memories.

Once and for all.

He pulled in a slow breath and released it again, mentally preparing himself for round three with Brynn Dixon…and realized he was smiling again.

How was it possible the woman could stir up equal measures of amusement and frustration?

She was used to getting her way, that much was evident in the way she curled up on his sofa, with his dog, in front of his fire.

Used to giving orders, too.

What had she said that morning?

Cut wood for a bonfire. Get the horses in shape to pull the sleigh.

Because she'd overheard him tell Esther that the horses were lawn ornaments.

If he didn't know better, he'd think Brynn Dixon was an honorary member of the Friends of Frost committee, too.

David knew he was partly to blame for her interference. He still couldn't believe he'd confided in Brynn about the sale of the inn when he'd done everything in his power to keep it a secret.

The Realtor he'd chosen to work with lived in another county. David hadn't wanted anyone in Frost to get wind of his plans until he'd signed the paperwork, but it had backfired on him. Martin, Esther's husband, had noticed he'd been trimming in the plantation and assumed it was a sign that the Christmas-tree farm would be open for business this season.

And then there was Grace, who'd not only entered some contest and thrown open their door to a best-selling author and who knew how many enthusiastic fans, but thought, mistakenly, the book tour took priority over her exams.

He was outnumbered. No way around it.

David stepped into his living room, ready to deliver the polite reminder that this side of the house was off-limits to guests, but the words died in his throat.

There was a pile of smoldering ashes instead of the fire he'd stoked before he'd left the house.

And an empty sofa.

Patch was stretched out on the rug in front of the hearth, soaking up the last bit of heat, a reproachful this-is-your-fault look on his face.

David ignored him and veered toward the woodpile in the corner. There might be some embers hidden among the ashes so that he wouldn't have to start from scratch.

He grabbed a few pieces of kindling and was about to move the grate aside when a book on the hearth caught his eye.

It hadn't been there when David had left, so he picked it up for a better look. The cover was butter-soft leather, no words or markings on it at all.

David would have expected some flowers or curlicues, maybe even glitter or a few sequins, if the book belonged to Brynn, but it was possible that Lucy or Caleb had left it behind while he was gone.

He flipped open the cover so he could return it to its proper owner and realized it was a journal.

Half the pages had been torn away from the binding, leaving rows of jagged white teeth in their place. On the first one that had been left intact, the owner had drawn a gigantic question mark. David quickly thumbed through the rest, looking for a clue as to who it might belong to, but every single one that followed was blank.

He buried a sigh and looked at Patch.

"This wouldn't happen to be yours, would it?"

The dog's ears twitched, but he didn't bother to open his eyes.

David's second and more likely guess was Lucy Gable. Every time she'd entered a room, she had a smile on her face and a tablet tucked under her arm, but it was possible that working for Brynn Dixon required an outlet for her emotions.

Which meant David couldn't rule out Caleb, either.

But leaving the journal on the hearth would only encourage someone to break the rules again, so David decided to track down its rightful owner.

He pushed open the doors and caught Lucy at the stove.

She'd knotted a dish towel around her waist, the wooden spoon in her hand slashing the air like a conductor's baton, dispersing the cloud of steam rising from the pot.

In that moment, she reminded David so much of Grace that he smiled, momentarily forgetting about the journal in his hand.

"Oh. Mr. McCrae." Her cheeks flushed pink, and the guilty expression on her face reminded David of his daughter, too. "I'm sorry. I didn't realize you were here." The pink deepened to rose. "It *is* your kitchen, of course, but I thought you were still outside."

Which explained why Lucy thought the coast was clear.

Had he really turned into such a grouch that a confident, articulate young woman like Lucy Gable got flustered in his presence?

"Whatever you're making smells delicious." David wasn't going to confess that he'd already looked in the pot. "Are you expecting company for dinner tonight?"

Lucy winced.

"It's chili." She gave the contents of the kettle a quick stir. "And no. I did a lot of the cooking for my siblings when I was growing up, so I automatically double...or triple...the recipe. You're more than welcome to join us for supper."

Lucy was a guest in his home. Inviting him for a meal.

If Lynette were here, she would have slapped David upside the head with the wooden spoon.

"Thank you," David heard himself say. "I think I'll take you up on that."

Lucy beamed. "I told Caleb five o'clock. I'm going to whip up a batch of corn bread to go with it, if that's all right with you."

David nodded. "I'll set up another table in the dining room."

Lucy's expression changed. "Brynn won't be joining us," she said briskly, changing into the efficient personal assistant in the blink of an eye. "She's...working and requested a tray."

David might have believed Lucy if she hadn't averted her gaze.

"Where did you find that?" She'd spotted the book in David's hand.

"It's yours?" He handed it back to her. "It was by the fireplace in the living room."

Lucy hugged the book almost protectively against her chest. "It belongs to Brynn."

"Brynn?" he echoed, the sequins and curlicue theory falling apart when she nodded.

"She'd be the first to tell you that she's old-school when it comes to writing. She starts a new journal every time she starts another book. Fresh page, fresh inspiration."

David guessed the last part was a direct quote from Brynn.

So why the torn pages? The question mark?

If he asked, Lucy would know he'd glanced through it.

And something told David that Brynn's personal assistant had no idea the pages were blank.

Chapter Twenty-Two

Lucy had changed into her favorite pair of joggers and a long-sleeved T-shirt and draped the wool throw from the sofa over her shoulders as an extra layer of insulation against the chill that had permeated the walls and settled over the library. She was about to start unraveling another set of white lights when her cell phone buzzed.

Ben again.

Honestly, her little brother, the guy who could have coined the phrase *It is what it is*, had suddenly become obsessed with all things wedding-related since their conversation earlier that morning.

Over the course of the day, Lucy had gotten two emails, a voice mail and half a dozen text messages. If Ben sent any more menu ideas, photographs of bouquets or helpful suggestions about the timeline of events on Christmas Eve, she'd have to start a spreadsheet and name the folder *Groomzilla-in-training*.

Her lips twitched as she reached for the phone.

It really was kind of adorable, though.

My essay was good? I have to submit it by midnight.

Lucy groaned.

She'd totally forgotten about proofreading Rachel's exam. She glanced at the clock on the wall and sent back a quick message.

Sorry. Long day. I'll get back to you in half an hour.

A smiling emoji popped up in response.

Lucy set aside the tangle of lights for the moment and grabbed her tablet so she could pull up Rachel's last email.

Q and A for Meet and Greet popped up on the screen.

Caleb had joined her and David McCrae for dinner, but the Christmas-tree farm had been the main topic of conversation. Caleb had asked a lot of questions about the kind of work that was involved, and David recited a list of tasks that rivaled Lucy's in terms of number and execution.

She'd had no idea there was more to the process than handing an axe to a responsible person over the age of eighteen and turning them loose into the rows of trees. Just when she was beginning to wonder how one man could possibly run what sounded to her like a complicated operation, Caleb had volunteered to be point person in the warming house if David decided to open the tree farm to guests. He could hand out tags and axes when visitors arrived and oversee the cash register after they found the perfect tree.

If only he'd been that agreeable about the waiver.

Was he offended because Lucy had asked him to do something that put him at the same level as a temporary employee, or did the thought of the Q and A being recorded make him uncomfortable?

Lucy had no idea.

Caleb hadn't provided an explanation. Just a simple, decisive *No* before he'd walked out the door. End of discussion.

Refusing to sign the waiver had put Lucy in a difficult situation, though. Talking to Brynn about it seemed like tattling, but in certain situations, like this one, following protocol was important, too.

She closed her eyes and firmly pushed thoughts of Caleb and waivers to the back of her mind.

Focus, Luce. One project at a time.

And right now, it was Rachel's exam. Even though she had to reread the opening paragraph of the essay to remember what the topic was about...

"I know your secret."

Lucy's head jerked up at the sound of Caleb's voice.

Caleb had gone to bed at ten o'clock and then tossed and turned for almost two hours before he finally gave up and went downstairs. His mission was to raid the kitchen for leftover corn bread—until he noticed a sliver of light shining underneath the door of the library. And since David McCrae kept to his side of the house and Brynn hadn't ventured from her room all evening, Caleb had a hunch he knew who was on the other side.

Lucy hadn't contributed much to the conversation at the dinner table, and when he'd asked her to pass the butter, she'd managed the transfer without making eye contact.

It wasn't hard to figure out why.

But Caleb hadn't expected their mock Q and A to end in an ambush. When Lucy had casually mentioned the waiver, all the possible ramifications of signing on the dotted line had made him, well, panic a little, so his response had come out a little more abrupt than Caleb had intended.

He'd seen the flash of surprise—followed by hurt—in Lucy's dark eyes.

It was the hurt that had lodged in Caleb's memory the rest of the day.

The temptation to sneak back up to his room was strong, but his conscience ended up winning the round. He might not be able to explain his decision, but he could do some damage control.

Lucy was so engrossed in whatever she was reading on her tablet, she hadn't heard the door open.

Caleb's eyes swept around the interior of the room, another space she'd turned into a Christmas wonderland. Two nutcracker soldiers flanked the wall of bookshelves. The crèche and hand-carved wooden Nativity pieces Caleb had found during another quick search of the basement took over the surface of the coffee table. Lights winked inside a trio of bronze lanterns on a shelf and sprigs of holly and bright red berries had been tucked inside a vase.

But it was Lucy he couldn't tear his gaze from.

She sat cross-legged in the middle of the floor, eyes glued to the ever-present tablet in her hands. He'd gotten used to seeing her wearing black from head to toe, but tonight's ensemble— T-shirt, sweatpants and a plaid blanket with tassels draped around her shoulders like a cape—was an eclectic clash of style and color and comfort that made him smile.

A tuft of hair stuck up from the sleek fringe of bangs over her forehead, and while Caleb watched her, Lucy knuckled her eyes like a kid refusing to admit she was tired.

Caleb had been going for a casual, Trace Hunter–style entrance. Instead, he'd blurted out the first words that popped into his head, startling Lucy in the process.

Now those black velvet eyes were focused on him.

"Secret?" Lucy echoed.

"You have Santa's elves on speed dial."

Her shoulders visibly relaxed. "It's a small space," she said. "And the McCraes have a lot of decorations."

"Well, I think you used them all." Caleb crossed the room and sank down on his haunches to study the Nativity set. Each piece had been meticulously carved, from the bristly mane on the donkey to the expression of awe on the faces of the shepherds.

His mom had owned one, too, although hers was made of glass. Few items were considered off-limits in the Beauchamp household, and the Nativity wasn't one of them. It had a special place of honor on the coffee table, fully accessible to little hands. Caleb never got scolded if a toy action figure turned up next to the angels or a plastic car joined the caravan of wise men and camels on their way to Bethlehem.

The manger would remain empty until Caleb woke up Christmas morning. He'd take a detour on his way to the tree and look for Baby Jesus, who'd mysteriously appeared in the manger between Mary and Joseph during the night. Caleb's parents would wander into the living room, blurry-eyed but smiling, as he towed them over to the crèche. Then, he'd plunk down between them on the couch, and his dad would read from the Gospel of Luke before Caleb opened his presents.

Caleb wondered what had happened to the Nativity set. Had Shae gotten rid of everything in the house the way she'd gotten rid of him?

A few months into his first semester of college, Caleb had spent the weekend at home. He'd gone downstairs to the kitchen to get something to eat and overheard Shae and his dad talking in low tones. Or rather, Shae had been doing the talking.

I understand you feel responsible for Caleb, but he's an adult now, Glenn. And he's not your son. Not by blood, anyway. You can try to change his behavior, but there's no changing his DNA.

Whether by accident or design, Shae had voiced Caleb's greatest fear. That he didn't belong. Wasn't really part of the family.

He wanted to believe it wasn't true, but his dad had remained silent instead of sticking up for him. And when Caleb's grades continued to fall, he'd waited for his dad to deliver a loving lecture and straighten him out, the same way he did whenever Caleb got out of line. Instead, Caleb had had to prove his worth before he could come home again.

The reason he had no idea what Christmas at the Beauchamp house looked like now.

Because why put in the effort when Caleb knew he'd only mess up again?

Lucy's groan broke the silence that had fallen over the room.

"Great. The battery is almost dead." She began to sift through the mounds of lights that formed a circle around her. "I unplugged my charger when I was testing to see if these worked."

Caleb spotted the tail of a silver cord underneath one of the piles and gave it a tug. "Here you go."

"Thanks." Lucy scooted across the rug to the closest outlet and plugged it in. "I have to finish this by midnight."

His gaze strayed to her bare feet. "It looks like you already lost your slippers, Cinderella."

Color swept into Lucy's cheeks. "I promised my sister I would proofread an essay she wrote for her final exam."

A sister.

Since they'd met, Caleb had only thought of Lucy in terms of her connection to Brynn, but suddenly he wanted to know more.

"What's her major?"

"Rachel is premed but this is for one of her electives, thankfully." Lucy shuddered. "No cell biology or organic chemistry."

"Tough classes, I'll bet." Caleb tried to remember what Lucy had said when he'd asked about her degree.

He couldn't—because she'd changed the subject.

"She ranks third in her class." A mixture of affection and pride kindled in Lucy's eyes. "But it's more than grades. Rachel is compassionate. Wise. Understanding... And I might be a wee bit prejudiced, is that what you're thinking?"

"I was thinking I hope your sister knows how blessed she is to have someone like you in her corner."

Instead of smiling at the compliment, a tiny crease appeared between Lucy's brows.

Because he'd sounded envious?

"Rach has a lot of people in her corner. I happen to be the only one who has time to read an essay, though."

It didn't look like she had time. Not when she had to fit it in long after everyone else went to bed.

"How many siblings do you have?"

"Five."

"*Five?*" Caleb echoed. "And where are you in the birth order?"

"The oldest. There's Kristin, Rachel, Sean and Boo are the twins, and Janie."

That was a lot of names but Caleb latched on to one of them. "Boo?"

The guy who'd made Lucy's face light up when she'd answered the phone and triggered an irrational wave of envy.

Lucy winced. "I should have said *Ben*. At six foot four, he's kind of outgrown the nickname, but I've been calling him that since he was born, and it's a hard habit to break.

"He's proposing to his girlfriend on Christmas Eve, so I should get used to the idea he's all grown up. What about you?"

Caleb was still trying to figure out why he was relieved to discover Lucy had a brother named Boo, so it took a moment to understand what she was asking.

"Only child." He steered the conversation back to her family again. "When did your sister know she wanted to be a doctor?"

His attempt to deflect and distract must have failed because instead of disappearing, Lucy's frown deepened.

"She was ten. I had to hide the box of bandages because Rachel would use them all on her stuffed animals and dolls. Every time I'd go into her room to tuck her in at night, she'd have a triage unit set up on the floor. I'd have to wait while she took everyone's temperature with her toy thermometer before she got into bed."

"*You* tucked her in? Did your parents work second shift or something?"

"Mom was…" Lucy's gaze dropped to the tablet again and

her fingers danced over the keyboard. "Busy with my little sister, Janie."

"The baby of the family?" he guessed.

"Yes." She hesitated, almost as if she were going to say something else, before she expelled a quiet breath. Tapped another key. "Sent."

"With five minutes to spare before your coach turns back into a pumpkin."

"I can't be Nancy Drew *and* Cinderella, you know." Lucy's lips curved in a smile. "That would be mixing genres."

"Like Brynn did?"

"She didn't... A missing necklace in the last five chapters of the book doesn't make it a mystery."

"Would it be so bad if it did?"

The flash of panic in Lucy's eyes told Caleb the answer to that question was *yes*.

The real mystery was why it mattered, though. Lucy would have a job no matter what kind of books Brynn wrote.

"It wouldn't be the first time a writer went in a different direction, right?" Caleb pressed. "Even I could tell Brynn enjoyed writing those scenes with Trace Hunter."

In the blink of an eye, Lucy changed from glowing big sister to efficient personal assistant and troubleshooter again. "Caleb... about the waiver."

Inwardly, he chided himself for letting his guard down. While he'd spent the day battling guilt over his abrupt refusal to sign a piece of paper, Lucy must have been plotting a strategy, waiting for the right opportunity to convince him to change his mind.

He regarded her warily, wishing he'd chosen the corn bread over his conscience now.

"I think I figured out a way around it."

A way...what?

Not what he'd expected her to say. "What do you mean?"

"After Brynn's meet and greet, I can collect everyone's cell phones before your Q and A. Tell them that we have something special—something only for the readers who came to this particular event. There've been some rumors Trace will make an appearance, but no one is really expecting to see him. A little mystery isn't a bad thing."

"It's a good idea." A really good idea. "Do you think it'll work?"

"I have no idea," Lucy admitted. "Asking people to give up their cell phones these days is like asking for their firstborn child, but I'm hoping they would happily give up a selfie with you for bragging rights on the message boards.

"It would be a way to protect Brynn from any awkward situations if your image ends up in a meme that doesn't, um, line up with Brynn's values or those of her readers. And it protects your privacy, too."

If possible, Caleb felt like more of a jerk.

It hadn't occurred to Caleb that his refusal might affect Brynn. Caleb assumed Lucy was just being a stickler when it came to standard protocol, when the truth was she'd been looking at the bigger picture.

Looking out for him, too, it seemed.

Caleb wasn't sure what to do with that.

Except maybe tell her the truth.

"What did Brynn tell you about me?"

Her eyes widened.

"Only that you're her son, but she chose adoption." Lucy reached for the pendant around her neck, and it helped a little, knowing she was as uncertain as Caleb about venturing into this new terrain. "But I know Brynn, and she must have a good reason for keeping it a secret all these years."

"The reason Brynn chose adoption was the same reason she didn't tell anyone. Her parents had a lot of influence over her at the time. The reason she's *still* keeping it a secret is because of me."

Chapter Twenty-Three

Caleb regretted opening the door to his past the moment the words slipped out. He thought about cracking a joke, pretending it was no big deal or changing the subject.

But instead of peppering him with questions, Lucy remained silent. Which, strangely enough, gave him the courage to go on.

"I always knew I was adopted," Caleb said slowly, not knowing quite where to begin. "My parents always wanted a large family but found out they couldn't have children of their own. They worked with an adoption agency, filled out all the paperwork, but the social worker warned them that they might have to wait months, years even. And then they got a call one morning. A young woman had given birth to a baby boy. Were they ready to be parents?

"It was a closed adoption. A lot of people want details about the birth parents and vice versa, but Brynn didn't even choose them from a list of candidates. She signed the papers and left me in the hospital." Caleb understood why, but it didn't completely reduce the sting.

"They never met Brynn?"

Caleb shook his head. "Mom told me once it didn't matter that she hadn't carried me for nine months. I belonged to her the moment the nurse put me into her arms. She called me her *miracle baby*, and that felt a lot better than being someone's mistake."

"I like your mom," Lucy whispered.

Caleb's throat closed.

She would have liked Lucy, too. And Brynn, if they'd ever had the chance to meet.

"She was pretty great," he managed.

Lucy was a details person, and Caleb could tell the moment it registered that he'd spoken in past tense.

"Caleb." She breathed his name. "I'm so sorry."

"It was cancer." A word that didn't begin to describe what his mom had gone through during the last few months of her life.

The pancreas was one of those organs no one thought much about until there was a problem. The oncologist had been honest with the family from the beginning. The treatments would make her more comfortable, but there wasn't a cure.

But while Caleb's faith had slowly unraveled, Marianne Beauchamp's had only grown stronger. He'd wanted her healthy and well and *here*. With them. He hadn't leaned on God. Turned to Him for strength, the way his mom did. Caleb had blamed Him for taking her away.

"How old were you?"

"Fifteen." His lips twisted. "Because it's not like you're dealing with anything else at that age, right?"

Lucy saw right through his awkward attempt to lighten the moment. Her hand settled on his arm. A light, warm touch that burned through Caleb's sleeve and chased away the chill of the memories.

"My dad remarried less than a year after Mom died, and every fairy tale about wicked stepmothers… Well, let's just say Shae didn't go against type."

"It must have felt like you lost both your parents," Lucy murmured.

"I could have handled things better." Caleb was old enough to recognize that now. "I was angry and grieving, and I didn't know how Dad could just...move on, I guess. Especially with a woman who wasn't anything like Mom. Every time Shae and I butted heads, she'd run to him. Make comments about my *background*, as she put it. Telling him that in my case, the apple must not have fallen far from the tree. Stuff like that."

"That's terrible." Lucy couldn't hide her shock. "Was she *trying* to create a wedge between the two of you?"

"I think so." If it was so obvious to Lucy, why hadn't his dad seen it, too? "Eventually, Shae made my dad pick a side. He picked her, and things went downhill from there. I applied to about a dozen colleges my senior year so I wouldn't have to stick around any longer than necessary."

But that hadn't gone very well, either.

Caleb spent the majority of his first year partying instead of studying. He'd been put on discipline his sophomore year, and Shae, who begrudged every penny Caleb's dad spent on him, convinced him to withhold the money Glenn and Marianne had set aside for his education.

Caleb asked for a chance to improve his grades, but the man who'd laughed with him, cheered him on, and taught him how to throw a ball and ride a bike informed Caleb that he needed to change his ways before he was welcome in the house again.

The house Caleb had grown up in. The one that his mom had made a home.

The house his dad now shared with Shae.

"College and I got along about as well as me and my dad, though, so I ended up dropping out." Caleb didn't want to tell Lucy all the other ways he'd failed. The girls whose names he couldn't remember and the friends who drank too much. "I got a job at a factory. Dad and Shae didn't seem to care what I did as long as it didn't involve them."

The Christmas that Caleb had swallowed his pride and called his dad, he could hear Shae in the background, grumbling about something. His dad cut the conversation short. Told Caleb they'd booked a cruise for the holiday and he would call when they got back.

Three months later, Caleb had still been waiting for that call.

For the first time, he'd felt totally adrift. The things that had kept him grounded—things like faith and family and feeling like he belonged—permanently severed.

"Is that why you decided to look for your birth mom?" Lucy ventured. "Because things weren't going well with your dad?"

To fill a void in his life?

"No." It was a reasonable guess. But unfortunately, Caleb hadn't been feeling very reasonable at the time. "And it wasn't like I was trying to find her…it was more like a fact-finding mission."

He'd decided if there was some fatal flaw in his character that made him so unlovable he was going to trace it to its source. Confront the first person who'd rejected him.

"And then you found Brynn."

"And then I found Brynn." It hadn't been as difficult as Caleb had thought it would be. Brynn had honored the terms of the private adoption and hadn't tried to find him, but she'd given the agency permission to share her name if Caleb tried to find her.

Lucy smiled. "Major plot twist."

"Major." Caleb smiled back, and this one stayed in place. "I was all set to unload ten years of baggage on her when she opened the door and she…she hugged me. Told me that she'd been waiting…praying…for us to meet."

Tears sparkled in Lucy's eyes. "That's Brynn."

"That kind of response does make it hard to be angry with

someone," Caleb admitted wryly. "And when I found out why she gave me up for adoption…let's just say she had a lot of reasons to be angry, too."

"She wasn't married, was she?"

"No. Brynn was nineteen when she found out she was pregnant. She wouldn't tell me anything about my biological dad except that we were both better off without him. When she scraped up the courage to tell her parents, they gave her an ultimatum. Give me up for adoption or become a single mom and figure it out on her own."

"Brynn was an only child. I can't believe they would have cut her out of the family."

"It may have been a bluff, but who knows? It worked. The pressure she must have been under…" Caleb took a deep breath. "I don't think she cared about being cut off financially, but emotionally they'd backed her into a corner. I can't judge my mom for a decision she made when she was practically a kid herself."

Lucy's fingers laced together in her lap, and she averted her gaze. "N-no. You can't."

"She invited me in, and I ended up staying a few days. I even dropped by a bookstore during one of her signings. That's when I made her promise not to tell anyone about me. If it came out that Brynn had had a child out of wedlock, she's famous enough that some reporter might do some digging and find out that my biological father was married. A detail he'd conveniently left out when they met, by the way, but it was one of the reasons her parents didn't want anyone to know she was pregnant. Image was everything to them."

In a way, though, finding out that Brynn was a public figure had only made things more complicated. Caleb had never dreamed his biological mother would be a best-selling romance novelist with a fan club that circled the globe.

The world could be an unforgiving place. Something he'd learned from experience.

"You thought it would hurt her reputation?" Lucy frowned. "Brynn wouldn't care about that."

She hadn't. If Caleb had given Brynn permission, she would have announced to the whole world that she had a son.

"That's what I told her...but it wasn't the whole truth."

Understanding dawned in Lucy's eyes. "It was because of your stepmom, Shae, wasn't it?"

Once again, Lucy's insight astonished him.

"She's a user. Shae pretended to be compassionate and sweet because she wanted someone to take care of *her*. She knew how to insinuate herself into my dad's life, and he totally fell for it. I knew if she found out that Brynn Dixon was my birth mom, no matter how she felt about me she'd use it to her advantage somehow."

Brynn had respected Caleb's decision, but he knew she wasn't happy about it. He'd done it to protect her, though. The woman who'd given birth to him and the woman who'd raised him were a lot alike in that respect. They saw the best in everyone.

Caleb wasn't going to put Brynn in a position where she had to set boundaries, so he'd done it for her.

"That's why you didn't want to sign the waiver. If your picture or a video ended up on social media, Shae might see it and wonder why you're playing a character in one of Brynn Dixon's books."

"I might be a little paranoid, but it's the first thing that crossed my mind when you brought up the waiver. I guess I didn't realize Trace Hunter was such a big deal."

"That makes two of us," Lucy muttered.

"Anyway, I know I overreacted, but I didn't want to take the chance." He gave in to the temptation to tease her a little. "Although, some people don't see the family resemblance."

Lucy actually blushed. "Yes, well, in my defense I didn't see the dimple right away."

Seriously?

"I don't have a…" Caleb wasn't sure he could even say the word "…dimple."

"You do, too. Right—" Lucy tapped his cheek "—here."

Her touch was light, almost playful this time, but Caleb felt a flash of heat that made it all too tempting to think more about the future than the past.

Caleb hoped his legs weren't as shaky as his voice as he pushed to his feet. "We'll have to agree to disagree, I guess. I better turn in. I promised David that I would help him in the morning."

Lucy's voice stopped him at the door.

"Caleb?"

She waited until he turned around.

"What you said…about being a mistake? That isn't true, you know. Brynn knows life is precious. A gift.

"There was a newspaper article a long time ago…early in Brynn's career. A reporter asked where *her* one and only love was. She said he wasn't in her life but he was in her heart." Lucy paused, not breaking eye contact with him. "Given the situation, she couldn't have been talking about your biological father. I think…I think she was talking about you."

Chapter Twenty-Four

It was David's fault Brynn kept breaking the rules.

On Thursday morning, he'd turned on the gas fireplace and set an urn of fresh coffee on the sideboard. An attempt to lure her into the gathering room or a not-so-subtle reminder of the demarcation between shared spaces and his private quarters. Or possibly both.

But the gathering room wasn't nearly as appealing as a cup of French press and a toasty fire blazing in the living room.

Plus, David made it all too easy for trespassers when there was no one guarding the premises.

The low growl of an engine woke Brynn before dawn. She'd looked out the bedroom window just in time to see the faint red glow from the taillights of a pickup truck before it disappeared behind the barn.

Brynn had felt a stab of envy.

Like David, she'd always been a morning person. She would jump out of bed at six and get dressed. Take a cup of coffee out to the patio and then walk the two-mile loop through the neighborhood. When she returned, Lucy would be waiting for her in the atrium, and they'd eat breakfast together while going over the plan for the day.

Now her routine had changed.

Now Brynn stayed in bed and stared up at the ceiling, experimentally flexing joints and muscles. A test she performed every morning to see if there'd been an improvement. So far, her body had failed every single one. Not only that, the pain followed her into the day like a shadow, making it difficult to concentrate on the most mundane of tasks.

Brynn had spent the last twenty-four hours holed up in her room, eating dinner alone, because she was afraid the give-and-take of a simple conversation would require more energy than she could muster.

Lucy had knocked on Brynn's door later in the evening, a concerned look on her face and Brynn's notebook in her hand.

Her assistant hadn't said anything, but Brynn knew what she was thinking. Brynn plotted the old-school way, with pen and paper. She'd led Lucy and Caleb to believe she'd been working all day only to find what Brynn teasingly referred to as her *creative brain* abandoned on the hearth in David McCrae's living room.

The logs in the fireplace shifted and sent up a shower of sparks, a signal their host would be returning shortly to serve breakfast. When she'd cut through the kitchen, Brynn had paused to lift the lid on the slow cooker and gotten an instant facial from the steam that rolled out.

And David claimed he didn't run a day spa.

Steel-cut oats weren't particularly glamorous, but like the flannel sheets and down comforter on Brynn's bed, they paired well with the drifts of snow and the icicles that trimmed the windows.

Brynn reached for her notebook and the Montblanc pen that had been a gift from her publisher the first time she'd hit the bestseller list. Winced when fire shot through her fingers.

There was no visible swelling around her joints. When Brynn looked down at her hands, all she could see was the festive red polish on her nails.

Somehow, that made it more difficult. On the outside, she looked fine. Looked like herself. On the inside, it felt like she was battling for every ounce of energy.

An autoimmune disease. That's what the doctor had said they'd be testing for if Brynn was still experiencing symptoms after the book tour. She'd done some research online and been completely overwhelmed by the mile-long lists of causes, treatments and side effects.

God...

Brynn, who'd never been at a loss for words, spoken or written, wished her prayers lately didn't always start and stop right there.

She opened the cover of the notebook. Standing out against the crisp white page like the gigantic letter *E* at the top of an optometrist's chart was the question mark she'd drawn the day before they'd arrived in Frost.

Because that was all she had right now.

Questions.

God's timing might not be hers when it came to answers, but Brynn knew it was best to keep the lines of communication open. And that His presence in the waiting was something she could count on.

But the waiting itself...

So hard, Lord.

The muffled hum of an engine warned Brynn she should have relocated to the gathering room with her second cup of coffee by now, but the temptation to linger a few more minutes was something Brynn didn't want to dwell on.

If it wasn't for the promise David had made to his daughter to act as their host during the book tour, Brynn was sure he would have helped them find other accommodations without an ounce of regret.

The door between the porch and the kitchen opened. Patch's tail began to drum a cheerful beat on the sofa cushion.

"Easy for you," Brynn whispered. "You have permission to be here."

"Hellooo?"

"David?"

Not one but two female voices, and the only barrier separating Brynn from David's early-morning visitors was a set of half doors.

Brynn's gaze bounced around the room, but the only exit she could see was a window that would require a ladder to reach.

"He's not here," one of the women stated. "Do you think someone tipped him off that we were coming?"

"No, but Esther did warn us an ambush wouldn't work on an ex-military man."

The words snagged Brynn's attention, momentarily disrupting any thoughts of escape.

Ex-military?

Brynn had noticed a photograph of a coast guard cutter on the wall in the lobby but hadn't understood its significance until now.

It didn't tax Brynn's imagination to imagine David serving his country in that role. He was strong. Confident. Could convey a thought in a few short words. Brynn had always admired that particular quality, but she was a storyteller at heart. If words were roses, why not offer an entire bouquet?

"I thought we were being strategic," her partner in crime said. "David refuses to attend our meetings, so it made sense to have our next one right here, where he can't avoid us. Once he realizes our ideas will draw more people to Frost, he'll want to do his part."

"I don't know. All the other businesses had a booth at the

harvest festival in September, but David didn't offer so much as a flyer for Spruce Hill Farm."

"There might be a reason for that." A disapproving cluck followed the statement. "Take a peek at what's inside this slow cooker. *Oatmeal*. And the website advertises a locally sourced, farm-to-table breakfast."

"I'm sure he bought the oats at Eddie's Corner Market."

Brynn hadn't heard another person enter the kitchen, but she instantly recognized Esther's lilting voice.

"It isn't that David doesn't *want* to attend our meetings," she continued. "I think it's difficult for him now that Lynette is gone."

The quiet statement invoked a sympathetic murmur of agreement from her friends.

Until Lucy had shown her Grace's essay, Brynn hadn't known why David was alone. Hadn't known he was running the inn because he was a widower.

My mom died a few years ago, but she always talked about leaving a legacy of love. She loved Spruce Hill Farm, and she loved people, and it was her dream to bring them together. It's my dream, too.

Brynn, who couldn't recall leaving her notebook behind in the living room, was somehow able to remember the words Grace had written.

"David might not consider himself an official member of the Friends of Frost but he's still part of our community," Esther said. "We just have to keep reminding him of that."

Brynn's heart sank.

She didn't know these three women at all, but something told her they would be crushed if they knew David didn't feel the same way.

"You can remind him, Esther. I'm resorting to bribery. I have a dozen cranberry pecan muffins in this bag to sweeten his disposition. We'll set up camp in here until he gets back."

Before Brynn could react—or hide—the doors parted, and a woman trundled into the living room.

At least a decade older than Brynn and several inches shorter, she had elfin features and a cloud of snow-white hair that stuck out in every direction like dandelion fluff. Underneath an ankle-length down coat that rustled with every step, she'd dressed for the day in a navy turtleneck, jeans and boots with sensible heels.

Unlike Brynn, who hadn't changed out of her lounge pants and an oversize sweater with the words *Got Mistletoe?* spelled out in red sequins on the front. Clothing that had seemed like an acceptable substitute for pajamas when Brynn was getting ready for bed the night before.

She burrowed a little deeper into the cushions in an attempt to blend in with her surroundings, but it had the opposite effect. The woman noticed the movement and braked so hard the wool cap perched on top of her head dipped over one eye. She reached up and righted it again, the expression on her face almost comical.

Brynn, who'd twisted her hair into a topknot before she'd come downstairs, automatically patted down some of the stray curls that had popped free from the elastic band and stuck out like rusty bedsprings.

Her attempt to look more presentable also backfired spectacularly because the woman's eyes got even wider.

"I… Excuse me. I'm so sorry," she babbled. "I didn't know David had, um…company."

Company.

Brynn suppressed a groan.

An honest mistake, given the fact that if Brynn were a B and B guest, she wouldn't be barefoot and curled up on the sofa in David's private living quarters.

"Darlene? What's…" The thin brunette in a pink ski jacket

who appeared behind her jerked to a standstill as her gaze locked on Brynn. "Oh." She finally blinked. *"Oh."*

Brynn's sentiments exactly.

She pasted on a smile, knowing anything she said would come out in the Tennessee twang that had amused David the first time they'd met. Brynn still wasn't sure why. The man had an accent, too.

"Uh...we should go." The woman in the beret—Darlene?—whirled around, almost colliding with the last member of the trio, who'd entered the living room behind them.

Today Esther had traded her bib overalls for jeans, but the silver braid trailing over the shoulder of her canvas jacket gave her identity away. Unlike her companions, though, she didn't appear the least bit shocked.

"Ms. Dixon." Esther smiled at Brynn. "Good morning."

Now the women turned to gape at her.

"Esther," Darlene muttered. "It can't be. Brynn Dixon is much taller...and she wears white cowboy boots."

Brynn felt a bubble of laughter form in her chest when the woman in the pink coat stepped forward and peered down at Brynn's bare feet.

"But she wouldn't be wearing them with pajamas," she reasoned, not even attempting to whisper. "Would she?"

Brynn wanted to point out that she wasn't wearing pajamas. But not only would her cover be blown the moment she spoke, Brynn suspected that *not* speaking would only leave room for further speculation. Like who was the strange woman lounging on David McCrae's couch at eight o'clock in the morning, and why was she there?

"Would you?" Darlene asked, deciding to settle the matter by including Brynn in the conversation again.

Across the room, Esther's eyes met Brynn's, and it looked like she was struggling to suppress a laugh, too.

Lucy wouldn't be happy, but at the moment, Brynn was more

concerned with protecting David's privacy and his reputation in the community than keeping her arrival in Frost a secret.

She wasn't sure she wanted to, either. She'd wanted to get to know Esther, and here was her opportunity.

"It's nice to meet y'all."

A moment of absolute silence followed, and then the brunette rushed toward her. "It's so nice to meet you, Ms. Dixon! I'm Patricia Vanderlee—Posey to my friends and family—and I'm the secretary of the Friends of Frost committee. I have every single one of your books, but *Meet Me under the Mistletoe* is my absolute favorite."

Brynn's hand was taken in a firm grip and pumped like the handle of a dried-up well before Posey released her and waved at Esther. "And this is Esther Lowell, our president."

Laughter still sparkled in Esther's sapphire-blue eyes. "Welcome to Frost, Ms. Dixon."

"Please, call me Brynn."

"Esther is the one who founded our group," Posey continued. "She also owns the quilting shop, Sew Happy Together, in town."

Brynn grinned. "I love that name."

Darlene wedged in between them. "Darlene Walters. Publicity and head baker at Lovin' from the Oven," she added.

"She's the only baker," Posey murmured.

Without waiting for an invitation, Posey settled into a chair next to Brynn. "That David! I can't believe he didn't tell us you were here!"

"The last Mistletoe Stop was canceled. We had some extra time and decided to spend it at Spruce Hill Farm," Brynn explained, not mentioning the exact day they'd arrived. "David found out about our change in plans a few hours before we showed up at the door."

Darlene plopped down on the sofa next to Brynn. "And you'll be staying here until the book signing?"

"I believe that's the plan."

Darlene cast a meaningful glance at Posey and Esther before she leaned forward and planted both hands on her knees.

"Well, the Friends of Frost have some plans, too. And now that you're here, our Countdown to Christmas celebration will be even better."

Chapter Twenty-Five

It didn't surprise Lucy that Brynn had broken the house rules and returned to David McCrae's living room again. No, what surprised her was the sound of voices on the other side of the swinging doors, proof that someone else had found Brynn first.

She drew in a breath and swept through the doors, ready to rescue her employer, and saw not one, not two, but *three* women clustered around Brynn.

They didn't look like reporters, but who knew what Ainsley was up to? Brynn hadn't hired the publicist for this particular tour, but Ainsley considered herself a big-picture person, which gave her license to involve herself in anything that had an effect on Brynn's career. Lucy wouldn't put it past her to contact the local media and set up an interview of her own.

"Lucy." Brynn lifted her hand in a wave, and the light bounced off the sequins on the…festive…sweater Lucy vaguely remembered a book club gifting to Brynn on their first Mistletoe Stop. "Good morning."

"Good morning." Lucy's smile expanded to include the women who'd turned toward her. Smiles wreathed their faces.

Lucy looked for cell phones or cameras and, when she didn't see any, relaxed a little. "Ladies."

"You must be Brynn's assistant, Lucy." An attractive woman who reminded Lucy a little of *Frozen*'s Elsa with her bright blue eyes, porcelain skin and silver braid smiled at Lucy. "Grace mentioned your name in an email she sent the Friends of Frost about the contest. I'm Esther Lowell." She motioned to her friends. "Darlene and Patricia."

"Posey," the woman sitting next to Brynn corrected. She peeled off her cotton candy–pink coat and draped it over the arm of the sofa, an indication she planned to stay awhile. "We're part of a committee made up of local business owners. There aren't a lot of us, but what we lack in size we make up for in heart."

"And creativity," her friend added.

Grace might have mentioned Lucy's name, but this was the first time Lucy had heard about a committee.

And why did the word *creativity* send a shiver of unease down her spine?

"Lucy is the one who keeps my life running smoothly," Brynn said. "I'm blessed to have an assistant I count as a friend."

And as her assistant and friend, it was Lucy's job to rescue Brynn from the impromptu gathering in David McCrae's private quarters.

Where was their host, anyway?

"David drove off a little while ago," Brynn said, almost as if she'd read Lucy's mind. "I'm afraid I've made a sizable dent in the woodpile over there, so he might have gone out to cut more."

"Esther always claims things happen for a reason," Posey sang. "We wanted to surprise David, and look who ended up being surprised."

"Us," Darlene added cheerfully, just in case Lucy hadn't figured it out.

A quick look at Brynn told Lucy she was handling the situation with her usual grace, but the lavender shadows under her eyes told Lucy she hadn't slept well.

But then, neither had Lucy.

She'd spent the majority of the night replaying the conversation with Caleb and worrying about Brynn.

Battling guilt.

For the first time since she'd started working for Brynn, Lucy had broken one of her own rules when it came to boundaries.

She'd opened Brynn's notebook.

Instead of plot points and character sketches and arcs, all Lucy saw was blank pages and a question mark.

But even more disturbing was the confusion in Brynn's eyes when she'd spotted the notebook in Lucy's hand. Brynn kept it so close Lucy sometimes teased her that it was another appendage. But not only had Brynn not missed it, Lucy had the sinking feeling she didn't even remember where she'd left it.

If Brynn wasn't writing, what was she doing in her room all day? Was she getting the rest her doctor had prescribed? Or was it a sign she was getting worse?

She was trying to find a tactful way of separating Brynn from the friendly group who'd taken over the room when Darlene reached into a quilted bag at her feet and retrieved a wicker basket. "Muffin? I hope David is feeding you." Her voice dropped a notch. "Grace did all the cooking before she went to college. The last few times there were guests, David ordered from the bakery."

"He's been..." Lucy searched for the right word.

"A wonderful host," Brynn supplied.

Not only had Darlene brought her own breakfast, she began to set out plates and napkins on the wooden pallet that David McCrae used as a coffee table.

"I'll take one of those," Posey said. "And you're right. We don't need to wait for David before we start the meeting. We have a lot to talk about!"

Lucy was losing control of the room. She was also distracted by the heady scent of cloves and cinnamon that wafted into the air. Patch, who'd been dozing with his head on Brynn's knee, roused from his nap, his nose twitching in anticipation.

"Brynn and I will leave you alone, then—"

"Everyone in Frost is so excited we're a Mistletoe Stop on Brynn's tour." Posey didn't seem to hear Lucy as she balanced a plate on one knee. "We want the whole community to feel like they're part of the celebration. Hannah, she's our local florist, has some ideas…" Posey stopped, her gaze fixed on something over Lucy's shoulder, and her cheeks turned as pink as her jacket. "H-hello."

David hadn't shown up yet, and since there was only one person unaccounted for, Lucy was pretty sure she knew who'd rendered Posey speechless.

Lucy glanced over her shoulder and tamped down a sigh. Insomnia must have been contagious, because it didn't look like Caleb had slept much, either. But the mane of tawny hair that looked as if it had been styled with casual fingers instead of a comb and the grain of stubble on Caleb's chin only added to his appeal.

Sometimes, Lucy thought, life just wasn't fair.

"Ladies." Caleb flashed a lazy smile. "I hope I'm not interrupting anything."

And that smoky voice…

Darlene grabbed a napkin off the table, and Lucy half expected the woman to start fanning herself. "N-no. Not at all."

"Caleb, Esther, Darlene and Posey are on the Friends of Frost committee," Lucy told him. Silently, she flashed an SOS.

Run. While there's still time.

Lucy should have known he would ignore the warning. He sauntered into the room instead and accepted a muffin from Darlene, who still looked ready to swoon.

"I'm Caleb Beauchamp. Brynn's…driver."

Technically it wasn't a lie, but Brynn didn't look happy with the description.

Neither was Lucy, now that she knew the truth.

"Oh." Posey looked disappointed. "I thought…"

Lucy knew what she'd thought. Caleb must have, too, because he leaned a hip against the fireplace. "What did I miss?"

He'd chosen the right question to ask.

"We've been brainstorming the past few days, and I think we've come up with the perfect plan," Darlene said.

Whoa. Back up the horse-drawn sleigh.

Lucy didn't mind decorating the inn in anticipation of Grace's arrival, but she already had a plan for their stay in Frost. A plan that involved *less*, not more.

She sneaked a glance at Caleb. The crease between his brows told Lucy that he wasn't sure what to make of the announcement, either.

"What kind of plan?" Brynn accepted a plate from Darlene, broke off a tiny piece of muffin and popped it into her mouth.

"We're calling it the Countdown to Christmas celebration," Esther said. "We'll host some special activities during the week leading up to Christmas to bring everyone in the community together."

Darlene set a muffin on a clean plate and handed it to Lucy.

Her stomach rumbled in appreciation, and the first bite practically melted in her mouth. She knew exactly who to hire to make the refreshments for Brynn's meet and greet.

"But first we have to get David on board," Posey added. "He can be a little…"

"Stubborn?" The dry comment drew everyone's attention to the man standing in the doorway. "So I've been told."

Lucy had no idea how long David McCrae had been listening in on the conversation, but he didn't appear the least bit shocked to find his living room filled with people. And the guarded look in his eyes gave her the impression he'd heard some, if not all, of the animated conversation that preceded his entrance.

Esther chuckled. "You're just in time, David. Darlene's muffins are disappearing faster than the last snowfall of June."

"We were just telling Ms. Dixon about our Countdown to Christmas celebration."

"The Countdown to Christmas." David turned to look at Brynn. "Is this part of your...*Kiss Me under the Mistletoe* tour?"

"*Mistletoe Stop tour,*" Darlene corrected before Brynn had a chance to answer the question. "*Meet Me under the Mistletoe* is the title of the book...and it wasn't Ms. Dixon's idea, but she was definitely our inspiration."

David bypassed the muffins and went straight for a coffee mug on the hearth. "I take it that Spruce Hill Farm is part of the countdown?"

"We'd like you to host the kick-off event," Esther said. "Offer afternoon sleigh rides and Christmas carols around the bonfire in the evening. I looked into it and came to find out there *is* an ordinance against lighting fires on Main Street."

Lucy could have sworn she saw David's lips twitch.

"But that's just the start," Posey said irrepressibly. "We're going to have winter games. Ice-skating and hot chocolate. Snowmen and snow angels." Posey's eyes drifted closed for a moment. "The way it used to be when our kids were growing up. The schools start their holiday break on a Monday, so Pastor Zach suggested we host a few family-oriented activities, like a movie night. *It's a Wonderful Life* is always a favorite."

"We want to start with the sleigh rides because everyone has missed them since..." Darlene seemed chagrined "...since they've been a tradition in the community for years."

"I realize it sounds like a lot to pull together at the last minute, David," Esther said. "But if you agree to the sleigh rides and bonfire, we'll hold everything else on Main Street or at the pavilion in the park."

Darlene grinned at Brynn. "And people will be more excited when they find out there will be a Queen of Ceremonies."

Queen of...

The bite of muffin Lucy had just swallowed lodged halfway down her throat.

Brynn's cup rattled against her plate. "Me?"

"You're our guest of honor," Posey said. "And you're kind of a queen already, right?"

Oh, this was worse than Lucy had thought.

Ainsley would have hired the Friends of Frost on the spot and added them to her creative team.

Brynn smiled and took a sip of coffee before she responded. No doubt waiting for Lucy to intervene.

So intervene already, an inner voice prodded. *Tell them Brynn is working.*

Even though she wasn't, a thought Lucy couldn't dwell on at the moment.

But Esther spoke up first.

"I think we may have gotten a little ahead of ourselves here, girls." She gave Brynn an apologetic look. "My mother always said *Ask before you assume*, and we didn't ask, did we? Frost might be small, but we have a big heart—"

"And snow," Posey whispered.

"And snow." Esther smiled. "You chose our town for a reason, and I believe I'm speaking on behalf of everyone when I say we'd love it if you joined our celebration, in whatever role you choose."

Lucy finally found her voice. "Ms. Dixon appreciates this—"

"And would love to be your Queen of Ceremonies and spend some time with y'all," Brynn interrupted.

Darlene and Posey beamed.

"We'll spread the news," Darlene promised.

"David?" Esther turned to their host. A man that was now Lucy's ally.

David had plans, too, and there was no way he'd agree to open the property to guests. If the kick-off hinged on his participation, the committee might be forced to, as Ainsley liked to say, *go in another direction*. Which would give Lucy time to come up with a way to minimize Brynn's involvement.

"Tell everyone there will be sleigh rides starting at one o'clock on Saturday afternoon."

"What about the bonfire? And the hot chocolate?" Darlene wanted to know.

David's gaze rested on Brynn now.

"I think it makes the most sense to have everything in one place...so when you're spreading the news, let everyone know that Spruce Hill Farm will host all of the events."

Chapter Twenty-Six

On Friday morning, Lucy woke up to a cloudless, denim-blue sky, an outside temperature that registered a balmy twenty-four degrees and a dozen blueberry muffins—still warm—nestled underneath an embroidered tea towel in a basket on the sideboard in the gathering room.

Darlene had clearly gotten a jump start on the day while Lucy was still trying to play catch-up. And not only with her to-do list.

After Esther and her friends left the day before, Brynn had joined Lucy and Caleb in the gathering room for breakfast, but Lucy couldn't talk to her about the Countdown to Christmas celebration. Not in front of Caleb, anyway. Brynn had agreed to participate, so he might wonder why Lucy would question his mom's decision. Which might lead to questions about why Lucy thought Brynn should pass up an opportunity—*on her book tour*—that would give it more exposure.

Why *had* Brynn agreed to participate? That's what Lucy couldn't figure out.

Yes, the women on the Friends of Frost committee were sweet. Enthusiastic.

A force to be reckoned with.

A force for good, yes. The committee cared about their town so they'd pulled out all the stops in the Mistletoe Stop tour and wanted to include Brynn in the festivities.

The only thing wrong with their plan was…everything.

"Don't you worry about a thing!" Darlene had told Brynn and Lucy as they were walking out the door. "We'll handle all the details!"

Words that had struck fear in Lucy's heart.

When David McCrae showed up, Lucy had found herself hoping he would be the voice of reason. Tell the committee there was no way the town could pull off half the things they wanted to do with no promotion and in such a short time frame. But suddenly, the man who hadn't wanted to roll out the welcome mat for guests had done a complete about-face and offered to host *all* the events.

Lucy poured a cup of coffee and took a bracing sip.

There had to be a way to keep Brynn's involvement to a minimum, in spite of her being the guest of honor. Or *Queen of Ceremonies*, the title the women had bestowed upon her. Lucy had come up with a solution about the waiver so Caleb didn't have to worry about Trace Hunter complicating his life the way he'd complicated Lucy's.

Oh, who was she kidding? Caleb had complicated her life, too.

Because *he* was complicated. And it was easier for Lucy to keep her distance when she could put a label on Caleb, the way she did her files.

From the day she'd started wiring money to Caleb on Brynn's behalf, Lucy had questioned his dubious career of hopping from continent to continent on what appeared to be someone else's dime. Questioned his motives.

How could she have known Caleb was trying to protect

Brynn, not only from trolls that could damage her reputation but from his stepmother, Shae?

Or that living in different times zones might be his way of protecting Brynn, too.

Caleb had given Lucy a brief summary of his family life, but it was the things he *hadn't* said that made Lucy's heart ache. The way his jaw tightened when he'd talked about losing his mom to cancer. His adoptive father abandoning Caleb when he needed him the most.

Lucy and Caleb had been the same age when tragedy struck. Her sister Janie's accident had changed the entire Gable family, but unlike Caleb's, it had brought them closer instead of tearing them apart. Something Lucy hadn't recognized as a gift until she'd seen the pain in Caleb's eyes.

The floor creaked, giving Lucy a second to blink back her tears before David entered the gathering room. It was barely seven in the morning, but he was already dressed for the outdoors in a fleece-lined coat, dark jeans and thick-soled boots.

"I smell cinnamon." David tilted his head back and sniffed the air. "Did you make breakfast? Because if you keep this up, I'm going to have to add you to the payroll as the inn's official chef and interior decorator."

He'd noticed the changes in the lobby.

After Esther and her friends left the day before, Brynn had retreated to her room, giving Lucy an opportunity to finish the decorating. She'd found a stepladder in the utility closet and hung a flock of tiny glass cardinals from the chandelier in the lobby. Replaced batteries in the luminaries she'd found at the bottom of one of the boxes and arranged them on a corner of the registration desk. Threaded a mile of garland through the spindles on the staircase until she reached the second floor.

Caleb had followed David outside shortly after the women left, too, and other than a brief appearance at dinner, Lucy hadn't seen or spoken to him. But that hadn't stopped her thoughts from gravitating to the man like a needle on a compass seeking its true north.

"Lucy?"

David was looking at her expectantly, and she realized he must have asked her a question. Further proof her thoughts had gone rogue again.

"I'm sorry." Lucy wrangled them back into line. "It was Darlene." She pointed to the basket of muffins next to the carafe of coffee on the sideboard. "She promised to keep us stocked with baked goods."

"How did…" David stopped, as if questioning how the woman had sneaked inside the inn before anyone else was awake was a mystery he didn't want to contemplate at the moment. "You asked about the warming house and the firepit at dinner last night?"

Lucy nodded cautiously. She had, but only because she'd been wondering how to best accommodate Brynn without arousing anyone's suspicions. Other than the early-morning forays to the kitchen and David's living room, Brynn's energy seemed to be decreasing since their arrival.

"I have to let the team stretch their legs a little before we open tomorrow afternoon, so I'm going to hitch them up and take them around the trails we'll be using," David said. "If you're interested in seeing the layout of the property, you're welcome to join me."

Two thoughts collided in Lucy's head.

The first was that checking out the distance between the inn and the warming house was something she'd already planned to do after breakfast, and the second, riding in a horse-drawn sleigh was one of those perfect, Christmas-card moments Lucy had always longed to experience.

"Thank you, Mr. McCrae. I'd love to go along."

David nodded. "Grace left some extra coats and hats in a closet by the back door. It's sunny today, but you still might want something a little more prac—*warmer*—than what you brought from Tennessee."

"When do you want to leave?" Lucy silently rearranged her schedule. Responding to Ainsley's last email and doing a cost analysis between seafood and prime rib for Ben's surprise engagement dinner would have to wait a few more hours.

"I could use a little more caffeine, too." David surprised her with a wry smile. "I've got a lumberjack special in the oven, and it takes an hour. I can have the sleigh ready to go in about fifteen minutes or you can eat breakfast first."

"I don't think I've ever had a...lumberjack special."

"Scrambled eggs, sausage, fried potatoes and cheese cooked in the cast-iron skillet. It's not gourmet, it's not even pretty, but it tastes good and should hold you until lunch."

Lucy reached for one of the muffins and set it on a plate rimmed in gold and holly leaves. "I'll let Brynn know that I'll be gone for a while...unless you've spoken to her already?"

Since David's living room seemed to be Brynn's favorite retreat in the morning.

His smile faded. "I haven't seen her yet."

Lucy smiled to cover her concern but wondered why the innkeeper, who'd pointed out the boundaries between the guest and private spaces on more than one occasion, didn't look happier to have the sofa and fireplace all to himself this morning. "I'm sure she'll come downstairs when she's ready for a cup of coffee."

David looked like he wanted to say something, but he shook his head instead, as if he already knew the answer. "I'll grab some carrots and meet you in the lobby."

"Oh, that's all right." Lucy reached for her plate. "I'll have one of these muffins to hold me over until breakfast."

"Carrots for the horses." David chuckled. "I may have to resort to bribery to get them out of the barn."

After he retreated to the kitchen, Lucy devoured the muffin

and decided to take David up on the offer to add a few additional layers to the outfit she'd chosen for the day.

She rounded the corner at the end of the hall and nearly collided with Caleb.

David had given Lucy permission to borrow some of Grace's outerwear, but Caleb, it seemed, had raided the box marked *Lost and Found*. The wool scarf loosely knotted around his neck gave him a rakish look, but it was the suede vest and trapper's hat with fur-lined earflaps that had Lucy wrestling down a smile.

Caleb spotted it anyway.

"What?" he growled.

Lucy had worried Caleb was avoiding her. That he regretted opening up and sharing something he'd never told anyone, not even Brynn. But his low growl wasn't the least bit intimidating, so Lucy had no other choice.

She laughed.

In the past twenty-four hours, Caleb hadn't seen much of Lucy. If anyone had asked, though, he would have been able to tell them where she'd been and what she'd been doing with her time.

Tiny glass birds hung from the ceiling in the lobby and the banister bristled with faux evergreen boughs from the base of the stairs to the landing on the second floor. He was pretty sure she was responsible for the elf peeking out from behind the coffee mugs on the sideboard, too.

But why was Lucy spending so much time creating a welcoming atmosphere with lights and faux greens and shiny ornaments when her laughter, the warm sparkle in her eyes, had the power to draw a person in?

Which was why Caleb had been avoiding her since the Friends of Frost had descended on the inn the day before.

But here she was, looking way too appealing in a chunky sweater and jeans that hugged her slender curves.

Breathe. Speak.

Caleb was having a difficult time managing both at the moment. He loosened his scarf a little just in case that was the problem.

"Were you looking for me?"

"No... A coat." Lucy had stopped laughing, but it lingered in her eyes, starlight against a background of black velvet. "And a hat that covers my ears."

"Don't even think about it." Caleb reached up and patted a furry earflap. "This one is mine."

"David said Grace left some extra things in the closet. He's taking the sleigh for a test drive and invited me to go along."

"He invited me, too."

"Oh." Lucy caught her lip between her teeth. "He didn't mention that."

David hadn't mentioned he'd invited Lucy, either. While Caleb's flight instincts battled against images of Lucy cozied up next to him in the sleigh, she sidled past him and opened the closet door. Pulled out a stocking cap with a glittery, softball-sized pom-pom and waved it in front of him.

"We could trade?"

Caleb grinned. "No, thanks."

She made a face, grabbed a purple vest sprinkled with snowflakes from its hanger and slipped her arms through the sleeves. "How do people move around in all this stuff?" She folded in half, the pom-pom on her hat almost clipping his nose, and began to fumble with the zipper.

"Let me do that." Caleb swept her hands aside. "And don't look down or you'll take me out with that pom-pom."

"I feel like a little kid," Lucy grumbled.

"You just don't like to ask for help."

Caleb zipped up the vest, following a path that ended up with him staring directly into Lucy's eyes. And she wasn't laughing now.

"Why would you say that?"

"Because it's true. How many boxes have you carried up from the basement? How many hours have you spent decorating the inn?"

"It's my job. And I couldn't ask…"

Him? Or Brynn?

Caleb wasn't sure what Lucy had been about to say because her expression changed and she waved at someone behind him.

He turned, expecting to see David, but it was his mom who stood at the bottom of the stairs. She'd always been petite, but this was the first time Caleb would have described her as fragile. The curls piled on top of her head sharpened her cheekbones, and although she'd always been fair-skinned, today she looked…pale. Tired.

Something cold and hard settled in Caleb's stomach, and his feet carried him down the hall.

She'd been working too hard without a break.

"You're just in time," Caleb said. "The sleigh leaves in ten minutes."

"Five." David emerged from the kitchen, Patch at his heels. "You're going on a sleigh ride?"

The interest that sparked in Brynn's eyes loosened the knot in Caleb's gut. His mom wasn't a complainer by nature, and based on his experience, a few sleepless nights in unfamiliar surroundings could take a toll on the most seasoned of travelers.

"Uh-huh." Caleb grinned. "A test run…trot…walk. It depends on the horses, I guess."

"There's room," David interjected. "You're welcome to come along."

Brynn's gaze shifted from Caleb to their host. "I appreciate the invitation, but my morning is already booked. No pun intended," she added lightly.

Caleb thought her smile looked forced. He glanced at Lucy,

expecting her to encourage Brynn to take a break, too, but she remained silent.

"Are you sure?" He pressed a little. "You've been putting in a lot of hours this week. Maybe you should take the morning off. Get out of your room and have some fun."

Spend some time with me.

That's what Caleb wanted to say. He knew Brynn was busy, but when she'd had supper in her room again, he'd realized how little time they'd been together since they'd arrived at Spruce Hill Farm.

For a split second, it looked like Brynn was tempted by the idea, and then she looked at David again.

"Y'all go on and don't worry about me." Brynn's lips tipped in a smile. "My cowboy boots are strictly for show. Horses pulling a piece of plywood on skis? Not my idea of fun."

"I've never thought of it quite like that, but okay. Your choice. I'll be down by the barn." David walked to the door without a backward glance.

"There are seats," Caleb pointed out, not quite ready to give up yet.

She chuckled. "I need one that doesn't bounce, though, if I'm going to get anything accomplished before the Countdown to Christmas starts tomorrow."

Now Lucy spoke up. "Esther sent an official itinerary, and I forwarded it to your email."

"See? Duty calls." Brynn patted Caleb's arm. "Be sure to take some pictures, and I'll see y'all later."

"Sure." What else could he say?

He followed Lucy outside. The door closed behind them, and she would have started down the steps but Caleb snagged her arm.

"What's going on?"

Lucy looked up at him, her eyes wide. "What do you mean?"

"Mom usually jumps at the chance to see the local sights

when she's on a book tour. Why won't she take a break from the project she's working on? She's been holed up in her room since we got here and…" Caleb didn't want to sound dramatic. Or needy. But he was getting a little frustrated, and Brynn wasn't the only one who had people counting on her. "I have to leave the day after Christmas."

An emotion Caleb couldn't quite identify skimmed through Lucy's eyes.

"Brynn didn't know you were going to join us," she said slowly. "She…she's doing the best she can."

Caleb blew out a sigh. Lucy was right. He'd invited himself along on the tour knowing Brynn would be busy, but the vibes he'd been getting had started weeks ago. Something was wrong.

His mom claimed she was happy with the way he was running her nonprofit, but Caleb knew he could be doing more. The next time he talked to Mel, retired medical missionary turned licensed mechanic, Caleb would ask if she could do some more networking. Expand their territory and show Brynn that she hadn't made a mistake by putting him in charge of the team.

A whistle pierced the air. Caleb wasn't sure if it was meant to get the horses' attention or theirs, but either way, it looked like their driver was ready to leave.

"I believe that's our signal." Lucy started down the path to the barn, the soles of her boots stamping a chevron pattern in the snow.

Caleb fell into step beside her. "So you don't think Brynn is acting…different?" He wasn't sure why he kept pressing the issue, especially when he was the only one questioning her decision to stay behind.

"I think she's acting like…Brynn."

Conscientious. Dedicated. That was his mom, for sure.

So why wouldn't Lucy look him in the eye?

Chapter Twenty-Seven

From the kitchen window, Brynn watched the sleigh disappear into the woods. David sat in the front, controlling a pair of long leather reins, Patch planted at his side. Caleb and Lucy had claimed a spot on the bench behind them.

A year ago, Brynn would have been right there with them.

Over the course of her career, she'd tried white water rafting, taken ballroom-dancing lessons and spent a weekend glamping on the edge of a cliff, all in the name of research.

It had been fun, too.

You've been putting in a lot of hours this week. Maybe you should take the morning off.

Brynn had wanted to throw caution to the wind when Caleb invited her to come along, but because she'd said yes to Esther and her committee, she had to store up as much energy as possible in order to get through the week leading up to the book signing.

Why she'd agreed to be Frost's Queen of the Countdown to Christmas was a question Brynn had been asking herself since yesterday morning.

Pride? Denial? Stubbornness?

Fear.

The same reason she'd stayed behind instead of going on the sleigh ride with her son.

After the notebook incident, Brynn no longer trusted her memory. No longer trusted that she wouldn't say something, do something, that would lead to more questions from Caleb. Questions she wasn't ready to answer yet.

Every year since her son had knocked on her door, Brynn had invited him to spend Christmas with her. And every year, he was in some remote location or a crisis came up so a phone call had to do. Now he was here, and Brynn could be spending hours with him, laughing, catching up. Dreaming about the future of Words with Wings.

And what had she done instead? Brynn had seen the disappointment on Caleb's face, but she'd stayed behind. By her actions, she was implying that her work was more important than him.

The woman who valued honesty in her relationships had outright lied to her son.

Brynn's hands fisted at her sides, and she ignored the pain that shot from fingertips to elbows.

Lord, this is harder than I thought it would be.

She wanted to tell Caleb the truth, but in some ways, he still hadn't made peace with the past. Or with Glenn Beauchamp, the man who'd turned his back on Caleb at a time when he'd needed him the most.

Brynn understood that people grieved in different ways, but Caleb's adoptive father should have realized that Caleb had lost not only one, but two moms, by the time he was fifteen years old. No wonder he'd acted out. And although Brynn wished that Glenn had had a change of heart and welcomed him home, she thanked God every day that he'd found her.

Brynn had been sitting in the atrium eating lunch that day

when she'd heard a knock at the door. Delivery trucks were always coming and going through her gated neighborhood so she hadn't thought anything of it when she swept the curtain aside and saw a young man standing on her porch. He was dressed casually in jeans and a T-shirt, a rooster tail of tawny, sun-streaked hair poking out from the back of his baseball cap. And then Brynn had caught a glimpse of his face when he'd looked up at the window and her heart had plummeted all the way down to the toes of her cowboy boots.

Brynn had promised herself that she wouldn't look for her son, but she'd never stopped hoping, praying, that one day he would look for *her*.

Brynn was barely able to breathe by the time she opened the door. They'd stared at each other, and when Brynn saw the emotions simmering in his blue eyes, she knew it wasn't longing or even simple curiosity that had brought him to her door.

Caleb had been angry at the world.

At her.

And even though Caleb hadn't said the words out loud, Brynn had seen the tears in his eyes, heard the bitterness in his voice when he talked about his adoptive mom's cancer diagnosis and her unwavering faith. His father's ultimatum.

Brynn's heart had broken for Caleb because he was angry with God, too. His faith shaken by the death of someone he loved and grief over losing another parent, too.

Spending time with people like Mel and a team of people from all walks of life who'd loved Caleb back together had strengthened his faith, but Brynn didn't want to be a burden. Or the reason he began to doubt God's goodness again.

If Caleb found out she was sick, he would either insist on staying at her side or he'd stay as far away from her as possible. After twenty-five years without her son, both possibilities struck fear in Brynn's heart.

She turned away from the window, ignoring the flare of heat in her joints, and saw David's coffee mug beside the sink.

Guilt dug deep. Because yes, not only had she disappointed her son, she'd offended their host, too.

Brynn had felt David's gaze resting on her, heard a hint of challenge in his tone. And because his clipped comment about there being room sounded more like a test than an invitation, she'd been forced to remind him that divas had better things to do with their time.

But now that she had an hour to herself, Brynn wasn't sure what to do with it.

The emails from her agent and editor asking about her next book were a gentle reminder to Brynn what she *should* be doing. New characters who, by now, should have been vying for her attention hadn't made an appearance, though, and her attempts to draw them out, to coax them out of hiding, had been half-hearted at best.

She wasn't sure if it was Frost or the thick blanket of snow that covered the ground like a down comforter, but she was starting to lean into the quiet instead of fighting it.

Or maybe she was giving up?

That had crossed Brynn's mind, too.

Her eyelids suddenly felt heavy, even though the sun had made an appearance a few short hours ago. There were times she felt like the Tin Man in *The Wizard of Oz*, her limbs frozen in place. The spirit willing but the flesh oh, so weak.

One foot in front of the other, Brynn Elizabeth.

And once again, those feet carried her into David's living room.

Brynn sat down on the sofa and pulled a blanket over her knees. She'd expected David's morning fire to be embers by now, but a neat tower of logs burned brightly as if they'd been expecting her.

A carafe and a muffin dusted with cinnamon had been placed

on the table in front of the sofa, along with a cloth napkin and the coffee cup Brynn had claimed as her own. The careful attention to detail was a sign that Lucy had been expecting her, too. Knowing her assistant, she was the one who'd most likely sneaked in a few extra logs in the fireplace as well.

Brynn leaned back and closed her eyes—for just a minute—and then she'd take the coffee upstairs to her room.

The soft snick of a door nudged her awake.

Brynn rubbed her eyes and looked at the clock. An hour instead of a minute.

Wonderful.

Now they'd catch her napping instead of working, and how was she supposed to explain that?

Brynn straightened and pinned on a smile, but the footsteps coming toward the Dutch doors were too light to be Caleb's or David's and too measured to be Lucy's.

"Hello?"

Relief washed over Brynn. And she looked a little more presentable today in leggings and a cashmere sweater.

The footsteps paused, and Brynn realized that David's neighbor wouldn't venture any farther than the kitchen. If she didn't answer, she could be back in her room before anyone else returned.

But this was *Esther.*

"In here," Brynn heard herself say.

The Dutch doors parted, and David's neighbor glided into the room. All Brynn could see was the brim of her hat and sparkling blue eyes over the top of the plastic bin cradled in her arms.

"The house was so quiet I didn't think anyone was here." Esther set the box down on the floor. "Hannah asked me to drop off the mistletoe decorations on my way home. As you can imagine, there's quite a stir in town today." She grinned. "I'll have to let David know that he'll be handing out axes tomorrow. A tree from Spruce Hill Farm is a tradition around here."

"Please…sit down." Brynn motioned to the empty chair. "David isn't here right now. He took the sleigh out for a test drive with Lucy and Caleb." Hopefully Esther wouldn't ask why Brynn hadn't gone along with them.

"Confession?" Esther's smile held a hint of mischief. "I was hoping to see *you*. I should have called first, but the three-year-old class from Kasey's day camp came to the shop this morning, and we made patchwork heart ornaments for their parents. I got so distracted I was almost to the inn when I realized I'd left my cell phone there." She stripped off her coat and draped it neatly over the back of a chair before she sat down.

"I feel like I owe you an apology for yesterday. Like I said, we got a little carried away. The committee had been hoping you could join us for the bonfire, but the whole week? That was a blessing we weren't expecting."

Neither had Brynn, but she couldn't help but feel she was the one who'd been blessed. There'd been an instant connection with Esther and her friends. The same soul-deep peace Brynn had experienced the first time she'd set eyes on Spruce Hill Farm. She wasn't sure how she could pull it off, but a Queen of Ceremonies didn't participate, she *observed*. Delegated.

Brynn could do that.

"I'm looking forward to it," she said honestly.

"I brought you a little something as a thank-you." Esther reached down, pried the lid off the bin and handed her a gift wrapped in silver tissue paper. "You don't have to wait until Christmas, either," she teased.

Brynn untied the braided cord around the package. It took a moment for her to realize the thick block of fabric nestled inside the tissue paper was a quilt.

"Esther…" Brynn ignored the burning joints in her fingers as she unfolded it.

The background was a night sky, a mosaic of tiny squares in shifting shades of blue from indigo to cobalt. A swirl of gold and silver in the center broke into shards of light that stretched to all four corners of the quilt.

A Christmas star. And more like a work of art, intricate and beautiful enough to be preserved in a frame, not folded up at the end of a bed or tossed over a chair.

Brynn remembered Darlene had mentioned that Esther owned a quilting shop.

"You *made* this?"

"I finished it a few days ago."

"It's beautiful, Esther, but I…I can't possibly accept it. A quilt like this should go to a family member or a special friend."

"I always let God tell me who the quilt will belong to," Esther said. "While I'm stitching, I ask Him to wrap His arms around them and remind them that they're loved. To know they're covered in prayer. Yesterday, I felt a nudge and knew I was supposed to give it to you."

Brynn ran her fingers over the perfect stitches along the hem, so small and fine they were barely visible at all.

Fear Not.

Brynn hadn't realized she'd read the words out loud until Esther nodded.

"Most quilts follow a pattern." She smiled. "Mine have names."

The reminder meant more to Brynn than Esther would know.

She'd been feeling forgotten, left out, and God had brought Esther and a beautiful reminder of His love right to Brynn.

"It's hand-sewn, isn't it?" Brynn traced her fingertip along the hem. "Esther…this must have taken months to complete."

"I do most of my quilting by machine now. My vision isn't what it used to be, but I still love to quilt the way Rose, Lynette's grandmother, taught me."

The name stirred in Brynn's mind. "Lynette… David's wife?"

Esther nodded. "Lynette visited Frost a lot while she was growing up. She was a real sweetheart, full of energy but never a handful like some kids can be. She helped Wes and Rose with the chores and got so good at baking, Rose let her take over the kitchen when she was here."

"Was it an inn then?"

Esther chuckled. "That was Lynette's vision. For Wes and Rose, the tree plantation kept them busy enough.

"Everyone in town was sad when Rose and Wes decided to move. The house needed a lot of updating, and with Wes's health declining, keeping up the property got to be too much for him. I couldn't imagine anyone else living here, but we were all tickled pink when we found out Lynette's husband was retiring and they were going to move to Spruce Hill Farm."

"David was in the coast guard?" Brynn prompted, suddenly hungry for more details about his life.

"Lynette said David would have made admiral if he hadn't retired early. She and Grace had followed him from base to base during his career, and David knew she wanted to put down roots. It was her idea to turn Wes and Rose's house into a bed-and-breakfast. Some folks around here weren't too sure they could make a go of it." Esther's eyes crinkled at the corners. "Frost isn't exactly a tourist destination, but we had faith in Lynette.

"David took over the renovations while she focused on the hospitality part of the business." Esther's smile trembled at the edges. "They were the perfect team."

"What happened to Lynette?" Brynn was almost afraid to ask.

"She was in a car accident three years ago. It was February, and Lynette had driven up to the Upper Peninsula to meet with an antique dealer. David stayed behind to finish up some painting, and Grace was studying for a test.

"We'd had a stretch of warm weather—fake spring, some would call it. There was a dense fog advisory, and David thought he'd convinced Lynette to spend the night there. He didn't know she'd decided to drive home until a sheriff's deputy came to the door. They determined that because of the fog, Lynette miscalculated a turn and lost control of the car. We were all devastated, but David..." Esther's voice thinned. "If it hadn't been for Grace, I don't know what he would have done. He wanted to be strong for her.

"Pastor Zach, Martin, the men in our church, they've tried to reach out to David, but he keeps to himself. I have to tell you I was worried about him when Grace went off to college, but yesterday...when he told us he'd decided to open the tree farm again... Well, I hope it's a sign that David is opening up a little, too."

Or he was hoping some of the visitors would become potential buyers once the property went up for sale.

Not that Brynn could tell Esther that.

"I hope so, too," she murmured.

"Martin rounded up a few of his friends, and they're coming over to lend a hand this morning. Don't tell David, though. If he gets wind of the plan, he'll claim he has everything under control."

"I won't say a word," Brynn promised.

Fortunately for Esther, she was good at keeping secrets.

Chapter Twenty-Eight

Now Lucy understood why the people who lived here didn't mind bundling in layers of fleece and flannel every time they went outside.

It was because they didn't just listen to songs about a winter wonderland, they got to be *part* of it. Got to feel the cold pinch their cheeks and turn every breath into a puff of frost. See the branches of the trees flocked with snow and the delicate rows of stitches crossing the trail, made by tiny feet.

Lucy had thought the woods would be silent. The cards and calendars depicting sleigh rides made them look so serene. But the squeak of the harnesses, a crow perched low on the branch of a tree, cawing out a warning there were trespassers nearby, and the chatter of a red squirrel in response brought the silver-and-white landscape to life.

Lucy didn't want it to end. Especially when Caleb's hand shot out to steady her when David urged the team up a hill.

He'd barely spoken to her since they'd left the inn, and Lucy wasn't sure if he was taking in the beauty of their surroundings or still thinking about Brynn.

Caleb had tried to hide it, but Lucy could tell he'd been disappointed Brynn had opted to stay behind.

The team slowed, and David pointed at something just off the trail. A whitetail deer with liquid brown eyes stood a few yards away, her ears lifted as she watched the strange contraption pass by.

Caleb lifted his cell phone and snapped a photo of the doe before David clicked his tongue, a signal for the horses to pick up their pace.

Lucy closed her eyes, enjoying the feel of the wind against her cheeks and the scent of pine and snow.

When she opened them again, Caleb was looking at *her*. A smile rustled at the corners of his lips.

"I know… I look like Rudolph." She scrubbed the tip of her nose with her mitten to jump-start the circulation again. "But it's so beautiful out here."

His gaze dropped to her lips, which were probably chapped. Or blue. Or…

Maybe neither of those things.

Because the warmth in Caleb's eyes told Lucy he wasn't thinking about the beauty of the woods at all.

And suddenly, neither was she.

Lucy was wondering what it would be like to feel Caleb's arms around her, no secrets between them. To talk about the future instead of the past.

To have a moment that turned into hours. And days. And years…

"Hold on to something." David twisted to look at them, and the moment was broken. "When we turn the corner up here, the horses can get a little excited because they know we're going back to the barn."

Hold on…

Another woman might have taken advantage of the opportunity and flashed a teasing smile at Caleb, linked her arm through his. Lucy gripped the edge of the seat instead. Pretended she wasn't thinking that the something she wanted to hold on to was *him*.

The horses rounded a corner, and David hadn't been exaggerating. They found another gear and broke into a trot.

Patch barked as if he was urging them to go faster, and Lucy laughed.

David glanced over his shoulder, a smile on his face. "This is Grace's favorite part of the trail, too."

She won't want to give this up.

The thought swept through Lucy's mind as the horses settled into a more sedate rhythm again.

How could David think that he was looking out for Grace's best interests by selling the inn?

But was that any different than Brynn, who hadn't told Caleb the real reason she'd turned down a sleigh ride?

Lucy thought about the empty notebook for at least the thousandth time since David McCrae had handed it to her that night.

Brynn considered her a friend, but Lucy still wasn't sure it wouldn't be overstepping to admit she'd seen that tattered binding and the enormous question mark.

Do you think Brynn is acting different?

When Caleb had asked Lucy a similar question the first time they'd spoken on the phone, she'd had no qualms about telling him everything was fine. But now she wondered how she could share her concern without breaking a confidence with a woman who was not only her boss but someone Lucy trusted and admired.

And the notebook didn't mean Brynn wasn't working on her next project. She could have been having a bad day.

Or she could be getting worse.

Something Lucy didn't want to contemplate.

Caleb's low whistle cut through the whoosh of the sleigh.

Lucy realized David's route had taken them on a loop through the woods that bordered the plantation. They'd emerged from the woods onto a ridge across from the inn. Lucy could see the fenced-in pasture and another outbuilding, twice the size of the small barn with the same rustic charm as the warming house.

Her curiosity piqued, she leaned forward and tapped David on the shoulder when the sleigh drew even with the building.

He pulled back on the reins. The team slowed down and lumbered to a stop. David turned around again.

"Everything all right?"

"Is this yours, too?" Lucy gestured at the building.

"Uh-huh." David tugged his cap off and raked his hand through his hair. "It was used to house cattle when the original homestead was built. There was a cabin right over there." He pointed to the jagged outline of a stone wall jutting up from the snow. "By the time Wes and Rose bought the property, the cabin was long gone, and the owner had decided a Christmas-tree plantation was a better investment than raising animals. When Wes bought the horses, he put up a round pen and built a lean-to closer to the house so he could keep a closer eye on them."

"It would be a great place for the movie night," Lucy ventured. "It looks like it could hold a lot of people."

And Brynn would have a cozy spot out of the cold.

"My wife thought so, too." David stared at the building. "Phase Three of her vision for Spruce Hill Farm. She wanted to rent the building out for wedding receptions and graduation parties. Things like that. Right now, it's a storage unit for some stuff Wes, Lynette's grandfather, left there, oh, fifty, sixty years ago."

Patch whined and performed a little tap dance on the seat.

"Do you two mind if we stop for a minute? Patch is telling me that he wants to stretch his legs."

"Fine with me," Caleb said.

It was fine with Lucy, too. Even if half the shed was taken up by storage, it would still hold more people than the warming house. The Friends of Frost committee wanted their Queen of Ceremonies to make an appearance at all the events, but Lucy had already decided it was up to her to make sure Brynn was comfortable.

The dog leaped off the side of the sleigh and disappeared into the brush. The outbuilding was only a few feet off the trail, so Lucy hopped down, too. Snow crunched underneath her feet as she walked over to the window and tried to peer through the thick layer of grime on the glass.

"Want to take a look inside?"

Lucy hadn't realized David had followed her. He held up a set of keys, the ghost of a smile on his face.

"It's not that I don't believe you," she said quickly. "But maybe we could move some things out of the way to make room for the people who come to movie night."

David actually laughed. "As much as I appreciate the offer, I doubt it." He unhooked the chain that bound the heavy service doors together and pushed them open. Sunlight streamed through the windows, creating intricate stencils on the dirt floor.

Lucy's mouth dropped open. She backed up and bumped into Caleb, who'd stepped through the door behind her.

"Okay. I see what you mean." Lucy's low laugh echoed through the cavernous interior. "I was picturing a rusty tractor or old tires, not a…plane."

Technically, it was a Rockwell Thrush Commander 600.

Caleb had never flown one, but he had a bucket list when it came to planes, and the Thrush Commander was in his top five.

She was a beauty, too. Compact and sturdy with a canary yellow fuselage and white tips on both wings that looked flashy in spite of the thick coat of dust and pollen they wore.

He tried to hide his envy as he looked at David. "Was it used for crop-dusting?"

"I don't think it's been used at all. According to family legend, Wes bought it at an auction because he wanted a hobby. Rose found out about the purchase after the fact and convinced him to take up woodworking instead."

Poor guy.

Caleb moved closer for a better look and saw the name *Daisy Jane* written in scrolly black letters on the side.

"I'm not sure why Wes kept it," David said with a shrug. "Maybe he couldn't find anyone willing to take it off his hands, or knowing Wes's sense of humor, he liked to see the expression on people's faces when he told them he owned a plane."

Whatever the man's reason, if the *Daisy Jane* belonged to Caleb, she wouldn't be hidden in a building at the edge of the property. She'd be airborne, waving at the people on the ground.

Lucy didn't seem to understand that she was looking at a piece of history. While Caleb stood there starstruck, she was taking a lap around the perimeter of the building.

"This is a great space." She paused to look up at the exposed wooden trusses that crisscrossed the ceiling. "It's not far from the warming house, and the trees shelter it from the wind, so it wouldn't be too uncomfortable for people who are already bundled up against the cold. The back wall would make the perfect movie screen…" Her nose, kissed pink from their adventure in the woods, wrinkled. "If their view wasn't blocked by a plane, that is."

David tipped his head, considering her words. "I suppose we could drag it out of the barn, but there's a lot of snow in the way, and I'm not sure where to put it."

Caleb could almost see the wheels turning in Lucy's head. She was in full fix-it mode. "What if we left the plane here but moved it out of the way? It would fit in that corner—" she pointed to the opposite side of the doors "—and we'd just incorporate it in the decorations. String some lights around the wings."

"Put a big red bow on the propeller?" Caleb murmured.

"That's a great idea!"

Caleb gave *Daisy's* wing an apologetic she-knows-not-what-she-says pat.

David walked a circle around the plane. "I suppose that would work. I'd have to get the tractor up here and tow it."

"The engine doesn't run?"

David looked surprised by the question. "I'm retired coast guard, so if it was a boat, I might be able to answer the question."

Caleb squatted down and inspected the tail, wheels and prop. *Daisy Jane* didn't have any visible defects, but he would have to check her vitals to be sure.

"Mind if I take a look at her?"

"No…" David flipped a switch on the wall, and the overhead lights popped on. "You know something about engines?"

Aware that Lucy was watching, he shrugged and vaulted into the cockpit. A scratching noise underneath the seat warned Caleb he wasn't alone. "A little."

Most of the time, Caleb's drop-off points could be reached by a car or bus. The more remote regions, though, could only be accessed by plane. The small but aging fleet that Mel had on standby in various parts of the world, ready to deliver supplies and the occasional passenger at a moment's notice, could be as temperamental as the weather, however, so what Caleb knew about engines had come out of sheer necessity.

Lucy was looking up at him, hands planted on the ledge of her hips, an expression of disbelief on her face.

And why wouldn't she?

Brynn had been adamant that no one know about her connection to Words with Wings. Her vision and financial support kept the nonprofit going, but when she'd asked Caleb to help her make it a reality, she'd made it clear that putting books into the hands of adults and children who hungered to learn was a blessing to *her*, not the other way around.

Now that Caleb had gotten to know Lucy, he wasn't sure he agreed with Brynn's decision not to bring her assistant on board. Lucy had vision, too. Like converting a drafty barn into a movie theater complete with hay-bale seating and an old crop duster as a Christmas decoration. Over the last few years, Caleb had been slowly building his team, and Lucy, with her eye for detail, would definitely be an asset. And although Lucy tried to hide it behind the somber attire and to-do lists and the ever-present calendar that kept life running smoothly, there was an adventurous spirit inside of her, too.

Caleb hadn't missed the look of wonder on Lucy's face when the horses had broken into a trot. Suddenly, he was imagining her sitting next to him in the cockpit, looking down at a family of elephants splashing in a water hole or letting a golden eagle have the right of way.

What was happening to him?

Not only had Caleb thought about kissing Lucy—and probably would have if he hadn't remembered they weren't alone in the sleigh—but now he was imagining that she was part of his life.

"You all right?"

David's question yanked Caleb's thoughts back in line.

Because Lucy definitely wasn't thinking about spending more time with him. She'd put as much distance between them as possible in the sleigh.

Caleb expelled a breath. He wanted to see if *Daisy* was truly an oversize centerpiece or if she'd been biding her time, waiting to show off her stuff, but he couldn't. Not now, anyway.

Not when Lucy was looking at him as if he was having delusions of grandeur, and an *Oh, yeah—fun fact—I'm a pilot* would have opened the door to questions Caleb couldn't answer. At least not now.

But the fact he *wanted* to was a sign that his emotions had taken control of his head.

And that's why Caleb was not even close to all right.

The buzz of an engine in the woods set off Patch and drew a loud whinny from one of the horses.

David jogged toward the door to see what the commotion was about, and after a moment's hesitation, Lucy followed. Caleb muttered a quick apology to *Daisy* before he swung down from the cockpit.

A man straddling a snowmobile was already removing his helmet by the time Caleb joined them outside. He looked to be in his mid- to late sixties but it was difficult to judge his age, given the fact that his craggy features looked like they'd been permanently cast in bronze.

"Beautiful day!" Grinning, he tucked the helmet between his knees. "I'm Martin, Esther's husband, and you must be Caleb and Lucy."

Up until now, Caleb had always thought that small-town grapevines were a bit of an exaggeration.

"What brings you out here?" David asked, his wary expression no doubt stemming from yesterday's ambush in his living room.

Martin grinned. "I saw the sleigh parked over here and thought I'd give you a heads-up."

"A heads-up about what?"

Martin pointed down the hill. Caleb followed the invisible line from the man's glove to a small caravan of vehicles winding down the driveway toward the warming house.

"The tree farm isn't open to visitors until tomorrow," David said, his voice sounding a little strained.

"Oh, we know," Martin said cheerfully. "Those aren't visitors. They're your neighbors." He clapped David on the back. "Esther said you might need a little help."

Chapter Twenty-Nine

"Come with me."

Brynn pressed the sofa pillow against her chest like a shield and snuggled deeper into the cushions. "Are you following me?"

David rolled his eyes. "This is *my* living room."

For three decades, Brynn had created the perfect man every time she sat down at the keyboard. None of them had scars on their chins or crinkles in the corners of their eyes that had settled there permanently, imperfections that made David Mc-Crae more attractive in Brynn's eyes, even when he was sporting an attitude.

Laugh lines sounded sweet and romantic on the page, but now she knew that tears had done some of the carving, too.

Life lines.

That's what Brynn decided to call them from now on.

"I like it here." Patch wiggled closer and rested his chin on Brynn's foot, clearly on her side.

"Really? I couldn't tell."

His dry tone was one of the reasons Brynn liked *him*, too.

David crossed the room and held out his hand. Brynn hesitated, even though the temptation was strong to see if his touch would ignite that little flash of heat again. Remind her she was alive.

"Haven't you read the sign in the lobby?" she complained. "The one that says *Make Yourself at Home*?"

David ignored her. "On your feet."

Brynn half expected him to add *soldier* as she took his hand. He escorted her through the Dutch doors and into the kitchen. Brynn was released, and David grabbed what looked like a bearskin rug off the breakfast island.

"Are you going to smother me with that?"

"It's a coat."

Brynn's nose twitched as David draped it around her shoulders and stuffed her arms into the sleeves. Before she'd adjusted to the weight, she was handed a fleece-lined hat and mittens.

"I thought I was being kicked off your sofa, not the premises."

He gave her a look, and Brynn put them on, more curious than concerned about her upcoming banishment.

"Boots." David pointed to the hand-tooled Miron Crosbys Brynn had left on the mat by the back door the day they'd arrived. "Unless you brought a pair of real ones?"

"These are real." Brynn adjusted the bulk around her middle and bent over to retrieve them. "No one warned me I'd be marching through four feet of snow."

"Five." David waited for her to put the boots on before he opened the side door and ushered her onto the porch.

Brynn grasped the railing and gingerly made her way down the steps.

A full moon had risen above the trees and turned the snow-covered yard to silver. The chill in the air stole the breath from Brynn's lungs and stung her eyes. She'd been content watching the flames dance in the fireplace, but this felt...glorious.

"Where are we going?" Brynn didn't know why she was whispering, but it seemed appropriate since the wind wasn't speaking at the moment, either. David didn't answer, and the only sound was the crunch of their boots against the snow.

Gossamer snowflakes caught in Brynn's eyelashes and melted against her cheeks before she could blot them away with her mitten. She turtled deeper into the coat's fur collar and trudged behind David down the path. A welcoming chuff broke the silence as they neared the barn.

The two draft horses she'd seen standing at the fence during the day were hooked up to the sleigh. Brynn had the boots but zero experience when it came to real-life horses. And since the top of her head barely reached their massive shoulders, she would have maintained a respectful distance if David hadn't urged her closer.

"Hey, Cinni." David fished a carrot from his coat pocket, and the horse delicately lipped it from his bare palm. Because, of course, Mr. Outdoorsman hadn't bothered with a hat, boots or gloves.

Brynn shuffled closer. "Cinni?"

"Short for Cinnamon."

"Hmm. What a surprise." Brynn grinned, and the heaviness in her limbs lifted. She looked at the horse's twin. "Don't tell me. Let me guess. Big Red? Autumn?"

"Lysander." Was that a smile in David's eyes or the reflection of the moonlight? "Grace named him. She played the part of Hermia her junior year." He offered Brynn his hand, and once again his intent was clear. "Up you go."

"David." Brynn straightened her shoulders, a futile attempt to look imposing given the fact David couldn't see them underneath the shaggy black pelt she wore. "I said I wouldn't enjoy a sleigh ride."

For some reason, Brynn's attempt to imitate her mother's lofty tone fell flat when the sky was a velvet dome above their heads and ice crystals winked in the air like hundreds of fireflies.

"I remember what you said. And I'm not buying it. Up."

Brynn could have leveled David with a sassy comeback about bossy backwoodsmen, but she spotted a thermos in the middle of the seat, holding a neat stack of fleece blankets in place like a red-and-white-checked paperweight.

He'd *planned* this in advance. Even though Brynn had been what her mother would have called a *pill* that morning.

"Fine." She stepped onto the running board and somehow managed to maneuver herself and the extra twenty-five pounds of fur and fleece onto the seat without David's help. He hopped up beside her, shook out one of the blankets and draped it over her legs.

He picked up the reins. "Ready?"

"What if I said *no*?"

"Wouldn't matter, and I was talking to the horses." David clicked his tongue, and Lysander tossed his head. The bells on his harness jingled, a perfect accompaniment to the whisper of the wind in the trees.

The horses set out at a brisk clip until they turned into the woods. The path narrowed, and Brynn could have reached out and touched one of the evergreen branches with a mittened hand.

They sat in silence, and Brynn realized the moonlight had stolen her ability to deflect or tease. Now that they were alone, snippets of their brief conversation in the lobby that morning cycled through her mind.

She'd been wrong about the sleigh being bumpy. Brynn could have poured a cup of coffee from the thermos without spilling a drop. She drew in a breath and released it again.

"I'm sorry I was rude."

David eased up on the reins as the team approached a corner, and Brynn sneaked a glance at him. His profile looked like it was etched from granite, his lips set in a firm line.

"David?"

Directed by some unseen cue from the driver, the horses stopped on a ridge overlooking the inn. All Brynn could hear was their breath coming out in puffs of frost and the creak of the leather harnesses. Frost was small, but the lights in the windows created a soft glow in the distance.

"Is it cancer?"

The air emptied from Brynn's lungs and with it a shaky "N-no."

"What, then?"

Brynn swallowed hard. They were really going to do this? Suddenly, she wanted the warm fire and the good-natured banter again. She opened her mouth to tell David the question crossed a line between host and guest but heard herself say "Stress. At least that's what my doctor says."

David turned to look at her now. "What do you say?"

"I'm scared." Brynn couldn't believe she'd admitted that. And to David, of all people. Someone she'd known less than a week.

He waited, letting her decide where the conversation would go from there, and Brynn realized she was tired of holding everything inside. Tired of pretending she was okay.

"I was on my way home from a conference in Connecticut when I got sick. I didn't think anything of it. It was spring, and half the people there had colds.

"I came home, stocked up on tissues and lemon tea and figured it would go away. It didn't. I was so tired I could hardly get out of bed in the morning. Lucy noticed and insisted I see a doctor, who ordered tests and more tests and finally came to the conclusion that my body was telling me I needed to rest."

"Is he right?"

"No. Maybe. Every day I wake up and think, *This is the day you're going to start feeling better.* But it hasn't happened yet. Lucy knows I've been tired, and that it's difficult for me to concentrate, but I haven't been completely honest with her about what's been going on over the last few months."

Lucy, God bless her, had already gone above and beyond her duties, writing the last five chapters of Brynn's novel so she'd been able to make her deadline.

"And you're scared because you don't think it's stress."

"My publisher is waiting for a proposal, readers are asking about my next book and my brain is so fuzzy I can't think about putting words on a page. Writing was always as easy as breathing, and now it...isn't. People are depending on me but right now, life is..."

"A question mark?"

He'd looked at her notebook. "Kidnapping *and* invasion of privacy."

Now David smiled. "This isn't kidnapping. This is a moonlight sleigh ride. And invasion of privacy?" He hiked a brow, reminding Brynn she was guilty of the same offense.

"I don't even remember leaving the notebook in the living room," Brynn admitted. "My memory... I had an episode not too long ago. I forgot an important interview. Conversations are difficult now because I'm afraid I'll forget something important."

"Lucy has been covering for you, hasn't she? Does Caleb know?"

"No." Guilt washed over her again. "He travels for business, and I don't want to worry him until I know what it is I'm dealing with."

"You need to tell him, Brynn."

"It's not that simple."

"Is it ever, when it comes to our kids?"

He'd figured that out, too.

"When... How did you know?"

"I didn't at first. But today, when Caleb saw the plane stashed in one of the outbuildings, he smiled, and I saw you."

"Caleb's mother was diagnosed with cancer when he was a teenager. I can't... I don't want him to worry."

"Mother?" David looked confused. "I thought you were his mom."

"I am."

He slanted a look at her. "More secrets?"

"Says the man who wants to sell this little piece of heaven."

David flinched. "We were talking about you."

Yes, they were. And Brynn still couldn't quite figure out how that had happened.

"He is my son, but I didn't meet Caleb until he was twenty-five years old." Tears burned the backs of Brynn's eyes. "My parents were very strict. After I graduated from high school, I convinced them to let me go abroad for a few months before I went to the college they'd picked out for me. I felt free, independent, for the first time in my life." Without closing her eyes, Brynn could picture her eighteen-year-old self, practically skipping down London's cobblestone streets, staying up until dawn and buying flowers from the outdoor markets. "I met someone while I was sightseeing in London. Clarke was sophisticated and handsome and funny and…married. Which he didn't bother to tell me until I found out I was pregnant."

Brynn tilted her head back, silently traced the handle in the Big Dipper until she found the North Star. "When I got home, I had to tell my parents. They were furious, as you can imagine. They said if I couldn't be trusted to make good decisions, how could I raise a child on my own? I was telling myself the same thing, so adoption seemed like the right thing to do."

"We make the best decisions we can," David murmured, and Brynn knew he was thinking about the inn.

"Caleb is doing so well… He was angry at God when we met, and I don't want to be the reason he doubts His goodness again."

"I think that whatever happens now," David said quietly, carefully, "you'll be the reason that he doesn't."

"You don't know that."

"I know you could have been bitter and angry, too. Someone you trusted took advantage of you. You went through some tough trials, but you write books about love and hope. You believe in second chances. You care about people.

"Maybe you didn't raise Caleb from a baby, but you've influenced the man he's become and that's no small thing, Brynn."

In spite of Brynn's best efforts to hold them back, one rogue tear broke over her lashes and trickled down her cheek.

"I want to tell Caleb everything will be fine."

"You can tell him that whatever happens next, you'll go through it together."

Is that what David had promised Grace when he'd told her Lynette was gone?

Brynn's heart ached for him.

"Christmas is only a week away, and with everything going on, I'll wait until we get back to Nashville."

"About that…" David slanted a look at Brynn. "Why did you agree to be part of the Christmas chaos if you want to keep a low profile? Because I seriously doubt a book tour was what your doctor had in mind when he told you to reduce your stress."

Brynn's lips lifted in a smile. "I've been asking God what to do—and you're going to laugh—but I really think He brought me here. I said *yes* because of Frost."

"You surprise me, Ms. Dixon."

"What about you? Why did you agree to host all the events? Looking to expand your pool of potential buyers?"

David didn't answer right away. And just when Brynn was starting to wonder if she'd offended him, David broke the silence.

"I said *yes* because of you."

"Me?" Brynn echoed.

"I figured there was a reason you camped out in my living room every morning and then disappeared for long periods of time. Frost is small, but they'd have you running all over town. If everything takes place at Spruce Hill Farm, the Queen of

Ceremonies can make an appearance, wave and smile, and sit by her hearth again."

"David McCrae."

A wary "Yes?"

Brynn couldn't tell him how grateful she was. Couldn't tell him that she no longer felt cold. Or alone.

Couldn't tell him that she wished they'd met before her future was so uncertain. Because David stirred up feelings that made Brynn want to hold on to every tomorrow. Hold on to him.

What she could tell him was the truth.

"You surprise me, too."

Chapter Thirty

At one o'clock on Saturday afternoon, a steady stream of cars and pickup trucks funneled through the gate.

Caleb lost count at thirty.

If David had been banking on the fact that everyone in Frost already had their Christmas tree up and decorated, he was in for a shock.

Red ribbons tied around the wooden posts guided visitors down the driveway and into a parking lot that hadn't been there twenty-four hours ago. Only one of the transformations that had taken place after Martin Lowell and a crew of David's neighbors descended on the property.

After yesterday's sleigh ride, Lucy had disappeared inside the warming house with Posey and Esther to set up tables and chairs and stock supplies for the hot-chocolate bar.

Caleb was drafted into service cutting and stacking firewood with Pastor Zach, an easygoing guy not much older than Caleb who seemed to have more energy than the group of teenagers he'd brought along to help. Everyone had worked until dusk, stringing lights across the roofline of the warming house and lining the walkway with ice candles.

This morning there'd been coffee, fresh fruit and boxes of cinnamon rolls from Darlene's bakery on the sideboard along with a Help Yourself note from David, who'd gone out to feed the horses before they were called into active duty again.

And judging from the squeals of excitement Caleb heard as the doors of vehicles popped open and kiddos bundled from head to toe spilled out, the team would be getting a workout today.

Martin was stationed in the lean-to, having been given a brief tutorial on how to run the baler. Caleb hadn't seen Lucy since she'd helped Darlene set out platters of Christmas cookies before gliding off to use her organizational superpowers again.

From his vantage point in the doorway of the building, Caleb watched the parents make a final check to make sure noses, ears and fingers were covered and coats were zipped up tight against the chill.

He remembered his mom doing the same thing when he was a kid.

What was it about Christmas that stirred up so many memories?

And for the first time in a long time, it was the good ones, not the bad, Caleb was remembering.

He had Lucy to thank for that.

"Heads up!"

A split second after the warning shout, a snowball exploded near Caleb's foot.

He looked up and saw a boy about seven or eight standing on top of one of the snowdrifts. Another boy crouched near the corner of the warming house, a small pile of icy missiles at his feet.

Caleb had been caught in the crossfire.

"Sorry!" The stricken look on their faces brought back another memory, too. Only Caleb's had hit its unintended target—the blow-up reindeer in their neighbor's yard.

He waved at the boys and smiled. "No harm, no foul."

Bells jingled, Caleb's signal that the sleigh was returning from the tree plantation with another group. He'd offered to be point person in the warming house, not realizing it was the central hub for people looking for a place to thaw out with a cup of hot chocolate after they found the perfect tree.

He ducked back inside and tossed a few more logs into the woodstove before taking his place behind the counter.

A young woman in her midthirties stepped inside and cast a bright smile at Caleb. At her side was a little girl wearing a purple coat and a sequined beanie topped with a slightly lop-sided unicorn horn instead of a pom-pom.

The girl's mother veered left to examine the mistletoe decorations the Friends of Frost had dropped off earlier that morning while the girl skipped toward the table to peruse the cookie tray.

Caleb smiled.

Priorities.

"Honey?" A young man in a hoodie and jeans poked his head inside the warming house. "Alex was trying to help me with the tree and poked his finger on a branch. Do you have a Band-Aid handy?"

His wife blanched. "He's *bleeding*?"

The guy glanced over his shoulder. "Not too much…"

Even Caleb, who didn't have children of his own, knew a mother needed more information.

The woman set down the wreath she'd been examining and was already digging in the oversize purse slung over her shoulder. She glanced at her daughter, who'd chosen a cookie and perched on one of the folding chairs by the table, before following her husband outside.

"They'll be right back." Caleb gave the little girl a reassuring smile.

She dipped her head shyly, cheeks turning the same shade of pink as the sprinkles on her cookie.

A couple wearing matching ski jackets drifted inside and stepped up to the counter.

"We just chose a Fraser fir, and I'd like one of the wreaths on the display outside, too," the woman said.

Caleb could have done the math in his head, but punching in numbers on the ancient adding machine was a perk of the job as far as he was concerned.

He took the money and gave her the change. "Merry Christmas."

"You, too!" They wandered out the door, hip to hip, giggling like newlyweds.

Caleb glanced over at the little girl, but the folding chair was empty. She'd returned to the buffet table and was reaching for the stack of cups next to the urn of hot chocolate when her elbow bumped the pitcher of cranberry juice.

As if it were happening in slow motion, Caleb watched the pitcher wobble in place before it tipped over. The girl's shriek pierced his eardrums. She jumped back to avoid the liquid flowing over the side of the table, and her boot hit the leg of the folding chair, causing it to slide across the floor. The shrieking increased in volume as the girl lost her balance and sat down hard on her bottom.

Caleb was at her side in an instant. "Hey! It's okay," he crooned. "Accidents happen."

Instead of being comforted, tears streamed from her eyes, and she gestured wildly at the puddle of juice expanding beneath them.

"Don't worry. I'll clean it up—" He tried to take hold of her hands, an awkward attempt to comfort her that backfired spectacularly because the trickle of tears turned into a flood.

"Caleb?"

Suddenly Lucy was there, kneeling beside him. "I'll take care of her while you clean this up."

"Works for me." Given the circumstances, it sounded like the ideal division of labor to Caleb.

He grabbed a roll of paper towel from behind the counter, righted the pitcher and began to wipe up the floor.

Out of the corner of his eye, he saw Lucy help the girl to her feet. The crying and the tears had subsided, but she was still gesturing at the dripping tablecloth.

It took Caleb a moment to realize there was nothing wild about the gestures at all. She was using sign language to communicate.

And not only did Lucy understand what she was saying, her hands and fingers were moving rapidly in response.

"Mia? What happened?" The girl's mother directed the question at Caleb as she burst through the door of the warming house. Her husband was right behind her, a wide-eyed toddler bouncing on his hip.

"Your daughter accidentally bumped the table, but the only casualties were half a pitcher of juice and her snow pants," Caleb said quickly.

"She's fine," Lucy confirmed as the woman hurried over. "I'm Lucy, by the way." She fingerspelled her name and the little girl offered a tremulous smile in return.

"I'm so sorry." The woman wrapped her arm around her daughter's shoulders. "I thought Mia would be fine for a minute or two while I checked on my son."

"The cups were just a wee bit out of reach, and that's my fault," Caleb said.

Mia's mother gave him a grateful look.

By the time Lucy had poured three cups of hot chocolate and handed out cookies, everyone was smiling again.

The horses stopped outside the warming house, and Mia's dad jumped to his feet. When his wife looked at him in alarm, he shrugged and gave Lucy and Caleb a bashful grin.

"Sorry. My parents used to bring me here when I was a kid," Mia's dad told them. "I've been stationed in the Philippines so this is our first Christmas home in quite a few years. I couldn't believe it when I heard the tree farm was open today. Mia and Alex have never ridden in a sleigh."

"I suppose we better get in line, then!" Mia's mother lifted the brown-eyed toddler from her lap and tucked him against her hip. "Thank you for the cookies and hot chocolate—and for looking after Mia."

The little family hustled toward the door before the sleigh filled up, but Mia hung back, her eyes fixed on Caleb, her expression troubled again.

Did she think he was still angry with her for spilling the juice? He knelt down in front of her.

"Merry Christmas, Mia." He said the words slowly.

Mia signed something back, and Caleb looked up at Lucy.

"She wants to stay here." A smile backlit Lucy's eyes. "She says the horses are too big."

"Ah." Caleb nodded. That he understood. "Will you tell her they're friends of mine, and I promise she'll have an awesome time?"

Lucy signed what Caleb had said, but Mia still looked uncertain.

A group of senior women wearing red stocking caps and necklaces with blinking Christmas bulbs around their necks funneled through the door, laughing as they dispersed throughout the room.

Mia's dad rapped on the window and motioned for her to come outside. Her thin shoulders slumped, but she obediently trudged toward the door.

"Can you hold down the fort for twenty minutes or so?" Caleb asked Lucy.

"Twenty… You're going with them?"

Caleb snagged two apples from the fruit bowl, tucked them into his coat pocket. "I have to keep my promise and make sure it's awesome, right? By the time we get back, Mia will be driving the sleigh."

★ ★ ★

Lucy submitted an order for a floral arrangement to be delivered to her parents' house on Christmas Eve—the last thing on her to-do list for the day.

"Darlene just dropped this off and said something about needing it for the bonfire tomorrow."

Okay. So not the last thing.

Lucy set down her phone. She still hadn't gotten used to the happy little skip her heart performed whenever Caleb walked into the room. They hadn't spoken since he'd returned from the sleigh ride—with Brynn in the front seat next to David. At some point during David's loop around the property, he'd picked up Brynn and brought her to the warming house to say hello to the visitors who'd braved the cold to spend an afternoon at Spruce Hill Farm.

Lucy had kept a watchful eye on Brynn, but it hadn't been necessary. She'd mingled with the guests, asking about their favorite traditions. Sipped hot chocolate with the committee members, and purchased a handmade ornament from one of the local artists who'd put up a display in the warming house.

Lucy scooted backward to open up a little more space, and Caleb set the box down on the floor.

"Who is it for?"

"She didn't say." Caleb dropped down beside her and stretched out his long legs. "I make it a personal rule never to open suspicious-looking packages, and now that I've seen what these people can accomplish in a short amount of time, I'm not only suspicious, I'm a little terrified, to be honest."

Lucy slipped her finger underneath the piece of masking tape holding the flaps together, and they popped open. It was only because her younger brothers' antics had made her immune to pranks that Lucy didn't yelp and shove the box away.

Caleb stared at the contents. "Is that…alive?"

"I think it might have been at one time." Lucy reached into

the box and pulled out a fur muff and a matching cape. A deeper dive inside the box revealed a velvet cloche hat trimmed with silk flowers and a man's top hat and wool scarf.

"She wants us to toss this stuff in the fire?"

Lucy elbowed Caleb in the side. "Or wear it while we sing carols."

"You told them the theme was an old-fashioned Christmas, didn't you?"

"Maybe?"

He rubbed his neck. "Did I mention my throat is feeling a little scratchy?"

"That's what the scarf is for." Lucy smiled. "Think of it as a disguise. Trace Hunter would wear one."

"Trace. Right. So I'm supposed to use it as a disguise to hide my superpowers." Caleb plopped the cloche on Lucy's head. "Like you do."

"I don't have superpowers."

"Really?" He drawled the word. "You can cook. Deck the halls with boughs of holly. Oversee an event you didn't know about forty-eight hours ago. Oh, and you just happen to be fluent in sign language, too."

Chapter Thirty-One

Lucy had been wondering if Caleb would bring it up.

When she'd walked into the warming house, Lucy had seen Mia signing *I'm sorry* over and over, but Caleb had inadvertently upset her more by taking hold of her hands.

"My youngest sister is deaf."

"Janie?"

Lucy nodded, surprised—and a little touched—that Caleb had remembered her name.

"From birth?"

"There was an accident…a head injury," Lucy said. "Janie survived, but it was a long recovery."

Not just for her little sister but for Lucy's entire family.

The medical bills began to pile up, and her dad, a truck driver, took on more work and was gone for longer periods of time. Janie was so young, her injuries so severe, it was natural she wanted her mama close by. Lucy kept an eye on her siblings so their mom could be at Janie's side until she came home.

But home wasn't the same. Not for a long time.

"A head injury," Caleb repeated. "Like a concussion? And she lost her hearing?"

An image of her sister's tiny frame swaddled in crisp white sheets flashed in Lucy's mind. Stubble where Janie's dark curls had been shaven off, angry red gashes and metal staples standing out in sharp relief against her pale skin.

"She had a skull fracture, and the bones in her inner ear were damaged. Sometimes after a concussion a person's hearing returns, but in Janie's case, it was…permanent."

The condensed version of the story didn't begin to describe the extent of Janie's injuries, physical and emotional. The curious, talkative little girl whose smile lit up a room had been confined to a bed for months. She couldn't go to school. Play with her friends. Quiet moments and privacy were a thing of the past as an endless flow of people came and went through the front door. Night nurses and therapists. Friends from church who dropped off meals.

Lucy's siblings were older, but they needed a semblance of normalcy, too, so she did her best to keep the household flowing as smoothly as possible. She created spreadsheets of her siblings' extracurricular activities and arranged for rides until she got her driver's license. Did her homework during her lunch period so she could help with theirs in the evenings.

"But she's okay now?" Caleb asked the question almost tentatively.

In her mind's eye, Lucy saw Janie grinning as she shuffled across the stage in her cap and gown, Percy, her service dog, at her side as she accepted her high-school diploma.

"She's…amazing. She's in first year at college now. Elementary education. Even before the accident, she wanted to be a teacher when she grew up."

"How old was she when it happened?"

"Six." So much time had passed, and yet the word still stuck in Lucy's throat.

Janie was the baby of the family, and she'd loved to tag along behind her older siblings, especially Lucy. Their dad drove long-distance and their mom worked full-time at a bookstore, so it was up to Lucy to hold down the fort on the weekends.

On a rare Saturday morning their mom wasn't on the schedule at work, Lucy had made plans to meet some friends at the park. Janie found out and begged to go along. Ordinarily, Lucy would have relented, but she wanted to talk about Isaac and knew that Kristin and Rachel would bribe their little sister with ice cream to get her to repeat everything she'd heard.

It was always hard to say no to Janie. The entire family doted on her. But Lucy ignored the fussing and pouting and told Janie she had to stay home this time.

Right before Lucy hopped on her bike, she saw Janie disappear into the attached garage and assumed she'd finally given up and gone back inside the house.

She was halfway down the block when she heard the squeal of tires.

Lucy glanced over her shoulder and saw a car stopped in the middle of the street. In front of it, upside down, was a pink-and-white bicycle with streamers on the handlebars.

And Janie...

Lucy's heart had felt like it was going to explode in her chest as she spun her bike around and pedaled back.

The next few minutes had unfolded in slow motion. The distraught driver, who swore he hadn't seen Janie until her bicycle had rolled into the street. Neighbors rushing outside. Her mom folding over on herself when she opened the door and saw Lucy kneeling next to Janie. The scream of sirens as first responders arrived at the scene.

Thirteen years had gone by, but the image of her little sister lying motionless next to the curb was permanently etched in Lucy's memory.

Their dad was working out of state at the time, so Lucy had

stayed home with her younger brothers and sisters while their mom rode in the ambulance with Janie and the paramedics.

The news, when it finally came, hadn't been good.

Not only had Janie fractured her pelvis and several ribs, in her haste to catch up to Lucy she hadn't taken the time to secure the chin strap on her helmet. The doctors had put her into a medically induced coma until the swelling on her brain went down.

Three months later, right before Christmas, Janie had opened her eyes. After months in the hospital, she was transferred to a long-term rehab facility. When she'd finally come home, she still needed round-the-clock nursing care as she recovered from her injuries. Milestones she'd reached during the first few years of her life—walking, feeding herself, reading—had to be mastered again. After months of physical therapy, her strength had slowly returned, but some of the damage had been permanent.

With the medical bills adding up, Lucy's dad took on more work so her mom could be there for Janie.

Lucy had been there for everything else.

Six years old.

Caleb mentally did the math. Lucy would have been a teenager at the time of the accident.

As an only child, Caleb couldn't imagine how Lucy had dealt with that kind of trauma.

"I'm so sorry," he murmured, knowing how empty the words sounded. "No one is prepared for something like that."

"I should have been."

Lucy averted her gaze, and Caleb saw the faint tremble in her hands as she slid the hat from her head and set it on her lap.

Was it possible she blamed herself for her sister's accident?

"Lucy...you said it was an accident. And you were a kid, too. There wasn't anything you could have done to prevent it."

She flinched. "Yes, there was. I was going to meet some

friends at the park. Janie asked if she could come along, but I told her no.

"If I hadn't been so selfish, Janie wouldn't have tried to follow me. I was halfway down the block when I heard the tires. I looked back and she…was lying on the side of the street. The driver got out of his car, and he was a wreck. He said Janie didn't stop to look both ways. She was just right there…in front of him. I ran over to her, and I knew she couldn't hear me, but I…I promised her everything would be okay."

Lucy's fingers closed around the heart-shaped pendant Caleb had teased her about when they'd first met, and he called himself all kinds of stupid. Because he'd never thought about *why* it meant so much to her.

"Did Janie give that to you?"

Lucy's gaze dropped to the necklace and a hint of pink crept into her cheeks before she nodded.

"It was a Christmas present. Janie saw it advertised on TV and made our mom order it for me." Lucy turned the necklace over, revealing a tiny hole in the back. "There were two necklaces in the package when it arrived. Janie gave me this heart and kept the chain with the gold key." Lucy smiled now. "I'm sure she lost her half a long time ago, though."

But Lucy hadn't, Caleb realized. She kept it close. Just like the memory of that day. A reminder to be diligent. Prepared.

Perfect.

Because she didn't dare make another mistake.

Oh, yeah. Caleb could relate.

"Janie gave you the necklace after the accident?"

Lucy nodded. "The first Christmas she was home to celebrate with us, I put up a tree in her room and lights in the window. She'd already gone through so much, and I didn't want her to feel left out."

Caleb was sure Lucy had done that and a whole lot more to make that holiday homecoming special. And every single one that came after it. She hadn't gotten cynical or bitter like he had, though.

Shutting yourself off from possibilities...from hope...in order to avoid disappointment doesn't leave a lot of room for joy, either.

Maybe Caleb wasn't trying to avoid disappointment at all. Maybe he was trying not to *be* a disappointment.

Ever since Caleb had pounded on Brynn's door that day, she'd invited him to spend Christmas with her. But he'd always had an excuse. One more flight. One more delivery. One more fire to put out. All in the name of doing good. Proving his worth.

Caleb didn't want to think he'd been running away. Afraid that if he spent time with Brynn she would see his flaws. Decide Caleb wasn't the person she thought he was and walk away, leaving him alone again, like his dad had.

Lucy's life had been turned upside down, but she'd stuck it out. Hadn't lost hope.

Caleb had walked away from everything.

Maybe it was time to find his way back again.

He flipped the top hat in the air and planted it on his head. Because yes, it was easier to be in disguise when he told Lucy the truth.

"I happen to think, milady, you're pretty amazing, too."

Chapter Thirty-Two

Brynn had noticed a strange phenomenon since she'd arrived at Spruce Hill Farm. Every day she woke up to trees dusted in snow and clouds as soft and plump as a goose-down comforter layered against the blue flannel sky, she wanted to add another day. And another.

And maybe another one after that.

And wasn't she just the greedy one? Wanting what she didn't have?

Or is it possible to have both?

What had started as a whisper in Brynn's soul had been getting louder, making it more difficult to ignore.

She leaned back in her chair, watched a column of sparks rise into the air and disappear above the trees and into the night sky.

Over the course of the afternoon, a team of architects in denim and flannel had constructed a tower of logs tall enough to not only illuminate the people gathered around it, but the entire county, too.

"Are you warm enough, Brynn?" Esther whispered.

Between the bonfire, the red velvet cape Darlene had draped

around Brynn's shoulders—borrowed from the high-school drama department—and the blankets tucked around her, if Brynn were any warmer, she'd be in danger of spontaneous combustion.

"I'm good," Brynn whispered back.

Pastor Zach's wife, Rebecca, had enlisted the children's choir to lead the caroling that evening. They were dressed in Victorian costumes, too. Capes and matching muffs for the girls, and cardboard top hats and wool scarves for the boys.

Brynn's gaze lit on Caleb, and she smiled. Darlene had somehow convinced both her son and Lucy to join the chorus, too. Caleb wore his top hat at a rakish angle and had tucked his scarf into the lapels of a long black coat. Lucy looked stylish in a fur cape and a hat embellished with tiny red flowers.

Brynn couldn't help but notice they stood side by side instead of circling each other warily, like boxers in a ring, although they may not have had a choice with the number of people who'd turned out for the bonfire and old-fashioned sing-along.

The only person missing was David, who'd delivered her to the bonfire in the sleigh and then promptly disappeared.

Because the music, the laughter, brought back painful memories?

Or because he'd confessed things on their moonlight sleigh ride that he regretted saying now?

An enthusiastic burst of applause reminded Brynn to turn to the next page in the sheaf of music she'd been given. And although she knew the words to "Silent Night" by heart, tonight, under a dome of stars, she *felt* them.

At the end of the song, Pastor Zach, a young man with kind eyes and a ready smile, rose to his feet and encouraged everyone to give Rebecca's choir another round of applause. When it subsided, he pulled a small leather Bible from his coat pocket.

"If you were in church this morning, you already had to listen to me once today, so don't panic." He grinned at the group of teenagers clustered by the fire. "I'm not going to preach a sermon. I'm going to tell you a story that comes from the book of Luke." He opened the Bible and thumbed through the pages.

"And there were in the same country shepherds abiding in the field, keeping watch over their flocks by night. And lo, the angel of the Lord came upon them, and the glory of the Lord shone around them and they were sore afraid.

"And the angel said unto them, fear not! For behold! I bring you tidings of great joy, which shall be to all people. For unto you is born this day in the city of David a Savior, which is Christ the Lord. And this shall be a sign unto you. Ye shall find the babe wrapped in swaddling clothes, lying in a manger."

Zach tucked the Bible into his pocket again.

"A lot of people think the opposite of fear is courage, but it's not. The opposite of fear is love. There's a passage in scripture that says *'perfect love casteth out fear.'* And because God's love for us is perfect, He doesn't make promises He can't keep.

"We go about our ordinary days, and then something unexpected happens that shakes up our family...our job...our dreams and plans. It's always a choice, though...to fear or to trust. Mary. Joseph. The shepherds. They could have said no. We can, too. But think about what we might miss out on if we let our fears get in the way. We miss out on the miracle.

"Jesus was called Emmanuel, which means *God* with *us*. His very name means we don't have to be afraid. If you ever doubt that, if you ever doubt God's goodness, His love for you, I want you to read this story again. It's not just for Christmas... It's for all of us every single day."

Pastor Zach took his seat again, and the choir sang the opening lines of "Joy to the World," but Brynn couldn't even pretend to sing along.

Fear not.

Esther's quilt. Luke's telling of the Christmas story.

Brynn almost smiled.

I get it, Lord. And whatever happens, I'll trust You for the rest of my story, too.

"Patch." David tracked pieces of white fluff to the stuffed reindeer lying upside down on the rug in front of the fireplace. "You know better."

Patch's head dropped to his paws, but his reproachful look told David he didn't deserve a scolding.

You weren't doing anything with it, those liquid brown eyes seemed to say.

Christmas ornaments didn't exactly qualify as chew toys, but it wasn't like David could disagree.

He scooped up the ornament and assessed the damage. The reindeer had definitely lost weight, and one of its felt antlers looked a little crumpled, but thanks to the generous dollop of glue that Grace had used to secure the red pom-pom, its nose was still intact.

David was about to toss it back into the box with the rest of the ornaments when a movement in the corner of the room caught his eye.

With all the pre-Christmas chaos over the past few days, it had been easy to ignore the tree in the corner of the living room.

But now, warm air flowed through the vent on the floor and the balsam's spindly branches were waving, almost as if it was trying to attract David's attention.

Why is this so difficult, Lord?

The question slipped out before David could stop it, and he wondered if God was as surprised as he was that David had opened the lines of communication again.

Or maybe they'd always been open but David hadn't been inclined to talk. Or listen.

Just like he hadn't been inclined to unpack the box of ornaments yet.

"You're decorating a tree, not deactivating a bomb," David muttered. "You do this every year."

But in past years, he'd had help.

He carried the box of ornaments over to the tree and set it down, wincing when he saw the needles scattered on the floor.

Because yup, he'd forgotten to water it, too.

Lynette had always put up several trees at Christmas, each one decorated with a different theme. The one in the living room belonged to their family alone, the majority of the ornaments works of art created from scraps of fabric, cotton balls, wooden sticks and googly eyes. If someone insisted on giving it a label, David would have called it *Grace through the Years*.

He peeled back layers of tissue paper until a crystal heart appeared, one of only a handful of ornaments purchased from a store.

Our First Christmas Together.

David's throat tightened.

He'd been gone the entire month of December after they were married and wondered if Lynette would resent spending their first Christmas alone. But she'd picked out a tree as spindly as this one and filled in the gaps with lights and tinsel. Hung the heart on the tree until he came home the first week of January.

They'd finished decorating it together, a tradition that had continued even if they were separated for the holiday. While Grace was growing up, she and Lynette had started making ornaments together, and their homemade creations began to outnumber the ones from a store.

David had always looked forward to decorating the tree because it was something they did as a family. And while the past three years had been difficult, he stuck to tradition because he knew how much it meant to his daughter.

It had been difficult enough to trim the family tree when the heart of their family was no longer with them, but David hadn't realized it would be doubly hard without Grace's running commentary.

There were traditions within the tradition. Pajamas were a must. So was a bowl of popcorn—extra butter—hot chocolate and Christmas carols playing in the background.

Grace would sit cross-legged on the floor and carefully remove each ornament from the box. Unwrap the tissue paper slowly, the same way she opened her presents on Christmas morning. Then she would hold the ornament up and study it, a look of wonder on her face as if she were seeing it for the first time.

Remember this one, Daddy? I made it for you when I was in second grade.

I can't believe you haven't thrown this gingerbread man away! It looks like Patch took a bite out of his arm.

Mom loved this little dancing penguin. She said it reminded her of me, but I have no idea why.

Only now, Grace wasn't here. Which was probably why carrying the box of ornaments up from the basement after he'd cut down the tree she'd picked out had required a monumental effort on David's part.

He'd actually been looking forward to a December without guests. A December he didn't have to smile and pretend everything was all right when celebrating felt so wrong.

"Are you going to glare at that poor snowman until it melts, or are you going to hang it on the tree?"

David was no longer surprised when Brynn showed up. Nor was he irritated. After all the times she'd invaded his space, he was getting used to seeing her in his living room.

When he'd dropped her off at the bonfire, she'd been wearing a voluminous cape that covered her petite figure from chin to knees. But in the interim of the caroling and eating a bowl of the chicken soup David had delivered to the dining room, she'd changed into jeans, a flannel shirt that looked suspiciously like the one he'd hung on a hook by the back door, and those ridiculous slippers that looked like cowboy boots. With her auburn curls piled in a loose knot on top of her head, she looked more small-town than big-city.

She looked tired, too, although she hid it well. David had noticed that Lucy made sure Brynn always had a place to sit so people could come to her. Her smile was genuine as she asked questions and listened to the answers, drew laughter whenever she repeated words and phrases in her Tennessee version of a Midwestern accent.

More than once, David had wanted to whisk Brynn back to the inn, pour her a cup of coffee and park her in front of the fireplace in his living room.

"Is there something you needed?"

Defaulting to host to his guest was David's only survival skill at the moment.

Ineffective, too, because Brynn saw right through it.

"Conversation. And don't suggest Lucy and Caleb because I told them I was going to bed early."

"You lied?"

"Of course not." Brynn smiled. "It's only eight o'clock. I've got at least two more hours until it's a lie."

David wasn't going to argue with that logic. "Just out of curiosity, what is it we'll be conversing about? Because I'd have thought you were tired of people talking to you."

"Never. I love your town."

"Frost isn't my town."

"I think you're the only one who believes that."

Brynn sank down on the floor beside him and picked an ornament from the box. "I wondered what you were going to do with these."

"I have to decorate this tree before Grace comes home." David stopped fighting the inevitable and reached for another decoration.

"She doesn't want to help?"

"Grace doesn't think she'll have time, but she asked me to save the star for her."

Brynn picked up an intricate paper snowflake and smoothed down a wrinkle on one of the points. "I loved making these when I was in elementary school, but mine never turned out like this."

"It's all in the wrist."

Brynn chuckled. "You did not make this."

"I certainly did."

She looked so skeptical that David decided he had to prove it. He hoped making paper snowflakes was one of those skills you never forgot. Like riding a bike.

He opened a drawer in the bookshelf and pulled out a pair of scissors and some loose sheets of copy paper. He sank onto the rug and carefully made the cuts. When he opened it, a snowflake emerged.

"Believe me now?"

Brynn scooted closer to see. A ribbon of auburn hair had escaped from the elastic band, but she didn't seem to notice. David breathed in the scent of roses and December snow, a heady combination when coupled with her grin.

"My turn."

Chapter Thirty-Three

Brynn winked one emerald green eye, and David's breath snagged in his throat.

I can't lose anyone else.

And there it was. The reason he'd kept his distance from Brynn since their sleigh ride. The reason he'd put her in Lucy's and Esther's hands during the bonfire and hidden in the warming house.

He'd stepped outside after "Silent Night," the final song in years past. But Martin spotted him and waved when Pastor Zach began to speak, forcing David to linger in the doorway and pretend to listen to a story he'd heard at least a thousand times.

Fear not.

The words had been circling in the back of his mind ever since.

Only David wasn't afraid. He was terrified.

He would have thought his career in the military had prepared him for every possible situation, but the *possibility* there was room in his heart—his life—for love again was something he'd never considered after Lynette died.

"Okay, Nashville." Even to his own ears, David's voice sounded a little uneven. He handed her the scissors. "Let's see what you've got."

Brynn folded the piece of paper into a neat square and eyed it critically before she set to work.

"Don't watch me," she said without looking up. "It makes it hard to concentrate."

David felt the same way.

Brynn caught her lower lip between her teeth, brow furrowed as the scissors sawed through the folds. When she winced, it took every ounce of David's self-control not to snatch them from her hand.

"Done." She handed him the finished product. "You can do the honors."

David separated the folds until a snowflake that resembled a lopsided spiderweb emerged.

"Not bad for a beginner, huh?" Brynn's elbow nudged his ribs.

She made him smile without even trying, and David found that a little terrifying, too. "Not bad," he allowed.

Brynn dipped her hand in the box again and pulled out a pine cone with a beak made from a sunflower seed and little pipe-cleaner feet.

"Is this a chicken?"

David glanced at the ornament. "A cardinal, I think. Lynette and Grace made ornaments together every year, but some of them look a little worse for wear now."

"I love it." Brynn hung it on the tree. Her smile turned pensive. "I wish I'd been able to do things like that with Caleb. I missed out on so much of his life, but I try and remember to look forward, not back."

"Easier said than done."

"But not impossible," Brynn said softly. "It took me a long time to forgive my parents. Myself. I know the memories can be painful, David, but you *have* them, and that's something to be thankful for. None of us know what the future holds. I thought I'd die with a smile on my face and a pen in my hand, but I want to let go of the things I can't control, which is just about everything, really, and find joy in the right now."

Joy.

Another one of those elusive things that seemed to have disappeared from his life after Lynette died.

Brynn had missed out on the first twenty-five years of Caleb's life. Birthdays and holidays. The sweet, ordinary moments like visits to the park and eating an ice-cream cone together on a summer day. And still she wrote stories about hope because, unlike him, Brynn didn't want to dwell on the things she'd lost. She wanted to celebrate the moments she'd been given.

When he and Lynette had met in the café that night, exchanged vows less than a year later, David hadn't known they wouldn't grow old and gray together. But if he had, David wouldn't have walked away. He still would have chosen Lynette.

"Brynn—" David wasn't sure what he'd been about to say, but the doors swung open.

"Hi, Daddy!"

David's head snapped up.

"Grace." David couldn't believe his eyes. But his daughter danced into the room, her backpack shedding snow on the carpet. "What are you doing here?"

"I, um, kind of live here?" She stopped and paused to greet Patch, who was performing figure eights around her feet. "Hey, Patchy," she crooned. "I missed you, too, buddy." She cast a mischievous grin in David's direction.

"What about your final exam on Wednesday?"

"I talked to Ms. Wallace, and she's going to let me take it online." Grace shrugged off her coat. Underneath it she wore a pale blue hoodie with the words *Snow Is My Favorite Season* printed on the front.

"Why didn't you give me a heads-up that you were on your way home?"

"Oh, I don't know." Grace tipped her head. "Maybe for the same reason you didn't tell me that Ms. Dixon was here or about the Countdown to Christmas? Because I didn't want you to worry?"

David sighed. He should have known someone on the committee would spill the beans.

"And it looks like I made the right decision." Grace's gaze bounced from the half-decorated tree to Brynn. "Please tell me that my dad hasn't been putting you to work, Ms. Dixon."

"It's Brynn. And I volunteered." Brynn smiled. "It's nice to finally meet you, Grace."

Patch let out a happy yip and detached himself from Grace's side to greet Lucy and Caleb as they filed through the swinging doors into the living room.

The gang's all here, David thought. But at least their arrival took the attention off Brynn as she slowly rose to her feet.

"Lucy?" Grace covered the distance between them in a single bound and stretched out her hand. "I guess I don't have to email you now!"

Lucy chuckled and shook her hand. "I guess not."

Grace's gaze shifted to Caleb, and her mouth dropped open. "Oh my... *Wow.* You're Trace Hunter!"

Trace Hunter?

Who was that? And why was there a starstruck look in his daughter's eyes when Brynn was the only celebrity in the room?

"Caleb Beauchamp, actually," he said easily.

"Oh." Grace sounded a little disappointed, although David had no idea why.

"Grace just arrived, and I'm sure they have a lot to talk about," Brynn murmured.

Caleb and Lucy took the hint, but David found himself wishing that Brynn would stay a little longer.

"If you need anything else this evening, please let me know." Grace escorted them to the Dutch doors. "Tomorrow morning

I'll be serving crepes with maple crème fraîche, warm cranberry compote and rosemary sausage links before the winter games start."

The sparkle in his daughter's eyes told David that Grace was in full hostess mode already, and she looked so much like Lynette in that moment David's throat closed.

Brynn was right. They did have a lot to talk about.

But for the first time since he'd decided to sell the inn, David wasn't looking forward to the conversation with his daughter.

Chapter Thirty-Four

A persistent hum woke Lucy up before the sun.

She rolled over and almost knocked the lamp over in the quest to locate her phone.

A missed call from Ben.

Lucy dropped the cell between the folds of the down comforter and closed her eyes again.

Too late.

Her brain was already uploading her to-do list.

The winter games started today, and Lucy was almost relieved that Grace McCrae was stepping into her duties again. She hadn't had an opportunity to talk to Brynn all weekend, and with the book signing only five days away, there were a few details that needed to be worked out.

The timeline, for instance. Choosing an excerpt to read out loud. The Q and A with Trace.

Caleb was prepared to answer questions from the readers who attended, but was Brynn? Someone was bound to ask about her current work in progress. What would she say?

Lucy gave up and tossed the covers back. Now that she was wide awake, she might as well use the time to her advantage.

Her wardrobe had been reduced to the one pair of black pants thick enough to keep the chill at bay and a sweater with three-quarter-length sleeves. She pulled it over her head and the fabric caught on the chain of her necklace.

Lucy carefully separated the two, but it wasn't as easy to separate what Caleb had said from the loop of *if onlys* that continued to play in her head.

No matter what Caleb had said, it didn't change the fact she'd said *no* instead of *yes* to Janie that day.

Lucy padded downstairs and slipped into the gathering room, only to find Grace already there, filling a cup from the carafe of coffee on the sideboard.

"Hi, Lucy." Her voice barely broke a whisper. "Dad didn't mention you were an early riser."

"Not quite this early." Thank. You. Ben.

"Cream? Sugar?" Grace picked up another cup.

"Yes."

Grace giggled, added a generous amount of each to the cup and handed it to Lucy. "Dad said you've been making some of the meals since you got here…but breakfast? It's been all right?"

What Grace was really asking was if her dad had been feeding their guests.

Oatmeal counted, right?

"It's been wonderful, Grace." Lucy smiled to put the girl's mind at ease. "Really."

"I still can't believe he didn't tell me your last Mistletoe Stop was canceled." Grace reached for Lucy's cup and topped it up. "I would have come home a lot earlier if I'd known you were here."

Which was why David hadn't said anything to his daughter.

"And the decorations." Grace's gaze swept around the room

and lit on the windowsill. "It looks beautiful. We haven't put the village out...for a few years."

"I hope that's all right," Lucy said quickly. "Caleb and I found it in the basement with the rest of the decorations. We never had one while I was growing up, and I kind of fell in love with it."

But maybe Grace felt more like Caleb. Maybe seeing the lights winking in those tiny buildings, her name painted on the tiny sign over the door of the hot-chocolate shop, triggered painful memories.

"I love it, too," Grace murmured. "Mom added to the collection every year." She drifted over to the coffee table and knelt down until she was eye-to-eye with the caroler figurines. "She called the town Frost, and Dad would laugh and tell her it didn't fit because this town was a lot bigger. We don't have a skating rink, either."

"Um, you will," Lucy said. "Some of your neighbors are getting together this morning to shovel off the pond before the winter games."

"Really? I should add it to the list of activities on our website."

The sparkle in Grace's brown eyes made Lucy's heart sink. She had such big dreams for Spruce Hill Farm. Was David really going to sell?

Lucy carried her cup over to one of the chairs and spotted a copy of *Meet Me under the Mistletoe* on the cushion.

"Oops. That's mine." Grace scooped it up with a bright smile and tucked it behind a pillow. "I'm reading it again, but don't tell my dad. He thinks I should be studying for finals."

"I won't." Lucy sketched a quick X over her chest. "Brynn's books are hard to put down."

"It must be so fun, working for her. Are you a writer, too?"

It wasn't the first time Lucy had been asked that question, but it was the first time she hesitated.

Was tempted to say *yes*.

Fortunately, Grace didn't seem to expect an answer. And the timer beeping on her phone propelled her toward the door.

"That's my reminder to start the crepes!" She tossed a grin over her shoulder. "I don't want my guests to leave a bad review!"

After she left the room, Lucy retrieved Brynn's book and thumbed through the pages until she reached the end.

What's next?

That's what everyone wanted to know.

Paisley and Fletcher had left for their honeymoon, and no one knew what happened to Trace.

Except for…Lucy.

Because suddenly Trace stepped out of the shadows of her imagination and blocked the path of the event planner who'd threatened to call security at Paisley and Fletcher's wedding reception.

"I knew I'd see you again."

"What are you doing here? Is crashing parties you weren't invited to a hobby of yours or something?"

"Ellie—"

"It's Eleanor, and I'm calling security—again. Wait… How do you know my name?"

"Eleanor Rose Brantley. Date of birth April fifth, age thirty-two. Ambassador's daughter. Speaks four languages, three fluently, one would benefit from a little more practice. Dropped out of your Ivy League college a year before you graduated—I'm sure Mom and Dad weren't happy with that decision—and took a job bussing tables at corporate retreats before starting your own event company at the age of twenty-five."

The scene continued to unfold in Lucy's mind. Through a set of French doors, she could see a four-piece orchestra and couples dancing. Eleanor—how it came about the event planner had suddenly acquired a first, middle and last name was a mystery—wore a white blouse with her company logo embroidered on the pocket and slim-legged pants. This time, Trace wasn't wearing a tuxedo, though. Every piece of clothing—jeans, T-shirt and leather jacket—was black.

"A stalker, too, it seems."

"Private investigator. Trace Hunter, if you were wondering."

"I wasn't."

"You asked why I'm here, though. In a room on the third floor of this mansion is a painting that doesn't belong to the people you're working for tonight. It was stolen during World War Two from the family that hired me."

"What am I supposed to do about that?"

"I need your help to steal it back."

"Steal… So you're a party-crasher, a stalker and a thief." Eleanor crossed her arms over her chest and glared at Trace. "I guess it explains what you're wearing, though. Was there a sale at Ninjas-R-Us?"

Lucy had no idea the event planner was so…salty.

"I don't have time for this now," she told the characters. "I have to call Ben back and help with setup for the winter games."

Suddenly, something Brynn had said at a workshop swept through Lucy's mind.

Do you want to know when you're a writer? It's when you don't just write down what your characters are saying to each other, you start having conversations with them, too.

"Lucy?" Grace poked her head around the corner of the door. "A delivery guy just dropped off a package for you."

"Great!" Lucy had ordered extra swag for the signing on Friday night.

Because this is what she did best—she solved problems for real people, not the imaginary ones walking around in her head.

"And don't you forget it," she told Trace.

Lucy scanned the crowd that had steadily grown in number after David opened the gate that afternoon. There were babes in arms, cocooned in blankets, and seniors lined up on makeshift bleachers made from hay bales. Pastor Zach pulled up in a van, and the doors popped open, releasing a dozen teens from his youth group onto the grounds.

The Friends of Frost committee had arrived in a caravan of mismatched vehicles, Esther's half-ton pickup in the lead. There were half a dozen members, men and women, but all of them wore bright red sweatshirts over their coats and lanyards with snowflake-shaped tags that marked them as volunteers.

A piercing whistle cut through the buzz of conversation, and the crowd quieted, looking expectantly at Darlene.

"Good afternoon! The Friends of Frost would like to welcome everyone to our first annual Winter Games! Pastor Zach and his wife, Rebecca, will be supervising the competition for our middle- and high-school students. Elementary kiddos will meet by the skating rink for a scavenger hunt."

After the exodus, Darlene waved her arms in the air to get everyone's attention again.

"On behalf of our guest of honor, the Queen of Storybook Endings herself—" Darlene paused to smile at Brynn, snug in a cocoon of blankets on a chair by the campfire "—I'm going to ask all our single men and women to come forward. The Friends of Frost will be giving away a special prize for the winners today."

Lucy wasn't sure if it was the promise of a prize or simply the thrill of the competition, but suddenly Darlene was surrounded by men and women who abandoned their apple cider and hot chocolate and formed a circle around her.

"Before the Great Mistletoe Matchup event, you'll be dividing into teams of two." Darlene pointed to an old wooden barrel. "All the women will toss one of their mittens or gloves in here.

"When Martin gives the signal…" Darlene glanced at Esther's husband, who dutifully lifted the silver whistle suspended on a chain around his neck for all to see "…the men will choose a glove or mitten from the box and find the woman who has its mate. Once he does, they'll be partners for all the games this afternoon."

Lucy glanced down at Brynn. The lower half of her employer's face was hidden by a scarf, but the shifting of fabric told Lucy she was smiling. And no wonder. The committee had chosen to recreate a scene straight from the pages of Brynn's newest book. Minus Paisley and Fletcher, of course.

Darlene hopped backward as the women surged forward like a group of bridesmaids eager to catch the bouquet and dropped their mittens and gloves into the barrel.

As the container filled, Darlene scanned the crowd, searching for stragglers. Her gaze lit on Brynn again, and she marched across the snow.

It hadn't occurred to Lucy that Darlene might insist Brynn take part in the event. She *was* their guest of honor—and single, too.

"No hiding, now." Darlene stopped in front of Brynn's chair and waggled a finger. "We've got a lot of games planned and only a few hours of daylight left. Let's have that mitten."

Lucy was so busy trying to come up with a reason why Brynn couldn't participate, it took her a moment to realize that Darlene was talking to *her.*

Lucy's hands fisted at her sides. Technically, the mittens weren't hers. They'd come straight from the Lost and Found box, but Lucy had a feeling Darlene didn't care about specifics.

"Darlene…" How to phrase this without admitting that cheering from the sidelines at her siblings' basketball and soccer games didn't exactly qualify as athletic ability? "The winter games are for the community. I wasn't going to participate today."

"You're part of the community." Darlene swept out her arm, encompassing the bustle of activity around the warming house as proof. "And you're single, aren't you? Today you're here to have fun."

But Lucy loved her work. And her idea of fun involved curling up on the sofa with a mystery novel, a pastime best enjoyed indoors, without boots, hats and one mitten, but she could see there was no getting out of it.

"All right." Aware that Darlene was watching, Lucy shuffled up to the barrel. Peeled off a mitten and added it to the colorful assortment that belonged to the women who were looking forward to meeting their mistletoe match.

"All right, gentlemen." Now that the last holdout had complied, Darlene clapped her hands. "Form a line, and when you get to the barrel, close your eyes before you pick. And no peeking! The fun is not knowing who your partner will be. After you choose a mitten or glove, you'll have to find your mistletoe match." Darlene turned toward the cluster of women and made a shooing motion with her hands. "Scatter, girls!"

The women quickly dispersed, but Lucy came up with a better plan.

Hide.

Chapter Thirty-Five

Lucy quickly calculated the distance to the sleigh David had parked between the warming house and skating pond. Fifty yards at the most.

The men were lined up in front of the barrel, waiting to make their selection, and she made a break for it. The snow was deeper than Lucy thought it would be. Kind of like jogging through concrete that hadn't quite set. Snow funneled into her boots, slowing her progress.

When Lucy finally reached the sleigh, she used the spokes of the wheel as a ladder and ended up performing a half roll, half somersault before landing in the space between the seats.

If the Friends of Frost had come up with a winter game that involved creative ways to fall, Lucy was their girl.

For a moment, she lay flat on her back, the sky a pale blue canvas above her. She was panting from exertion, and each breath turned into a little cloud of frost.

Lucy hoped a relay race wasn't on the list.

Her heart continued to thump in her ears, but it didn't drown out the squeals of laughter that mingled with the Christmas music pumping from the speakers in the warming house.

Or the piercing shriek from Martin's whistle, signaling the games had officially begun.

Lucy's fingertips, pink from the cold and extracting the snow from her boots, began to tingle. She wiggled them a few times to get the blood flowing again before shoving her bare hand into her coat pocket.

Was this even a good idea? How long did it take for frostbite to set in?

And how long would it take for her teammate to find her?

As the laughter subsided, Lucy's curiosity began to rise.

Finally, she couldn't stand the suspense anymore. Crawling across the floorboards on her hands and knees, Lucy peeked over the side of the sleigh to see what was going on.

Her view was blocked by the man grinning down at her.

Caleb.

Lucy hadn't seen him standing in the line. Hadn't seen him all morning—not that she'd been looking, of course.

"How did you find me?"

Caleb swung her fluorescent orange mitten back and forth before handing it to her. "Are you kidding? It looked like you were waving a flare when you were running across the yard."

Lucy slipped the mitten on and frowned. She suspected the mittens she'd pulled out of the Lost and Found box hadn't been lost at all. They'd been abandoned on purpose.

Caleb reached out his hand. But instead of helping Lucy out of the sleigh, he grabbed on to the side and, in a graceful movement a man his size shouldn't be capable of achieving, vaulted into the sleigh and sat down on the bench, seasoning the air with the tang of pine and a hint of peppermint.

Lucy slanted a look at him. "I didn't know you were going to participate in the games today."

"That makes two of us."

"Darlene?"

"Posey. I was stacking wood for the bonfire, and she handed me this mitten. Told me to find the woman wearing its mate."

"She *handed* you the mitten? You didn't pull it out of a barrel?"

"A barrel? Nooo. I'm pretty sure she pulled it out of her pocket."

A setup. Paisley's friends had pulled the same stunt in chapter twelve, forcing her to spend time with Fletcher.

"Lucy? What aren't you telling me?"

Caleb's innocent question pricked Lucy's conscience. She couldn't admit it was possible that Esther's friends had taken the whole life imitating art concept to a new level.

But Caleb?

If the women knew the man, they wouldn't have matched him with Lucy.

Caleb was outgoing. Confident. Traveled all over the world.

Lucy's career and family obligations kept her close to home, and she preferred it that way.

What could she possibly bring to the relationship? Unless Caleb needed help booking flights and hotels.

There is no relationship, Lucy reminded herself. After Christmas, Caleb would be flying off to some exotic locale, and Lucy would be back in Nashville, keeping Brynn's life running smoothly while she started her next book.

"Earth to Lucy. Come in, Lucy."

"I'm terrible at this kind of thing." It wasn't the whole truth, but right now, it was the only thing she was willing to admit to.

"What kind of thing?"

"Anything that involves speed. Hand and eye coordination."

Caleb laughed. "I don't believe it. I've seen how fast you type."

"I doubt that's one of the events, but it should tell you everything you need to know about your partner."

Caleb pulled a colorful flyer out of his pocket. "Let's see what we've got here. Broom Ball Blitz. Shovel Shuffle. Reach for the Star. They don't sound too terrible."

Lucy wasn't quite ready to agree. She leaned over and skimmed the list. "Is this a cheat sheet? Where did you get it?"

"Esther was handing them out when people arrived."

Well, that explained why Lucy hadn't been issued a copy. Responding to an email from Ainsley, who wanted an update on the book signing, had her running late.

"Who are Dasher and Dancer?" Lucy pointed to the names scrawled across the top of the page.

"I think we are." Caleb's grin coaxed the dimple out of hiding, and Lucy's breath hitched in her lungs.

"We better get going, then."

"Are you sure?"

Lucy nodded.

Because suddenly, staying here with Caleb seemed a lot more dangerous to her peace of mind than the competition.

Caleb handed Lucy the broom and tried not to smile when she used it to clear a dusting of snow from the ice.

In spite of her claim that she wasn't fast or coordinated, Team Dasher and Dancer had inched into first place. They'd aced the Shovel Shuffle and Reach for the Star. Now they stood together in the center of the skating pond, facing off with the group of teenagers who'd formed a line in front of the net, determined to block Lucy's shots.

"No pressure," he murmured. "I'm sure there's a consolation prize for second place."

"That's your idea of a pep talk?"

No, but he'd made Lucy smile.

It wasn't Caleb's turn yet, but it felt like he'd scored a point.

The orange mittens lay on the ground at Lucy's feet so she could get a better grip on the broomstick.

Martin blew the whistle. While the other competitors hadn't worried about finesse as they smacked the beach balls into the net, Lucy *dribbled* each one toward the net and looked for an opening between the goalies before she took the shot.

And in the sixty seconds of time allotted, over half of the beach balls made it into the net.

Martin tallied up the points and pointed at them. "Dasher and Dancer are still in the lead."

Without thinking, Caleb picked up Lucy and spun her around. "I knew you could do it!"

Laughter shimmered in Lucy's eyes, and all he wanted to do was hold on to the moment. Hold on to her.

Kiss her.

So he did. A quick, light kiss that made Caleb forget where he was. Forget everything but the way Lucy felt in his arms.

"Attention, everyone!"

Darlene's voice echoed around the yard, and Caleb released Lucy immediately. He didn't know whether to apologize or kiss her again, but Darlene was waving everyone over.

"Our final event will be held in the warming house. Grace is in charge of this one, and she's waiting inside to give you directions."

The paired participants trooped through the snow to the warming house, and the blast of warm air from the ancient wood burner was a welcome change from the temperature outside.

"Whoa," Prancer said.

Caleb silently agreed.

In their absence, the outbuilding had been transformed into something that resembled the set of a cooking show. Tables had been arranged in a square in the center of the room, and down the middle of each table were tiny glass bowls filled with every decoration imaginable. Jelly beans. Sprinkles. Edible pearls and miniature doughnuts dusted with sugar.

"I think Grace has the North Pole on speed dial," Lucy whispered as David's daughter took the floor.

"Today you'll be making a gingerbread house," Grace announced. "The gingerbread pieces are precut and baked, but the design, the decorations, are up to each team. You will have one hour from start to finish before Brynn Dixon, our guest judge, chooses a winner."

"We're sunk," Caleb heard Cupid mutter.

"The only rule is that you must complete the gingerbread house together," Darlene added. "This is a team effort, from preliminary sketches to the finished product."

Preliminary sketches? For a gingerbread house?

"Have you ever made a gingerbread house?" Caleb whispered in Lucy's ear.

"One? No." A smile lifted the corners of Lucy's lips, and if they hadn't had an audience, Caleb would have been tempted to kiss her again. "Closer to a dozen, I think."

Caleb had a pretty good feeling about their chances of winning now.

He had a pretty good feeling about a lot of things.

Martin raised the whistle to his lips, caught Esther's eye and said, "Go!" instead.

The teams dispersed to find their tables, but Lucy didn't look panicked. Caleb surveyed the edible construction zone, gingerbread squares stacked neatly beside bowls of white icing, gizmos and gadgets he didn't recognize, and would have happily repeated the Shovel Shuffle.

"What should we build? A castle? Santa's workshop?" Caleb plucked a tiny chocolate bar from one of the bowls and popped it into his mouth.

"Don't eat the shingles!"

"Grace didn't say we can't sample the building materials."

"It's Lucy's rule." She lowered her voice. "And we're going to make a replica of the warming house."

"The warming house?" Caleb repeated. "But…it's kind of plain, isn't it?"

"Trust me." Lucy picked up one of the gingerbread squares. "It won't be when we're done with it."

"Okay." Caleb stripped off his coat. "Let's get to work."

Spectators wandered between the tables to watch the gingerbread houses take shape, but Caleb was too busy to be self-conscious of the attention.

"You have fifteen minutes left!" Grace sang out.

Caleb took a step back and eyed the structure. The walls were in place, connected at the seams with glossy white icing. Lucy was bent over the table, her forehead puckered, molding a tiny pair of pink hiking boots from a Play-Doh-like substance she'd called *marzipan*.

Fifteen minutes was cutting it close, but Caleb felt confident they could finish in time.

He picked up a piping bag—a mysterious tool he hadn't known existed until half an hour ago—and used a dot of icing to secure one of the black jelly beans he'd been using to build the chimney.

A quiet chirp broke through Caleb's concentration, and it took a moment to realize the noise was coming from Lucy's pocket.

She must have realized the same thing, because she began digging through several layers of clothing to get to it.

Caleb leaned over. "Why do you still have your phone?"

When they'd joined the other couples before the first event, Darlene had sent Posey around to collect all the cell phones in a basket for supposed safekeeping.

Caleb had left his cell at the inn, but he remembered seeing Lucy add hers to the mix.

Guilt flashed in Lucy's dark eyes. "I may or may not have dropped my makeup mirror into the basket instead."

To say Caleb was shocked was an understatement.

"You used a *decoy*?"

"Shhh." Lucy cast a furtive look around the room to see if anyone was listening. "I told Boo..." she winced "...I mean

Ben that I'd have my phone with me today. He has to work on Christmas Eve morning, and the jewelry store is closing early so he can't pick up Chloe's engagement ring. I told him I'd see if we could catch an earlier flight out that day."

"You? Isn't there someone else who can pick up the ring?"

"I don't think so."

"Did you ask?"

The confusion in Lucy's eyes gave Caleb his answer even before she shook her head.

The phone, which had lapsed into silence for ten seconds, began to hum. Lucy glanced at the screen and bit her lip.

"It's Ben."

"Ten minutes before the judging begins!"

Caleb looked at their gingerbread warming house. They were getting down to the detail work now, but it was the jelly-bean chimney, the chocolate shingles and the sparkling coconut snow on the walkway that would set their creation apart from the others.

"Go ahead. I'll keep working on the chimney." Caleb picked up another jelly bean while Lucy turned her back on the flurry of activity that Grace's last announcement had triggered.

"Hey, Boo." She covered her ear with one hand to block out the cheers from Comet and Cupid's fan club as the team put the finishing touch on their Victorian house. "What's going on? I'm kind of in the middle of something right now."

Kind of in the middle of something?

Caleb tried to tamp down his frustration as another couple whooped and bumped their fists together. "Lucy? Do you want me to start the sign?" He hated to interrupt, but Lucy was the one with the artistic ability, and she'd told Caleb she had something special planned for the sign on the door.

"Ben? I didn't catch that last part. Ben?" Lucy sighed. "The call dropped. I'll have to go back to the inn."

"Now?" Caleb struggled to hide his disbelief.

"I should call him back, Caleb." Lucy slipped the phone back into her pocket. "He sounded upset. We're so close… You can finish without me."

"We'll be disqualified," Caleb pointed out. "You heard the rules. We're supposed to work together. Your brother is a big boy, Lucy. I'm sure he can wait a few minutes."

Lucy stared at him, a mixture of confusion and hurt in her eyes, like Caleb had suddenly turned on her and joined another team.

"I don't expect you to understand. You do whatever you want to. There's no one depending on you…" Lucy's voice trailed off, but it was too late. Caleb felt the sting.

"You're right. This is just a contest." He forced a smile, but Lucy didn't see it.

She was already halfway to the door.

Chapter Thirty-Six

"I'm never going to complain about sticky armrests at the movie theater again." Esther chuckled and rubbed the small of her back. "I think I'm too old to sit on a hay bale for two hours."

David felt the same way, but at least Brynn's Queen of Ceremonies title meant she always had a comfortable seat for all the activities. Lucy made sure of it, and David was silently grateful for that.

He'd been keeping an eye on Brynn from a distance throughout the evening. She'd sat through *It's a Wonderful Life*, munching her way through the bag of caramel corn Grace had handed out at the entrance to everyone who'd shown up to watch the movie.

And once again, the number of people seemed to double every time they hosted an activity. But this was the last official event before Brynn's book signing, and life would go back to normal again.

If David said it enough times, maybe he would actually begin to believe it.

He crumpled an empty paper sack stained with butter and tossed it into the trash bin.

"I have to say, it was genius to show the movie in here," Esther said. "And the plane... Not your usual Christmas decoration, but it's a very nice touch."

"That was Lucy's idea." But David had a hunch she'd joined forces with Grace. In the whirlwind day sandwiched between the winter games and the movie night, heaters placed in the corners had slowly raised the temperature in the cavernous building to tolerable. The crop duster was wrapped in lights, and the antique grain barrels were filled with evergreen boughs.

The entire inn smelled like butter and vanilla, and David had heard giggling in the kitchen at midnight while the young women filled bags with caramel corn.

He'd barely seen his daughter since she'd come home. At least she was too busy to ask why no one other than Brynn and her entourage had booked rooms for the month of December and beyond.

Guilt scraped against his conscience. After everyone left, he would tell her. Grace was an intelligent young woman. She had to know that even if the Countdown to Christmas celebration became an annual event, it wouldn't change the fact that Spruce Hill Farm was more of a novelty these days than a vacation destination.

Wouldn't change the fact that Grace should be free to pursue her own dreams.

"When do you think this will be finished?" Esther asked. "Because I'm hoping the Friends of Frost can rent this space for the harvest market and craft show next fall."

"Finished?" David repeated. "It is finished."

"Lynette told me that you planned to eventually convert the loft into a private suite where brides could get ready for the ceremony or guests who wanted more privacy could stay instead of the inn."

David knew Lynette had dreamed of fixing up the outbuilding as a venue, but she'd never mentioned anything about a private suite.

"I have no idea if that will happen now," David said truthfully. Decisions like that depended on the new owners.

A cup suddenly sailed past David's nose and bounced off the side of the trash can.

"Oops." Brynn had left her cozy chair by the heater and sneaked up behind him.

"The Queen of Ceremonies isn't supposed to help with cleanup," he told her. "You're supposed to let the common folk take care of that."

"*Many hands make light work.* Isn't that how the saying goes?" Brynn said lightly.

And pride goeth before a fall, David wanted to shoot back.

If he'd learned one thing about Brynn Dixon, though, she had a stubborn streak. She was pretty good at pretending she wasn't in pain, too.

But then, so was he.

Still, David was tempted to scoop Brynn up and carry her back to the inn. Which sounded a little Neanderthal and would probably draw the attention of the committee members who'd volunteered to help that night.

Brynn might have something to say about it, too.

David couldn't help it. He was a protector by nature. It was why he'd joined the military. But he hadn't been able to protect Lynette, and he couldn't protect Brynn from whatever illness was slowly stealing her energy.

Less than two weeks ago, he'd never heard of Brynn Dixon, and now he couldn't imagine walking into his living room and not seeing her curled up on the sofa, the firelight picking out threads of gold in her hair. Hearing her laugh. Putting him in his place.

She'd worked her way past his defenses as effortlessly as sunlight melted the snow in May.

"It was a wonderful evening." Esther picked up another abandoned cup and tossed it into the can. "I think Martin had more fun playing referee at the winter games than the pairs who participated in the events."

Warmth stole into her eyes as she watched her husband grab one of the hay bales and drag it across the floor where it would once again act as insulation instead of seating. "A year ago, he could barely walk from the kitchen to the living room."

David frowned. "I didn't realize it was that bad."

"Neither did I. At least, not at first." Esther winced. "Folks our age tend to complain about achy joints and fatigue, don't you know? Martin doesn't remember getting a tick bite, and by the time they tested for Lyme disease, he was too weak to walk the trails or chop wood for the fire." The memory stole the smile from Esther's eyes. "Once he started on antibiotics, he turned a corner, but it wasn't until a few months ago that I got my Martin back."

Shame washed through David. Esther and Martin were his closest neighbors, and he hadn't known what they were going through. He could have helped Martin with his chores. Stopped in to check on them once in a while. But no. Grief had blinded David to anything else.

Something Lynette, who'd always kept her heart and eyes open to the needs around her, wouldn't have wanted for him.

"Looks like we're done here." Martin trudged up to them. "And just in time... There's a football game starting in ten minutes."

Esther gave her husband an indulgent smile and David a quick hug. "Thank you for hosting tonight."

"Did I have a choice?" he asked dryly.

"You always have a choice." She grinned and turned to Brynn. "I'll see you in a few days!"

David flipped off the lights after the volunteers left the building. Brynn was waiting outside, staring up at the sky.

"It's so quiet here." She drew in a breath and exhaled. "I could get used to this."

So could David.

And there was the heart of the problem.

Brynn had reminded David that he still had one. A little worse for wear, sure, but intact enough to break again if he wasn't careful.

"I'm sure you'd miss civilization." David opened the passenger side door of his truck. "The horses are enjoying their break, so I'm afraid my pickup has to stand in as your carriage tonight."

Brynn lapsed into silence as the truck rumbled down the road toward the inn.

"How are you holding up?" David finally asked.

"I'm still upright." She stifled a yawn. "For now."

Lights glowed from the windows of the inn and painted the snow silver and blue. It reminded David too much of the night he'd taken her on the sleigh ride, so he stepped on the gas a little harder.

"It looks like everyone is still up," Brynn murmured as they pulled up next to the porch.

"Caleb offered to do the barn chores tonight, and Grace said she and Lucy were going to clean up after the tornado that went through the kitchen." David hopped down from the cab and jogged around the front of the truck. He opened the door and extended his hand to Brynn.

"Thank you." Her smile frayed a little at the edges, belying the claim she wasn't tired.

"Your hands are cold," David heard himself say. "If you want to sit by the fire to warm up, I make a pretty decent cup of tea."

"I accept."

There was no sign of Grace or Lucy. The kitchen had been put back in order, the appliances gleaming and the countertops wiped down, no evidence there'd been a pop-up caramel-corn factory the night before except for the faint scent of vanilla that lingered in the air.

"I'll boil the water while you give Patch some attention. He's probably sulking because I wouldn't let him come to the movie."

Brynn disappeared into the living room, and David spent the next five minutes silently berating himself for lying to Brynn.

He hated tea. Hardly made it enough to know whether it was decent or not.

Patch was draped across Brynn's lap when David set the tray down on the coffee table and checked the fire—*stalling*—before he sat down.

Brynn leaned over and sniffed the steam rising from her cup. "What is it?"

David hadn't paid attention. It all looked like grass clippings to him. "Green? What do you usually drink?"

"Coffee." Brynn's mischievous smile arrowed straight through him. A direct hit to the heart. "I don't really like tea."

But she'd accepted his invitation.

David was in so much trouble…

"Daddy."

Grace swept into the room. David took one look at her face and rose to his feet.

"Gracie? Did something happen?"

His daughter barely glanced at Brynn before she stopped in front of the sofa. "A man called the desk a few minutes ago. He said he has time to survey the property next week and asked what day worked best for us." She exhaled a shaky breath. "I told him I had no idea what he was talking about. Do you?"

David remembered the Realtor mentioning a survey but assumed it had been put on hold, along with his signature on the final paperwork.

"Daddy? What's going on?" Grace prodded.

Brynn rose to her feet. "It's been a long day," she murmured. "If you'll excuse me, I'll finish the tea in my room."

David felt a gentle squeeze on his arm before she left the room.

"Grace...I was going to tell you but you were so excited about the Mistletoe tour I decided to wait."

"Tell me what?" She dropped into the chair across from him, her face pale. "What is it? You're scaring me."

"I decided to sell the inn." Before she could say anything, David went on. "It's for the best, Grace. You know it is. Running an inn was your mom's dream, not mine. And now that she's gone, you should be free to live your own life. Pursue your dreams, too."

"The inn *is* my dream." Grace's voice cracked with emotion.

"Think of all the things you'll miss out on. The inn will tie you down. You won't be able to travel, sweetheart. Experience new things."

"I *want* to stay in Frost. It's home. Did you know that Esther sends care packages to my dorm? And every week, Pastor Zach calls and asks how he can pray for me."

David shook his head.

"I'm not keeping Mom's dream alive. The inn *is* my dream."

"Your grandparents want me to buy the condo. It's a good plan, Grace."

She recoiled as if David had physically slapped her.

"It's *your* plan." Grace vaulted to her feet. "You just said I should be free to live my own life, and I want to live it here! The only reason you don't want to stay is because Mom is gone."

"Grace—"

"I can't talk about this right now. And what does it matter, anyway? Nothing I say is going to change your mind. You used to love Spruce Hill Farm, too! I know you did. And selling the inn won't make you stop missing Mom, you know."

Grace headed toward the door that led to their rooms upstairs, and it snapped shut behind her.

David closed his eyes.

Even his eighteen-year-old daughter had figured out what David hadn't wanted to see. It wasn't Spruce Hill Farm he wanted to leave. He was running away from the memories.

Chapter Thirty-Seven

"We have to talk, Lucy."

As usual, Ainsley skipped the preliminary *hello* and got straight down to business.

From the window of the gathering room, Lucy watched the snow continue to fall and coat the driveway David had cleared earlier that morning. She'd been watching the forecast, and the white Christmas the local meteorologist predicted had the potential to wreak havoc with their travel plans again. Lucy hadn't been able to book an earlier flight home. Any delays along the way on land or air would mess up Ben's proposal plans, and Lucy had promised she would be there to help with the final details.

Lucy turned away from the window, but the Victorian gingerbread mansion that had earned a place of honor on the coffee table didn't do anything to even out the spike in her heart rate. She'd been trying to apologize to Caleb since the winter games, but helping Grace with the preparations for the movie night had consumed most of Lucy's time. She'd barely caught a glimpse of Caleb because he'd been busy, too, but Lucy couldn't shake the feeling he was avoiding her. Again.

Or maybe he regretted kissing her...

Lucy hoped not. Because the only thing she regretted was that it hadn't happened again.

"Lucy? Are you still there?"

No. She'd been in Caleb's arms, but Ainsley's question brought her back to reality.

"Everything is coming together for the book signing," Lucy told Ainsley, assuming she'd called for an update. "Grace Mc-Crae is here now, and she has some amazing ideas that go along with the old-fashioned Christmas theme."

"Speaking of amazing ideas...that's the reason I called."

Lucy stifled a groan. Didn't Ainsley have other clients who needed attention?

"Brynn is going to make an announcement at the signing. A special Christmas gift to all of her fans."

"What kind of an announcement?" And why hadn't Brynn mentioned it before now?

"About her next book. And you're going to record it!"

"Ainsley...did Brynn agree to this?"

"Publicist," Ainsley reminded her cheerfully. "She trusts me to make decisions that further her career."

And Lucy had promised to protect it.

"Let me run it past Brynn and see what she thinks," Lucy said carefully. "She might have something else in mind."

Silence. And then, "Is there something you aren't telling me, Lucy?" Ainsley demanded. "I thought we were on the same team, but for the last few months you've been shooting down every suggestion I've made for promoting her new book."

"Of course we're on the same team," Lucy said. "All I'm saying is that Brynn might not be ready to make that announcement yet."

"You'll just have to trust me, too, Lucy, and tell her the timing is perfect. Imagine receiving a cyberpackage wrapped in shiny paper along with a card that says *Don't Open until Christmas Eve*. You're curious and you're excited because it's from your favorite author, and you and your fellow booklovers can't stop talking about what's inside.

"And then on December twenty-fourth, a new link shows up. You tap on the big red bow and see Brynn standing there in her red leather dress and cowboy boots. Then she delivers a special message that will put Trace Hunter's book at the top of your next Christmas wish list."

"Trace isn't going to be the hero, Ainsley."

"If that isn't true, why is he there? I saw a photo of a guy who looks a lot like Trace on Frost's official website."

Dread pooled in Lucy's stomach.

"You *didn't* send the gifts out to them yet..." She paused, waiting for confirmation.

She'd been so caught up in the committee's pre-Christmas festivities she hadn't had time to skim through the message boards for several days.

"The Mistletoe Stop tour was a cute idea, Lucy, but the small-town venues drastically reduced the number of people who would normally attend one of Brynn's events. The mystery gift will make everyone feel like they're getting in on the fun."

"So that's a *yes*?"

"I had to act quickly. Like you said, timing is everything. You record the announcement, send it to me, I'll play Santa and deliver it around the world on Christmas Eve."

What if Brynn didn't have an announcement to make?

"I'll talk to Brynn, but it's up to her."

"Her readers will love the idea, and that's why Brynn will love it, too. I've got another call coming in, but I'll check back with you tomorrow."

Ainsley ended the call, and Lucy immediately went to the virtual coffee shop where Brynn frequently chatted with her fans. She clicked on the personalized coffee cup that welcomed her to the site and winced when a package wrapped in shiny paper popped up. There was the big red bow Ainsley had mentioned and a tag with a message from Brynn.

A special gift from me to you! No peeking until Christmas Eve!

The comment section was so long it would have taken the next two days to read through them all. And the virtual coffee shop was only one place where Brynn's readers met on a regular basis.

Lucy took a lap around the room.

It was a brilliant idea...if Brynn had an announcement to make.

And Trace.

Lucy could tell Ainsley that it was a coincidence she'd seen a man who looked like the PI, but she'd probably demand that Lucy hire him for the meet and greet.

Her cell phone buzzed. A text from Rachel.

Flight comes in half an hour after yours. Can you give me a ride to Mom and Dad's?

"Lucy? Grace asked me to tell you that breakfast is ready."

As Caleb walked into the room, she had a split second of regret that she hadn't taken Ainsley's call upstairs.

"You're pacing." His smile vanished. "What's wrong?"

Lucy shook her head, but a tear traced a crooked path down her cheek, outing her.

"Did something happen with your family?" Caleb crossed the room in two strides and stopped in front of her, close enough for Lucy to rest her forehead against his broad chest.

She took a step backward instead.

"No..." Lucy wished she'd had time to collect her thoughts before Caleb had found her. "They're fine."

"Then, what?"

The genuine concern in his aquamarine eyes was Lucy's undoing.

"This." She lifted her phone and showed him the Christmas present. "Ainsley posted it this morning, and now thousands of Brynn's fans are trying to figure out what's inside."

Caleb's brows dipped together, as if he were trying to figure out why Lucy would be upset about that. "From what I've seen, Mom's put out teasers on social media for all her previous books. She has to know something about the next one. She's been working on it while we've been here, hasn't she?"

If only he hadn't ended with a question.

Caleb's eyes narrowed. "Hasn't she?"

"I can't do this now."

"Yes, you can."

"I don't think so."

"But…all the time she's spent in her room. All the meals she's eaten alone. What has she been doing?"

"Caleb…" Lucy bit her lip. "You should talk to Brynn."

"I've been trying, but she won't talk to *me*." Understanding dawned in his eyes. "You know what's going on, don't you? I sensed something was wrong, but you assured me everything was fine." He pressed down on the last word. "But Mom's not fine, is she?"

"No," Lucy whispered.

He stared at her. "I can't believe this. You're telling me she's…what? Burned-out?" His voice hitched. "Sick?"

"She went to some specialists, but they haven't been able to pinpoint the cause of her symptoms yet."

Specialists?

The word almost took Caleb out at the knees.

The pieces began to fall into place. How had he been so blind? He hadn't questioned the times his mom had retreated to her room. Skipped meals. Encouraged him to help David McCrae.

Turned him over to Lucy for so-called coaching lessons.

Because Lucy had totally covered for her.

"If there's something wrong, why did Mom agree to this book tour?"

"Brynn doesn't want to disappoint anyone, and she always goes on tour after a new release. I came up with the Mistletoe Stops to keep the venues small. The doctor told Brynn to cut back on her commitments, and fewer demands meant more time to rest and get her energy back."

No wonder Lucy had reacted the way she did when he'd shown up at the hotel that morning.

"It hasn't happened, though, has it? Your plan didn't work."

Lucy shook her head.

"You claim to be looking out for her best interests, but it didn't occur to you that the best place for her would be in Nashville? Close to her doctors? A hospital? Instead of towns with no zip codes?"

Lucy flinched, and Caleb realized he wasn't being completely fair. His mom might look as delicate as wisteria, but she could be just as stubborn, too.

If Brynn wanted to keep her health issues a secret, it meant sticking to her normal routine as much as possible.

"I have been looking out for her! I've been running interference with Ainsley for months, and now everyone loves Trace Hunter, and things are even more complicated."

"Trace?" Caleb didn't follow. "What does he have to do with any of this?"

"He...he's my character."

"Your idea, you mean?"

Lucy didn't answer, and another piece clicked into place. Caleb had thought it strange his mom had let Lucy read her manuscripts before she sent them to her editor. Now he remembered she'd dodged his question about that, too.

"Lucy?"

"Brynn...she was having a hard time concentrating and asked me to finish the last five chapters of the book."

"You're a writer?"

"N-no."

"That didn't sound very convincing. Is that why you took the job as her assistant? You were hoping it would give you an in with her publisher?"

Lucy recoiled. "I can't believe you'd even think that!"

"And I can't believe you kept this a secret."

"I promised Brynn I wouldn't tell anyone."

"I'm her *son*."

"And I didn't know you existed! In the past three years since I started working for Brynn, we'd never even met. She never mentioned you. Your last name is different from hers, and I thought..."

"You thought what?"

"That you were taking advantage of her. All the traveling. The...checks."

"Wow." Caleb breathed the word. "Mom hired me to run the nonprofit she started a few years ago."

"But...I don't know anything about a nonprofit."

"Neither does anyone else. That's the way she wants it. My mom is a generous person, and putting books in the hands of as many children as she can is her way of giving back. Her name isn't attached to Words with Wings so no one can accuse her of using it as a marketing tool. She wants God to get the glory.

"I stop at major hubs and do paperwork, check in with my contacts in other countries. Depending on where the books are going, sometimes I have to rent a plane and fly them in myself."

"Fly?"

"I'm a pilot."

Under different circumstances, Caleb would have been amused by the stunned look on Lucy's face.

"You never told me what you did for a living."

"So you assumed I was a freeloader and then, after Brynn introduced us, a deadbeat son?"

Caleb knew he wasn't being fair. In the beginning, he hadn't trusted Lucy, either.

But that didn't mean she was off the hook.

Promise or not, Lucy had known there was something seriously wrong with Brynn and kept it to herself.

Turns out that some of his suspicions about Lucy were right. He *had* been played.

"I thought I was doing the right thing," Lucy murmured.

"See? That's the trouble. You always think you have to do something. You blame yourself for Janie's accident, and you've been trying to make up for it ever since. But the people who love you will understand if you make a mistake or can't drop everything to answer a phone call once in a while.

"Has it ever occurred to you that maybe you aren't supposed to fix everything, Lucy? That maybe God has something else in mind, and things are *supposed* to change? That maybe the best thing to do sometimes is get out of His way?"

She looked so stricken that Caleb wanted to pull her into his arms, but fear for Brynn stoked his anger.

He'd already lost one mom. Caleb didn't know what he'd do if he lost Brynn, too.

"I'm so sorry, Caleb."

He pivoted away from her.

"So am I."

Chapter Thirty-Eight

Brynn heard a quiet tap on the door and reluctantly set her notebook and pen aside.

From the time Grace had confronted David until well after midnight, Brynn had stared out her bedroom window, praying for David and Grace before she'd finally fallen asleep. And then inspiration had struck at 4:00 a.m., and she'd been jotting down notes for several hours, missing her first cup of coffee in front of the fireplace and whatever delicious breakfast Grace had served in the dining room.

The brain fog had dissipated slightly, chased away by the thoughts whirling through Brynn's mind, and she didn't want to stop—not yet—but she'd also received a text from Ainsley, telling her to check her email, and knew Lucy must have seen the unexpected gift sent out to Brynn's readers, too.

"It's open."

The knob turned, but it was Caleb, not Lucy, who stepped into the room.

"Good morning!" Brynn wished she'd taken the time to get dressed and do something with her hair, but with a fleece blanket tucked around her, maybe Caleb wouldn't notice she was still in her robe. "It looks like we'll be staying inside today. Every time I look out the window, I feel like I'm living inside a snow globe."

Caleb didn't even glance at the window.

"Why didn't you tell me?"

The sheen in his eyes, the tightness of his jaw, stripped the breath from Brynn's lungs.

He knew.

"Caleb." She motioned at the empty chair by the window. "Please. Sit down."

He didn't. He was only three feet away, and Brynn already felt the chasm between them.

Please, God. Give me the right words to say.

"I didn't want you to worry until I knew what I was dealing with. What you went through with your mom…" Brynn swallowed, but the lump that had formed in her throat didn't budge. "I didn't want to put you through it again."

"I'm not a kid anymore, Brynn."

Brynn. Caleb was always careful to call her by name in public, but more often than not now, she was *Mom* when they were alone. A title that stirred a sense of wonder and gratitude inside of Brynn. But now he was angry, the very thing she'd been trying to prevent by keeping a secret from him.

She remembered the expression on Grace's face when she'd confronted David about the phone call and realized both she and David had made the same mistake. They'd let fear guide their decisions.

"I know you aren't," Brynn said softly. "But I wanted to believe it was stress and if I just got some extra rest, the symptoms would go away."

Caleb sank onto the edge of the bed. "But they're getting worse, aren't they?" His eyes dared her to deny it.

"Yes. I'll be undergoing more tests when I get back."

Caleb's jaw worked as he struggled to keep his emotions in

check. "Lucy shouldn't have encouraged you to do this book tour."

"She's done everything she can, short of sending me to a deserted island to lighten my schedule."

"Like finishing your book?"

Brynn had suspected Lucy was the one who'd told Caleb about the recent struggles with her health, but his question confirmed it.

"She only did it because I asked her to—and I don't regret that." Brynn managed a tremulous smile. "What I regret is not being honest with you. When you showed up at the hotel, I was scared you'd figure it out. I pretended I was writing so you wouldn't get suspicious."

Caleb's lips twisted. "I was already suspicious. That's why I came back. Whenever I called, you always found a reason to cut our conversation short. You didn't return my texts right away. I was concerned, and Mel encouraged me to take some time off and come home. See if my theory was right."

"Theory?"

"I thought Lucy was manipulative. Trying to control your career."

Brynn would have laughed if Caleb hadn't looked so serious.

"Lucy was protecting it. And me. Don't be angry with her, Caleb." Brynn met his eyes. "She's a loyal friend, and I made her promise she wouldn't tell anyone what was going on. I'm glad she confided in you, though. I should have trusted you, too."

Caleb raked his hand through his hair.

"Lucy didn't confide in me." She hadn't trusted him, either. "She was upset, and the truth slipped out."

"Oh." Brynn's brow furrowed. "At the winter games, I thought you and Lucy..."

His mom didn't have to finish the sentence. Caleb knew what she meant because he'd thought the same thing.

His stomach knotted.

Lucy had looked devastated when Caleb told her that it wasn't her job to fix everything.

But it was true.

Lucy *did* blame herself for Janie's accident. Her parents and her siblings had relied on her to keep things running smoothly while Janie recovered, but somewhere along the line, Lucy started to believe their love for her was dependent on what she did for them, not because of who she was. The older sister they all adored.

And Caleb had been doing the same thing. If Brynn's nonprofit were a success, if she were happy with the results, then she'd be happy with him.

It was his turn to be honest now.

"I had another theory," Caleb admitted. "I thought you regretted putting me in charge of Words. I'm a newbie, and I'm still trying to figure things out. I was afraid I was messing up and you were disappointed in me."

That it was only a matter of time before she decided to walk away when he didn't live up to her expectations.

Like his dad's.

Brynn rose to her feet and the blanket puddled on the floor. She took two steps forward, and Caleb thought she was going to hug him. She poked her finger at his chest instead.

"You're my *son*, Caleb. You don't have to earn my love. I've loved you from the moment I found out I was carrying you, and nothing is going to change that."

Now she hugged him.

"I've only been a mom for seven years," she whispered. "I'm still a newbie, too. From now on, no matter what happens, let's promise each other that we'll figure things out together."

Caleb's arms tightened around her.

No matter what happens.

"I promise."

That was one he could keep.

★ ★ ★

"Lucy? I just got a call from the leader of the Lattes and Lit book club in Jackson Lake. They're concerned about the storm and might not be able to make it to Ms. Dixon's book signing tomorrow night."

Grace was looking expectantly at Lucy, waiting for her to come up with a plan to make sure the storm that the local news anchor claimed would have the dubious distinction of being the first blizzard of the season wouldn't ruin all their plans.

But Lucy had…nothing.

Well, that wasn't quite true. What Lucy had was Caleb's voice in her head, telling her that it wasn't her job to fix everything.

Has it ever occurred to you that things are supposed *to change?*

The words had cut deep because if anyone knew about change, it was Lucy.

And she'd been trying to reduce the collateral damage with calendars and schedules, lists and notes, ever since.

"Whatever happens, it'll be okay, Grace," Lucy heard herself say.

Now, if only she could convince herself of that, too. Because she still hadn't talked to Brynn. And Caleb? Lucy doubted if he'd ever speak to her again.

He'd been angry with her. But it was the hurt in his eyes that had cut Lucy to the core.

Every moment she'd spent in Caleb's company since they'd arrived at Spruce Hill Farm had revealed his character. Yes, he was charming. Confident. Better-looking than a mere mortal had the right to be. But he was also funny. And kind. Lucy had accused Caleb of being a Scrooge, but that hadn't stopped him from pitching in to help with all the activities the Friends of Frost had planned. To accompany a child on a sleigh ride because she was afraid of the horses.

Lucy had seen Caleb's face light up at the sight of that old plane. When he'd climbed into the cockpit and settled in as if it were something he'd done a hundred times, she hadn't let herself wonder why.

Assuming Caleb had made a lucrative career out of being Brynn Dixon's son was easier to believe because it had given Lucy a reason to keep him at a distance. A way to protect herself and the way Caleb made her feel.

Because he *saw* her. The girl who liked being invisible. The girl who liked taking care of people but never asked for help because she had to be strong.

Didn't want to disappoint the people she loved or let them down.

"I don't expect you to understand," Lucy had told Caleb. "There's no one depending on you."

Knowing what she knew now, Lucy was surprised Caleb hadn't dumped her headfirst into the nearest snowbank. Instead, he'd let her bail on the competition so she could call her brother. Whose emergency, as it turned out, was a question about the flowers she'd ordered.

Some Nancy Drew she'd turned out to be. When it came to the really important things, Lucy had missed all the clues along the way.

"Our road is one of the last ones the county snowplows clear," Grace murmured. "If we get a lot of snow or ice, I wouldn't want anyone to risk it."

The undercurrent of sadness in Grace's voice tugged at Lucy. They'd spent a lot of time together over the course of the week, and the college student's sunny personality coaxed a smile from everyone she met.

Lucy looked more closely at Grace and noticed the droop in her slim shoulders. The sparkle in her brown eyes that had hardened to a diamond-bright sheen.

She didn't want Grace to think the success or failure of the event depended on her.

According to Caleb, Lucy had dibs on that.

"Hey, it'll be great. If there are fewer guests, it means there will be more of your delicious sugar cookies and maple fudge to go around."

Grace returned Lucy's smile with a half-hearted one of her own.

"I'll put a fresh pot of coffee on in case Ms. Dixon comes down." Grace swept the dirty dishes onto a tray and scuttled out of the dining room.

Lucy's cell buzzed, and her heart plummeted to her feet when she read a text from Brynn.

Do you have a minute?

A minute to apologize for breaking a confidence?

A minute before Lucy started looking for a new job?

There was no sign of Caleb when she walked through the lobby and hiked the stairs to the second floor.

Brynn didn't wait for Lucy to knock. She was standing in the hallway outside her room.

"Brynn—"

Brynn shook her head and waited for Lucy to enter her room before closing the door.

"There isn't much room, but I thought we'd have more privacy here," Brynn said.

A minute before Lucy started looking for another job, then.

"I'm so sorry, Brynn. I was upset, and I let my guard down, and Caleb is just so…*smart*…and he started asking questions, and I told him everything. I broke your trust, and I—I don't blame you for letting me go."

"Letting you go?" Brynn actually laughed. "I asked you to come up here so I could thank you, Lucy."

Thank her?

"Why? You asked me to keep a secret—"

"And that was another mistake," Brynn interrupted. "Not

telling Caleb was the first one I made. I'm glad you told him, Lucy. My son and I had the first honest conversation since the day we met. It seems both of us have been keeping secrets."

"He told you about Shae?"

Brynn looked confused and... Oh no. Caleb *hadn't* told her about Shae.

She'd done it again, and now Caleb would have another reason to be angry with her.

Brynn held up her hand. "Don't worry. I won't ask." She leaned forward. "But I will ask why you were so upset that Caleb was able to figure it out."

"I put you in a terrible position," Lucy admitted. "I should never have encouraged you to go on this book tour." Caleb had been right. Brynn should be closer to her doctor. A hospital. "Ainsley orchestrated this big announcement, and I didn't know women were going to fall for Trace Hunter."

Or that she would fall for Caleb.

"There's a snowstorm coming, and Frost might be in its path," Lucy rambled on. "If the roads are bad, people won't venture out for the book signing."

"You're suggesting we cancel it?" Brynn asked slowly.

Lucy hadn't suggested it. But now that Brynn had brought it up...

"It might be the wise thing to do."

Wise? Or safe?

Lucy ignored her inner voice. She was beginning to think she didn't know the difference anymore.

"If we decide to cancel, we can leave today after lunch, before the storm hits. There's an evening flight out of Madison. I can change our tickets, and we'd be back in Nashville by midnight.

"I know all the activities this week were hard on you. People are used to adjusting their plans during the winter, and a storm is a legitimate reason to cancel the event."

And Lucy wouldn't have to worry about announcements or Trace Hunter or the fact she'd made a huge mistake about Caleb. In spite of what Caleb had said about the people who cared about her understanding when she made a mistake, Lucy wasn't sure he would forgive or forget the one she'd made with him.

Brynn was silent for a moment.

"If I leave today, I'd be letting fear win, and I'm not going to do that anymore," Brynn finally admitted. "Like Pastor Zach said, I don't want to miss out on what God's going to do next."

You could watch Him at work from your comfortable patio in Nashville, too, Lucy wanted to protest.

"But that doesn't mean you have to stay here," Brynn continued. "If you want to catch a flight home this evening, you have my blessing, Lucy. Your family is expecting you for Christmas, and I don't want to do anything to jeopardize your plans."

It was a good thing Lucy was sitting down or she would have fallen off the chair.

"I can't just *leave* you here. What about the meet and greet with Trace? The announcement?"

"Grace is here to help." Brynn's eyes twinkled. "And the announcement? I'm not sure yet. By tomorrow night, maybe I'll have something to say."

Maybe?

Lucy doubted that would satisfy Ainsley. Or the thousands of fans waiting for news about Brynn's next book.

"The storm... You could get stranded here over Christmas."

"One last secret?" Brynn put a finger to her lips, but it didn't quite cover her grin. "I couldn't think of a better gift."

Chapter Thirty-Nine

David hadn't gotten the silent treatment from Grace since she was thirteen years old, when he'd accidentally cut a slice from the pie she'd planned to enter in the county fair. It had taken a double scoop of mint chocolate chip to smooth things out again.

Unfortunately, ice cream wasn't going to cut it this time.

Out of the corner of his eye, David watched Grace sprinkle brown sugar into the pot on the stove. She wore Lynette's denim apron with the cardinal embroidered on the pocket, a gift from Esther the first Christmas they'd moved into the house.

This was when David missed his wife the most. Parenting had been a team effort, and Lynette always seemed to know what Grace needed.

David had tried to guess and messed up big-time.

He lifted a corner of the flour-sack dish towel draped over a ceramic bowl on the counter. The scent of yeast rose into the air, a familiar aroma that reminded David of laughter and leisurely Saturday mornings.

"You found the recipe for Mom's Christmas bread?"

What started out as an accident when Lynette had accidentally mixed up the ingredients for fruitcake and her almond tea rings had become a family favorite. David and Grace had looked through every one of Lynette's files, hoping she'd written it down but eventually conceded defeat. At least David had. Grace must have continued the search on her own.

The sweet little girl David had rocked in his arms, carried on his shoulders and sat across the table from while she conquered algebra barely spared him a glance. "I decided to try it from memory."

Unlike her father, who'd been trying to shut them down.

David wasn't always great at reading between the lines, but Grace's meaning was clear. At least she was talking to him, though.

"Even if it doesn't taste exactly like Mom's, I'm sure it will be delicious."

"It's for the guests."

"Grace." David sighed. "We have to talk about this."

"Why? You already made up your mind." She whirled around to face him. "It isn't an inn you're selling, Dad. It's our *home*. We made memories here, even after Mom died. Or do you want to forget those, too?"

Insert knife. Twist.

"Grace, please. You know I don't."

"I don't think I know you at all. And you must not know me, either, or you wouldn't have done this."

A melodic ding punctuated Grace's passionate statement.

It took David a moment to realize someone had rung the bell on the desk in the lobby. He hadn't heard the front door open, but then again, David hadn't been listening to anything but Grace and his conscience chewing him out.

David was about to tell Grace he'd see who it was, but she didn't give him the opportunity. He followed her into the lobby and saw Brynn standing at the counter, beautiful as always in ankle-length pants and the plaid flannel she'd claimed as her own.

Did Brynn think he was a first-class jerk for not telling Grace his plans sooner? Or did she understand because she'd kept a secret from her child, too?

It was impossible to tell from Brynn's expression.

"Ms. Dixon. I'm so sorry, I didn't realize you were out here." Grace glided forward. "What can I do for you?"

"I was wondering if I could speak with y'all for a few minutes."

"Of course." Grace had composed herself more quickly than David. "Would you prefer the library? Or the office?"

Brynn smiled. "If there's a fire going in the living room, I'd rather go there."

The three of them trooped through the kitchen into the living room, Grace in the lead. David paused to toss another log on the fire and realized Brynn had claimed the recliner, forcing Grace to share the couch with him in an awkward truce.

He wondered if she'd done it on purpose.

Grace broke the silence. "If you're worried about the snowstorm, Ms. Dixon, there's a good chance it will shift farther north. That happens a lot around here."

"I'm not worried about the snow," Brynn said. "Or the event. I can see how hard you've been working."

Brynn accomplished what David hadn't been able to do. Put the sparkle back in Grace's eyes.

"I have a little more shopping to do this morning, but most of the food is prepared. The number of guests who plan to attend has been rising since the Countdown to Christmas, so I'm going to set up a round-robin in the library, gathering room and dining area so people won't feel crowded. There will be heavy appetizers, a chocolate fondue and an assortment of traditional cookies and candy. If we need extra room, I'll set up the beverage station in the lobby."

Two thoughts swept through David's mind. One, his baby

girl actually looked excited about another ten-hour day in the kitchen; and two, he hoped she'd put as much time into her finals as she had the preparations for Brynn's book-signing event.

"That sounds absolutely perfect, Grace."

His daughter beamed. "If you can think of anything I missed, let me know."

"There is one more thing." Brynn's smile warned David the *one more thing* had been the reason she'd called this impromptu meeting to order in the first place.

"Sure!" Grace, who didn't know Brynn as well as David, leaned forward, an eager look on her face.

"At the first two Mistletoe Stop events, the people who entered the contest shared their winning essays. I was wondering if you'd be willing to read yours tomorrow night."

Grace sat back. Blinked. "Out loud?"

Brynn pressed her lips together to keep the smile from expanding. "Out loud."

"I don't know." Grace didn't appear quite so confident now. "I'm not good at public speaking, Ms. Dixon. And I'll be busy in the kitchen," she added quickly.

"Promise you'll think about it," Brynn urged before turning toward David. "We weren't planning to venture this far north, but Grace's description of Frost was the reason Lucy added it to the tour. Grace might claim she's not good at public speaking, but she's a wonderful writer, isn't she?"

"I haven't read it," David admitted. He glanced at Grace, but her gaze dropped to the floor.

Brynn pulled out her phone. "Lucy sent me a copy if you'd like to read it."

Grace vaulted to her feet. "I have to check on something in the kitchen."

She disappeared through the Dutch doors but not fast enough to hide the tears that flooded her eyes.

"Brynn, maybe this should wait…"

"I don't think so." She handed him the phone. "You need to read this, David."

Why? So he would feel worse about selling the inn than he already did?

"Please."

A sigh slipped out before David could prevent it, and he nodded.

Why Frost Should Be a Mistletoe Stop
Hi! My name is Grace McCrae. I love Brynn Dixon's books, but that's not the reason I think Frost should be included on her Mistletoe Stop tour. A lot of people think their hometown is special, but mine really is.

I know it's not perfect. Nothing is. But I love that people know my name and wave when I'm walking down the street. Everyone who lives here is family. We take care of each other. Some people want to travel the world and experience new things, but every time I look out my window, there's something different. I see the change of seasons. I hear a quiet so loud it wakes me up at night.

Frost is my retreat. My haven. My inspiration. It's home.

The lines blurred when David read what Grace had said about Lynette's legacy. He blinked several times until they came into focus again.

My dad likes to work outside, and I like to be in the kitchen, so we make a great team. I love making guests feel like part of the family, and if Brynn chooses to come to Frost, she'll become part of our family, too. We'll feed her and give her hot chocolate and cozy blankets and snow, because everyone should have snow for Christmas. And if she doesn't want to leave, I guess we'll have an author-in-residence ☺
Merry Christmas and Happily-Ever-After!
Grace McCrae

David closed his eyes. Felt Brynn's presence before she sat down next to him.

"Don't you know a man prefers to be alone when he gets emotional?"

"There's nothing wrong with emotions," Brynn countered softly. "They're a gift, David, not part of the curse."

Brynn was a gift, too. One he hadn't expected and certainly didn't deserve.

Two weeks ago, David had tried to convince Brynn Dixon to cancel her reservation. Now he couldn't imagine her leaving.

"Your daughter's heart is in that essay, David," Brynn said softly.

"Grace is only eighteen. She has her whole life ahead of her."

"Did you see your whole life at eighteen? Maybe the most important thing is to stay in step with God, moment by moment. Trust that no matter what happens tomorrow, we *lived* today."

David felt himself getting emotional again.

The doors opened, and Grace came back, carrying a tray with the sterling-silver carafe and china cups Lynette had used on special occasions. A typical teenager might have retreated to her room, but Grace had not only returned, she'd brewed a fresh pot of coffee to share.

Lynette, you'd be so proud of her.

David was proud of her.

He rose to his feet as she set the tray down on the table.

"Grace…I'm sorry for the way I handled this. You're an adult, and I was wrong not to include you in this decision."

Hope glowed in her eyes. "You changed your mind about selling?"

"I don't know." David couldn't lie. "You have three years of college left, and I don't want to run the inn anymore, Grace. You were right about me. I'm not a people person. I'd rather be pounding nails or outside splitting wood than making small talk with the guests."

"Daddy—"

"I'm glad you said that, David," Brynn interjected. She pointed to the sofa. "Now, both of you sit down, please."

There was no missing the hint of steel in the usually dulcet voice. They sat.

David's eyes narrowed. "Is this an intervention?"

"I would call it a…proposal." Brynn took a sip of coffee. "Grace, you aren't just a phenomenal hostess, you have the gift of hospitality, and that's what makes the difference. You welcome people into your home, make them feel special, cared for, because it's who you *are*, not what you do. Everyone needs a place to retreat. A haven." She smiled. "Inspiration."

She turned to David. "You love to be outdoors and find satisfaction in working with your hands. You enjoy being the caretaker and running the tree farm."

He opened his mouth to deny it, but both Brynn and Grace gave him a look, and he closed it again. He'd forgotten how much he'd enjoyed taking families out in the sleigh. Seeing the wonder on their faces as they absorbed the beauty around them.

"It's the way God designed you, too," Brynn said. "Being an introvert isn't a character flaw. I don't think you really want to leave Spruce Hill Farm." Their eyes met, and David saw the warmth, not judgment, in the emerald green depths. "You just don't want to run an inn."

But Grace did.

"You have a solution?" he asked.

A smile kindled in Brynn's eyes.

"Separate the two."

"Separate?" David repeated cautiously. "What do you mean?"

"Only take reservations during the summers when Grace is home from college…and maybe the month of December, because she's right about the Christmas snow. You'll be the caretaker the rest of the time, and after Grace graduates, you both can decide where to go from there."

David slanted a look at his daughter. Her shining eyes told him that she was already on board with Brynn's plan.

And then she frowned. "But Dad will still have to share the house with the guests in the summer."

"No, he won't. Your father will be living in the very comfortable apartment he's going to build above the event barn."

And Brynn claimed her brain was foggy.

As far as compromises went, her idea wasn't half bad, though.

The landline in the lobby began to ring, and Grace winced. "I'll get it."

"Wow," David murmured after she practically skipped out of the room. "You could have warned me."

"What do you think?" Brynn looked a little apprehensive now, and he laughed.

"You're asking me that now? You just sentenced me to a year of hard labor, because that's how long it'll take to get my *comfortable apartment above the event barn* livable."

"You're already looking forward to it."

It was a little scary how well she knew him.

"From a business aspect, I'm not sure the inn will be able to support itself if we're only open in the summer," David said slowly. "Frost holds seasonal events, but the tourists tend to bypass us and go farther north."

"Oh." Brynn caught her lip between her lower teeth. "I didn't think about that," she admitted.

"Unless there was something special to draw people here. An author-in-residence, maybe? Like Grace mentioned in her essay?"

"David." Brynn was already shaking her head. "I don't know what's going to happen. I can't make any promises—"

"*Semper paratus.*"

"What?"

"It's the coast guard motto. It means *always ready*. I wasn't ready for you, though." David smiled. "So don't think you can change my life and then walk out of it again, Brynn Dixon."

Brynn's eyes misted over. "David."

"Whatever happens, I'm not going to let you go through it alone, okay? You're stuck with me now, Nashville."

Stuck with him.

Brynn liked the sound of that. Too much.

She released a shaky breath and returned his smile. "Okay."

David stared at her as if he couldn't believe she'd agreed. In fact, for the first time since they'd met, he looked uncertain. "I have a question, then. It's a little awkward, though…"

"Yes, you can kiss me," Brynn heard herself say.

David's eyes widened for a moment, and then he was drawing her into his arms. His hands tunneled into her curls, and he claimed her lips in a kiss that was sweet and searching. Tender and a little untamed. A kiss that told Brynn that, like her, he'd been thinking about it for some time. When David released her, he looked as dazed as Brynn felt.

"Wow," she murmured.

"I agree." David chuckled. "But, uh, that actually wasn't the question I was going to ask."

Brynn should have been embarrassed. But no. She wasn't. Not at all. "I'm sorry?"

"I'm not." And to prove it, David kissed her again.

When it ended, Brynn rested her head on his shoulder and sighed. "I believe you. Now, what were you going to ask me?"

"When your doctor ordered all those tests?" David looked serious again. "Did they check for Lyme disease?"

Chapter Forty

Lucy looked out her bedroom window just in time to see the rental car disappear through the open gate.

She had no idea where Caleb had gone or when he planned to return, but that particular vehicle was her only mode of transportation if she was going to catch the nine-o'clock flight.

Lucy opened the weather app on her phone again and saw the ominous purple cloud creeping over the Minnesota border.

If she didn't leave tonight, there was a chance a slow-moving storm would impact travel on Christmas Eve, and Lucy would be stranded in Wisconsin over the holiday, too.

And Ben was counting on her. Everyone was counting on her. Her family. Brynn.

You always think you have to do something.

Caleb had left the building and Lucy still heard his voice in her head.

I'm listening, God. Please tell me what to do.

As if on cue, Lucy's cell rang. She knew God didn't communicate that way, but she hoped it wasn't Ainsley again. She picked it up and saw the SOS of her brother's name on the screen.

"Hello?"

"Hey, Luce!"

He sounded…cheerful.

Lucy's heart settled into its normal rhythm again. "Hey, your-self. I was going to call you later and let you know there's a winter-storm warning where I'm staying. You may have to pull Kristin into the fold and ask her to pick up the engagement ring in case the weather affects my travel plans."

"Hold on a sec."

A request for a face-to-face call popped up. Lucy tapped the green button, and her brother's face appeared, his grin the width of the screen.

"Yeah. About the ring." Ben scrubbed his chin. "That's why I called. You don't have to worry about it."

"I don't?"

"It's right here."

A hand with a gorgeous diamond ring appeared and waved at Lucy before Chloe's face popped into view.

"Hi, Lucy!"

"You…proposed?"

"Last night." Ben looked sheepish. "It just kind of happened."

After the elaborate scheme he'd concocted, it just kind of *happened*?

"Ben is so romantic," Chloe gushed. "He took me out for pizza at Sully's, and there was this cute old couple at the table next to ours. Barbara and Sam. It was Barbara's birthday, and after they ate dinner, Sam surprised her with a cake. She asked us to help her blow out the candles—there were eighty of them, Lucy. *Eighty.* The waitresses were crying, and people were tak-ing pictures of them. It was so sweet.

"When Ben and I sat down at our table again, he took my hand and told me that he wanted that to be us someday. Old and gray and happy. Then he got down on one knee right there and asked me to marry him." Chloe stared adoringly at Ben. "It was perfect."

"Congratulations!" Lucy heard the wobble in her voice. "I'm so happy for you two. Have you told anyone else?"

"We were going to wait until you got home and tell everyone on Christmas Eve." Ben frowned. "You'll be here, right? Because Chloe already has her ugly sweater and a gift for the white-elephant exchange. She's been alone for Christmas the past few years because her family is scattered all over the country, and she misses their Christmas-carol karaoke contest. I told her we'd have to ask you before we started a new tradition."

Christmas karaoke.

"New traditions are good," Lucy said. "You won't be stepping on my big-sister toes."

Chloe smiled and snuggled against Ben, who whispered, "See? I told you she was great."

"I'll try to make it home," Lucy promised.

"Luce? We want you here for all the fun, but if the weather's bad, don't take any chances, okay? I'd rather have you than the awesome gift you're going to give me."

He yelped when Chloe's elbow sank into his side.

"What? She knows I love her."

"I love you too, Boo," Lucy whispered.

Ben's face loomed larger in the screen. "You aren't crying, are you?"

"No. Yes. Just a little."

Ben sniffled. "Allergies," he muttered. "We gotta go. Chloe's anxious to tell her parents, but I wanted to tell you first."

Lucy tried to swallow past the lump in her throat. "Bye."

"Bye!"

Their voices wove together in a duet as Lucy hung up the phone. Outside the window, snow was already filling the tire tracks in the driveway.

Ben's brand-new fiancée loved Christmas, and Caleb had stolen the car.

Well, she hadn't expected an answer to her prayer this soon.

Lucy smiled and closed the suitcase lying on her bed.

It looked like she was staying, too.

Thank you, Lord.

"Three more cancellations, Lucy." Grace hung up the landline on the desk. "We'll be eating fudge until Valentine's Day."

Lucy didn't bother to look outside. For one thing, the sun had disappeared hours ago, snuffed out by a bank of dark clouds that unfolded over the sky like a flannel comforter. Like an unexpected houseguest, the storm had arrived early and showed no signs of moving on.

So far, tomorrow's Christmas Eve flight hadn't been canceled, but Lucy figured it was only a matter of time before she received a text from the airline.

Brynn would get her Christmas wish, after all.

Caleb had been helping David clear the driveway and the roads around the property since early afternoon, an exercise in futility in Lucy's mind. If no one could get to the side road that led to the property, it didn't matter if the driveway was clear. But it gave Caleb an excuse to continue to avoid Lucy while she and Grace finished the final preparations for the meet and greet.

If there was going to *be* a meet and greet.

Lucy had given Ainsley a heads-up the county was under a winter-storm warning, but the publicist didn't seem to care that Grace had spent hours preparing for the event. The only thing that mattered was the Announcement.

Never mind that Brynn had been fighting a migraine all morning and barely touched the tea and toast Lucy had brought to her room. Or that the road to Spruce Hill Farm was becoming more impassable with every downy snowflake that drifted to the ground.

Grace came around the desk. She looked adorable in skinny jeans and a sparkly sweater. Christmas bulbs danced on the gold hoops through her earlobes, and felt snowflakes circled the hem of the apron tied around her waist.

Lucy's dress was still hanging in her closet, but there was an hour before the event officially started. She would change when she went upstairs to check on Brynn again.

"Everything is ready." Grace walked over to the beverage station. The scarred wooden table they'd dragged up from the basement had been given a makeover with a silver tablecloth and crystal vases filled with lights and boughs cut from one of the cedar trees near the barn.

Lucy had tried to make things easier on Grace. Tried to give her a memory of her last Christmas at Spruce Hill Farm. It would be memorable, all right, but not in the way Lucy imagined.

"I'm sorry you went to all this trouble, Grace."

"It's not trouble when you love it." Grace grinned. "It's practice. And now we know what happens to homemade caramels when you don't get the temperature right."

"A delicious mistake."

They said the words together and laughed.

Grace poured a cup of hot chocolate from the carafe and handed it to Lucy before filling one of her own.

"Lucy?" Grace looked solemn now. "Don't feel bad. I started praying about the Mistletoe Stop from the moment you called and told me you'd chosen Frost.

"One of my mom's favorite verses says that *faith is the substance of things hoped for, the evidence of things not seen.* It doesn't matter how many people come tonight." A mysterious smile touched the girl's lips. "Last night God reminded me that He's been working behind the scenes. Just like He was the night Jesus was born."

Lucy wanted that kind of faith. She believed in God but had

always been reluctant to bother Him, thinking she could handle the day-to-day details of life. Thinking she had to work for His approval. Prove herself instead of just being...loved.

The landline on the desk rang again, and Grace set her cup down before she jogged over to answer it.

"Spruce Hill Inn." A frown creased Grace's brow. "No. She's upstairs resting." She slanted a look at Lucy. "Right now? All right." She hung up the phone. "That was Esther."

Lucy's heart skipped a beat. "Is something wrong?"

"She said we're supposed to stop whatever we're doing and look out the window...on the third floor."

Grace was already jogging toward the stairs so Lucy followed. "There's a third floor?"

"It's more like an attic. We talked about fixing it up for guests someday, but it's not at the top of the list." Grace continued past the guest rooms to a part of the inn Lucy hadn't explored and opened a door at the end of the narrow hallway.

A rickety wooden staircase appeared on the other side.

Grace flipped a switch on the wall, and a bulb hanging from the low ceiling flickered to life.

The temperature seemed to drop ten degrees with every step. By the time they reached the top, Lucy was wishing she'd grabbed her coat.

"What are we looking for?"

"Esther didn't say."

There was one small window centered in the wall, and they reached it at the same time. Lucy spotted David and Caleb shoveling the walkway to the barn, and her pulse evened out a little.

Until Grace gasped.

"Look!"

Lucy scratched at the layer of frost on the window. From this height, she could see a single, unbroken strand of lights on the sliver of road that connected the roads between the inn and Frost. "Is that a...train?"

A look of wonder spread across Grace's face. "I think it's a convoy."

"A convoy?" Lucy leaned forward until her nose was almost touching the glass. Now she could see the lights weren't a single strand at all but a line of cars and trucks winding slowly down the snow-covered road. "Are they coming *here*?"

Grace pressed her hands against her face. "Yes?"

"How long?" Lucy squeaked.

"Half an hour?"

"I have to change my clothes." And tell Brynn there was going to be a meet and greet after all, because the town she'd fallen in love with had fallen in love with her, too.

"Lucy?"

Lucy tossed a glance over her shoulder as she reached the stairs. Grace looked excited. And panicked.

"I don't think there's going to be enough fudge."

Chapter Forty-One

"Are you sure you're up to this?"

Brynn smiled and reached for David's hand, let him help her to her feet. The migraine had subsided, but she still felt a little light-headed. "I'm sure."

"Good." He smiled back. "Your loyal subjects are waiting. They're thirsty, too. Grace is making her third batch of hot chocolate."

"Your daughter is amazing. I hope you know that."

David leaned in, his breath stirring a curl by her ear. "I have been blessed with a lot of amazing women in my life. Love the tiara, by the way."

Brynn reached up and touched the jeweled comb in her hair. "It was either this or my cowboy hat with the red feather."

The sound of laughter was almost deafening as they reached the top of the stairs. Brynn paused for a moment and took in the scene. People milled around the lobby, balancing cups of hot chocolate and plates piled high with Christmas cookies.

She caught Esther's eye, and her friend winked.

Brynn exhaled a slow breath and passed it on to Lucy, who

waited at the bottom of the stairs. Tonight, she had cast aside her usual black and was wearing a stunning velvet green cocktail dress and heels.

More changes.

Brynn smiled, tightened her grip on David's arm. His hand folded over hers, infusing her with a warmth that danced across her nerve endings and spiked her heart rate.

Brynn couldn't believe she'd thought David was cold the first time they'd met.

But it turned out they were both at a crossroads in life, and by divine intervention they'd met there. Stepping into the future was a little terrifying. And exhilarating.

Kind of like a moonlight sleigh ride.

"Fifteen steps to the library. I counted," David whispered in her ear. "Or I can carry you?"

He wiggled his eyebrows, and Brynn laughed.

The chatter instantly ceased. As they reached the bottom of the stairs, a feeling of peace stole over her.

There was no sign of Caleb in the crowd, but Brynn saw familiar faces from town. Darlene. Posey. Martin. A week ago, they'd been strangers, but now she counted them as friends. Friends who'd organized a convoy to her book signing and bribed the driver of a county snowplow with the promise of a buffet of Christmas goodies when they reached their destination.

Grace waved, a grin on her face, as David escorted Brynn through the lobby. She pulled up short in the doorway of the gathering room and would have toppled over if David hadn't been holding on to her.

"Y'all..." Brynn choked.

An ornate wooden chair twice the size of the others that had been removed from the room had taken up residence next to the fireplace. Some enterprising elf—Grace, judging by the wide grin on her face—had braided a garland of faux ivy with tiny white lights and red and gold ribbons and woven them around the arms and legs and through the latticework on the back of the chair.

"It's a *throne*, David. I can't sit on that." Brynn smiled the words behind gritted teeth.

"You *are* the Queen of Storybook Endings."

"I'm going to look like Mrs. Claus."

His hazel eyes warmed. "Hmm. Interesting," he murmured. "Does that mean I get to tell you what's on my wish list?"

Brynn knew what would be on *hers*.

The temperature in the room spiked a few degrees, and Brynn could feel his reluctance when he guided her into the chair and released her hand.

People worked their way into the room. Those who didn't fit crowded in the doorway.

Brynn spent the next hour signing books until her fingers began to cramp. When she handed back the last copy, Brynn caught Lucy's eye and waved her over.

"I'd like to thank everyone for braving the snow and cold to come here tonight." Knowing she was about to go off-script, Brynn gave Lucy a reassuring smile. And her cell phone.

Lucy's eyes went wide but she understood. Took a few steps backward and lifted the phone.

"I was asked to make a special announcement tonight be-cause a lot of you have been asking about my next book. The past few months have been challenging. I've been struggling with some health issues and have decided to take a sabbatical from writing.

"Being here the past two weeks made it clear it's the right thing to do. Grace promised that if I came to Frost, I would feel like family. But even more than that, I feel like I've come home, and that's because of you. So thank you."

Lucy slowly lowered the phone, a look of shock on her face.

"Now, if you'll excuse me, I am going to have to say goodnight before I fall asleep in this wonderful chair. But please… stay here and enjoy some more refreshments and the McCraes' wonderful hospitality. And Merry Christmas to y'all."

The buzz in the room increased in intensity as Brynn rose to her feet.

A woman in the back of the room tentatively lifted her hand. "But you can't quit," she said. "What about Trace Hunter?"

A murmur of agreement stirred the air, and Brynn paused.

"My talented friend and assistant, Lucy Gable, and I collaborated on *Meet Me under the Mistletoe*. She refused to take any credit, but she's the one who should answer that question." Brynn smiled at Lucy. "I believe it's your turn."

Chapter Forty-Two

*H*er turn?

Lucy froze when Brynn rose from her chair and left the room with David at her side.

But…she had no script prepared. No plan.

Just the tiniest seed of a dream that had been planted in her heart when she was fifteen years old, waiting to be noticed. Waiting for light and air.

So why did Lucy feel like she was suffocating?

Don't be afraid.

The words broke through the pounding in Lucy's ears.

Brynn had stepped out in honesty, in courage, but she wasn't sure she could do the same.

Caleb had insinuated she'd finished Brynn's book because she wanted to be a writer, but that couldn't have been further from the truth.

Even though she'd loved it.

She'd been ignoring Trace for weeks. Letting her doubts drown out his voice.

Lucy cleared her throat. "Trace—"

"Did someone say my name?"

The low murmur of conversation Brynn's exit had triggered turned into a cheer when Caleb sauntered into the room. Lucy heard a whistle from the back of the room and saw Darlene fanning herself with a napkin.

He wore a rakish smile...and a black tuxedo with a red satin pocket square.

Lucy was rendered speechless again.

Caleb, on the other hand, appeared calm and confident as he took his place at her side.

She'd been pretty sure he would never speak to her again, and now here he was, standing beside her, a mischievous twinkle in his aquamarine eyes.

Too late, Lucy realized she'd made another terrible mistake.

"Wait..." she tried to tell him, but Caleb ignored her and flashed a charming smile at the audience. "I was told some of you might have questions..."

A dozen hands shot into the air.

Caleb nodded at a woman wearing leggings and a chunky-knit sweater with a herd of reindeer prancing around the hem.

"Why didn't you call the police when you found out it was Rex Rodgers who took Paisley's heirloom necklace? A man like that deserves to go to jail!"

Lucy blinked.

Not one of the questions they'd practiced, but Caleb didn't look the least bit rattled. He leaned forward instead.

"It's true the necklace was in Rex's possession, but there was no evidence he was the one who'd taken it. The charges wouldn't stick." Caleb's voice had dropped a notch, and everyone in the room leaned closer, too. "I know Rex from way back. We were in the same foster home when we were kids, but he chose a different path, unfortunately."

The same foster home?

What on earth...

"So you're hoping Rex changes?" The woman's friend asked.

"I believe in second chances."

Lucy swallowed hard.

And what did that mean, exactly?

Caleb had been so angry...and Lucy didn't blame him. She should have encouraged Brynn to tell him the truth. Even before Caleb had told her about the nonprofit, she'd realized that he wasn't taking advantage of Brynn. Caleb cared about and respected her. Wanted to protect her.

Lucy had been trying to protect Brynn, too, but of course, Caleb hadn't seen it that way.

"You have a question?" Caleb nodded at Posey.

"At the end of the book, you got a text message while Paisley and Fletcher were dancing at the wedding reception and you left right away. Was it a new case?"

No, Lucy wanted to shout. She'd simply realized it was high time she focused on the bride and groom, who also happened to be the main characters in the story.

"That's classified information, I'm afraid." Caleb winked at Posey and pointed to one of the women Lucy remembered from the winter games.

"Is Trace dating anyone?" She batted her spiky lashes flirtatiously.

"The event planner," someone spoke up. "What was her name again?"

"Eleanor," Lucy heard herself say. "Eleanor Brantley."

All eyes shifted to Lucy now.

"Does that mean Trace is going to get his own book?" Darlene called out.

Lucy looked at Caleb for help, but he grinned.

"Don't look at me," Caleb murmured. "You're the writer."

"Yes." The word tumbled out with a shaky breath. "Trace will get his own story."

The applause and the whistles drowned out the carols playing in the background. When it subsided, Caleb tipped his head thoughtfully.

"I'm not sure one book is enough," he drawled. "I think I deserve a series, don't you?"

Based on the second round of applause, everyone in the room did, too.

A series.

Lucy's head was spinning. With ideas…

"Well?" Caleb prompted. "What do you think, Lucy?"

"I think…" If he kept looking at her like that, Lucy was going to start stammering again. "We'll start with one and see where it takes us."

That seemed to satisfy their audience. And Caleb, too, because he unleashed a slow grin.

Rebecca, Pastor Zach's wife, raised her hand.

"Can you tell us about your most memorable Christmas?"

Caleb looked at Lucy, and this time his smile was for her alone.

"I think…it's going to be this one."

"I forgot to collect the cell phones." Lucy had tracked Caleb to the library while Grace, David and a small group of volunteers took down tables and the beverage station in the lobby. He was stacking the extra chairs. In his tuxedo. "You took selfies, too! They'll be all over social media tomorrow."

"It's okay, Lucy."

"How can you say that? Ainsley will try to find out who you are. The woman is tenacious. If she figures out you aren't a model, she'll keep digging. What if she finds out your relationship to Brynn?"

"Brynn and I aren't going to keep it a secret anymore," Caleb said.

"Is that one of the reasons she's taking a sabbatical?" Lucy asked.

Brynn's announcement had shocked Lucy down to the stilettos that had gripped her feet in a vise all night.

Almost as shocking as telling everyone in the room that she was going to write a book.

A *book*.

"No, she's been writing for thirty years, and I think she's ready for a change."

Changes again.

"What about Shae? Just look at you! Pictures of you are probably all over the world… And where did you get that tuxedo, anyway?"

A smile touched his lips. "Darlene let me raid the costume closet at the high school. I thought it was a nice touch."

That explained why he'd gone into town earlier.

"I wasn't thinking about the cell phones because I didn't think you'd show up."

"I made you a promise, and I like to think I'm a man of my word."

"You are," Lucy said. "Even before you told me about the nonprofit, I knew you weren't taking advantage of Brynn. But it was easier to believe you were a villain than…" She stopped. Stepping out of the familiar into uncharted territory was harder than she thought.

"The hero?" Caleb prompted.

Lucy swallowed hard. "Someone who shows up and changes the way the story is supposed to go."

"Ah." Caleb nodded. "But what if that's the way it was meant to be all along?"

Then, Lucy had messed things up more than she'd thought.

"Caleb…I'm a homebody, and you travel all over the world." The thoughts that had been tumbling through Lucy's mind slipped out before she could stop them. "I make lists and try to organize everyone's life, and what if…what if I drive you crazy—"

"Lucy." Caleb stopped her. "I realize we haven't known each other very long, but the only thing that would drive me crazy is not being with you. You're the woman who makes me laugh. Keeps me on my toes. Makes me want to be better." He drew her slowly into the circle of his arms. "Everything else? As long as there's an *us*, we can figure it out one day at a time."

Lucy leaned into the word. Leaned into Caleb and met his gaze.

"Us," she repeated. "I like the sound of that."

Caleb unleashed a slow smile. "Great." He nodded at the ceiling. "Because we can't let this go to waste."

Lucy looked up. A bouquet of mistletoe she didn't remember putting up swayed gently on a silver ribbon above her head.

The twinkle in Caleb's eyes gave him away.

"You put it there?"

"I can plan ahead when the situation calls for it. Besides that, someone told me that traditions are important."

"They are," Lucy breathed.

And then she couldn't because Caleb was kissing her. Lucy tasted the sweetness of hot chocolate and promises and something that felt like coming home. When they finally broke apart, his lips moved to her ear.

"So…is this the start of a new tradition?" he whispered.

Lucy rested her forehead against his chest. She could hear the rapid thump of Caleb's heart, beating in time with hers, and smiled.

Mistletoe and Caleb.

Lucy was already looking forward to next Christmas.

"New is good."

Chapter Forty-Three

Early the next morning, Lucy scrolled through the messages on her phone and smiled.

Brynn's Christmas wish had come true.

She finger-combed the spikes out of her hair and wrapped the pashmina she'd tossed into her carry-on at the last minute around her shoulders for an extra layer against the chill before she tiptoed down the stairs to the lobby.

"Our flight?"

Brynn's voice came from the gathering room, startling her.

Lucy changed course and found Brynn. She was tucked into one of the chairs by the gas fireplace, a gorgeous quilt in blues and silvers draped over her lap. A cup of coffee was cradled in her hands, and Lucy went to the sideboard to fill hers before she sat down.

"The storm shifted again," Lucy told her. "The airport is right in its path. No flights going in or out until tomorrow."

Brynn tried not to smile, but it broke through anyway. "Did you reschedule?"

"Not yet." Lucy was trying not to smile, too. "I didn't think you'd want to leave on Christmas Day."

"I don't want to leave at all." Brynn bit her lip. "Did I say that out loud?"

"It's a great place for a sabbatical," Lucy said.

Brynn winced. "Yes. About that. I'm really sorry I didn't tell you ahead of time, but I didn't know what I was going to say... until I did. Which probably makes no sense at all. And then I put you on the spot." Her eyes twinkled. "You're welcome, by the way."

Panic seized Lucy by the throat again.

"A *book*, Brynn," she croaked.

"A story," Brynn corrected. "I read those five chapters, Lucy, and you have one that isn't finished yet. Don't let fear get in the way."

Lucy drew in a breath, held it and slowly released it again.

Maybe Caleb hadn't been totally off base when he'd questioned her reason for taking a job with a best-selling novelist. Maybe subconsciously, Lucy wanted to be part of something she'd dreamed about when she was solving mysteries with Nancy Drew. Dreams she'd tucked away after Janie's accident.

"You can't quit your day job, though," Brynn went on. "Unless you want to, that is. I still need my amazing personal assistant to handle all the phone calls and the emails that flooded my inbox last night. I need my friend Lucy, too."

"That's good," Lucy said softly. "Because I wasn't going to let you fire me. Trace Hunter keeps talking to me, Brynn. I either need a good counselor or a mentor."

"Sometimes you'll need both." Brynn grinned. "You set your hours, though. You'll need time to write."

Anticipation overrode the panic, and Lucy felt her heart lift.

Just wait, Trace. You think finding a missing painting is a challenge? Wait until you join forces with Eleanor Brantley.

"Hey, no one told me the Christmas Eve celebration was

starting at dawn in here," Caleb complained. He wandered into the gathering room, blurry-eyed and rumpled and incredibly good-looking even when he was wearing sweats instead of a tux.

"Morning, sweetheart." Brynn pointed to the carafe on the sideboard. "Help yourself."

"Your flight is canceled." He shot a glance at Lucy. "I checked this morning."

"I'll call Mom and Dad a little later, but I have a feeling they'll be so thrilled to hear that Ben proposed to Chloe they won't even notice I'm missing."

"They'll notice." The look in Caleb's eyes melted Lucy's heart like butter on a warm griddle.

Patch trotted into the room sporting the festive red bow Grace had attached to his collar for the signing event. David was right behind him, dressed in faded denim and the fleece jacket he wore down to the barn every morning.

"Why is everyone up so early?" His gaze swept over Caleb and Lucy before it lit on Brynn. "It's not like you have a plane to catch."

Wait a second…

Was he *happy* they were stranded here a few more days?

Judging from the smile on David's face, the smile aimed at Brynn, the answer to that question was *yes*.

"Do I have to set my alarm for four o'clock in order to get the coffee ready?" Grace flew into the room, set down a tray of muffins and peered into the carafe.

"I'll have a cup, if there's any left," David said. He claimed the chair next to Brynn, and now Lucy had no doubt that Brynn hadn't been spending as much time alone over the past two weeks as she'd thought.

Her cell phone began to hum, and Lucy rose to her feet. "It's my mom. Excuse me."

She walked over to the window and saw a blush of pink and lavender in the sky.

"Hey, Mom. What are you doing up so early?"

"I'm making cinnamon rolls for breakfast. Ben called last night, and he's coming over with Chloe before your dad and I pick up Janie."

Lucy had a hunch she knew why.

"Was the book signing canceled last night?" her mom asked.

"Yes and no. I'll tell you all about it when I get back."

"And when will that be, exactly? Your dad has been glued to the weather station since yesterday, and he said it looks like you're getting bad weather there."

"Our flight was canceled. I'm sorry, Mom. I'm going to miss out on the fun."

"No, you aren't. We decided to put everything on hold until you get here."

"Mom!"

"An insider told me there's going to be karaoke, too."

"You don't have to do that," Lucy protested.

"We want to. It wouldn't be the same without you." Her mom's voice thinned. "I'm just thankful Brynn is with you. I'd hate to think you'd be alone for Christmas."

In the window's reflection, Lucy saw Brynn and David, their heads bent together as they talked in low tones. Grace was arranging muffins on a platter and surreptitiously dropped a piece on the rug for Patch.

"I'm not alone," Lucy said, her heart full again. "And, Mom? I may be bringing someone over for karaoke."

"Trace Hunter?" she heard Kristin shout.

"Am I on Speaker?" Lucy demanded.

"Of course you are, sweetheart," her mom said mildly.

Lucy heard a cheerful chorus of "Merry Christmas" in the background.

"Merry Christmas to everyone who's listening," Lucy called back before hanging up the phone.

"I love karaoke, by the way."

Lucy jumped a little at the sound of Caleb's voice.

"How did you know I was talking about you?" Lucy teased.

"Trace isn't the only guy who's good at eavesdropping."

Trouble. Both of them.

Her lips curved in a smile. "Where are we going?"

Caleb slipped his arm through Lucy's as he drew her toward the door.

"To find some mistletoe."

Merry Christmas.

The text popped up on Brynn's phone before her alarm went off, and she smiled, typed a message back.

Merry Christmas.

Fire going. Coffee on. Join me?

Yes.

Yes, yes, yes.

Brynn exchanged her pajamas for jeans and the official Friends of Frost sweatshirt she'd been given, before slipping out into the hall and making her way downstairs.

The kitchen was dark, a sign that Grace hadn't come downstairs to start breakfast yet. Still, Brynn was a little surprised—and thrilled—to find David alone in the living room.

"No one else is awake?"

"I heard Grace's door close around midnight. I think that's when the Monopoly game finally ended." David poured another cup of coffee, and Brynn moved a sofa pillow aside and saw a copy of *Meet Me under the Mistletoe.*

"Did you hide this from Grace?" she teased.

"That's my copy. I bought it at the signing, but I'm only on chapter ten."

"*You're* reading it?"

"Isn't that what you do with books?" he teased her back.

"Yes. But…" Dare she ask? "What do you think?"

To Brynn's dismay, David's smile faded a little. "I think Fletcher is a pretty tough act to follow. He has all the right moves. Knows exactly what to say. I've never been very good at that." He shot her a wry glance. "Confession? Lynette asked me out on our first date. I'm not very wordy, as you probably noticed, and not creative enough for the grand gestures. I have no idea how to woo a woman." David shook his head. "And the fact I said the word *woo* just confirmed I'm probably too old for it."

Brynn would have laughed, but she had a confession to make, too.

"When I was in London, Clarke swept me off my feet," she said slowly. "I got the flowers and the chocolate and the candlelight dinners. He made promises he wasn't free to make. Or keep.

"For thirty years, I've been writing the kind of stories I *wanted* to believe in. That people fall in love and it lasts. But all this time, I never really believed it would happen for me. After what I'd done…and giving Caleb up for adoption…I didn't think I deserved it. I told Lucy that I'm tired of being afraid." Brynn pulled in a breath. Released it again. "That's why I'd like to stay here a little longer. My next appointment with the doctor isn't until the first week of January…" She stopped. Because David was shaking his head. The expression on his face made her heart sink.

"Grace and I won't be here."

"You've decided to go to Florida? Are you…are you going to sell Spruce Hill Farm after all?"

"No." A smile kicked up the corners of David's lips. "We'll be spending Grace's break in Nashville."

"Nashville?"

"We've never been there. Lucy will be visiting her family, and Caleb has to go back to work, right? So we decided you might like some company and…you do remember me saying that you're stuck with me?"

How could Brynn forget? It was right before he'd kissed her. Kissing seemed an appropriate response this time, too.

"So is that a *yes*?" David finally said.

"Yes." Brynn snuggled against him. "David?"

"Mmm?"

"Nashville…it qualifies as a grand gesture, you know."

His smile made Brynn's toes curl in her slippers.

"I was hoping you'd say that."

Chapter Forty-Four

Christmas—One Year Later

"Is anyone else having a déjà vu moment?" Lucy pointed at the window.

Esther paused and looked up from the table. Sandwiched between Darlene and Posey, the three women were embellishing the pine-bough centerpiece with stems of bright red berries, pine cones and ribbon. "It's not déjà vu." A smile curved her lips. "It's December in Wisconsin."

Right. But the bits of fluff sifting from the sky, the evergreens swaying in rhythm with the wind, still reminded Lucy of her first visit to Spruce Hill Farm.

A year ago, Lucy had been a guest here. Now it felt as if she'd become grafted into another noisy, wonderful, extended family.

"I'm not worried." Darlene didn't so much as spare a glance at the falling snow. "I talked to Stan this morning, and he's ready to make a detour with the county plow if necessary. This is our first event, and it's going to be perfect."

Grace, who'd been flitting from table to table, checking the satin tablecloths for wrinkles, caught Lucy's eye and grinned. Lucy didn't know if it was Darlene's use of the word *our* or if she was remembering it was Darlene's brother who'd blazed a trail for the convoy that traveled from Frost to the tree farm for Brynn's last book signing.

People had been stacked three deep like cordwood, filling every inch of available space in the inn to show their support for Brynn. Not because they counted themselves as fans. Because they counted Brynn as one of their own.

"I'm glad we have more room this time." Grace had read Lucy's mind. "Dad and Martin have been working around the clock to finish everything, and I think they did a wonderful job."

Wonderful didn't quite describe it. Lucy still couldn't get over the transformation that had occurred in the event barn over the past few months.

Chairs replaced the hay-bale seating, and an actual furnace, not space heaters, warmed the air, making the room feel downright cozy even while the temperature outside continued to fall. Vintage chandeliers hung from the ceiling. A towering Fraser fir cut from the plantation was the focal point of the room. Dozens of ornaments—silver stars, delicate snowflakes, crystal hearts—reflected the white lights glowing in the branches.

Lucy's gaze swept over the antique bins filled with boughs and lit on something in the corner.

She smiled.

Well, not everything had changed.

Daisy Jane, who sported an enormous silver bow on her propeller, had earned a place of honor in the event barn. Over the summer, the crop duster had developed a fan club of her own, serving as a backdrop in almost every photograph taken by the guests who'd stayed at the inn.

Caleb tinkered with the engine whenever he visited, and although he fretted that *Daisy* was destined to live out the rest of her days as a whimsical prop for selfies, Lucy wasn't worried. The plane was going to be featured in her next book, transporting Trace and Eleanor to their next adventure.

And Lucy couldn't wait for hers.

She'd turned in her final edits on *Without a Trace* a week ago. Brynn no longer required an assistant, so Lucy had officially resigned from her position and accepted another one.

Brynn had convinced Caleb to make her home in Nashville the official headquarters of her nonprofit and hired Lucy to oversee the day-to-day operations.

Lucy would continue living in the carriage house while she balanced her time between writing and working closely with Caleb. The latter was the best perk of her new job as far as Lucy was concerned.

Posey tipped her head to one side. "I hear bells."

"Already?" Grace looked panicked. "We aren't finished with the decorations yet!"

"It's probably my husband," Esther said. "He was tickled pink when David put him in charge of the sleigh rides today. My guess is that he couldn't wait to take the team out for a quick spin before the guests arrive."

Grace peered out the window. "It's Martin." She glanced over her shoulder and cast a mischievous smile at Lucy. "He's not alone, though."

"Who…" Lucy's throat closed.

Caleb.

She'd been counting the days until she saw him again.

The past three weeks, Caleb had been abroad, finalizing details so he could pass the torch to Mel. He called Lucy every day, but it wasn't the same.

She'd missed his smile. Missed the way he teased her brothers and doted on her sisters. Missed the blue flames that danced in his eyes whenever he drew her into his arms.

Missed *him*.

The door opened, and a gust of frosty air preceded Caleb's entrance. If Lucy had any doubts that he'd missed her, too, they dissolved when his gaze locked on her.

Lucy ignored the knowing looks that passed around the table. And in a move that would have made Brynn's heroines proud, she all but threw herself into his outstretched arms.

"Why are we never alone?" he murmured.

"Because we're blessed."

"True."

"And because you set a precedent," she teased.

"Also true." Caleb's sigh shivered against her ear, but Lucy knew he wouldn't have it any other way.

He'd proposed at her parents' Fourth of July picnic in front of her entire family. Lucy's younger sisters were already conspiring with Grace, plotting bridal-shower menus and games before their June wedding.

"All right, you two." Darlene clucked her tongue. "There will be plenty of time to…catch up…later. There's only an hour until the guests start to arrive."

Caleb looked as if he wanted to argue, but Grace was already reaching for her coat. "We have to get back to the inn. I still have to get dressed and check on Dad."

"Soon." Lucy mouthed the word to Caleb as Grace towed him toward the door.

"It's time for you to get dressed, too, Lucy," Esther said. "We'll finish up here."

Posey bobbed her head. "Go on." She made a shooing motion with her hand. "Esther's right. We've got this, sweetie."

Lucy shooed. It felt good not to be the one in charge this time.

She ducked into the private entrance that led to the spacious suite above the event barn and tapped on the door at the top of the stairs.

When it opened, tears sprang into Lucy's eyes.

"You look beautiful!"

She and Grace had helped Brynn pick out her dress. The bodice was encrusted with pearls, and a cloud of sparkling netting floated over an underskirt of champagne-colored satin.

"So do you." Brynn's gaze swept over Lucy, and she chuckled. "Even in jeans and flannel."

"When in Frost," Lucy quipped. "And can I admit I'm a little envious that you'll be living here?"

Brynn reached out and squeezed Lucy's hands. "This is your second home, you know. David is already talking about adding another suite on the third floor of the inn."

"Just one?" Lucy teased. "The last time I talked to Grace, there was already a waiting list for the writer's retreat next summer, thanks to the new author-in-residence."

Brynn shook her head. "Thanks to the Friends of Frost," she corrected. "They've been spreading the word."

Lucy should have been as stunned as Brynn's readers when her sabbatical had taken her down another path. But Brynn was a natural mentor. Encouraging. Truthful. Patient. Insightful.

She'd been all those things to Lucy during the roller-coaster ride that had become Trace and Eleanor's story, so it wasn't difficult at all to picture Brynn in her new role at Spruce Hill Farm.

Outside the window, Lucy caught a glimpse of Pastor Zach's van chugging through the gate.

And speaking of new roles…

"I better finish getting ready." She plucked at the hem of her flannel shirt. "Is there anything you need?"

"I can't think of a single thing."

Except the groom.

The door closed behind Lucy, and Brynn smiled.

I know I say it a lot, Lord, but thank You.

Brynn's gaze settled on the mountain of packages under the Christmas tree Grace had helped her decorate the night before. The living room still smelled like wet paint, and there was a ladder propped against the wall, but the space was warm and inviting.

Lucy had claimed she was envious that Brynn had made the move from Nashville to Frost, but Brynn was still in pinch-me mode.

Not in a million years would Brynn have guessed that the suite she'd encouraged David to build above the event barn would become her new home.

Their new home.

Brynn padded down the carpeted hallway and dared another glance at the mirror in the walk-in closet.

She'd wondered if her dress looked too youthful, but Grace and Lucy had declared it perfect and insisted that she ring a little gold bell to announce it to the world.

Brynn had chosen the white cowboy boots decorated with tiny rhinestones because she knew they would make David smile.

She slipped them on her feet and heard another soft tap on the door.

This time, her son stood on the other side.

"Caleb." Brynn trapped him in a fierce hug. "Lucy said your flight was delayed. When did you get here?"

"About half an hour ago." He hugged her back. "I didn't mean to cut it so close, but the last storm had a snowball effect on my flights." His eyes twinkled. "No pun intended."

"You're here now." Brynn's eyes misted over.

"Hey," he teased. "You aren't nervous, are you?"

Brynn shook her head, careful not to dislodge the cluster of white rosebuds pinned in the curls behind her ear. "Is David?"

Caleb grinned. "Would I be able to tell?"

Brynn would.

Over the past year, she'd learned a lot about the man who'd stolen her heart.

He was gorgeous. Funny. Patient.

Stubborn.

David had revealed that particular trait when he'd spent Grace's last winter break accompanying Brynn to appointments instead of sightseeing. David had been at her side when the doctor finally confirmed she was showing all the symptoms of untreated Lyme disease. Symptoms Brynn would never have connected to the ones she'd been experiencing if it hadn't been for David.

Another reason to thank the One who'd brought her to a little town that was barely a dot on the map. But He'd known it was where Brynn belonged.

She retrieved her bouquet, a cascade of white roses, juniper and cedar that Hannah had sent over that morning.

At the bottom of the stairs, the murmur of conversation subsided, and everyone turned to look their way.

Tears stung Brynn's eyes. The faces of the people gathered together to watch her and David exchange their vows blurred for a moment before she blinked them away.

"Just so we're clear," Caleb murmured, "I'm not giving you away. I'm getting more family."

Brynn's breath hitched in her throat.

She was getting more, too.

How a smaller life could somehow feel...*bigger* was one of those inexplicable, beautiful mysteries that Brynn couldn't quite figure out.

"Ready, Mom?"

Caleb's whispered prompt made Brynn realize that she hadn't moved. She took a step, and her eyes met David's. The warmth, the promise Brynn saw, made her heart swell with emotion.

She was *so* ready.

Ready to start a life with this man. Ready to call Spruce

Hill Farm, a place that made room for both memories and dreams, home.

Ready to choose love over fear.

David reached for her hand, and Brynn smiled up at him.

Ready for the next chapter to begin.

★ ★ ★ ★ ★